"A lady, untrained, serving the Princess[...] herself. "What is the Baroness thinking?"

Liza's stomach began to churn; she couldn't lose the post now. "Mrs. Strode, I'll work hard and I learn quickly."

"Until you fail, I don't suppose I have a choice." Mrs. Strode sighed. "The Baroness takes morning tea at eight o'clock. On Mondays, you must be ready to help her with her bath. You'll lay out the Baroness's clothes and assist with her hair." She tapped the claw arm of her chair. "You will have one afternoon off each month."

"Per month!" Liza cried, certain she had misheard. *Slavery was abolished in '33!*

"Per month, and I'll thank you not to take that tone with me again," Mrs. Strode said, frowning. "In my experience, the more liberties you give a servant the more they take. You will have free time when you are not needed by the Baroness or the Princess. Finally, you'll be paid twenty-three pounds per annum, paid quarterly," the housekeeper concluded.

Papa gave me more than that for my dress allowance!

 PRAISE FOR *PRISONERS IN THE PALACE*

★ "A great read." —*School Library Journal,* starred review

"A whip-smart, spunky protagonist and a worthy heroine to root for." —*Publishers Weekly*

"Themes of friendship and romance give the story teen appeal." —*Booklist*

"I loved getting to know Victoria before she was Queen, but she's only one of the rich characters. I enjoyed it immensely and recommend it highly." —Karen Cushman, Newbery Medal winner for *The Midwife's Apprentice* and honoree for *Catherine, Called Birdy*

A Junior Library Guild Selection

For Margaux, Rowan, and Rob
—M. M.

A hardcover edition of this book was published in 2010 by Chronicle Books LLC.
First Chronicle Books LLC paperback edition published in 2013.

The Library of Congress has cataloged the original edition as follows:
MacColl, Michaela.
Prisoners in the palace : how Princess Victoria became queen with the help of her maid, a reporter, and a scoundrel / by Michaela MacColl.
p. cm.
Summary: Recently orphaned and destitute, seventeen-year-old Liza Hastings earns a position as a lady's maid to sixteen-year-old Princess Victoria at Kensington Palace in 1836, the year before Victoria becomes Queen of England.
ISBN 978-0-8118-7300-0
[1. Orphans—Fiction. 2. Household employees—Fiction. 3. Self-reliance—Fiction. 4. Victoria, Queen of Great Britain, 1819–1901—Childhood and youth—Fiction. 5. London (England)—History—1800–1950—Fiction. 6. Great Britain—History—William IV, 1830–1837—Fiction.] I. Title.
PZ7.M13384Pr 2010
[Fic]—dc22
2010008257

Interior design by Amelia Mack. Cover design by Sara Gillingham.
Photo by Marta Syrko/Trevillion Images
Typeset in Bodoni.

ISBN 978-1-4521-1958-8

Manufactured in the United States of America.

1 3 5 7 9 10 8 6 4 2

Chronicle Books LLC
680 Second Street, San Francisco, California 94107

Chronicle Books—we see things differently.
Become part of our community at www.chroniclebooks.com/teen.

PRISONERS in the PALACE

How Princess Victoria Became Queen
with the Help of Her Maid, a Reporter, and a Scoundrel

A NOVEL OF INTRIGUE AND ROMANCE BY

MICHAELA MACCOLL

chronicle books · san francisco

Contents

I

In Which Liza's Circumstances Change for the Worse

LIZA HUDDLED in the armchair near the window, her mother's shawl wrapped tightly around her shoulders. Despite the fire, she couldn't seem to get warm. The blinds were drawn against the morning's winter light.

It shouldn't be sunny.

There was a discreet knock at the door. A maid in a black dress with a white apron entered, carrying a meal on a tray. "Miss Liza, you mustn't shut yourself away like this. It's not like you." With a quick motion, she deposited the tray and jerked the blinds open. Liza blinked and held up a hand to shade her eyes.

"Cora!"

"With all due respect to your bereaved state, Miss, the staff is beginning to talk," Cora scolded. "This is no life for a young lady such as you. Go out of doors, put some color back in those cheeks."

"There's nothing for me outside."

The hotel suite had been her refuge since the day she had walked behind the black carriage drawn by four black horses and watched the shovelfuls of black earth rain down on her parents' coffins. And now what? Her family had come to London to join society. But without Mama's letters of introduction, there would be no welcome for Liza in the best homes. There would be no glittering season followed by a brilliant marriage. She was alone in a strange country; she had neither friends nor family. When her parents' cabriolet had plunged into the Serpentine a fortnight ago, it had desolated Liza's life too.

"I have a letter for you," Cora said enticingly.

Hiding her face in the protective wing of the chair, Liza's answer was muffled. "Leave it on the table."

"The notation says 'Urgent.'"

Liza peeked out from under the shawl. "Who sent it?"

A satisfied smile spread across Cora's face. "I don't know." She handed Liza the letter. "Look for yourself."

Liza stood up and brought the letter to the window. "It's from Papa's lawman, Mr. Ratisbon."

Cora's bright smile dimmed. "I never knew good news to come from a lawyer." She picked up Liza's dressing gown from the floor and bustled into the bedroom.

Liza broke the seal and began reading the letter half aloud. "Assets . . . liens . . . five hundred pounds owed? . . . creditors . . . legal action. . . . Oh my goodness." She sank back into her chair. "Papa left nothing? Less than nothing." Her breathing was shallow as if her lungs had shrunk along with her expectations. "How am I to live?"

For the first time, she looked at her luxurious hotel suite and realized it must be expensive. Two bedrooms, a sitting room, meals on trays, a maid . . . it all cost.

Did Mr. Ratisbon include the hotel in his list of creditors? She would be a thief if she slept here another night or ate another meal. How could she afford to pay for Cora?

What on earth am I to do?

Liza began to pace. "How could you do this, Papa?" she whispered to the sumptuous room. "You and Mama were my whole world. How could you leave me with nothing?"

The crinkle of paper in her hand recalled her to the last paragraph of Mr. Ratisbon's letter. Her heart beat faster. After informing her she had lost everything, the lawyer presented her with the opportunity of a lifetime.

"Cora!"

"Miss?"

"I have to get dressed! I'm to go to court!" Liza exclaimed, waving the letter. "More precisely, I have an interview at half past one o'clock to be a lady in waiting."

Cora's eyes widened. "To the Queen?"

"No, to the Princess Victoria at Kensington Palace."

"Court is where the King is, Miss Liza," Cora corrected. "But the little Princess is just as good. She'll be the Queen someday. I saw 'er once, picnicking with 'er mother, the Duchess, in 'yde Park. She's ever so pretty."

"She's not so little. I read in the broadsheets she's sixteen, a year younger than I," Liza said. "If I suit her, I'm to live at Kensington Palace."

"Your good mother would have been proud." Cora's face fell when she saw Liza's stricken expression. "I'm sorry, Miss."

Liza rubbed her sore eyes. "You're right, Cora. My mama would have been so pleased. This was all she ever dreamed of—but now she'll never know." She straightened her back and tilted her chin. "We must pay particular attention to my toilette," she said. "This appointment is the most important of my life."

Liza carefully folded Mr. Ratisbon's letter while Cora hurried away to fetch Liza's clothes. Liza ran her fingers across the crease, thinking hard. What if she didn't find favor with the Princess? Or rather, Her Highness's governess, the Baroness Lehzen? Mr. Ratisbon said that the Baroness would make the decision. This interview *must* go well. It must. Liza had nowhere else to go.

"Your black lace?" Cora asked from the bedroom.

"No! Not that . . ." Liza's voice faltered as she recalled her parents' funeral, but then she forced herself to be practical. "Never mind, it's the best I have, even if it reminds me of terrible things."

She slipped her dressing gown off her shoulders and stood in her chemise. Cora fastened a wide petticoat around her waist.

"The corset?" Cora asked.

Mama would have insisted. "No," Liza said, with a twinge of guilt. "It's wretchedly uncomfortable."

"Your waist is tiny enough as it is," Cora said, fastening the dark skirt around Liza's middle. The black silk was heavy with fine lacework from Brussels. Liza remembered the rainy afternoon she and her mother had spent in the milliner's shop poring over dozens of styles. Cora buttoned the sleeves into the armholes. They were wide below the elbow but narrow at the shoulder. She tut-tutted, "This style looks more like a leg of mutton every season."

Liza stared at her reflection in the mirror. "Mama always told me I looked washed out in dark colors."

"But you have to wear your blacks, it's disrespectful else," Cora said.

"To honor Mama and Papa properly, I will," Liza said. Tears rolled down her cheeks. She sighed; this had to stop. The Princess would send her away if all she did was cry.

Cora avoided looking at Liza's face. She finished joining the hooks and eyes at the back of the bodice. "That looks lovely," she said. "Your shape is 'ourglass perfection."

Taking a deep sniff, Liza pursed her lips and set her shoulders back, fighting her tears. "With these huge sleeves and wide skirt, anyone would look like an hourglass." But even as she said it, she remembered laughing with her mother, discreetly of course, at the ladies who insisted on the latest styles even though they did not have the natural tiny waist.

"'Tis the fashion, Miss." Cora's voice was firm.

Liza said, "Fashion isn't everything." She swallowed past the lump in her throat; her mother would have swooned had she heard Liza say such a thing. Fashion had been their consuming passion, save for the opera and theater. But now Liza had more important concerns.

"What about jewelry, Miss?" Cora asked briskly.

"My gold and enamel locket." It contained a small length of her mother's hair. "And the jet bracelet and pin. I must look my best."

"A pretty girl like you is sure to please the Princess. They say she 'as no friends 'er own age. You'd be a boon to 'er, you would."

"I hope so." Liza fastened a black bonnet on her head and arranged the black ribbon to display becomingly in her blond curls. "It would be a boon for me to go where there are no memories."

The lobby was filled with its usual denizens, well-to-do young ladies and their mothers and, on occasion, pompous fathers. Two weeks ago Liza had been utterly at home here; she had grown up in fine hotels in the most elegant cities around the world. A murmur spread through the room when she appeared at the top of the stairs. Behind gloved hands or strategically held fans the ladies whispered, speculating. Liza blushed.

Stop being self-centered, Liza. They can't possibly know the money's gone. They are curious because I've been a hermit in my rooms this past fortnight. They can't possibly know.

"Miss Hastings!" A peremptory voice drew every eye to her. It was Mr. Arbuthnot, the hotel's manager. Though portly, he insisted on wearing gaudy vests that emphasized his girth. "Miss Hastings, I must speak to you about your account."

Liza wished she could sink into the lush red carpet. Instead, she took a breath and made one foot follow the other down the stairs. Now everyone was staring at her and she knew they weren't admiring the lace on her mourning dress.

"Good afternoon, Mr. Arbuthnot," she said formally.

Recalled to his manners, he said, "Of course. Good afternoon. May I speak to you in my private office, please?"

Liza looked for any possible reprieve, but his piggish, black eyes were implacable. "Why, certainly, Mr. Arbuthnot, although I only can spare you a few moments. I have an important appointment."

He led the way through the crowded lobby. Liza followed as slowly as she dared. Her father's lawman had said she wasn't responsible for her father's debts. But did Mr. Arbuthnot know that? Perhaps the bailiffs were waiting to take her to debtor's prison?

Mr. Arbuthnot opened the door. Liza craned her neck to see past his bulk. Her knees weakened with relief; the room was empty.

Mr. Arbuthnot sat behind a too grand mahogany desk. Most discourteously, he didn't offer her a seat, but Liza's legs were trembling so, she sank unbidden into the deep chair opposite him. Immediately she regretted her choice; the chair dwarfed her petite frame and she felt like a small child.

"Do you know why I've asked to see you?" he began.

"You'd like to offer your condolences?" Liza asked hopefully. But she had spied a letter with Mr. Ratisbon's handwriting on his desk; the manager would not be commiserating with her over her tragedy.

"Your account is in serious arrears, Miss Hastings." He frowned and picked up the letter. "Your father's solicitor tells me you have no fortune at all and no prospects," he said as though it were her fault.

Two weeks ago, he had fallen over himself to indulge their every whim. Violets in winter? Of course, Lady Hastings. Seats to the opera for *Don Juan*, starring the famous tenor Luigi Lablache? Consider it done, Miss Hastings. But his courtesies had a price.

"Mr. Arbuthnot, my father was a valued client of yours."

"Indeed he was . . . when he was alive to pay his bills."

Liza gasped. "How much is the amount outstanding?" she asked, when she trusted her voice again.

"Forty-three pounds, two pence," he said.

Liza recoiled as if from a blow to her body. Her gloved fingers twisted around the handle of her little reticule, which contained only a few pounds and a handful of change.

"That is the amount due immediately," he continued. "If you stay another night, it will be more."

"Of course," Liza said. "My parents would have—," she began again.

"The hotel is deeply sorry for their deaths, but even our generosity has its limits. Have you no one to pay your debts?"

"As you know, we have only just arrived in London from Munich. I know no one." Liza struggled out of the chair. "As it happens, I have an appointment this morning that will provide me with a new home." She smoothed out her full black skirt. "I will pack my trunks and leave as soon as possible."

Mr. Arbuthnot's fleshy lips quivered with impatience, "And your account?"

Liza's stomach was full of angry butterflies. "I have no way to pay right now, but it will be settled," she promised.

"I don't see how," he replied, his tone snide. "But Claridge's will not be the loser; I'm sure I can sell your personal chattel for at least some of what you owe."

"You cannot!" Liza cried.

"But I can." He tapped the letter on his desk. "Ask your solicitor."

"You can't sell my clothes to strangers! And certainly not my mother's jewelry and my father's books . . ." As Liza listed the other possessions she could not bear to lose, her voice grew louder and more shrill.

"Miss Hastings, calm yourself." He stood up and made sure the door was closed. "I'm the maître d'hôtel of the finest hotel in London, what will my paying guests think if they hear your caterwauling?" He shoved a handkerchief at her.

With so little money in her reticule, how could Liza buy some time? Looking up at him from under her damp eyelashes, she said, "I'm so sorry, Mr. Arbuthnot, but I'm an orphan, at my wit's end."

Mr. Arbuthnot shifted from foot to foot, his eyes looking everywhere but at Liza. "There's nothing I can do."

With a sudden air of inspiration, Liza sat up straight saying, "Perhaps I should throw myself on the mercy of your guests? Once I tell them the hotel is going to cast me out onto the street, someone will help me."

"You'll do no such thing!" he snapped. "I've the hotel's reputation to think of."

"You have left me no choice," Liza sniffed, dabbing at her eye with his cologne-laden handkerchief.

"Perhaps I could let you have one trunk with your personal effects," Mr. Arbuthnot grudgingly offered.

"That would be exceedingly generous," Liza said, hating the necessity of sounding grateful.

"But the rest . . ." he said.

"You may hold my other belongings until I pay the debt," Liza interrupted.

"For ninety days," he countered. "Then I sell everything."

"A twelvemonth at least. You must give me time to find my feet, sir," she said. Surely that would be time enough to make her fortune or at least to find a suitable husband at Kensington Palace.

"Half a year. And that's my final offer."

"Thank you. I appreciate your kindness." She stood up and waited for him to remember to hold the door open for her. She was about to sweep through when she remembered another problem. "One more thing," she said.

"What?" he said sourly.

"I have a meeting at Kensington Palace, but I've no money to pay for a hansom cab."

"You could walk."

"I could," she mused. "But how would it reflect on Claridge's? A young lady, walking unescorted through Hyde Park?"

He snorted. "Miss Hastings, I think if you had been in charge of your father's business interests, there would be an estate worth inheriting."

Liza waited, her face impassive.

"Very well, I'll pay the fare," he said at last. "But first you pack your things. I have an Italian nobleman arriving this evening. He can afford to pay for your suite."

When Liza came back downstairs, Mr. Arbuthnot was waiting for her. He rushed forward to take her arm and shepherd her through the crowded hall, and Liza rewarded him with a genuine smile. To her surprise, she felt grateful to Mr. Arbuthnot for forcing her to pack so quickly. She would have mourned every item; cried over every glove, cufflink, and book had she more time. Instead, her single trunk was bursting with her favorite things and clothes appropriate for a grieving daughter.

Mr. Arbuthnot accompanied her to the door and instructed the doorkeeper to pay for a hansom cab to Kensington Palace. Then he turned on his heel and retreated to the comfort of London's finest hotel.

Liza was left standing with the doorkeeper, her eyes blinking against the cold sunlight. He blew a shrill whistle and was answered with the clip-clop of hooves and the rattle of a cabriolet driven by a tiny man in an oversize greatcoat and a battered top hat.

"Miss, it's nice to see you taking the air again," the doorman said loudly. He lowered his booming voice. "I'll ask the driver to take the long way around, avoid the river."

Liza swallowed. She had not considered that she might have to cross the bridge where the horse had bolted, plunging Mama and Papa to their deaths in the muddy waters of the Serpentine. Liza smiled at him, grateful for his thoughtfulness. With a practiced hand, he helped her into the carriage.

As she sank down to the cushioned seat, Liza forced herself to breathe deeply. Her exhalation hung suspended in the chilly air, like a promise or a threat. Whatever the future held for her, it was about to begin.

2

In Which Liza's Position Is Clarified

THE CARRIAGE wound its way through Hyde Park. Liza averted her eyes from the cold grayness of the river in the distance. They traveled along Rotten Row, where even in these frigid temperatures, society's finest showed off their clothes, horses, and social connections.

The carriage wheels crunched up a long gravel drive studded with weeds and stopped at an imposing iron gate. Streaks of rust marked the gate and the ornate pineapples topping the gateposts had long ago lost their gold leaf. The red brick building beyond the gate looked like an ordinary country house. Large enough certainly, but Liza spied a broken windowpane and brickwork in need of repair.

"This is Kensington Palace?" Liza asked the cabbie doubtfully. "Are you sure?"

"'Tis cert, Miss," he said, his bright blue eyes twinkling. "It don't look like much, I know, but thems that live 'ere can't afford better. The King dumps all 'is poor relations at Kensington."

Liza got out of the carriage and rooted around her reticule, looking for some loose coins, but before she could find a tip, the cabbie touched his white hat in a salute and clicked to his horse. The cabriolet lurched forward and she watched him go, feeling very alone.

The tall, black gate was locked. Liza spotted the porter's box just inside the gate, but no porter to ask what her business at the Palace might be. Glancing around the empty courtyard, she spied a smaller pedestrian's gate. It swung open at her touch, the metal's coldness seeping through her fashionable gloves. She shivered, although not from the cold.

Cowardice is a luxury you cannot afford.

Climbing the wide, stone steps to the tall, oak door, Liza touched her mother's locket for luck and struck the brass knocker to a reverberating thud. No response.

Shouldn't Kensington Palace have a footman or a butler to open the door?

Growing bolder, Liza knocked again. Still no answer.

"Hello?" she called out. "Is there anyone here?"

She shifted from one foot to the other and tapped her fingers against her wrist.

She knocked a third time. No sooner had the knocker hit the strike plate than a tall footman jerked open the thick door. Clad in dark green livery with a powdered wig atop his head, he looked flustered, no doubt due to the furious old woman standing behind him. She was short and stout and dressed in gray muslin; a chatelaine with keys jangled at her waist.

The housekeeper, Liza concluded.

"Miss Elizabeth Hastings to see the Baroness Lehzen." Liza's voice squeaked like a door that hadn't been opened for months.

The housekeeper squinted at her, her shrewd eyes taking in every detail of Liza's fashionable ensemble. "Are you certain?" she asked.

"Of my name or that I am here to see the Baroness?" Liza responded sharply.

Pursing her lips, the housekeeper said, "You have come to the wrong entrance." She pointed. "Go along the length of the Palace to the small, red door there."

"My apologies. Had there been a *proper* porter, I would have inquired." Liza gestured around the empty courtyard.

"I am responsible for the inside of the house, not the exterior," the housekeeper snapped. "I'll admit you at the *proper* door." She gestured to the footman. He closed the heavy door in Liza's face. Liza's jaw dropped.

The standards for royal help must be very low.

As she trudged around the house, Liza could not help but take note of the gardens surrounding the Palace. Even with the trees bare of leaves in late winter, its beauty encouraged her to take heart with the early crocuses, pale yellow and blue, forcing their way through the soil. She reached a nondescript, red door, its paint peeling. Just as her knuckles came down to knock, the door swung open.

The housekeeper must have run the length of the Palace to meet her so quickly. "So slow, Miss Hastings? We do not tarry here at Kensington Palace." Her words came between puffs for air.

"I'm sorry, Miss . . ."

The housekeeper's eyebrows lifted halfway up her forehead. "*Mrs.* Strode. Housekeepers are always referred to as Missus." A plump index finger beckoned for Liza to follow her.

Before the door could swing closed, Liza jumped inside. She bit back a sharp comment. Once she impressed the Baroness, then she could chastise the help.

The door led into a round room with a cold flagstone floor and doors leading off in every direction. The only light came from narrow windows and a few cheap, tallow candles hanging from the walls. Mrs. Strode opened the third door on the right curve of the room and led Liza up a damp stairwell with spots of mold on the plaster walls.

Despite her warm woolen cloak, Liza shivered. "The Palace is very chilly," she said.

Mrs. Strode stopped short and turned, glaring down at Liza from the step above. "I am sorry Kensington does not meet your expectations, Miss Hastings," she said, her syllables soaked with sarcasm. "The Duchess's means may be slender, but let me assure you, we know how to respect our betters in this house."

Abashed, Liza dropped her eyes and mumbled, "I beg your pardon." Perhaps she'd do better to guard her tongue. Who knew how much influence this odious housekeeper had with the royal family?

With a sniff, Mrs. Strode continued her ponderous progress up the stairs and down a shabby hall. She stopped without warning and Liza trod upon her skirts. "You'll have to be more graceful if you are to serve the Princess," the housekeeper said sharply.

"Yes, Ma'am." Mrs. Strode seemed to expect something more, so after a moment, Liza said, "I'll bear it in mind."

Mrs. Strode opened the tall, white double doors. "Baroness Lehzen, Elizabeth Hastings."

This room was another disappointment. It did not fit Liza's idea of a royal parlor at all. With a long table in the center facing a desk, it resembled a faded schoolroom. Cracks ran up and down the walls. Though the sun streamed in—through windows marred by fingerprints and streaks of weather—the room still felt chilly. Liza thought she saw a black beetle skittering into the cold fireplace. The carpets were threadbare and the curtains frayed at their hems.

At least they match.

A tall figure was sitting stiffly on a faded blue velvet armchair. Her dark hair, shot through with gray, was piled high in a braided crown. Liza had not expected an older woman; the Baroness looked at least fifty. In all the novels she read, the governesses were young and pretty.

"Mrs. Strode, you may go." Baroness Lehzen flicked her bony hand in dismissal. Liza stepped forward and after a moment's hesitation, curtsied prettily.

"So you are Miss Hastings." The Baroness made the statement sound like a question. Her hand disappeared into a pocket in her navy skirt and emerged with a handful of caraway seeds. She crammed them into her mouth.

"Yes, my lady," Liza answered.

"That's wrong." She shook her head irritably, chewing the seeds all the while. "You must call me Baroness." Her English was thickly accented. "Mr. Ratisbon tells me you are an orphan?"

The familiar wave of dark pain hit Liza and threatened to sweep her feet out from under her. "Yes, Baroness."

"How did you lose your family?" she asked, making it sound as if Liza had misplaced them.

"A carriage accident in Hyde Park."

The Baroness gave a little nod, dismissing the parents. "Elizabeth is too grand a name," she said. "What were you called at home?"

Liza forced the words past the lump in her throat. "My family called me Liza."

"Liza." The Baroness rolled it on her tongue. "How old are you?"

"Seventeen, Baroness."

"Victoria will be seventeen next month." A tender smile flitted over her lips, then passed. "Have you had any education?"

More than you.

"Yes, of course. I'm very good at parlor games and anagrams. I can also play the pianoforte." Liza's mother had ensured she was well versed in all the tools a lady of leisure required to combat boredom.

"None of that is of use here," the Baroness frowned.

Liza had never heard the Princess was so serious-minded. It might be very grim at Kensington Palace.

"Can you sew?"

"Sew? Of course I can." For a moment, the memory of her mother's golden head leaning over her embroidery, patiently showing Liza a new stitch, was more real than the Baroness.

The Baroness coughed, bringing Liza back to the moment. Liza managed to say, "I am quite handy with an embroidering needle."

"If you can embroider, you can mend," the Baroness said. "Let me look at you." The top of her body ramrod straight, she levered herself out of the upholstered chair. Circling Liza, as though she were a horse on sale at the fair, Baroness Lehzen muttered, "Not too tall. Pretty enough, although the complexion is pasty."

"Black is not my best color," Liza felt compelled to say.

The Baroness scowled. "Did I ask you a question?" she said.

"No, Baroness."

Control your tongue!

"Too much jewelry. And the dress is too fashionable," the Baroness continued. "The Princess prefers bright colors."

"I'm in mourning for my parents," Liza said. Her nervous fingers plucked at her mourning locket.

"That is irrelevant here, Miss Hastings. Nor am I accustomed to being contradicted," the Baroness said, as she lowered herself back into her seat.

Liza willed her tone to be respectful. "I apologize, Baroness, but my nerves have been strained by my tragedy."

"A maid is not permitted to have nerves."

There was a long silence while Liza's heart sank.

"M . . . maid?" Perhaps she had misheard.

"What else?" the Baroness said, her eyebrows nearly touching her ornate crown of hair.

"I'm here to apply to be a lady in waiting!" Liza winced, hearing her own shrillness.

"A commoner?" The Baroness laughed. "Even if the Princess was permitted a lady in waiting, she would have to be, at the very least, a countess."

"I can't be a maid," Liza protested. "I'm a lady."

The Baroness frowned. "Mr. Ratisbon told me your father was in trade."

"He was," Liza admitted. "But his products were such a favorite with the late king, he was knighted." Papa had been so pleased. It was then that he and Mama began to speak of an auspicious match for Liza.

"Knighted!" Baroness Lehzen made an impatient noise. "This interview is over. I have no wish for you to demean yourself. Mrs. Strode will show you out."

Liza's last bits of pride disintegrated into dust as she imagined begging Mr. Arbuthnot for another night at Claridge's Hotel. She couldn't do it. "Wait!" she cried. "What kind of maid?"

"The Princess's maid. And as needed, mine also." The Baroness's face tightened. "But it's impossible now. You are a lady. And one with too much pride." She reached for the bell on the table. "You can go."

Liza's chest contracted, squeezing her heart of every drop of blood. Her thoughts raced: what could she do to change the Baroness's mind?

The double doors slammed open, banging against the wall. A King Charles spaniel, dressed in a red tartan vest and blue velvet trousers, scampered in, yipping loudly. Following on his heels, a girl in a white muslin day dress with pink trim walked in. Her long, fair hair was tied back, like a little girl's might be, with a matching ribbon. Behind them both, a parlor maid followed, panting for breath.

The Princess!

The newspapers sometimes published drawings caricaturing her prominent blue eyes and her lips, pursed together like a cupid's bow. And here she was—in the flesh. Liza liked the look of her immediately.

"Oh darling Lehzen, look at Dash!" cried the girl, with a hint of a German accent. She held up her hand and the dog jumped on its hind legs and turned in a circle. "Isn't he *mignon?*"

"*He* may be adorable, but your manners are not, Princess." With a gesture, the Baroness directed the dog to sit. The spaniel whimpered and obeyed, as intimidated by the Baroness as Liza was.

Victoria pulled herself up tall and held her weak chin unnaturally high. "Lehzen, please forgive the intrusion," she apologized. Then she turned to Liza with manners just as exquisite. "And do pardon me for interrupting."

With a pang Liza realized the Princess assumed she was a proper visitor.

The Baroness hastened to correct her mistake. "Victoria, this is no one."

"Lehzen, she's clearly someone!" Victoria giggled. "Look at her dress." She held out her hand. "I am the Princess Victoria."

Liza curtsied as her mother had taught her. "Your Highness," she said. "My name is Liza Hastings."

The Baroness bustled in front of Victoria, as if to protect her from riffraff. "Victoria, go to your room, Liza is here to apply for Annie Mason's job, but as you can see, she is clearly unsuitable."

Victoria's eyes went from Liza's fashionable slippers to her jet and enamel earrings. "I think she is suitable in every way, Lehzen."

"It is not for you to say."

"No one consulted with me about Annie's dismissal." The Princess put her hands on her hips. "At the very least, I should choose my new maid."

"I will find someone better. One who is not so well born," said the Baroness.

"Can anyone be too well born to serve me?" Victoria asked, frowning.

Liza smothered a smile as she saw the Baroness did not have an answer to that.

"Victoria, go to your room, we will discuss it later."

"Lehzen, I shan't be disappointed again," the tiny Princess stomped her foot, daring her giant governess. "I insist you hire Liza."

Liza racked her brain, searching for anything that might help Victoria persuade the Baroness. She remembered her father complaining the royal family was more German than British. Though her mother had teased him that his own daughter was half-German, Papa still grumbled that the monarch should be British through and through.

"*Bitte Baroness, benötige ich diese Beschäftigung.*" Please, Baroness, I need this position.

Both the Baroness and Princess stared.

"*Sprechen Sie Deutsch?*" Baroness Lehzen asked. You speak German?

"*Ja.*"

"How?" the Baroness asked, her voice sharp with suspicion.

"But your face, your voice . . . you are English," Princess Victoria said, her voice full of delight.

"My father was from Leeds, but my mother was born in Munich. We traveled a great deal for his business, but I always spoke German with Mama and English with Papa."

The Princess was intrigued. "What kind of business?"

"He imported delicacies. He supplied the King's table with sauerkraut and sausage."

The Baroness interrupted with a guffaw. "Ah! I knew the name was familiar. Your parents were Sir Sauerkraut and his Lady Bratwurst!"

The Princess giggled.

"How dare you say such a thing!" Liza exclaimed.

The Baroness's eyes narrowed. The Princess gasped.

Liza froze. "Excuse my outburst, Baroness. It is just my parents died so recently . . ."

"Is that why you are wearing such dreary mourning?" the Princess asked. Her face was filled with morbid interest.

"Yes, Your Highness, I am an orphan."

"That's appalling," said the Princess. "And I know exactly how you feel. My father died when I was a baby. He was English too, while my Mama is from Germany. Just like you!"

Liza tried to drag the Princess's attention back to her plight. "I have neither friends nor family in England."

"You are utterly alone?" Tears welled up in the Princess's eyes. "You have no one?"

"No one, Your Highness. I need this position quite desperately." Liza let herself hope.

Victoria snatched the Baroness's hands and held them to her lips. "Lehzen, don't you see, it would be a good deed to hire Liza. And it would be so amusing for me to have someone to talk to. And she speaks German; that will be easier for you."

"Perhaps." The Baroness looked at Liza, her lips pursed as she looked her over a little more closely. "But if I do, Victoria, you must promise not to be too familiar with her."

Liza fixed her eyes on the floor.

I hugged Cora farewell not two hours ago!

"Of course not. I shall be as stern as you." The Princess embraced the Baroness. "Thank you, my darling Lehzen."

The Baroness tried not to smile as she said, "Go write in your journal. Your mother will look at it tonight."

"It isn't as though anything ever happens worth writing about," the Princess said. With a becoming pout, she called to her dog. Dash followed Her Royal Highness out of the room, barking cheerfully as he trotted behind her.

3

In Which Liza Goes Below Stairs

As though Victoria's presence had thawed the Baroness's frozen demeanor, her face had more color. "I cannot deny my Victoria anything," she said with a pleased smile. "They say in England she is spoiled ripe."

"Spoiled rotten," Liza corrected. "The Princess is spoiled rotten."

The Baroness frowned and without warning pinched the flesh above Liza's elbow.

"Never be disrespectful of the Princess," she hissed.

Liza bit her lip to prevent herself from crying out. She closed her eyes until the pain subsided, reminding herself of all she had at stake.

The Baroness rang for a maid and told Liza she would be interviewed by Mrs. Strode next. Liza followed the housemaid through a labyrinth of stairways and halls. Rubbing her sore arm, Liza's eyes fixed on the maid's white apron and starched cap.

"Will I have to wear a cap and apron too?" Liza asked.

The maid stopped in surprise. "Of course not. A lady's maid wears proper street clothes. Ain't you never been in service before?"

Liza hesitated. "No," she said finally. "This is my first position."

The maid glanced sideways at Liza, paying particular attention to her dress and accessories. "You weren't born to it," she said flatly.

Liza shook her head ruefully. "My name is Liza."

"I'm Nell. Don't worry. If you worship the Princess, you'll be in good odor with both 'er and the Baroness." She wrinkled her nose and laughed at her little joke.

"The Baroness seems very devoted," Liza offered, cautious of saying the wrong thing.

"Like a dog guarding a whelp. She acts more like Victoria's mother than the Duchess does."

They came to a white door with a crystal doorknob. Every great house had a door just like it—separating the gentry from the servants. Nell pulled it open to reveal a narrow, gloomy hallway. The other side of the door was lined with green baize and the doorknob was made of plain gunmetal.

"Why is the door covered with fabric?" Liza asked.

"Muffles the sound from our side, I suppose. And keeps smells in. The family don't want to smell dinner until it's on the table."

Liza stepped through. Without a stairwell in sight, she had gone from above to below stairs. They were back in the round, stone room where Liza had first entered the Palace. Nell opened one of the doors to reveal a stifling, hot kitchen with two large, coal-burning stoves and deep, stone sinks lining the walls. A cook and two scullery maids bustled around cleaning up one meal and preparing the next.

Nell led Liza past a narrow room with a battered, oak table and long, wooden benches. There were no windows.

"The servant's 'all, where we eat." The smell of stale beer and onions reminded Liza she hadn't eaten anything from the breakfast tray at the hotel. Her stomach twisted with hunger. Claridge's Hotel had already assumed a dreamlike haziness, as though it were someone else's life. Nell went on, "Most of the time, you'll eat upstairs, off a tray."

"By myself?"

Nell snorted. "You'll be grateful after you've met the others."

She pointed to another door. "The still room where Mrs. Strode makes 'er cordials." She indicated a door at the end of a long corridor. "The butler's pantry. But you won't 'ave much to do with Mr. Jenkins. Fortunately, since 'e's usually three sheets to the wind." She winked. "He keeps the keys to the wine cellar and it's 'is job to be sure the wine 'asn't gone off—takes a lot of tastin' that does."

"Where will I spend my time?" Liza asked.

"Not down 'ere with us. You'll be above stairs. You 'ave to maintain your position."

"What position?" Liza asked bitterly. "I'm a maid."

"A lady's maid," Nell corrected. "You rank at the very top."

"There's rank below stairs?" Liza had never considered the lives of servants once they left her hotel suite.

"Of course there is. I remember the airs Annie Mason put on when Lehzen was 'Baronessed.' Everyone had to greet her first in the morning because her position had improved, except for one French maid I won't name." Nell's smile was tinged with sadness. "I do miss Annie."

Liza touched Nell's arm to stop her. "The Princess mentioned Annie Mason left suddenly. What happened?"

Nell's open countenance clouded, "Miss, I don't 'old with gossip."

"Please. If I'm to take her place . . ."

"Miss, you're a proper lady," Nell interrupted. "You won't make 'er mistakes."

They arrived at a plain door and Nell's relief played across her face. She knocked immediately. "Wait, I'll tell Mrs. Strode yer 'ere," she said as she slipped behind the door, leaving Liza alone in the hall. Liza remembered how she had tried to put Mrs. Strode in her place and her cheeks grew warm. Nell reappeared. "Go in," she whispered. "'er bark is worse than 'er bite." She gave Liza a little push.

The warmth of the room struck Liza like the heat of an oven. Sitting ensconced in a large wing chair near a coal fire, Mrs. Strode sipped from a cup of tea and looked like the mistress of the house.

"Apparently, Miss Hastings, the Baroness has decided you will suit." The perfect enunciation of her vowels questioned the soundness of the Baroness's judgment.

"Yes, Mrs. Strode."

Eyebrows lifted, Mrs. Strode stared at Liza, tapping her fingers against her teacup. Liza realized she expected a curtsy. Staring straight ahead, eyes wide to keep from focusing on Mrs. Strode's forbidding face, she bobbed.

"Sit down," Mrs. Strode said.

Liza sank gratefully into a chair. She slipped her shawl off her shoulders to prevent perspiring in the overheated room.

"Your duties will start tomorrow," Mrs. Strode said. "You may move your things here tonight. Your room is on the second floor, near the old state apartments. You will be the only person in the wing." She paused.

"I'll be alone?"

"If you wish, you could share a room with another servant," Mrs. Strode said.

"I'd prefer my own room," Liza replied quickly. So long as she had privacy, that wing of Kensington Palace could be haunted for all she cared.

"Very well. There's no water closet on that floor, but Nell will supply you with a chamber pot. You'll bathe in the kitchen with the rest of the female servants every Friday. We have standards at Kensington."

Liza thought wistfully of the gleaming water closet at Claridge's.

Mrs. Strode kept talking. "Unless the Princess or the Baroness says otherwise, you are always on duty."

"Always?" Liza asked. Mrs. Strode's scowl told her to mind her tongue. "I'm sorry, Mrs. Strode, but, you see, I've no experience. I know what my maid at Claridge's did for me, but I'd be very grateful if you would explain my responsibilities."

Mrs. Strode stiffened in her chair. "Your maid . . . at Claridge's?"

"Yes, ma'am."

"A lady, untrained, serving the Princess." Mrs. Strode fanned herself. "What is the Baroness thinking? Especially after the last one . . ." She trailed off, dismayed.

Liza's stomach began to churn; she couldn't lose the post now.

"Mrs. Strode, I'll work hard and I learn quickly."

"Until you fail, I don't suppose I have a choice." Mrs. Strode sighed. "Do you have something to write with?"

Nodding vigorously, Liza pulled out her notebook from her reticule and began taking notes. Spying Liza's favorite gold pencil, Mrs. Strode's face tightened. "The Baroness takes morning tea at eight o'clock. On Mondays, you must be ready to help her with her bath."

Liza remembered the enormous claw-footed hip baths at Claridge's. Even there, the poor maids carried heavy pails of steaming water to fill the tubs every morning.

"Do I fill the tub myself?"

"Certainly not. That is the housemaid's job. I'd never be able to hold my head up amongst the other royal housekeepers if a lady's maid did such a thing."

Liza breathed a small sigh of relief and scribbled, "No Pails."

"You'll lay out the Baroness's clothes and assist with her hair."

Liza and her mother had often whiled away a rainy afternoon dressing each other's hair. The task would not be onerous— although the Baroness's wiry gray loops were a far cry from her mother's golden curls.

"The Baroness will instruct you regarding your duties with the Princess." She tapped the claw arm of her chair. "You will have one afternoon off each month."

"Per month!" Liza cried, certain she had misheard.

"Per month, and I'll thank you not to take that tone with me again," Mrs. Strode said, frowning.

Slavery was abolished in '33!

"I'm sorry, Ma'am," Liza mumbled. "I am only surprised to learn servants have so little freedom."

Mrs. Strode harrumphed. "In my experience, the more liberties you give a servant, the more they take. You will have free time when you are not needed by the Baroness or the Princess. I expect you to occupy yourself decently by reading the Bible or suitable poetry—Coleridge or Wordsworth."

Liza's mischievous sense of humor surfaced despite her best intentions, "What about Byron?"

"That reprobate! Certainly not. If you must read something modern, you may read Miss Austen's novels."

"Thank you, Ma'am," Liza forced herself to say. "I'll do exactly as you say."

"Finally, you'll be paid twenty-three pounds per annum, paid quarterly," the housekeeper concluded.

Papa gave me more than that for my dress allowance!

Though Liza was learning not to complain openly, her face was not so disciplined.

"You could do far worse, Miss Hastings." From her expression, Mrs. Strode clearly thought Kensington Palace was getting the sharp end of the bargain.

Liza calculated quickly. At that rate it would take more than two years to pay her account at Claridge's. Her things would be sold long before then. She began negotiating in earnest.

"It might be the usual wage for a maid, Mrs. Strode. But I think my situation warrants more."

With a bark of laughter, Mrs. Strode said, "Pray tell?"

"Victoria . . ."

"The Princess or Her Highness, and don't you forget it."

Darting her tongue over her dry lips, Liza began again. "The Princess insisted I be hired. She is sympathetic to my personal tragedy. And my education and experience offer the Princess more than a typical maid ever could."

Mrs. Strode's face was impassive. She stood up abruptly. "Wait here," she said and left the room. Liza didn't know if that were a good sign or not. For all she knew, the housekeeper might return with that stout footman to throw Liza out for impertinence. She felt suddenly overheated and edged her chair away from the fire.

Mrs. Strode returned as brusquely as she had left. "I've spoken with the Baroness. Against my advice, she has authorized thirty pounds."

Liza opened her mouth, to be interrupted by Mrs. Strode.

"Miss Hastings, I don't know why the Baroness is offering you this outrageous wage." She paused. "But I will not tolerate any more negotiation."

"Yes, Ma'am," Liza said with a small smile. It was a start.

"Miss Hastings, you will be entrusted with a national treasure. Princess Victoria will someday be our Queen. Take excellent care of her."

"Of course, Mrs. Strode," Liza assured her. There was a gentle knock at the door. It was Nell calling Mrs. Strode to dinner. "Miss Hastings, you'll join us. On Sundays, all the servants eat together. Since you will rarely see the other domestics, it will be useful to introduce you to everyone at the same time."

"It's only three o'clock," Liza said, glancing at the crystal clock on the side table. Nevertheless, her stomach rumbled in anticipation.

"Naturally. Servants in a great house have to eat several hours before our employers. Otherwise, who will prepare the meal and wait at table?"

Liza had never once considered it. During those thousands of intimate hours with maids over the years, as they had dressed her, bathed her, and ministered to her every need, Liza had never once asked about their lives below stairs. Flushed with shame, Liza followed Mrs. Strode to the dining room.

The sounds of a dozen noisy people in an enclosed room struck Liza's ears like a hammer. The men sat at one end, the women at the other. A tall man in black with a red, bulbous nose punctuating his long face, stood at the table's head.

This must be Mr. Jenkins, the drunken butler.

All the chatter stopped as Mrs. Strode sailed into the room, her chatelaine jangling at her waist. The servants craned their necks to get a better look at the newcomer.

Mrs. Strode went to the far end of the table. She gestured to Liza, who smiled brightly. "This is Miss Elizabeth Hastings. She will be serving the Baroness and Princess Victoria."

Liza's smile faded before the curious stares. The men were looking at her face while the women were openly envious of her dress. She recognized the footman in green livery who admitted her into the Palace. He stared at her and boldly smiled at her discomfiture. Nell waved. One of the parlor maids giggled, only to be hushed by her neighbors.

"Mademoiselle Blanche, please move down a seat for Miss Hastings," said Mrs. Strode. She addressed a superior-looking woman arguing in a lisping whisper with her neighbor. Like Liza, she wore street clothing, not a uniform. Another lady's maid then, Liza decided. Perhaps she served the Duchess.

"She sits below me," Mademoiselle Blanche answered in a French accent, with a shake of her jet black curls. "I outrank her."

Mr. Jenkins cleared his nose with a honk. "Mrs. Strode, I don't want to presume, but Mademoiselle Blanche's mistress is a Duchess while Miss Hastings will only serve a Baroness."

"*Exactement*," said Mademoiselle Blanche with a nod. "I serve the Duchess not *une baronne fausse*." Everyone looked blank. "A fake Baroness."

Liza frowned, trying to place Mademoiselle's accent.

"You forget, Mr. Jenkins, Miss Hastings will also serve the Princess, the future Queen." Mrs. Strode's nostrils flared and splotches of bright pink appeared on her round cheeks. "She sits higher than Mademoiselle Blanche."

"*Non! Je refuse*." Mademoiselle Blanche did not budge. She stared defiantly at the housekeeper, her nostrils flaring.

"I don't care where I sit," Liza said. She pulled out the chair below Mademoiselle Blanche's and sat down decisively. "What does it matter?"

The hostile expressions on everyone's face told Liza she had blundered.

"Miss Hastings, in the future, do not presume to substitute your judgment for mine," said Mrs. Strode. "Since Miss Hastings is already seated, we will discuss it another time."

Mademoiselle Blanche smiled triumphantly.

Eating alone might not be such a burden.

The door swung open and a scruffy kitchen boy strode in carrying a roast on an enormous platter. He placed it in front of Mrs. Strode, and handed her a carving knife and fork. Everyone watched reverently as she reduced the roast to thick slices, then the kitchen boy served everyone as though they were royalty.

"Excuse me, Mrs. Strode, is there any chicken?" Liza said. "Beef tends to give me indigestion."

Everyone at the table burst out laughing and the now familiar, forbidding look on Mrs. Strode's face gave Liza her answer. Mutely, she held out her plate and accepted a slice of roast beef.

Liza let the conversation flow over her head as she avoided bits of congealed fat floating in the meat's juices and wolfed down the overcooked cauliflower and stewed spinach. She looked up, startled, when she heard her name.

"Miss Hastings's belongings need to be collected, Mr. Jenkins," said Mrs. Strode.

Mr. Jenkins nodded. "I'll send Simon."

Simon turned out to be the handsome footman in green livery. He nodded to her, his mouth stuffed full of beef.

"I've only one trunk," Liza gritted her teeth to keep her jaw from trembling. "My other things are in storage." She prayed Mr. Arbuthnot would honor their agreement. "Should I accompany him?"

More tittering, instantly quelled by Mrs. Strode's glare. "Of course not! That would be unsuitable, Miss Hastings. Simon is perfectly capable of picking up another servant's trunk without your assistance."

Liza stared down at her plate, fingering her locket. Mama and Papa would be mortified to see her so humbled.

"What is the direction, Miss?" Simon asked, flashing her a glimpse of bright white teeth in a reassuring smile.

"Claridge's Hotel in Mayfair," Liza said.

There was a murmur at the name of the prestigious hotel.

With an avidity that Liza found distasteful, Mr. Jenkins asked, "With whom were you in service?"

"Pardon me?" Liza asked.

Mrs. Strode answered for Liza, "Miss Hastings was a guest at the hotel."

Each diner's fork stopped in midair as everyone stared at Liza.

Mademoiselle Blanche said to the table at large, "That explains her wardrobe." She leaned toward Liza and shamelessly inspected her jewelry. "Unless she learns to dress like what she is, she'll be on the street more quickly than the last one."

Liza's hand went protectively to her necklace.

Mr. Jenkins started to laugh, which turned into a fit of coughing when Mrs. Strode raised her eyebrows. "The Duchess will not countenance a maid dressing more fashionably than she," Mr. Jenkins said when he recovered.

"I'm in mourning," Liza protested. "I don't have many other clothes."

Mrs. Strode shrugged. "Make do. In time the Baroness will give you her old dresses. Once you've removed any frills which mark the dress as a lady's, you may wear them." She stared disapprovingly at the lace of Liza's dress.

"But I can't wear her clothes, she's much too tall," Liza blurted out.

Mademoiselle Blanche sniffed. "You alter them for yourself or sell them. It is a perquisite of the position. You will also get the Princess's clothes. Her clothes are beautifully made, even if they are not *à la mode*." She sounded envious.

Her curiosity about the Princess's oddly immature dress getting the better of her, Liza asked, "Why doesn't the Princess dress more suitably for her age?" The servants exchanged knowing looks.

"The Duchess feels the Princess is too young to follow fashion," Mrs. Strode said.

"She's sixteen!" Liza said.

"If the Duchess has her way," said Mr. Jenkins, "the Princess will always be treated like a little girl."

"*Pas du tout!*" Mademoiselle Blanche shook her head vigorously. "The Duchess is protecting Victoria, who is immature. She will protect her even when she becomes Queen, as her regent." She made a face in the housekeeper's direction. "Then she will be more important than the Princess. Which is why I sit higher at table."

Simon joined in, "But if Sir John Conroy lived in the Palace, his valet would sit higher than all of us."

"That man aims to be King in all but name," said Mr. Jenkins.

"King John," Mademoiselle said. "Or, as I hear the King calls him, 'Con-royal.'"

There was laughter all around the table.

Bewildered, Liza asked, "I've never heard of a Sir John. Who is he?"

"The Duchess's personal secretary and comptroller," Mr. Jenkins said. "He manages her accounts."

"More than just her accounts," Simon said with a leer.

"He's insufferable!" said the butler. "Yesterday, he suggested we were drinking too much port wine. I told him the household was drinking just as much as it always had." He hiccoughed.

"He accused me of eating the Duchess's bonbons," Mademoiselle Blanche added. "As if I could keep my figure if I stole candies. It must be the Princess. She is always sneaking food when she can get away with it."

Liza glanced around the table nervously. How was it a maid could speak so familiarly about the Princess? To her surprise, many of the servants, even Mrs. Strode, were nodding.

"Sir John thinks we've a thief in our midst," Mr. Jenkins pronounced.

"Aren't there guards at the Palace?" Liza asked.

"Who would pay for 'em?" Simon asked with a laugh.

"But the Princess is the heir to the throne!" Liza said. "Doesn't she need protecting?"

They all burst out laughing again. "The Princess barely has friends, much less enemies," Mr. Jenkins said. "Sir John and the Duchess keep her sequestered as much as they dare. They want her to rely on them for everything."

Liza felt a twinge of worry for the Princess.

Mrs. Strode gave a sharp glance around the table as though the conversation had gone too far. "It is not for us to question our betters." She took a sip of ale and then spoke to Mademoiselle Blanche. "Mademoiselle, as you are familiar with Miss Hasting's duties, I will look to you to help her settle in."

The maid scowled and began muttering under her breath in French. Liza listened carefully, not to the words, but to how she pronounced them. After a moment or two, she put down her fork and turned to Mademoiselle Blanche.

"Where are you from, Mademoiselle?" she asked sweetly.

Simon said in a smooth voice full of malice, "Mademoiselle is from Paris, where all the most superior maids come from. As she tells us. Frequently."

"I spent a summer in Paris once with my family," Liza said. "It's curious, but you don't speak like a Parisian at all."

Nell gasped, then giggled.

"You are mistaken, Miss Hastings." Spots of color appeared under the French girl's face powder. "I was born and trained in Paris."

Liza deliberately made her voice artless. "I heard your exact accent when we visited a pig farm in Normandy."

Simon chortled. "Miss Hastings has exposed you, Mademoiselle Pig-Keeper. What else have you lied about?"

"*C'est insupportable!* I'll not stand to be interrogated like this." Pushing back her chair, Mademoiselle Blanche leaned down and whispered in Liza's ear, "As the highest servants in the house, we might have been friends. But it will never be! *Jamais!*" She flounced out of the room, her nose in the air, like an insulted poodle.

"That will teach her to tangle with a real 'lady.' Silly cuckoo," Simon said, holding up his glass to toast Liza.

Liza cast her eyes to her plate to hide her flushed cheeks. Her first meal, and she had already won an admirer . . . and an enemy.

A BROADSHEET, PUBLISHED ANONYMOUSLY

PRINCESS VICTORIA: A TRUE HEIR TO THE HANOVERS?

Sources close to the little Princess living at Kensington Palace have alerted this writer to a worrisome situation. Princess Victoria, the heir presumptive to the throne, is woefully unprepared for her awesome destiny as Queen of the British Isles.

Our sources report she is mentally backward for her age, frivolous, and self-centered. Easily irritated by her tutors, she has been known to throw her schoolbooks at them in a fit of temper. Despite the devoted attention of her mother, the Princess is incapable of comprehending novels or poetry. She studies several languages, but speaks none of them well. English, which should be her native tongue, is pronounced with a noticeable lisp and, worse, a German accent.

Princess Victoria's weakness of mind leads this writer to question the Princess's readiness to rule. If the King, whose health worsens daily, should pass away before she achieves her eighteenth year, her Mother is designated to be regent. There could be no wiser choice. However, the nation might be even better served if the Duchess can be prevailed upon to remain regent until Victoria is at least twenty-one or perhaps even indefinitely.

4

In Which Liza Is Noticed and Not Noticed

LIZA WATCHED the hands on the fussy ormolu clock on the mantle tick the minutes away. The royals took their time over dinner. Liza willed them to hurry so she could complete her final interview with the Princess's mother, the Duchess of Kent.

"You will wait here until the Duchess comes," the Baroness had said an hour earlier.

"Here" was a grand drawing room in better repair than any room Liza had yet seen.

"How long will she be?" Liza asked.

The Baroness went on as though Liza hadn't spoken. "As far as the Duchess is concerned, you are English through and through. She will speak freely in German in front of a servant who she believes doesn't understand."

Liza realized her increased salary was not because Victoria liked her. The Baroness had her own reasons.

"You want me to be a spy?" Liza dared not be mistaken about the Baroness's intent.

"*Ja, eine Spionin.*" It was an ugly word in German or English.

"But why?"

"If you do your job properly, you will overhear the answer. If not, then you are too stupid and your linguistic skills are worthless to me."

Slowly, Liza said, "The Princess was very kind—I won't do anything against her."

The Baroness drew herself up. "And you think I would? Trust me, Miss Hastings, the Princess's interests and mine are exactly the same. Your information will serve us both."

"If it is to serve the Princess," Liza swallowed hard, "then I will do it."

The Baroness nodded, satisfied. "Keep your ears open. Do not speak unless spoken to. Your expression must be as blank as a sheet of paper."

Liza blinked. She had lost so much already. Was she to lose herself too? She looked up to see the Baroness's skirt disappearing out the door with a swish.

She examined the room more closely. At first glance it was all crimson, velvet, and luxury, but a second look revealed the walls had cracks as fine and wide as spiderwebs. The ceiling was stained from old leaks. Two marble fireplaces flanked the doorway, but only one had a meager coal fire burning. Near the windows, sunlight had faded the blood red carpet.

This Sir John must be a poor manager to let the house fall into such disrepair.

Click-clack. Click-clack.

A woman—it must be the Duchess, Liza decided—tottered in on high heels. She wore a scarlet velvet gown, with matching satin ribbons. It was chic, but designed for a debutante, not a mature Duchess. Liza's father would have noted, in his driest voice, that the Duchess was mutton dressed as lamb.

"Outrageous!" the Duchess cried in German. "It's disrespectful to me!"

Her hands gripped a broadsheet newspaper. Liza recognized the style. Hawked on the street for a few pennies, broadsheets were full of delicious gossip and innuendo. Since coming to London, Liza and her mama had bought several of them behind Papa's back. The Duchess paced furiously, her heels catching the threadbare patches of carpet. Peering nearsightedly at the newsprint, she collided with Liza and her pointy shoe nearly crushed Liza's toe. Liza cried out and the startled Duchess rocked backward.

So much for the unobtrusive servant.

"I beg your pardon, Your Grace." Liza was careful to follow the Baroness's instructions to speak English.

The Duchess stared at her, her quick glance taking in every detail of Liza's fine mourning gown. A crease appeared between her eyes as she began speaking English. "Who are you? We aren't expecting visitors today."

"I'm the Princess's new maid," Liza said, remembering to curtsy. Her toes stung from the Duchess's pointed shoes.

"A maid? In such a dress? When were you hired?" the Duchess asked, her expression puzzled, as if she were trying to remember a detail that had escaped her.

"Today, Your Grace."

"Oh. Very good." Turning her back on Liza, the Duchess returned to the broadsheet.

Liza rested her head against the wall. She had prayed Kensington Palace would be a refuge, but now she wondered if it were an asylum.

The door slammed open and a gentleman paused in the doorway. He was middle-aged, but extraordinarily good-looking. His dark trousers and tailored coat accentuated his broad shoulders and narrow waist perfectly. His gray silk cravat was impeccable and fastened with a diamond tiepin. Liza stared admiringly at the effect he made.

"My lady, what is this upset?" He also spoke in German as he made a beeline for the Duchess. He placed both hands on her shoulders.

"Sir John," said the Duchess, leaning into his embrace. "Thank goodness you are here." Her voice was breathy and pleased.

So this is what the servants mean about Sir John managing the Duchess.

The Duchess's coils of hair quivered with a life of their own. "Sir John, they're saying I'm a terrible mother!" She shoved the broadsheet at him. He harrumphed as he read.

"Do you see where they criticize Victoria's accent?" The Duchess interrupted. "How unfair, when I've been so careful to limit her German!"

Still scanning the article, Sir John said absently, "We can do something about that."

"I already have, Sir John," the Duchess simpered. "There's a new maid to wait on her. Her accent seems ladylike." She pointed to

Liza, who held herself motionless in the corner. Sir John started; he had not noticed Liza until that instant.

"I was not consulted," he said coldly. Disengaging himself from the Duchess, he strode across the room to Liza. "What's your name, girl?" he asked in English.

"Liza Hastings, sir," Liza replied in a low voice.

"No maid in this house ever wore a dress as nice as yours," he said.

"My parents died recently and I have to earn my living," Liza answered.

"As a maid?" He eyed her carefully.

"I prefer to make my own way, sir."

"Very commendable." He smiled, his dark blue eyes glittering with admiration. "But a word of caution: you must be careful not to outshine the Princess. She is not amused unless she is the prettiest girl in the room."

Liza felt a blush creeping up her neck.

Sir John might have paid her another compliment, but the Duchess interrupted. "Sir John, what is taking so long?" she cried in German. "Come away from the girl." She extended her hand to him, her wrist weighed down by a many stranded bracelet of precious pearls.

Sir John hurried back to the Duchess's side and led her to a settee. He stroked her palm with his thumb. His hands looked smooth. Liza's Papa had told her never to trust a man with a manicure.

"My lady," he said. "The girl seems quite suitable. Much more refined than the last maid."

The Duchess's kohl-lined eyes narrowed. "But you always seemed to like Annie . . . until the day you dismissed her."

Liza edged closer, hoping to hear something useful.

"She pried into my private business so she had to go." His dark eyebrows came together in a scowl and his fingers pressed the Duchess's hand harder as he rubbed.

"Sir John, you are hurting me!" the Duchess cried. She pulled back her hand. His cufflink snagged her pearl bracelet and the clasp came apart. Pearls spilled everywhere.

"Girl! Don't just stand there!" Sir John barked at Liza.

Liza scurried to chase the pearls rolling into every corner. Under a settee, she found a dusty embroidery hoop and gathered the pieces of the bracelet in the bamboo circle.

The Duchess, apparently forgetting Liza, turned back to Sir John. "What are we to do about this terrible newspaper?" she asked in German.

"My lady, this story can only help us."

"How can you say so?"

He glanced over at Liza. She was careful to appear uncomprehending, as she reached for a pearl in an unswept corner.

"Did you read to the end?" he asked.

"I was too upset to read that far," confessed the Duchess.

"The writer feels you are an excellent choice to be her regent."

"So I am." The Duchess almost purred with anticipation. "Victoria will be happy for me to assume her terrible burden, I'm sure of it," she said. "She is anxious about her future. You know what tempers she's had lately."

"Let her have her tantrums. In the end, she'll do as she's told," said Sir John. "We have a year to bring her to heel."

I never expected to feel sorry for a Princess.

"Unless the King dies before she's eighteen, we are left with nothing," the Duchess said, her voice dropping to a whisper.

Liza breathed as shallowly as she could.

Sir John smiled. "This reporter goes so far as to suggest your regency be extended."

The Duchess sat up straight. "Until Victoria is twenty-one?"

"Or longer!" he said, watching her intently. "We'd have years to ensure we . . . *you* get what you deserve."

The Duchess caught his thought and went further. "We could pay my debts, reward you properly for your service, commission a decent wardrobe . . ." She couldn't list the advantages quickly enough. "If only William would die, as he's been threatening to do these past six years!"

"Even if he lives past Victoria's eighteenth birthday, I have a plan," Sir John reassured her. "Parliament reads the papers. The Lords are worried they will have to deal with a featherbrained girl. They much prefer to work with us. Who knows, Your Grace?" He lifted her hand to his full lips. "Parliament may let you rule indefinitely. Victoria need never bother her head about the crown."

They want the throne for themselves!

Worn out by her fretting, the Duchess's body sagged against the padded arm of the settee. "I'm exhausted. I need to lie down."

"You must rest, before your responsibilities overwhelm you," Sir John said to the Duchess.

Envy coursed through Liza; she wouldn't mind a respite herself.

The Duchess leaned against his chest for a moment and her fingertips touched his sideburns, then she click-clacked out of the room.

Even before the sound of the Duchess's shoes faded, Sir John turned to Liza, where she still knelt on the carpet, chasing the Duchess's forgotten pearls.

"Let me be of assistance," he said in English. His voice was silky. Without warning, he placed his hands on her waist and effortlessly lifted her up. His hands lingered too long and Liza felt a blush creeping from her shoulder blades up to her cheeks. She wished she had heeded Mama's advice and worn a corset.

"Thank you, sir. I can stand on my own."

Sir John reached out and ran his finger through the long blonde curl hanging next to her cheek. "So charming. You're certain to win Victoria's heart."

Liza trembled from the effort it took not to pull away. She would do herself no favors by offending him for he had the Duchess' affection, and her ear. No doubt he could dismiss her as easily as he had the last maid.

"Perhaps you can do a small service for me," Sir John said.

Wary, Liza asked, "What?"

"I would like to get Victoria a special gift for her birthday. Find out for me what she particularly wants."

There's no harm in that. Victoria will probably thank me.

"Yes, sir."

Sir John reached into his pocket and pulled out a sovereign. He tossed it into her hoop full of pearls.

Liza stared down at the coin.

"I am generous to my friends."

"Thank you, sir," she mumbled. Though she was in no position to sneeze at the money, Liza was mortified at the casual way he assumed her loyalty was for sale.

His eyes looked her up and down. "Excellent," he murmured and turned on his heel.

Liza sank into a chair in the corner of the empty room. Finally, a moment to reflect on her changed circumstances. Her first day and she already had too many parts to play at Kensington Palace. And too many employers. To whom should she be loyal? Sir John, the Duchess, the Baroness, Princess Victoria?

Who will do the most for me?

It was almost six o'clock and the room was growing darker by the minute. Her breathing became quieter, almost imperceptible even in the silent room. Liza heard a slight sound coming from the cabinet built into the wall behind her. Kensington Palace was filled with black beetles, spiders, traitors; why not mice? She gathered her skirt tightly to protect her ankles and pounded on the cabinet door. The sounds stopped so abruptly, she wondered if she had imagined them.

Nell arrived with a lit candelabrum. "Why are you sittin' alone in the dark? Come 'ave a cuppa tea. Simon's fetchin' your trunk right now."

Liza was tempted to ask Nell about Sir John and his plans to steal the throne of England, but she thought better of it. In Kensington Palace, she might need a secret or two of her own.

5

In Which Liza Takes Up Her Duties

SIMON LIFTED LIZA'S TRUNK off his shoulder as though it weighed nothing. He dropped it on the wooden floor with a thud that echoed up and down the empty hallway outside her door. Liza winced, thinking of her fragile treasures.

"It's lonely up here," Simon said, glancing around the bare room. "Are you sure you won't be nervous?" In his fine livery, designed to show off his trim footman's figure, Simon looked like a tropical bird. His bulk pushed all the air out of the tiny room; there wasn't enough left for Liza.

"I'm quite used to being alone, now," she said.

"I can check on you, if you like," Simon offered.

"No, thank you. I'll be fine." She wished he would go; his attentions made her uncomfortable.

"It's not what you are used to, I suppose?" Simon asked.

Thinking of the luxurious suite at Claridge's, Liza almost laughed out loud. "It's very . . . quaint." She ran a gloved finger down the small bureau and frowned at the accumulation of dust.

"You must have a tale to tell, coming from Mayfair to here." He ran his hand from his forehead to the back of his neck, smoothing his thick hair down.

"My parents died, that's all." Liza licked her lips nervously, then instantly regretted it when Simon's eyes stayed locked on her mouth. "Thank you for bringing up my trunk, but I'm very tired. Good night."

With more refinement than she would have credited him, Simon took his leave. Liza closed the door after him, listening to his footsteps moving down the hall. Once certain he was gone, she shot the bolt home with unsteady hands. Finally, she was alone.

She pushed herself away from the door and began to explore her new living quarters. It didn't take long. The wind rattled the tiny window and threatened the flame of her cheap tallow candle. Her bed lay wedged under a slanted roof of bare wood and on the wall hung a tiny mirror with a crack that ran all the way through it. A battered chest of drawers and a tiny table and chair completed the furnishings. In the corner, as Mrs. Strode had promised, sat a battered chamber pot.

Resting in the center of the narrow room, Liza's single trunk reminded her of all she had lost. She braced herself and lifted the lid. On top lay a soft rose shawl, the last gift her father had given her mother. She lifted it as though it were a precious treasure and wrapped it around herself, inhaling her mother's jasmine perfume.

Exhausted and fighting panic, she flung herself down on the scratchy blanket that barely covered the bed and let herself cry. For the first time since her parents died, she didn't worry about anyone overhearing her sobs. The thin pillow became damp with her tears.

A long while later, she sat up, her eyes sore and her throat aching.

That is quite enough, Liza. Mama always said self-pity wastes energy and spoils the complexion.

She took a deep breath, held it, then tried to exhale all her troubles in one long sigh. If she were to have any sort of new life, she would have to build it herself. To begin, she must make this dreadful room her own. Placing the shawl on the bed, she went back to unpacking. She arranged delicate sea shells from a trip to the Ostend shore, a sketch of the Winter Palace in St. Petersburg, and a long feather from her mother's finest hat on the battered bureau. She tacked her favorite fashion drawings from the Paris papers on the wall. The miniature portrait of her mother, encased in pearls, she propped on the rickety table next to her bed. She hung her father's watch carefully on the bedpost. She draped her two mourning dresses over the chair.

At the bottom of the trunk, Liza found what she didn't even know she was searching for: a leather book wrapped in muslin. Her chest hollowed out as she relived the moment Mama had placed the journal in her hands. She opened the cover to the inscription in her mother's elegant handwriting, "Dearest Liza, the first year in society is a year like no other. I hope you use this journal to remember every detail of your adventures. Love, Mama."

So far, Liza had used it only once; the day she buried her parents. By the light of the sputtering candle, Liza found her pen and ink. She opened the journal, averting her eyes from the first entry, and began to write.

1 April 1836 Excerpt from the Journal of Miss Elizabeth Hastings

Who am I? A fortnight ago, I knew. Liza, beloved daughter of Matthew and Mathilde, ready for her first season. We looked forward to introducing me to society and finding me a suitable husband. But now? I am a boat whose mooring has been cut. I could come ashore anywhere. This next year will indeed be a year like no other.

My first(?) port of call is Kensington Palace. I came for one position, but was offered another. And then another. Am I still a lady? A maid? Or a spy?

Papa always said a businessman looks for opportunities to profit. The Princess Victoria's problem is my chance. The Duchess and Sir John are scheming against her; they want the throne for themselves. If I can help the Princess, who knows where her generosity might lead? Money, a title, a good marriage? All the things Mama and Papa wanted for me. The Princess already likes me. Next, she must need me. Who else will gather the information she needs to protect herself?

Rereading these words, I seem a cold and calculating stranger. What choice do I have? I must make my own way. But were our stations equal, Victoria is someone I could like. Perhaps I can serve her without losing myself. The first step will be to win her trust. To do this, I must separate her from the Baroness Lehzen. Surely the Princess must be alone sometime!

Liza closed the journal and carefully slid it between her mattress and the wooden pallet. She glanced at her father's watch. It was late. She wondered how to call a maid to help her undress. Then, like a wave of cold water drenching her body, she remembered there was no one to call.

I am the maid.

With a sigh, she began disassembling her outfit. Separating the sleeves from the arm holes proved relatively easy. Her skirt slipped off with minor difficulty. But the bodice closed with hooks and eyes in the back. Only after a struggle that would have done a contortionist credit, did Liza manage to unfasten them. The rest of the ensemble came off quickly, but she was at a loss when it came to putting the pieces away in her trunk. It was a sobering fact: she had never tidied up after herself.

Liza eyed the thin blanket and rubbed the scratchy sheets between her thumb and forefinger. Wrapping herself in her mother's shawl, she ducked into bed, careful not to hit her head on the sloped ceiling. She shifted her weight half a dozen times before she concluded there was no section of the mattress that was not lumpy.

She blew out her candle: Nell had given her only two for the entire week; she must learn to conserve. A tiny tear escaped her resolve to cry no more and in the dark Liza let it fall.

Too soon after Liza placed her head on her pillow, there was a tap at the door.

"Not now," Liza said, half asleep.

"Miss, unlock the door." It was Nell's voice.

Sitting up, Liza slammed her forehead on the slanted ceiling. She touched the sore spot as she got up and made her way through the dark, freezing room to slide back the bolt. The coconut matting on the floor felt damp to her bare feet.

Nell carried in a heavy tray with a pot of tea and a tiny piece of rock-hard sugar and a pitcher of milk. A lit candle stood on the tray. "Good morning, Miss. It's six o'clock." Her friendly face was a welcome sight in the cold room.

"Heavens, I've never been awake this early." Liza rubbed her eyes and looked at the tray. "Do I bring this to the Baroness?"

Nell snickered. "Lordy, Miss, you don't know anything. This tray is for you." She stepped back into the hall and brought in a basin of cold water for Liza to bathe herself.

"Oh, thank you." Liza yawned and accepted a cup of lukewarm tea. "Nell, you've been very kind. Can I impose on you further? I don't know what to wear."

"May I?" Nell carried the candle to look through the small pile of Liza's dresses. "Most of these would do, but they are too dark."

Although she knew how little that mattered here, Liza said once again, "I'm in mourning."

"Not for anyone in the royal family," Nell said flatly. "And that's the only mourning a servant in this 'ouse wears. Lady's maids should be pretty to look at." She held up a light gray dress. "P'raps this one, if we add one of these white collars," she said.

Liza pulled off her nightdress, and Nell helped her into her gown. Liza was particularly grateful to have someone to help fasten the row of tiny seed pearl buttons from the small of her back to the top of her neck.

"Miss, 'ow did you get yerself out of yer clothes last night?" Nell asked. "I'd 'ave 'elped if I'd thought of it."

"I managed," Liza said, grimly recalling her battle with her bodice. "When do I wake the Baroness?" she asked over her shoulder.

"Not until eight o'clock. The servants eat their breakfast at seven." Nell stepped back. "All finished." She yawned, and Liza suddenly noticed the wearied lines creasing her face.

"Nell, you look exhausted," Liza said. "When do you get up?"

"At four o'clock, Miss. I've ever so much to do. I sweep and dust the Duchess's drawing room, clean the grates, light the fires and wait on the lady's maids."

"I've added·to your work. I'm sorry." Liza was ashamed to think her whole life, she had lazed in bed until ten o'clock in the morning, or even later.

"It's my job, Miss," Nell said simply. "And I don't mind 'elping you. Yer a real lady. But Miss Frenchy's a different story. She's a proper terror. 'er tea is always too 'ot or too cold or too bitter. As if Mrs. Strode would give me extra sugar for the asking!"

The door banged open. Liza whirled around to face a fully dressed, and furious, Mademoiselle. Mademoiselle's artificially dark hair was gathered at the top and fell down in tight curls on either side of her face. Liza wondered if it might be a wig. Her heart sank. After the scene at dinner, Liza had hoped Mademoiselle could be avoided for a while.

"I have waited for my tea for twenty minutes," Mademoiselle cried. "And now I find you gossiping in here. I'll have to report you to Mrs. Strode."

"Again?" asked Nell.

Ignoring her, Mademoiselle's gunmetal eyes swept Liza's tiny room. "You have Annie Mason's old room. *C'est absurd!*"

"It's small and damp, but I am the newest . . ." Liza stopped because Mademoiselle looked like a pot ready to boil over. Nell smothered a giggle with her hand.

"What is it?" Liza asked.

Nell whispered between her fingers. "She has to share a room."

Liza's lips formed an O but no sound came out.

"*C'etait insupportable.* I am certain that you are no better than Annie Mason," Mademoiselle hissed like an angry snake. "She lowered the tone of the entire household."

"Mademoiselle, you need not worry about my morals," Liza said. "Since you only aspire to the gentry, whereas I have actually fallen from it, you may trust I know precisely how to behave."

Mademoiselle was sputtering in French, but Liza didn't cede an inch.

"Why are you here, Mademoiselle?" she asked. "I assure you I am perfectly capable of waking up without you."

"Madame Strode told me to show you the Dutch classic braid the Baroness prefers. But I will not stand here to be abused," said Mademoiselle, glaring at both Nell and Liza. "You and the vulgar Baroness are perfectly matched." She stormed out the door, her jet black curls bobbing down her neck.

"Well, I never," Nell stared at Liza with undisguised admiration. "That was a treat, Miss. Wait 'til I tell the others."

A belated twinge of caution gnawed at Liza. "Perhaps it should stay between us."

"She can be a bad enemy," Nell agreed. "But you won't have much to do with the Duchess's lady's maid. Especially since the Duchess and Sir John have fallen out lately with the Baroness."

"What do you mean?" Liza asked.

"The closer the Princess gets to bein' Queen, the more the Duchess pushes away the Princess's friends. She'd fire the Baroness if she could, but the King likes 'er. So you see, Miss Frenchy wouldn't be your friend for all the coal in Newcastle."

Liza worked it out. "Do you mean, if *her* mistress dislikes *my* mistress, then we are enemies?"

"Below stairs is the same as above." Nell grinned. "Not to mention what you said yesterday at table."

"Well, she can go to the devil for all I care," Liza said with a lot more bravery than she felt. "I have my own job to do. First, would you show me how to do this special braid?" She handed her tortoiseshell comb to Nell.

Nell showed Liza the hairstyle, a simple braided rope of hair wound around the top of the head.

"Trust Mademoiselle to make it sound difficult," Liza said. "Dutch classic braid indeed! I'll have no trouble doing the Baroness's hair now."

Nell caught a glimpse of Liza's father's watch. "Oh Lord, I must go or Mrs. Strode'll take my 'ead off." Turning to leave, she gave Liza an encouraging smile. "You'll do fine, Miss." Then she skittered out of the room.

Liza brushed her long hair quickly and with deft fingers twisted it into a demure chignon. Reluctantly, she left her locket on the bureau. It would not do for a maid. Examining her reflection in a hand mirror, she hoped she looked the part she was about to play.

After a meager breakfast of watery porridge, Liza met Nell at the Baroness's door. Without knocking, Nell entered the surprisingly small bedroom, laid the breakfast tray complete with eggs, sausages, liverwurst, and tomatoes on a table and opened the curtains to the narrow window. She winked at Liza as she withdrew.

"Girl, bring the tray here," the Baroness said from her narrow bed. The shelf hanging above her head on the wall overflowed with handmade dolls. From the corner of her eye, Liza recognized in each doll a past Queen of England.

The room was as cold as Liza's own and the damp mingled with the Baroness's lilac-scented perfume. Liza wrinkled her nose, trying without success to suppress a sneeze.

As if reading Liza's mind, the Baroness said, "It is the fourth room assigned to me in as many years. Each room is smaller and worse than before. But Sir John is sorely mistaken if he thinks he can drive me away." She smiled with satisfaction, as if her loyalty to the Princess was measured by her suffering.

Liza didn't know what to say, so she bobbed a quick curtsy.

"So?" The Baroness was intent on her excavation of a boiled egg.

"Baroness?" Liza asked.

"What was the Duchess so upset about yesterday? Or did you forget my instructions?"

Liza described the Duchess's reaction to the broadsheet and how Sir John comforted her. The Baroness did not seem surprised by the liberties Sir John had taken with the Duchess.

"Where is this newspaper?" the Baroness asked.

Liza wracked her brain. What had the Duchess done with it? "I think the Duchess kept it," she said.

"Find it," the Baroness ordered.

"I will look for it," Liza promised.

The Baroness seemed satisfied, so Liza decided to hold back Sir John's master plan to steal the throne. She'd keep the most valuable secrets to purchase the Princess's gratitude.

"Now, help me up!" barked the Baroness.

Once she was upright, the Baroness shook off Liza's help. Standing tall, she turned to face the wall, her back to Liza. Her plaits of gray hair hung down to her waist. She opened her arms wide.

Is she praying?

After a long moment, the Baroness said, "My dressing gown, Liza."

I missed my first cue.

Liza hurried to help her put on the dressing gown, a thick gray flannel that appeared dull but was lined with soft astrakhan wool. The Baroness tightened the dressing gown belt and sat down at her battered vanity table.

"My hair," Baroness Lehzen ordered.

Liza stepped forward and lifted one of the loose plaits of hair. They were heavy and smelled faintly of rancid grease. As Liza untied the rags, flakes of the Baroness's scalp scattered on her shoulders. Liza gagged and the Baroness glared at her.

"Excuse me, Baroness, it must have been something I ate," Liza lied, taking deep breaths to stave off nausea. She concentrated on the work her fingers had to do, and tried to keep her thoughts from drifting to her mother's golden hair.

The braid completed to the Baroness's satisfaction, Lehzen stood up, took off her dressing robe and then her nightdress. Liza found it easier to meet her black eyes than to look at her naked body.

"My corset." The Baroness pointed. Standing behind the Baroness, Liza fit the stiff fabric around the stomach and then moved to the front to fasten it around the Baroness's sagging abdomen. Her face frozen, Liza forced her fingers to lace it up.

"Tighter," the Baroness said. "A woman is only as virtuous as her corset is unyielding."

Only because she is too uncomfortable to think about sinning!

Liza pulled harder. She had performed this intimate service for her mother—but never had she realized how degrading it was to do it as a paid servant.

"Tighter."

She pulled until the corset strings made deep painful creases in her fingers.

"Enough," snapped the Baroness. "You're hurting me."

Holding back a sharp retort, Liza rubbed the welts on her hands. She muttered, "I'm sorry, Baroness."

"Tomorrow, I trust you shall remember to pull just so hard and no harder." Her lips pinched together as tightly as her corset laces. "Now, my gown."

The gown was hanging with a dozen somber dresses in an armoire in the corner. Pulling the Baroness's stockings up around her flabby legs carried its own humiliation. But finally, it was done: the Baroness was fully dressed.

"It is time to wake Victoria. The Duchess will still be sleeping, so be quiet."

"Why doesn't the Princess have her own room?" Liza asked. She wanted to see if the Baroness's story matched the one she had heard in the servant's hall. "After all, she's nearly seventeen."

"Victoria is our most precious jewel," Lehzen said. "She is never alone."

If the Princess was never alone, how was Liza to become her confidant? But at the moment she had a more urgent consideration: what was the proper distance for a lady's maid to walk behind her employer?

6

In Which Liza Tries to Win the Affection of the Princess

LIZA FOLLOWED THE BARONESS through several
antechambers until they entered a large bedroom
with high ceilings and a beautiful marble fireplace.
The room was warm and heavy with the cloying scent
of flowers: Liza felt as though she was walking into
a greenhouse. Although the room's proportions were
generous, it felt cramped. Glancing about, Liza understood why: there were two complete sets of furniture.
Two writing desks. Two crystal jars of bonbons. Two
wardrobes. Two ornate mahogany beds: one narrow
and the other impossibly wide. Both were occupied.
In her tiny bed, the Princess turned onto her stomach and groaned. The Duchess, a mask over her eyes,
snored in hers.

A noise behind her made Liza whirl around. Dash, the Princess's dog, slept in a miniature bed identical to the Princess's. He too, was lying on his stomach, snoring.

"*Prinzessin*, it is time to rise," the Baroness said.

"Not yet, Lehzen, just a few more minutes."

The Princess burrowed into her thick feather pillow. Liza sighed as she remembered begging her mother for a little more time to sleep.

The Baroness would not be denied. "The future Queen must not be indolent."

"'Fie, you slugabed,'" Liza quoted.

The Baroness glared at Liza. "Did you just call the Princess a slug?"

"No, no . . . it's from *Romeo and Juliet*," Liza stammered. "The nurse says it to the heroine."

From the bed came a muffled giggle. "At that point in the play, Liza, I do believe Juliet was dead. It's not a very auspicious way to begin the day."

Keeping her voice light, Liza replied, "O lamentable day!"

"Maybe not so much, now you are here," Princess Victoria replied, a smile in her voice.

Her face creased with ill-temper, the Baroness scolded the Princess, "Victoria, a Princess does not joke with her maid."

"Oh, Lehzen, don't be tiresome." The Princess sat up and stretched her arms wide.

"Liza, the lavender dressing gown from that wardrobe." The Baroness pointed. The Princess had at least six dressing gowns in various colors, all exquisitely trimmed with ribbons, bows, and lace. The Baroness went to another closet to find matching embroidered slippers.

As soon as the Baroness' back was turned, the Princess gave Liza a little wave. "I'm glad you stayed," she said. "I've been very bored."

Liza curtsied, feeling very daring. "I'll do my best to amuse you, Your Highness."

Dressed all in lavender, the Princess sat on a cushioned stool in front of her vanity table. The Baroness began to brush Victoria's long fair hair with a tortoiseshell brush. "*Eins, zwei, drei,*" the Baroness counted.

Liza stood by, idle, except to wonder how many strokes the Baroness could possibly manage.

"Lehzen, surely fifty would be enough," the Princess said, grimacing at her governess. "One hundred strokes every morning seems excessive."

"Don't be foolish, *Vickelchen.* Your hair is your best feature."

Liza suspected this was a conversation repeated every morning. *Small wonder she is so bored.*

When the Baroness reached fifty, she stopped brushing to knead her arthritic fingers.

Liza reached out. "Baroness, I can help."

The Baroness struck Liza's hand hard with the back of the brush. "I am the only one who brushes the Princess's hair."

Rubbing her stinging hand, Liza choked on her indignation. Never in all her life had she been struck. She glanced up at her reflection in the mirror. This girl, with sad, green eyes and red cheeks like splashes of paint on her pale skin, was a stranger.

Victoria gave Liza a small sympathetic smile. To her own surprise, Liza's spirits rose.

The Princess's morning toilette complete, the Baroness led the way to the schoolroom, where she had interviewed Liza the day before.

At the top of the narrow stairs, the Princess stopped and held out her arm.

Liza paused, unsure what to do. "Your Highness?" she asked.

"Take my arm," the Princess said, her face scarlet with mortification. "I'm not permitted to walk down the stairs alone."

Sixteen years old and not permitted to descend stairs alone?

"Victoria, you cannot take the slightest risk," the Baroness said over her shoulder.

Liza took the Princess's arm, trying to convey her support and sympathy with her eyes.

A solitary breakfast sat waiting for Victoria on the school table. While the Princess wolfed down her eggs and sausages, Liza stood in the corner trying not to think about food.

"Victoria, don't gobble your breakfast," the Baroness said, sipping her second cup of unsweetened tea.

"But it's delicious." Victoria shoved another sausage through her cupid's bow lips.

"Princesses should not be greedy. It reflects badly on their upbringing—and on their waistline."

The Princess put down her last sausage, gazing at it longingly. Liza stared too; her breakfast had been flavorless porridge and lukewarm tea. Her stomach made a long growling sound. The Princess giggled.

"Liza, why don't you have the sausage?" Liza stepped forward, only to be stopped short by the Baroness's scandalized expression.

"Victoria, what are you thinking? Your maid cannot eat with you!"

Liza slunk back to the corner.

"I don't see why I can't give away my own breakfast," the Princess muttered.

Click-clack. The Duchess arrived, dressed in an elaborate morning gown of mauves and pinks in a riotous bouquet of bows and silk flowers.

"Good morning, Victoria."

"Good morning, Mama."

"I expect to hear good reports from your tutors. What are you doing today?" The Duchess looked at Baroness Lehzen who answered quickly.

"The customary schedule, Your Grace. At half past nine, geography, at half past ten, history, and the rites of the Church of England at half past eleven."

The Princess sighed. "I hate the Kensington System. It is the bane of my existence. Why can't Sir John ever let me rest?"

The Duchess frowned. "Sir John and I have designed the Kensington System to prepare you for your destiny. Parliament and the bishops think very highly of it."

"But, Mama," the Princess wailed, "I never have any time to myself. I never have any fun."

"Time enough to have fun when you are grown, with the responsibilities of the nation on your shoulders."

Liza noted the Princess accepted the Duchess's ridiculous reasoning without question.

"Mama, you get to visit friends and go into town. Why can't I? I'm sixteen!"

"Victoria, your ingratitude pierces my heart. After all the sacrifices I've made for you!" The Duchess waited, tapping her foot, but the Princess only sighed. Finally, the Duchess nodded to Lehzen to continue the schedule.

"At two o'clock," the Baroness said in a monotone, "arithmetic, and at three o'clock, languages: Greek and Latin, followed by an hour of conversation in French."

"Excellent. Work hard, my dear. I must dress to visit the Duchess of Northumberland." With more click-clacks, the Duchess was gone. The Princess stuck her tongue out at her retreating back.

"Victoria!" the Baroness scolded. "What a rascal you are!"

"I'm sorry." The Princess glanced at Liza. "Tell me Lehzen, I study so many languages, why not German?"

The Baroness shook her head. "The people do not want a German Queen; they want a British one."

"The Queen's guests will speak the language she, I mean I, choose."

"All the more reason to be gracious. Queen Elizabeth spoke six languages."

"But who wants to be like Elizabeth? So mannish. And she had black teeth." The Princess ran her tongue delicately over her small teeth. "No wonder she never married."

"They named an entire age after her," said the Baroness with a sidelong smile. "You should be so fortunate!"

"A Victorian age. It has distinction," murmured the Princess. "It's a good thing they didn't change my name. Liza, did you know last year it was proposed in Parliament that my name be changed to Charlotte after my dead aunt. But it came to nothing." Victoria giggled. "Imagine, a Charlottian age!"

"Victorian is much better," Liza agreed.

Dabbing the corners of her mouth with a linen napkin, the Princess smiled.

"Victoria," the Baroness began. "Don't—"

"Be familiar. I know, Lehzen."

———

After breakfast Princess Victoria's school day began. Geography with Reverend Davys came first. The reverend was a bald elderly man, with one tuft of soft white hair on his chin. At first Liza thought his face seemed stern, but then she noticed the laugh wrinkles at the corners of his eyes. He was not smiling this morning, however; the Princess had not learned her capital cities.

"Princess, what is the capital of Spain?" he asked.

Madrid.

"Lisbon!" the Princess said.

"Princess, no, it's Madrid," the reverend said. "Of which country is Lisbon the capital?"

The Princess put her hands on her hips. "Obviously, I thought it was Spain."

"Princess, lack of preparation is not an excuse for rudeness."

Liza was impressed; this reverend was not overawed by the Princess's rank.

"What does it matter?" the Princess asked, shrugging her shoulders. "Spain hasn't been important in centuries."

"It may become so again. And in any case, Lisbon is not the capital of Spain." The Reverend beckoned to Liza, "Maid, fetch an atlas so Her Highness can look it up herself."

Liza placed the atlas on the table. Princess Victoria was pouting and barely looked up.

"Portugal," Liza mouthed.

"What did you say?"

Liza widened her eyes, trying to warn the Princess.

"Liza, speak up," the Princess insisted.

"Portugal," Liza said in a low voice.

Reverend Davys appeared behind Liza's shoulder. "So, Princess, your maid's grasp of European geography is better than your own?" he asked with a hint of humor in his voice.

The Princess turned an annoyed look on Liza.

"Your Highness, I was just trying to help," Liza said.

The reverend said, "Perhaps a little friendly rivalry is just the thing for you, Princess. I wonder I never thought of it before. Why don't we play a game?"

The Princess, her miff forgotten, clapped her hands. "I love games; I am very good at them."

With a slight smile, the reverend said, "I'll call out the country, and you girls can compete to answer first. Egypt."

"Casablanca," shouted the Princess.

"Cairo," Liza said.

"One to the maid," said the Reverend. "France."

"I know that one! Paris," said the Princess.

"The score is tied," he said. "Russia."

"Moscow!" crowed Victoria.

"St. Petersburg," corrected Liza.

"Two for the maid."

"Bother, Liza. How do you know all this?" the Princess asked. She stood up and stalked to the window, her arms clasped across her chest. Liza stared after her, dismayed her future Queen was acting like a sulky child.

The reverend murmured to Liza, "It would be prudent to remember Her Highness does not like to lose." He looked at the clock on the mantle, and said, "Princess, my time is up. I will see you tomorrow."

Victoria pointedly did not acknowledge his departure.

Liza hurried to Princess Victoria's side. "Princess, please don't be offended. I've been to many of those cities. My father traveled for his business and my mother and I often accompanied him."

"How interesting for you," the Princess said coolly. "I, on the other hand, have never been anywhere. My duty traps me on this island."

"My traveling days are behind me," Liza said. She had played on the Princess's sympathies once before; she'd do so again to regain her goodwill. "Since my family is gone, I shall never go anywhere interesting again."

The Princess's stiff posture softened a little.

"But when you are Queen," Liza obliged the Princess's obvious preference to talk about herself, "there will be no limit to the places you can go."

The Princess brightened.

That was the right thing to say.

"But even when I am Queen, my mother will be ruling for me. Over me. Instead of me. She won't let me go anywhere," the Princess retorted.

"But after the regency . . ." Liza said, wondering how the Princess would react to the news her mother wanted to be her daughter's regent forever.

"Then I can do as I like." The Princess positively glowed. "Where should I go first? Have you really been to St. Petersburg? Is it beautiful?"

"Very beautiful, but the most interesting thing was the *Beliye Nochi*, the White Nights," Liza said. "In June, the sky doesn't ever darken. Even at midnight, it's still bright. Everyone stays up all night and goes to parties."

"That sounds so amusing! Last year I danced with Tsar Alexander. He was very charming." The Princess clapped her hands. "And I love staying up late, but I never get to stay up past ten o'clock. Even if Mama is out late, I have to go to bed and Lehzen stays with me."

"The Baroness told me you were never left alone," Liza said, "But I thought she must be exaggerating."

The Princess shook her head. "No. It's true. I'm never ever alone."

"But that's dreadful!" Liza couldn't help herself. "Every girl, even a Princess, if I may be so bold, deserves a little privacy."

"It's for my own safety," the Princess said, as if it were a lesson learned by rote. "Sir John tells my mother there are assassins behind every tree in Hyde Park."

"The danger may be much closer to home," Liza said, with a deliberate air of mystery.

The Princess looked alert. "Whatever do you mean?"

"There are secrets in this house that even Sir John doesn't know." Liza dropped her voice to a whisper. "But I could find out for you."

"Really? That would be marvelous because no one tells me anything. And it would be quite a feather in my cap to know something Sir John does not."

"We must meet in private and I'll tell you everything I have discovered." Liza went to the door. She could hear footsteps, the Baroness was returning. "Not here. Come to my room tonight at midnight, Your Highness."

"Liza, haven't you been listening?" The Princess's face was full of frustration. "I can't!"

Baroness Lehzen was almost at the door. Liza whispered, "Wait until they fall asleep. Do you know where my room is?"

Princess Victoria nodded.

"I'll be waiting for you."

"I'll come tonight if I can."

Liza smiled. Her plan was working.

10 April 1836 Excerpt from the Journal of Her Royal Highness Victoria

I would give millions to behold but for a day, Brussels, Paris, Germany, Italy & Spain and envy all those who do. Perhaps another who was compelled to travel would long to be bound as I am to my native soil! But enough of these reflections & let me think of what I have and how grateful I ought to be for all God has given me.

7

In Which Liza Strikes Two Bargains

LIZA HAD RISEN at six o'clock in the morning and now it was half past ten at night. Repeatedly during the Princess's evening toilette and another one hundred strokes of her hairbrush, Princess Victoria had shot Liza meaningful glances. I will be there, her face seemed to say. Liza wasn't convinced the Princess could escape her adult guards, but if she did, Liza needed to be prepared. It was time to find the broadsheet.

I'm ready for my first spying mission.

Liza opened her door and listened for anyone stirring. Claridge's Hotel had gas lights in the corridors, but Kensington Palace's halls were pitch dark. Holding her candle in front of her, she tiptoed to the narrow servants' stairs. The light of the candle threw monsterlike shadows on the walls. She reached out to the rough plaster to guide her down the uneven steps. She stumbled and only saved herself by wrenching her body upright on the step.

Why don't the servants get banisters?

At the green baize door, Liza hesitated before opening it. Now she was truly committed.

She hurried to the Duchess's sitting room. The room seemed much larger at night. Apart from her flickering candle, the only light came from the remnants of a coal fire behind the iron grate and the moonlight shining in through the windows. She went to one of the windows to savor Kensington Gardens bathed in moonshine. A draught from the ill-fitting windowpane extinguished her candle. Irritated, Liza riffled in her pocket for a lucifer to relight it.

She froze when she heard a rustling inside the wall behind her. The slight noise came from a wood box built into the wall, a vestige of the old days when wood fires, not coal, heated the Palace. The sound was too loud to be a mouse. She backed away until she felt the corner walls against her back. The lid of the wood box lifted slowly and soundlessly. Liza caught her breath.

Ghosts!

Then, in the dim light, she made out a head of wild black hair atop a pale white face. The boy, for now she saw it was young boy, climbed out of the box. Liza watched him reach under the settee and begin feeling about. With a small exclamation, he found a pearl Liza had missed the day before. His smile gleamed in the light as he rubbed the pearl against his front tooth.

Liza held still in her corner. Should she call for a guard? But wait, there weren't any guards at Kensington Palace. She heard a growl. Liza recognized the sound. The boy's stomach was demanding to be fed. Bold as brass, he walked out of the room.

Her hand shaking, Liza relit her candle. With her other hand, she grabbed an iron poker from the fireplace. Listening for his return, she approached his lair and silently opened the lid. Her candle held high to better illuminate the box, she peered inside. Amazing. The wood box was deeper than it seemed. It extended three feet into the wall and made a snug and comfortable home for the strange boy. He had lined the inside with velvet pillows. In a corner, stood a half-full bottle of port, and scattered everywhere were candy wrappers. A silver candlestick and pewter tinderbox provided light for reading. Aha! A stash of newspapers. Liza would wager Sir John's golden guinea she would find the broadsheet. She rummaged through the papers and found it at the very bottom. Straightening up in triumph, she reclaimed her poker and turned to go.

The small boy, grimy and disheveled, stood at her back. Liza stepped back, gripping her poker tightly. He was small, but who knew how desperate he might be?

"'Oo the 'ell do you think you are, goin' through my things?" he demanded fiercely.

"Who am I? Who are *you*?" Liza's voice squeaked. "Help!"

Almost quicker than her eye could register, he stepped in close and put his grubby hand over her mouth. His other hand locked like a vise around her wrist, forcing her to drop the poker.

"Not a word, Miss. You don't want to get a lad in trouble, do you?" he whispered.

Liza struggled not to panic, breathing hard through her nostrils.

"I'm just making my way in the world, like you." He went on in the same urgent whisper, "Do you promise not to scream?"

She nodded and he lifted his sticky hand. She pushed it away from her mouth and exclaimed, "We are nothing alike."

Puffing himself up like a bantam rooster, the boy said, "And I s'pose yer not up to mischief sneakin' around in the night?"

"I'm neither a thief nor a housebreaker," Liza said. She stopped to consider, "Although, I suppose strictly speaking, you are a house-thief." She rubbed her dirty cheek with a handkerchief, glaring at him all the while.

Sheepishly, he pulled a crushed half-eaten bonbon from his shirt pocket. Liza recognized it as one from the Duchess's dressing table. Her eyes widened.

"Want one?" he asked, offering the nasty sweet.

As though her outrage was a balloon pierced by a pin, Liza burst out laughing, then smothered the noise with her own hand.

The boy gave her a tentative smile. "Did you call me a thief? That's just 'urtful, Miss. I'm just preventin' some perfectly service-able food and goods from goin' t'waste." Before she could remon-strate, he said, "And what are you doing 'ere at this 'our?"

"I'm on an errand for the Princess," Liza said. "Not stealing valuable knickknacks." Her fear of the amusing boy vanished like a candle flame being snuffed out.

He spread his hands out wide. "I'm just borrowin' some things that ain't needed at the moment."

"Like a fine bottle of port?" Liza asked with a small smile, "Or the Duchess's pearl?" His eyes shifted away and he put his hand deep in his pockets, as though to safeguard his treasure. "The Duch-ess won't miss one little jewel. And I'll put it to much better use."

"What if she thinks I took it?" Liza asked thoughtfully, although she suspected the Duchess was none too careful with her belong-ings. Except for the Princess, of course.

"She'd never. Sometimes Sourpuss Strode asks questions, but I wouldn't do it if anyone else got blamed. But—"

"No one cares," Liza finished. Two days ago, she would have been the first to tell the authorities about a theft. But now—let the royals look after their own goods; Liza had more important worries.

"You don't look like the sort of girl to shop a lad to the body snatchers," he said with a winsome smile.

A body snatcher? I've never heard anyone speak like him.

"Just promise me you won't steal from the Princess," Liza said. "It's thanks to her I have a job and a place to stay."

"I swear." The boy crossed his heart with a filthy hand, then stuck it out toward Liza. "Inside Boy Jones, at your service."

She shook his hand with the tips of her fingers. "Liza Hastings. What an unusual name, Inside Boy. Does it have anything to do with why you live in the Duchess's wood box?"

"Being Inside Boy is me claim to fame," he said, thumping his chest. He reclined on the Duchess's velvet settee, looking for all the world like a gentleman taking his repose.

"But why?"

He shivered dramatically. "The Duchess may keep lousy fires, but it's better than livin' rough."

"How old are you?" she asked. He was so unkempt it was difficult to say.

"I ain't celebrated a birthday since me ma kicked the bucket," he said. "Fourteen, fifteen, thereabouts."

"And how long have you been here?"

"Four months."

"Impossible!" Liza sat down on a hard sofa.

"Miss Liza, it's easy. No one's lookin' for me." His bright grin lit up his dirty face. "I've put a special lock on the lid from the inside so no one can find me by accident like. And at night, there's no one around. You were lucky to catch me."

She had a dozen questions, but if no one suspected him, she could guess the answers. The food at Kensington Palace would stretch easily to feed this skinny boy. The cabinet gave him a place to hide during daylight. As for bathing, he wasn't worrying, so Liza wouldn't either. She did wonder, though: "What about, when you need to . . ." She couldn't think of a delicate way to ask.

"A chamber pot ain't choosy. My piss or Their 'ighnesses—it's all the same."

Liza didn't know if she should blush or laugh.

"And no one suspects?"

"Miss, let me tell you 'ow Palace life works." He stroked his chin like an old wise man. "Kensington Palace is poorly run indeed. So many people are in charge, no one is responsible. An Inside Boy falls through the cracks."

Liza nodded, remembering her wait at the front door that first day. She also recalled Mrs. Strode disclaiming any responsibility for the Palace's exterior. "You've never been caught?"

"If anybody stopped me, which ain't never 'appened yet, I'd say I'm the chimney sweep's boy." He hesitated a moment, then said, "You've taken Annie Mason's place, right?"

Liza stared at him, eyes widening. "How do you know that?"

"I 'ear everything," he said with an impish grin. "I'll prove it. You speak the same funny spitting language they do. The Princess likes you. The Baroness wants you to be 'er very own personal spy. The Duchess barely knows you're alive. Sir John Conroy admires your looks."

The darkness hid the blush Liza could feel flooding her cheeks. "But how . . . those conversations were in different rooms. How did you hear all that?"

"Never you mind," he said. "But you watch out for Sir John. I tried to warn Annie, but she was stubborn, thinkin' she could 'andle 'im on her own."

"You knew Annie?"

"Knows 'er," he corrected indignantly. "She didn't die when she was booted outta the Palace. She's me friend."

Liza touched his arm in apology. "I'm sorry, but no one here will tell me about her. Do you know why she left?"

Inside Boy began moving about the dark room. Staring out the window, with his back to Liza, he said in a low voice, "Annie's well out of this."

So Inside Boy wouldn't talk about Annie either.

"So what could you be doing for the Princess down 'ere at this hour?" he asked, turning back to her.

"I needed this broadsheet." Liza held it up.

Inside Boy tugged at his collar as if to loosen it. "Funny sort of errand to do in the middle of the night. It's what I'd call risky for a maid."

"I wasn't always a maid," Liza said. "I'm going to help the Princess hold her own against Sir John. When she's Queen, she can make me a lady again. I could use your help."

"You'll need more than me to go up against Sir John." Inside Boy polished his fingernails against his pants. "What's in it for me?"

"Would you settle for knowing I owed you a favor?"

"You can do one for me right now," he said. "Get a note to Princess Victoria. From Annie."

"The Baroness would not approve."

"But the Princess would. You said you were workin' for 'er."

"Why can't Annie send it herself?"

"The Princess ain't allowed to open 'er own mail."

Liza thought that sounded quite likely. "What does it say?"

He drew himself up, the very portrait of injured pride. "I don't read other people's private letters."

Liza giggled. "You just eavesdrop on their private conversations, eat their sweetmeats, and steal space in their wood boxes?"

"I've got standards!" Inside Boy said, his voice raw and indignant.

Liza smiled to herself, remembering how Mrs. Strode had said the same thing.

"What can you tell me about the broadsheet?" she asked.

He grinned and they both knew they'd reached a deal. He stuck out a filthy hand and with barely a moment's pause, Liza shook it.

Inside Boy said, "I can bring you to the cove who publishes it. You can ask 'im yerself."

"Excellent. Where is he?"

"Fleet Street, of course, where all the newspapers are," he said, matter-of-fact.

"I'll have to find a way to leave the Palace. In the meantime, I'll try to deliver your letter."

He pulled out a folded square letter from a deep pocket, the edges smooth from handling. In the dim light, she could make out the letters P V penciled in with a blunt lead point.

"Annie asked me to get it to the Princess quick, but 'er 'ighness is never alone. I'd about given up."

"If there's a reply, how do I find you?"

He gestured grandly to his wood box. "You can always find me at 'ome. Now Miss, you should get back to your room. And mind your step around Sir John."

She pocketed the letter. "It's been a pleasure to meet you, Inside Boy."

"Likewise."

Liza turned back at the doorway to see the lid closing down over Inside Boy's impudent head.

———

Liza congratulated herself as she stole back through the silent house. In one evening, she had established her own source of information in the Palace, retrieved the broadsheet, and brought back something certain to interest the Princess. Hurrying down the deserted hallway, she slipped through her door. A figure in white was standing in the center of her room. Liza stifled a scream.

"Liza, for heaven's sakes, it's I." Despite her small stature, the Princess, in a billowing nightdress, seemed to fill the room.

"I'm sorry, Your Highness."

"Where have you been, I've been waiting," the Princess complained, a shiver racked her body. "It's terribly cold in here."

Liza glanced around her tiny room: it wasn't much of a haven, but it was hers.

"With all due respect, Your Highness, you are early. I didn't expect you for another hour." She spoke deliberately like a hostess might, confronted by an inconsiderate guest's arrival before the appointed time. "How convenient my door was open, so you could let yourself in."

It was the Princess's turn to be surprised and affronted. "Liza, I dare not be found in the hall."

"Of course not, Princess," Liza said graciously.

The Princess rubbed her arms and shuddered again. "Is the window open?" she asked. "There's a draught."

"No, the pane is broken," Liza said. The least Liza could do was make her guest comfortable. She pulled her mother's shawl from the chest and draped it around Victoria's shoulders.

The Princess pulled it tightly against her body. "This is beautiful," she said. "And so warm."

"My father brought it from Kashmir, in India; it was a gift for my mother," Liza answered. Perched on Liza's chair and burrowing in the colorful shawl, the Princess looked like an inscrutable eastern empress.

"Now, Liza, you were very mysterious earlier," the Princess said. "I couldn't lay still for wondering what all your enigmatic hints meant. *Dites-moi!*"

Liza went to the window and plugged the hole in the window with a rag. "I overheard something you should know about," she said.

"You were eavesdropping? How unladylike—best not let Lehzen know."

Marveling at the naiveté of the Princess, Liza said, "She told me to do it."

"Lehzen did?"

"As you know, I speak German . . ."

With a leap of logic proving how false the accusation of feeble-mindedness was, the Princess cried, "No wonder Lehzen hired you! She wants you to spy on Mama and Sir John! How diabolical! How delightful!" She smiled broadly.

"Your mother was upset yesterday because of . . . this." With a flourish, Liza pulled the broadsheet out from under her skirt.

The Princess took the paper closer to the candle and began reading. "I am mentally backward *and* self-centered." She snorted with laughter. "Heavens, what a combination! Mama must have been furious!"

"She was, but Sir John comforted her."

"Of course he did, that's why he is indispensable," the Princess said absently as she scanned the article. "What twaddle! It's not worth the time to read it." She crumpled the paper. "Liza, I hope this isn't all you have for me, because there are always silly stories about me in the papers."

Doggedly, Liza brought the conversation back to the danger. "Sir John was particularly pleased when he read it."

"But why?" The Princess's forehead crinkled. "Any criticism of me reflects badly on him."

Liza plunged in. "Not if, as the writer suggests, the regency be extended."

Victoria became very still. "Extended?" she asked icily. "For how long?"

"At least until your twenty-first birthday. Perhaps forever." Liza watched her carefully.

The Princess threw the balled up newspaper against the wall. She scrunched her hands into fists, squinted her eyes and huffed, like a young child whose sweet had been taken away. "I've been patient," she said. "I was prepared to wait until my eighteenth birthday. But not a day longer!" She paced about the room. "I won't let him. They will have to reckon with me . . ." She sank down onto the bed, her face blotched with unshed tears. Her anger seemed to evaporate. "Oh, what's the use? I can't stop him. He controls the Palace. He controls Mama. He controls me."

"But time is on your side," Liza insisted. "Like sand falling through an hourglass, the more time passes, the more power shifts to you." Liza played her card. "I'll help you."

The Princess's eyes widened. "How?"

"While we wait for you to reach your majority, we'll keep close watch on Sir John. We counter his plans until your eighteenth birthday."

"How?" the Princess repeated.

"When my father entered a new market, the first thing he did was learn whose opinion mattered. Sir John is relying on the press to make his case for him. Let's investigate this newspaper writer," Liza said. "He knew about your tutors; perhaps he knows other things. I've a friend who can take me to him."

"Oh Liza, do that. Find out what this miscreant knows." Victoria nodded eagerly. "At least then I can feel as though I am doing something."

Liza reached into her pocket and felt the gold guinea Sir John had given her. "Princess, there's one more thing." She explained Sir John would pay Liza handsomely to know what Victoria fancied for her birthday.

"I don't have any money." Victoria's protuberant eyes narrowed suspiciously. "Why are you helping me?"

"'A friend i' the court is better than a penny in purse,'" Liza quoted.

Victoria frowned quizzically for a moment, then: "*Henry IV, Part 2!*" she cried, identifying the quote with triumph.

"I mean one day, you'll reward me properly," Liza pressed.

The Princess looked disappointed. "If I couldn't reward you someday, does that mean you wouldn't help me?"

It was an important question, not just for the Princess but for Liza. It was one thing to be a paid spy for someone you liked, another to do it only for the money. She reached her decision. "Princess, I would. You rescued me when I had no home. And you will be my rightful Queen. Besides . . ." the Princess waited with cautious eyes, "of all the people in this Palace, I like you best."

Princess Victoria smiled. "It's a bargain then."

A little while earlier, Liza had sealed her bargain with Inside Boy with a handshake. But the Princess did not put out her hand. After an awkward moment, Liza curtsied. The Princess inclined her head regally.

"And for your birthday gift?" Liza asked.

"Don't tell him anything. Why should we help him with my present?"

"Perhaps we could get you precisely what you want," Liza prompted.

A broad grin lit up the Princess's face. "And instead of currying favor, Sir John, all unwitting, will be doing exactly what I wish. Liza, you are clever."

"Thank you, Your Highness," Liza said. "So, what do you want most?"

"I'll have to think on it. We have our marching orders: you find out what you can about Sir John's machinations and I'll decide on a birthday gift." She stood up and a gust of cold wind pierced the crack in the windowpane. The Princess wrapped the shawl around her more tightly. "I truly believe you have been sent here to give me hope."

Eyeing her property, Liza said, "Princess, my shawl."

"You wouldn't want me to catch a chill, would you?"

"Of course not, Your Highness."

"Good night, Liza."

"Good night, Your Highness."

From Miss Elizabeth Hastings to the Firm of Ratisbon and Ratisbon, Esq.

5 April 1836
Kensington Palace

Dear Mr. Ratisbon,

Thank you for your consideration during my recent troubles.

I am grateful for your efforts on my behalf. I wish to assure you I intend to honor all of my father's debts. However, I am concerned you have found no assets whatsoever. As the daughter of an old and valued client, might I prevail upon your magnanimity to do a last service on my behalf? Please ascertain the whereabouts of Mr. Ripley, my father's business manager. I am certain he can provide an explanation. The last I heard news of him, he was superintending a manufacturing site in Kashmir.

You can reach me at Kensington Palace, where, entirely through your kind intercession, I am now installed.

I have the honor to remain,
Miss Elizabeth Hastings

8 April 1836 Excerpt from the Journal
of Miss Elizabeth Hastings

I've survived my first week as a maid. The work is not hard; my duties have never been more onerous than on my first day. Boredom and loneliness are my enemies. I'm not permitted to have friends below or above my station. The only servant at my level, Mademoiselle Blanche, hates the ground I walk on. The sentiment is heartily reciprocated!

Despite our different ranks, the Princess is just as bored and lonely as I am. My plan is to keep her amused. To that end, I am withholding Annie Mason's letter. Although I promised JB (even within these private pages, I will keep his secret), I'll wait until the Princess requires a diversion. While I am mortally curious as to its contents, I can't bring myself to peek. A sorry sort of spy, am I!

The Baroness was pleased with me when I gave her the broadsheet. The only thing I've done properly since she hired me. Sir John has not forgotten our bargain. Whenever he sees me alone (something I avoid whenever possible), he asks what the Princess wants for her birthday. She doesn't know her own mind. One day she thinks she wants another spaniel. Other days, she wants a new mare. But Sir John wants to give her something special. I suspect he is looking for another way to control her—what Sir John giveth, he can taketh away. Since the Princess loves the opera, I'm going to suggest Signor Luigi Lablache, the famous tenor, might come to the Palace and sing for her.

Princess Victoria not only wants Lablache to sing, she wants him to teach her voice! Being a Princess has its advantages!

8

In Which Liza Sees Both the Carrot and the Stick

LIZA WAS ALWAYS PLEASED when Victoria had her piano lessons because those were times she didn't need to entertain the Princess. Besides, the Princess played very well indeed. Her Mendelssohn was always full of pleasant verve.

"And now the Wagner," said Mr. Hayes, the music instructor. He was a middle-aged, rotund man, whose bottom was much wider than his piano stool.

Victoria grimaced. "Liza, don't you detest Wagner?"

Avoiding the piano teacher's discomfiture, Liza answered, "No, Your Highness. I've always rather liked his music. He's German, as you know."

"Bother where he's from! It's all big notes and bombast to me," the Princess complained as she began to play. Mr. Hayes and Liza did their best not to wince at the flubbing of the notes.

Finally, Mr. Hayes could bear no more. "You've not practiced, Your Highness," he scolded.

Victoria shrugged her pretty white shoulders. "I don't like this piece."

"Sir John insists you learn the classics, including Wagner." Disapproval puffed out his cheeks. "Start again. Even princesses must practice."

Without warning, the Princess slammed the cover on the piano and shoved her chair back. The instrument continued jangling even as she stood up. "There is no MUST about it. We are finished for today."

Clutching her piano book as though it were a club, the Princess stormed out. Liza followed on her heels, barely sparing a glance for the embarrassed instructor. Victoria walked to the Duchess's sitting room in stiff staccato steps.

"Why should I learn Wagner if I don't want to?" The Princess slapped her palm with the book, over and over again. "Do you really think it makes one bit of difference whether the Queen can play Wagner or not?"

"It's not for me to say, Your Highness," Liza said, cautious of her answer with the Princess so out of sorts.

Victoria stomped her foot. "Answer me, Liza."

Liza grinned and let her guard down. "I don't see how it possibly could matter, Princess."

"Yet Sir John forces me to learn Wagner!"

At that moment, the door slammed open and the man himself walked in. He presented a dapper picture in his greatcoat and shoes shined to a high polish. Liza caught a glimpse of a fashionable chartreuse waistcoat. He held a top hat in his hands. "You dismissed your piano teacher?" he asked.

"Yes, I did, *Sir* John." Victoria emphasized his title in such a way as to remind him of hers.

"I will not permit any interference with the Kensington System. It is designed to maximize your instructional time. It is not for a little girl, pardon me, a Little Woman, to second-guess me."

The Princess's fingers turned white as she gripped her piano book tightly. "This 'Little Woman' will be your Queen, Sir John. Do not forget that in your . . . zeal for my welfare."

Liza wanted to cheer for Victoria.

"When you are Queen," he said sternly, "you will be prepared for your duties, thanks to my system."

"I'm sure the nation owes you a tremendous debt for making me practice the piano," the Princess replied in a tone that would wither a man less sure of his power.

Sir John turned his top hat in his hands, his long fingers running along the satin rim. "If you won't cooperate, I'll be forced to cancel your birthday surprise."

"What surprise?" asked Victoria, with a quick glance at Liza.

He turned his back on her and walked to the window.

No doubt, to make the Princess frantic with suspense.

"After all the trouble I've taken, it would be a shame to tell Signor Lablache not to come after all," he said over his shoulder. "I arranged for him to be your singing teacher during the season."

The Princess played the role of an astonished girl to perfection. "Lablache? Coming here? What a marvelous treat, Sir John. How did you know how much I admire his voice?" She winked at Liza.

"Anyone could see your passion for him," Sir John said, turning around to reveal a satisfied smile on his thick lips. "You practically fell out of the royal box applauding his last performance. Everyone was laughing about it."

Victoria's joy dissolved like a sugary confection in a downpour and Liza wished she could scratch Sir John's mean eyes out of their sockets.

"I thought he sang very well." Victoria's chin trembled from mortification.

Sir John's eyes never left her face, savoring every ounce of her humiliation. "And thanks to me, he will be your teacher."

The Princess retreated behind her exquisite manners. "Thank you, Sir John." She looked down, duty dripping from every syllable. "It is very kind of you and Mama."

"You will practice your Wagner?" He was implacable.

"Yes." Victoria's eyes stayed rooted to the floor.

"Excellent." He gestured to the door. "Shall we return to the music room?"

Victoria followed him like a puppy kicked by her master. Her back stiff with resentment, she settled herself in front of the piano. Sir John pulled on his kid leather gloves and without a word, turned and left, shutting the door behind him. Victoria and Liza listened to the sound of his footsteps fade. With a cry of frustration, Victoria hurled the piano book at the door.

"The gall of Sir John Nobody lecturing me! Me!" Victoria poked herself in the bosom. "To offer a carrot and turn it into a stick to beat me with the very next moment!"

"But what a carrot!" Liza said. "It's just what you wanted."

For an instant, Victoria let herself be pleased. "I've always wanted to meet Lablache and now I get to study with him!"

"Can you sing?" asked Liza, forgetting who she was and to whom she spoke.

"Of course, Liza." Victoria gave her a cold royal stare. "Do you think Lablache would instruct a complete novice?"

If the novice were the future Queen, he might.

"But I owe it to Sir John!" The Princess's pique returned in a rush. "It ruins everything. You didn't think of that, did you, Liza?"

Liza thought quickly. "Your Highness, you are mistaken." The Princess's mouth dropped open in surprise. Liza hurried on. "Signor Lablache is coming here because of your position. Any, any . . ." she searched her mind for a word to please, "any *flunkey* could have made the request."

The Princess beamed and Liza sighed.

"Lablache comes for me, not the odious Sir John. How clever you are to see it, Liza."

"Thank you, Princess."

"If I want the maestro, I had better practice." She sat on the bench and looked at Liza expectantly. Discomfited, Liza realized the Princess wanted her music score. She scurried to retrieve it and place it in on the piano.

"You turn the pages, Liza." The Princess set her hands delicately on the black and white keys. Her fingers were plump and looked like little sausages on striped cloth. But she didn't play yet. "You know, I won't have to suffer his insolence forever. Soon I will have all the carrots and all the sticks. Guess which Sir John Conroy will receive?"

The notes of the detested Wagner filled the room. Waiting for Victoria to reach the end of the page, Liza imagined a tiny Queen with an enormous crown, holding a huge scepter as she chased a frightened Sir John out of her royal presence.

The next Tuesday was cold and wet. But more importantly, it was the Princess's first singing lesson with Maestro Lablache. Liza was to chaperone. The Princess had been singing all week long in anticipation and Liza was wearied to death by her practicing. Her voice was pretty enough but pitched too high for Liza's tastes.

Victoria could barely contain herself as they waited for the great man. Dash had caught her excitement. The spaniel raced frantically around the large room yipping. He jumped up onto Victoria's full, pale pink taffeta skirt.

"Down, Dash, or else you will have to leave," the Princess ordered. She stroked his head and smiled. "I do think Tuesday will be the best day of the week," she said. "And what a privilege it will be for you, Liza, to hear the maestro."

"But I already have, Princess. Twice," Liza said without thinking. "His Leporello in *Don Giovanni* was wonderful. Mama took me to see it." It was the last opera she had seen with her mother. Steeling herself against the melancholy that came with remembering her parents, Liza went on, "My mother and I went to the opera whenever we could. My father never came; he called it caterwauling to a full orchestra. We often laughed about it."

The Princess's eyebrows drew together in a frown. "I wasn't allowed to go. Mama thought it unsuitable. But you and I are almost the same age." The Princess's face grew bleak.

Too late, Liza remembered the unpalatable facts: The Duchess was not the Princess's friend, the Princess had never known her father, and Liza had seen an opera the Princess had not. Liza almost felt sorry for her.

"Where is the man?" Victoria exclaimed, cross. "If he is late, I won't be able to have my full lesson."

At that moment, Simon came in, a dashing figure in his green livery. "Your Highness," he said, staring into the air above Victoria's head. "Signor Lablache has a touch of the ague and will not be coming."

"Thank you," the Princess said quietly. Though her spirit was crushed, Victoria was too well-trained to show her feelings in front of Simon. Dash was not so subtle. With a small whimper, he lay his body across her feet, his head pressed flat against his paws.

As the footman backed out of the room, his face filled with sympathy for the Princess. Liza rather liked him for it. She started to speak, but the Princess waved her silent, tears rolling down her cheeks. She sat at the piano and banged out a gloomy tune as though beating a carpet. After a time, her playing became more measured. The music trailed off slowly and silence overtook the room. Liza started when the Princess finally spoke.

"What a week! Every night I have wanted to visit, but Mama has been vaporish. She's cancelled all her evening engagements." She swung around on the velvet piano stool and faced Liza. "Have you talked to the publisher yet?"

"I haven't been able to leave the Palace," Liza said. "Mrs. Strode watches me like a hawk."

"Did you even try?" the Princess cried. "I can't rely on anyone!"

"That's not fair, Princess," Liza protested. "My livelihood is at stake."

"Don't be melodramatic." The Princess was neither amused nor sympathetic. "You have so much more free time than I do. The least you could do is find out about this broadsheet." She sighed. "I always have to wait for news."

"When I have a day off, I'll get it for you," Liza promised.

"As soon as you can," the Princess said. She walked over to the window and stared outside at the rain. "What am I going to do for the rest of the afternoon?"

Liza had kept Annie's letter with her all week, waiting for the perfect moment. "Princess, I have a letter for you." She pulled out the folded square.

"I never get letters." Intrigued, the Princess turned the letter over in her hands.

"Truly? No one writes to you?"

"Oh everyone writes to me, even people I don't know! But Mama and Sir John open all my correspondence first."

"It's from Annie Mason," Liza said.

"Annie?" The Princess looked as excited as a child with a surprise gift. But the paper was folded too tightly for her to open it. "Liza, open it."

Using her fingernails, Liza separated the folds to reveal a small piece of paper covered with writing. Annie had used every inch. Twice. She had written across the narrow side of the paper and then turned it and written again on the long side as well. Her face expressionless, Liza handed it to the Princess, whose excitement drained away.

"I can't read this! It's a mishmash. Why ever would she do that?"

"Your Highness, paper is expensive." Liza had learned this lesson since her parents' death when Mrs. Strode had begrudged her the writing paper to correspond with her solicitor.

"All the more reason to make it legible."

"You can decipher it, once you get the knack."

The Princess huffed, impatient. "I don't want to strain my eyes." She pushed the letter at Liza. "You read it to me."

The salutation was easy to make out. "Dear Princess Victoria," Liza read. "I hope you are well and Dashy is recovered from his nasty cold."

"Does she say why she left?" asked Victoria avidly.

Liza shook her head and squinted at the letter. "No. She says Sir John ruined her and he dared not let her stay at the Palace." Liza felt a knot grow hard in her stomach. "She says 'Do not trust him or his men.'"

"Sir John!" Victoria leaned forward, intrigued. "What did he do?"

"Ruin usually means one thing, doesn't it?" Liza asked in a low voice.

The Princess's eyes gleamed. "And under my mother's roof! If Mama found out . . . she's quite unforgiving about other people's lapses. Perhaps this is my trump card against him. *Brava,* Liza!" Standing up, she shoved the piano stool across the parquet floor. "Should I tell Lehzen? Perhaps she already knows." She began pacing around the music room, rubbing her palms together.

Liza felt as though she was looking on the scene from a great distance. She saw a tiny girl in a pink dress thinking ugly thoughts. The Princess had not given Annie's predicament a second's worth of consideration before she began to think of herself. Liza was ashamed for her. And frightened for herself.

"What about Annie?" Liza asked abruptly. "Have you forgotten her?"

"Oh, yes, of course." The Princess stopped her pacing. "Finish the letter, Liza."

Liza took the letter closer to a lamp. "She says 'I was let go without a reference and cannot find decent work. I have no money and am in desperate straits.'" Liza grew cold. She had reached the bottom of the page and turned it on its side to read the rest. "Annie describes how much everything costs. Then she says 'Please send money.'"

"She wants money!" The Princess sounded more annoyed than surprised. "She knows I don't have any. My pocket money is only a few pounds a month."

Liza was still staring at the letter. "It's well written," she said slowly. "I didn't realize Annie was educated."

The Princess was still brooding on her iniquitous allowance. Absently, she said, "Of course she was, Liza. Her father was a clerk. Lehzen won't allow just anyone to associate with me."

Not quite a gentleman's daughter, but not working class either.

"Will you help her?" Liza asked.

"I would hate to think you are deaf, Liza. I don't have any money to send." But the Princess wouldn't meet Liza's gaze.

"But she's desperate." Her recent personal experience gave Liza's words passion. "You don't know what it is to worry where you're going to sleep and how you will eat."

"Liza!" The Princess reminded Liza of their relative ranks with a word.

Bowing her head to hide her angry face, Liza said, "Your Highness, I forgot myself."

"It would seem so." Their positions reestablished, the Princess's mood softened. "Do you really think her need is dire?"

"Does she have any family?" Liza asked

"She's an orphan, like you."

Liza rubbed her hands together; they were suddenly cold. "Without a reference, she'll go through her savings. She'll end up on the street." She recoiled from thoughts of what might happen on the street.

The Princess pulled out her little notebook of accounts. "I do have a few pounds put away for charity. I could give that to her." She looked at Liza for approval, pleased she had come up with a solution.

"That would be exceedingly generous, Your Highness."

"Can you get it to her? Perhaps when you go to town on my other errand."

"I'll need permission to leave for the entire day."

"Go tomorrow. The King has sent us an invitation to court that not even my mother can refuse. You won't be needed. Can you find her?"

Thinking of Inside Boy's dirty face, Liza said, "We've a mutual acquaintance. He'll find Annie for me."

"Hand the money to her personally," the Princess said. "Sir John has taught me not to trust anyone."

I daresay he has.

9

In Which Liza Goes Outside with Inside Boy

THE NEXT MORNING the entire household ran about frantically preparing for the Princess to visit the King's court. Liza arrived at the covered porch, panting, carrying the Princess's warmest cloak. Sir John handed the Duchess into her waiting carriage. The Princess's face glowed with the excitement of having somewhere to go. As was her habit, the Baroness was scowling.

"Liza, you've kept us waiting."

Liza barely noticed the Baroness's tone, so accustomed had she become to her surly ways. "I beg your pardon, Baroness," she said as she held the cloak up for Victoria.

The Princess glanced at the carriage; her mother was paying her no attention. "We would have had to wait anyway. Sir John's business delayed us."

"Sir John is a man much occupied with other people's business, Princess," Liza murmured, laying the Princess's crimson wool cloak on her shoulders and fastening the black velvet ties in a becoming bow under the Princess's chin. The Baroness inspected the result. Satisfied, she followed the Duchess into the carriage.

"This is going to be such an amusing day," Victoria whispered. "I get to go to court and when I return, you'll have so much to tell me!"

Under her breath, Liza said, "I hope so."

"Victoria, what is keeping you?" An irritated voice came from the carriage.

"Coming, Mama." She touched Liza's hand. "Good luck."

"Princess," Liza whispered, "I don't have permission to leave the house. If I am caught . . ."

"Don't worry, you won't be! I must go." The Princess stepped away and Simon held the step so she could enter the carriage safely.

Liza had never seen Simon look so handsome. He was dressed in his most formal livery, the forest green with gold piping. His tight breeches set off his muscular thighs and his coat showed off his broad shoulders. He smiled at her before he climbed up to the box seat. Liza gave him a severe look, cursing the blush she could feel creeping up her neck. As the carriage rumbled off toward Windsor Castle, where the King was holding court, Liza hurried to the Duchess's sitting room.

"This is the perfect day to go to town," Liza announced to the empty room. "I'll be at the chestnut tree at the end of the avenue in a quarter of an hour." A rustling in the wood box made her smile. Shutting the door behind her, she jumped to see Mrs. Strode standing a few feet away.

"Miss Hastings, to whom were you speaking?"

Liza gulped, "No one, Mrs. Strode."

The housekeeper looked puzzled, glancing back at the sitting room door, then back at Liza. "I could have sworn I heard you speak—"

Liza said, "I'm sure I don't know, ma'am."

Mrs. Strode glared at her, but a crash from behind the servants' door distracted her. Quick to see her opportunity, Liza fetched her own cloak from the below stairs cloakroom and walked through the servant's entrance as if she hadn't a care in the world.

The day was crisp and clear. Liza fastened her wool cloak tightly at her neck, enjoying its cozy warmth even as the chill nipped at her nose. With a spring in her step, she set off down the avenue to the ancient chestnut tree. Inside Boy joined her a few minutes later.

He was dressed in a coat too big for him, and breeches a shade too small. His shoes were a collection of patched leather all polished black, regardless of their original color. His face was scrubbed pink; Liza didn't ask where he had found washing water. He grinned and fell into step.

"You look a treat, Miss," he said. "Bein' out and about agrees with you."

Liza couldn't take the smile off her face. Being outside was better than one of Mrs. Strode's tonics. "Stolen time is doubly precious," Liza said. "Mrs. Strode doesn't know I'm out."

Inside Boy's eyebrows rose high on his forehead. "Yer mission must be perishin' important."

"It is, to the Princess."

"And what about Annie?" he asked.

"I have money for her." She waved her little reticule full of coins.

"It's about time the Princess 'elped 'er." He looked her over and his face crinkled in disapproval. "Yer a dipper's dream, you are."

"What's a dipper?" she asked cheerfully.

"A pickpocket. They'll take your little purse and be 'alf a mile away before you knows it's gone. Tuck it under your cloak and keep one 'and on it at all times." He took the tails of his jacket and looped them around his arms. The ends were oddly weighted. "That'll thwart anybody after me goods."

"But aren't your trouser pockets easier to reach now?"

"That's what I want 'em to think. Instead I keep me valuables in the tails of the coat. And I keep the tails where I can see 'em."

"Do you have anything worth stealing?" Liza asked, laughing.

"You'd be surprised at the odds and ends you can pick up at Kensington Palace," he said with a mischievous grin.

Liza shrugged. What was some minor thievery of Inside Boy compared to Sir John Conroy trying to steal the throne?

"It's wonderful to be outside," Liza said. "I used to love riding in parks like this." Her wide gesture took in the bridle paths and rolling hills. Dandies were hacking about on gleaming horses and well-dressed matrons in sumptuous carriages maneuvered, with the nicest manners, to outshine each other.

"You went on one of those beasts?" Boy asked. "Voluntary like?"

Liza nodded happily.

"I'll keep to my wood box, thank you very much."

"Kensington Palace is smothering me to death," she said. "You can leave whenever you please. Why don't you?"

"I live in the Palace so I don't 'ave to be out." His face took on a wise expression of a man thrice his age. "Don't go romanticizin' the outside world. We 'ave it cozy at Kensington." His eyes widened and he nudged her. "Watch out for the peeler."

A tall man, wearing a swallow-tail blue suit with shiny metal buttons, walked toward them. His hat looked like a chimney pot.

He gave Inside Boy a suspicious look, tapping a short wooden club against his white-gloved hand.

Inside Boy's anxiety was infectious. "What's a peeler?" Liza whispered after the man had passed.

"These new policemen. We call them peelers because they're Sir Robert Peel's men. Some folks call 'em bobbies."

"Excuse me, Miss," the peeler had come back. "Is this young man making a nuisance of himself?"

Inside Boy looked as though he wanted to bolt, but Liza put her hand on his arm and smiled brightly. "Officer, thank you for your kindness, but I assure you my cousin is harmless."

The peeler's eyebrows rose high on his forehead. "Cousin?"

"Yes. He's not well." Liza touched her temple. "But he's quite safe."

Politely averting his eyes from Inside Boy, the peeler touched his tall hat. "G'day Miss."

"Good day," Liza inclined her head, rather pleased with her ingenuity.

Inside Boy could hardly contain himself. As soon as they were out of earshot, he burst out, "Brilliant, Miss Liza. I thought 'e knew me for a scrannin' cove. If 'e 'ad found the whack in me fork, I'd be off to boardin' school for sure."

Liza stared blankly for a moment. "What on earth did you just say?" she asked.

"It's flash patter," he said, glancing back at the peeler.

Liza's eyebrows rose high on her forehead.

"Thieves' talk," he explained.

"So you are a thief!" Liza teased.

"The Duchess isn't givin' me room and board." Inside Boy's grin was full of mischief.

"At least not to her knowledge." They both laughed. "But what does it mean?" Liza asked again.

"Well, a scrannin' cove is, not to put too fine a point on't, a thief. Whack is my ill-gotten gains, fork is pocket."

"And this takes you to boarding school?"

"Prison. If I'm lucky. If I'm unlucky I cross the 'erring pond—get transported to Botany Bay."

Liza had always been proud of her facility with language. She committed the new phrases to memory. "But why talk this way?" she asked.

"A peeler can't touch you if they can't understand a bloomin' word you say," he said.

They emerged on the far side of Kensington Gardens. Inside Boy grabbed her hand and began to run down the road.

"Where are we going?" Liza panted. "Is the peeler after us?"

"C'mon, Miss, we've struck it lucky. Me friend's omnibus is about to leave. That's our ride to town." He dragged Liza to a green enclosed carriage drawn by three horses that stood waiting. A driver sat on the seat, holding a stick with a long flexible whip. To Liza's surprise, he greeted Inside Boy very civilly.

"Boy! I 'aven't seen you in a bit. I thought p'raps you'd moved on."

"Naw, Bill. Kensington suits me fine for now." Inside Boy turned to Liza and performed the introductions. "This is Miss Liza. She works for the Princess."

The driver's hand moved respectfully to tip his cap. "Any friend of Boy's is bound to be a troublemaker. But a friend of the Princess— that's a different kettle of fish. Come aboard, only 'alf a crown."

Clutching her reticule, Liza turned to Inside Boy in a panic, "I don't have any money of my own."

Bill and Inside Boy burst out laughing.

"Ne'er you mind, Miss," Bill said. "It's my treat."

"Are you certain?" Liza asked.

"Guaranteed."

Inside Boy held her arm as she climbed in. "Bill ain't never charged me yet."

"Aren't we stealing the ride from Bill's employers?"

"Aren't you stealin' this day out from yours?" he shot back. "Besides, do you know 'ow long it takes to walk to Fleet Street?"

Still nervous, Liza climbed in. She looked around the empty interior lined with cushioned seats for about twenty passengers. Long straps of leather attached to the ceiling through iron rings disappeared out to the driver's end of the bus.

"Those reins are attached to Bill's arms," Boy explained. "When we want to stop, we tug."

Bill's booming voice came down from his perch. "But don't pull too hard. Some of these ladies are stronger than they look. I've got bruises all up and down me arms. Gee-up!" Bill clucked and cracked his whip and the omnibus lurched forward. Liza was heading into London.

"We'll be in town in no time," said Inside Boy. "We'll go to Fleet Street first."

"Then to Annie's house?" Liza asked.

Staring at the dirty straw on the floor, Inside Boy nodded.

"Boy, what aren't you telling me?"

"Nothin.'" The look on his face gave the words the lie.

Inside Boy tilted his head back and fell asleep. With an exasperated sigh, Liza turned her attention to the Kensington Road. At each stop, the car filled up with market farmers, ladies, and respectable families. Within a mile, Liza sat crowded into the opposite corner from Inside Boy, her face pressed to the window.

The green hills and wide bridle paths of Hyde Park soon gave way to upper crust Mayfair, with its well-paved roads and mansions. Peering out the window, Liza could make out the towering high spires of Westminster Abbey rising above the trees.

One day the Princess will be crowned there.

Somehow, Inside Boy knew to wake up just as the bus reached the market behind St. Paul's Cathedral. He and Liza clambered out.

"I'm headin' back around three o'clock." The driver winked at Liza and cracked his whip.

Inside Boy led Liza into the heart of the market. The wide square bustled, filled to the edge and beyond with shops, stalls, and hawkers.

"Chestnuts! All 'ot, a penny a core!" bawled a street vendor standing in front of a red-hot metal box.

"Who'll buy a bonnet for tuppence?"

"Bootlaces, pick 'em out cheap! Four pair for a 'alf-penny. Bootlaces!"

Liza desperately wanted to stop and drown in the lovely cacophony of noises, colors, and smells so unlike musty Kensington Palace, but Inside Boy tugged on her arm, "Look later. Right now, we've errands."

He led her past stalls bright with sparkling glass and others adorned with tin saucepans clanking in the light breeze. They stepped over a boy sitting by a makeshift display of used boots laid out on the curb. He shivered in his tattered coat; Liza wished she could buy him some hot chestnuts. Suddenly, Inside Boy pulled her out of the crowds into a deserted side street.

He sighed in relief. "The reason I live in the Palace is there ain't so many people. C'mon, Fleet Street is this way."

"Who are we going to see?" Liza asked.

"Will Fulton. 'e's a mate," Inside Boy said. "An orphan, like us."

An orphan like us.

The memory of her parents, more real than all the strangers in the marketplace, threatened to overwhelm Liza. Inside Boy prattled on, not noticing how his words cut.

"'is uncle is a printer in Manchester. 'e set up Will with a press a year or so ago and 'e ain't never looked back."

"A press sounds important."

"You don't know the 'alf of it." They emerged onto a new street and Inside Boy spread out his arms. "Fleet Street."

Liza knew Fleet Street was the center of newspaper publishing in London, but hadn't realized it would be so loud. The metallic rumble of machines filled the street. Men and boys dodged cabriolets and horsemen. Workers filled wagons with newspapers bundled up for sale. All along the street, hawkers sold the latest papers to passersby.

Inside Boy pulling at her sleeve, Liza dragged her feet to read the placards. She hadn't read any news since she arrived at Kensington Palace.

A young man was shouting the headlines in a hoarse voice. "'Princess Victoria Stark Raving Mad!' Halfpenny to read all about it."

Liza stalked over, hands braced on her hips. The young man grinned, revealing bright white teeth that stood out against the pale peach fuzz on his chin, and pointed to a placard pasted on the brick wall behind him.

"'Daft and Demented. The Princess Unfit to be Queen!' Read all about it," he shouted in a singsong voice.

Gritting her teeth, Liza asked for a paper. It was the same broadsheet as the one she had stolen for the Princess. Her fists crushed it in a ball.

"Hey! You haven't paid for that yet!" he said.

"It's rubbish!" Liza replied, filled with anger. "Who writes these lies?"

"I do!" he said, indignant. "And I had the information on excellent authority." A group of street urchins leaned against the building, enjoying the show.

"Your 'authority' is full of twaddle. And you are the worst kind of hack to repeat it," Liza answered.

"Who are you to call me a hack?"

Inside Boy's eyes were wide with glee. "Miss Elizabeth Hastings of Kensington Palace," he said. "Meet Will Fulton, publisher and hack."

Feeling a blush creep up to the roots of her hair, Liza stared at Will Fulton. His green eyes stared back.

10

In Which Liza Confronts a Newspaperman and a Fallen Woman

INSIDE BOY WENT ON TALKING while Liza and Will Fulton stood mute. "Will Fulton, I've got a bone to pick with you. I told you about the tantrums, but I never said the Princess threw a book at her teacher. And for certs, I never said the Princess shouldn't be Queen."

Fulton's eyes didn't leave Liza's face. "I've got more than one source."

Liza turned to Inside Boy. "You work for him?"

"Don't look daggers, Miss." Inside Boy looked sheepish. "Last fall I was stony-broke, and Will offered me a bit of coin to pass on interestin' facts and circumstances."

"But it's not true!" she cried.

"Miss Liza, that story didn't come from me. You forget I know these people. As if I'd prefer the Duchess to the Princess," Inside Boy said. "Will, 'oo told you such foolishness?"

"Yes, who fed you these lies about the Princess?" Liza asked.

Fulton leaned against the wall and folded his arms. "My sources are confidential." He went on, "And how do you know she's not a nitwit?"

"I live at the Palace." She held up the crumpled ball of newspaper and shook it in Fulton's face. "Her Highness is proficient in four languages. She has a good sense of history and economics. Her geography is not the best, but, I assure you, she's not feeble-minded."

Grinning broadly at her recitation, he opened the door with a neatly lettered sign that said Fulton's Press and called inside, "Stop the presses! The Princess isn't good at geography!"

Liza pressed her lips together to keep from betraying her knowledge of an unladylike word and stomped her booted foot. Noticing the curious bystanders, Fulton gestured to Inside Boy to pack up his newspapers and held the door open for Liza to pass within. "I apologize for my manners, Miss Hastings. Come in and we can discuss this in a civilized way."

The first thing Liza noticed was a loud rumbling coming from the back of the building. The clean room had a large desk in the center with several chairs scattered around it. Her eyes watered from the strong vinegary smell of printer's ink. Fulton offered her a chair and a glass of ale, apologizing he had not the means to make a proper tea.

"Ale is fine, thank you," she said, marveling that she was drinking ale alone with a young man.

Inside Boy came into the shop burdened with the broadsheets. "Is Jim in the back? I'd like to say 'ello."

Fulton nodded, and Inside Boy disappeared through a door in the back corner. The rumble became a roar when the door was opened. Liza caught a glimpse of a large, iron press, churning off broad sheets of newsprint. Fulton sat down across from her and placed two glasses on the desk. She noticed his ink-stained hands had long, well-shaped fingers.

"I should've realized the Princess's lady would be upset with my article."

Liza almost told him she wasn't a lady anymore. For a moment, Liza toyed with letting him believe she was still a lady.

But Inside Boy will tell him if I don't.

"I'm the Princess's maid," Liza said in a low voice, unable to meet his eyes.

"Her what?"

"Her maid."

He guffawed, displaying his bright straight teeth. "I don't believe it, not with that coat and that accent."

"I just started working there." She was anxious to turn the conversation back to Victoria. "But I've been present at the Princess's lessons. She's no fool."

He shrugged. "Sometimes sources disagree. What's a publisher to do?"

"Publisher? You're hardly older than I," Liza said.

Spots of red appeared high on Fulton's cheeks. "I may be young but I write news. I print it. I sell it. By definition, I'm a publisher."

"How can you call it news when it's all falsehood?" She slapped her hand on the desk.

He held up his arm warding off her anger, but a grin snuck onto his face. "It's all a matter of perspective, Miss Hastings."

"Truth is truth and lies are lies. There's no in between, Mr. Fulton." She cleared her throat and said in a stronger voice, "You should destroy them!"

"I can't afford to toss my profit in the trash," he protested. "Let the Princess buy every copy if she's so upset."

"Isn't the truth more important than profit?" Liza asked tartly.

"When I'm rich, I'll say yes. But for now, I've my living to earn." His voice was reasonableness itself. "I'll tell you what, I won't print any more. That's more than fair. This looked to be a popular edition."

Liza took a sip of ale. Licking the foam from her lips, she considered him. His hair was an agreeable sandy color. She tapped the crumpled paper with her gloved hand. "How much do I owe you?"

"Keep your money. I'll consider the Princess to be in my debt." His chair tilted back and his arms folded, Will contemplated Liza. "I could use information from someone well placed like yourself." He waited for Liza's reaction.

"Be one of your sources? I think not."

Why does everyone want me to be a spy?

"Why not?" He grinned. "Inside Boy brought you here for a reason."

Liza glanced toward the back of the shop, where Inside Boy had disappeared. "I asked him to bring me . . ."

Did I? Or was it his idea?

"Maybe he wanted to help you. I pay well." Fulton rubbed his thumb and forefinger together. "Boy's earned ten pounds since he moved into Kensington."

"But I couldn't possibly spy on the Princess," Liza said.

"Who asked you to spy? I want her willing participation. If her enemies are spreading rumors about her, this is a way to fight back."

Liza opened her mouth to protest, but then closed it with a snap. Fulton had a point. The Princess might leap at a chance to communicate with her future subjects. And Liza needed the money. She was sure Mr. Arbuthnot at Claridge's was just counting the days until he could sell her things.

Could this be how I pay my father's debts?

Catching her lower lip between her teeth, Liza said, "The Princess's life is very dull, you know."

"So are the days of most young ladies," he reminded her. "My readers will be reassured by her domestic doldrums."

"She's only sixteen."

"An age when most girls are launched in society, attending balls and dreaming of young men. Which handsome prince is Victoria dreaming about?"

Liza caught her breath. If her parents had lived, she would be one of those girls, planning her season, saving her dance cards. But she would never have met an enterprising young man like Mr. Fulton at a society ball. She stared at his stained hands.

"Well?" Fulton interrupted her reverie.

Liza came back to herself and half surrendered. "I'll ask her, but only on the condition you stop selling the paper."

His eyes gleamed and he seemed more delighted than discomfited. "You strike a hard bargain, Miss Hastings." He held out his hand and they shook. His grip was firm. "Talk to your Princess and send me word by Inside Boy."

Inside Boy came back in the room. "Miss, we 'ave to go."

Liza would not have minded more conversation with Mr. Fulton, but she was careful not to show it. "Mr. Fulton, thank you for your hospitality. It has been a most interesting discussion."

"Please, Miss Hastings. Call me Will. If we are going to work together—"

Inside Boy looked sharply at Liza. "''as 'e got you into 'is web? Lousy spider, 'e is."

"I'm undecided," Liza said.

Inside Boy shook his head in warning. "Remember Miss Liza, 'e's a newspaper man. 'tis job is to get people to say things they'll regret. But it's your funeral, Miss. Let's go."

"You know how to find Annie?" she asked.

Shooting a look at Will, Inside Boy said briefly, "We'll talk about it outside."

Will leaned forward and Liza saw the investigator's gleam in his eyes. "Annie. Would this be Annie Mason, late of Kensington Palace?"

"Yes," Liza said.

At the same moment, Inside Boy said, "'tis none of your business, Will."

Will's face was stern. "Why are you visiting her?"

Inside Boy drew his finger across his throat.

Taking his hint, Liza said, "It's not any of your concern, Mr. Fulton."

Will turned on Inside Boy. "I know Annie's a friend of yours, but she's not fit to meet Miss Hastings."

"'tis none of your business," Inside Boy repeated.

"It's any gentleman's business to protect a lady," Will retorted.

Liza felt lightheaded; no one had tried to protect her since her parents died.

"You're no gentry cove, Will Fulton," said Inside Boy in a sour voice.

"Miss Hastings," Will said. "You shouldn't go there." He stepped closer and she could smell the vinegar on his shirt and the yeasty ale on his breath.

"You can't stop us, Mr. Fulton," Liza said. Handsome or not, he was trying to keep her from her duty.

"I'll go with you then," he said. "Trust me, in that neighborhood, you want someone a bit more imposing than Boy here for protection."

———

Will locked up his shop and they set off through the crowds of Saturday shoppers, rushing past with their baskets and packages. Sea gulls screeched above and the wind carried the foul smell of the Thames River. Inside Boy led them through a series of narrow, dirty streets. The houses were poorly built and leaned against each other for support. Liza wondered, were one removed, would they all fall down? A stream of stinking waste was discarded from an upper window; fortunately Inside Boy was alert to such dangers and held Liza back. Will was not as lucky, his pants got splattered with the fetid liquid. He shook off as much as he could, disgusted.

Inside Boy finally stopped in front of a dilapidated wooden house. The windows sagged but the oak door was stout. Liza heard raised voices inside.

Will put his fist to the door. "Are you sure?" he asked Liza.

"I promised Her Highness."

"Stubborn," Will muttered. Liza hid a smile behind her gloved hand.

He pounded on the door, and the shouting stopped. Eventually a woman opened the door a crack and peered out. Liza stifled an exclamation when she saw the woman's face.

Pox!

The woman's face was covered with old craters that had once held the dreaded smallpox. "No snoozin' kens," the landlady said and tried to slam the door shut.

Will shoved his boot between the door and the jamb. "We don't want rooms."

Liza stepped forward. "I'm looking for Annie Mason."

"What do you want with that light skirt?" She spat on the doorstep, just missing Liza's boot. "You're no better than she is, no doubt."

Liza took a step back.

"Some friends want to see her," said Inside Boy, passing a coin through the door.

The landlady shoved the coin in her pocket, swung open the door and said, "Top o' the stairs, first door on the left. There'd better be no trouble."

Liza gritted her teeth and entered a small, dingy hallway. The smell of onions and an overpowering odor of too many unwashed people hung heavy in the hall.

"How many people live here?" she asked Will.

He shrugged. "I doubt the landlady keeps count. But she'll get her rent from each one of them, no question."

Inside Boy darted ahead. With foreboding weighing down every step, Liza followed. Will brought up the rear.

Annie's room was narrower than Liza's room at the Palace. A thin mattress of straw lay on the floor and a battered valise sat in a corner. Liza couldn't help staring at the woman standing just inside the door. She had imagined Annie like herself—petite and blonde. But Annie was an Amazon—very tall with red, curly hair and pale eyes. Her white Carrara marble–like skin gleamed against her blue velvet gown trimmed with tattered lace. Modest enough once, the dress had been altered to display more of her full bosom, though the bones at the base of her neck jutted out. Liza couldn't help but think how pretty Annie would be without her cut and swollen lip.

"Boy, I'm glad to see you," Annie said. Her gravelly voice made Liza wonder if she had just risen from bed, though the noon bells of St. Paul's chimed in the distance.

Inside Boy twisted his cap in his hands. "Annie, you asked for 'elp. Course I came."

"It took you long enough. Did you give Victoria my letter?"

"I gave it to 'er." He pointed to Liza. "She found a way to get it to the Princess. You know 'ow they are—she ain't ever alone."

"Who's she? One of those do-gooders who want to help but don't know how? Someone tried last month to get me into service again. As if I'd ever do that." Annie tugged her sleeves down to her wrists, but not before Liza saw the cruel bruises ringing her forearm.

"Quit it, Annie." Inside Boy's face tightened. "This is Miss Liza, 'oo's got your place with the Princess."

Annie stared down at Liza. "Didn't take them long to replace me," she said, bitterness twisting her mouth. "Don't start thinking of it as home, they'll throw you out like a used rag when they're done with you."

Liza couldn't contain her curiosity any longer. "Your letter said Sir John daren't let you stay at the Palace. What did you mean?"

"Did he send you?" Annie asked suspiciously.

"No, of course not."

"Then never mind what I meant. I'm safer if I say nothing. I never should have written that letter."

"But—"

"You're wasting your time."

There was a long moment of silence.

In the hall, Liza could see Will leaning against the wall, watching everything with an investigator's eye.

A large roach skittered across the floor and Liza drew her skirts close. Annie's plight was worse than Liza had imagined.

Annie was suddenly angry. "Don't sneer, Miss High and Mighty. I can pay my rent and feed myself. I'd like to see you do as well on the outside."

Stung, Liza replied, "I never said I could. But if you are doing so well, why did you beg the Princess for money?"

"When I wrote that, I had no friends, 'cept for old Boy here. Since then, I've found a protector."

"A fancy man," said Inside Boy in a flat voice.

"Then you don't need help?" Liza asked uncertainly.

Will muttered, "She needs help, but not the kind you can give."

Annie glared at him. "The Princess owes me. I did her dirty work, just like you're doing now. I'll take her money. How much did she send?"

"She doesn't have a large allowance," Liza said.

"You think I don't know that? How much?"

Liza fumbled with her reticule, pulling out the money Victoria had given her. Annie snatched the coins from her hand. As she counted them rapidly, Liza took note of the filth under her jagged fingernails. Heedless of the men in the room, Annie lifted up her skirt.

Liza gasped. She knew she should avert her eyes, but she couldn't help but stare.

Annie secreted the coins in a pocket attached to a strip of cloth tied around her waist, then smoothed the skirt down. Liza, as well as Boy and Will Fulton, could testify she was not wearing a corset.

Liza waited, expecting some sort of thanks.

"Well?" Annie challenged. "What else did you come for?"

"Nothing," Liza said. After a moment, she turned to leave.

Before Liza reached the door, Annie began to speak and the words came tumbling out as though she wanted to say her piece before she thought better of it. "Does the Princess miss me at all?"

Liza froze in the doorway. Annie had fallen so far from Kensington Palace; even farther than Liza had fallen from Claridge's Hotel. She answered gently, without turning around. "I think she does."

Will took Liza's arm without saying a word. He led her outside. Inside Boy stayed behind talking to Annie for a moment, then joined them on the street.

Shaken, Liza looked at the two of them.

"Does 'fancy man' mean what I think it does?" she asked.

Inside Boy and Will looked at each other, neither of them meeting Liza's gaze.

"Never mind," she said. She could guess. Annie had become a prostitute and the fancy man was her procurer. He took her earnings and treated her none too well by the look of her bruises. In just a few weeks, Annie had sunk so low. A chill ran up Liza's spine as she realized her own precarious position: she was out of the Palace without permission.

"I must get back," Liza said. "I'll lose my job if I'm out too late."

No one had to say what happened to maids who were dismissed from Kensington Palace.

II

In Which Liza Insists on the Privacy of Her Thoughts

Liza's feet were sore as she trudged to the servants' entrance alone. Inside Boy had disappeared as soon as they sighted the Palace. The memory of Annie's degradation made her feel dirty and fearful. Why had she left the Palace without permission? Before she could steel herself to knock, the door opened and Mademoiselle Blanche appeared. Liza's heart sank; this did not bode well.

"Miss Hastings, you've been missed," hissed the French maid. "My Duchess returned an hour since. She has sent me to find you two times."

Liza knew better than to expect favors from Mademoiselle. "What did you tell her?"

"What could I say, but the truth? You have not been seen for all the day!"

"I'd expect no less of you, Mademoiselle."

With a malicious smile, the Frenchwoman said, "My Duchess has spoken sharply to Madame Strode, who wants to speak to you, *immédiatement.*"

"*Merci beaucoup,*" Liza said sourly. She hurried to the house-keeper's private room. Her heart beat so hard it threatened to drown out her footsteps. A formidable voice bade her to enter. Mrs. Strode sat in her armchair knitting before the fire.

"Miss Hastings, you've been here less than a month and you're already sneaking out of the house," Mrs. Strode said, without looking up from her knobby blue scarf.

Liza's blood pumped even faster. "Mrs. Strode, let me explain."
But what can I tell her?

"Well?" said the housekeeper.

Picking at her skirt, Liza said, "It's confidential."

Mrs. Strode's needles clicked louder. "Miss Hastings, you will have to be more forthcoming, else you'll pack your bags today."

"I was . . ." Liza sought the right words. "I was on a confidential errand for the Princess."

Mrs. Strode's head jerked up and she gave Liza a look that penetrated through the city grime. "The Baroness gave you permission to leave the Palace?"

Liza hesitated. "No. The Princess did."

Click, click. Mrs. Strode's needles were moving faster now. "You work for the Baroness."

"I was told I also work for the Princess."

"The Princess is a child."

"The Princess is a month shy of seventeen," Liza retorted. "If she gave you a direct order, would you disobey her?"

Mrs. Strode said nothing for a few minutes. Her needles clicked louder and faster. Finally she muttered as though she had forgotten Liza's presence. "Twenty-seven years I've worked for the royal family, but never have I seen the like. A grown Princess treated like a child. A maid who doesn't know who her mistress is. I have to keep secrets from the Duchess, my employer, if I am to serve the Princess, my future Queen."

Liza nodded sympathetically.

"The Princess expected you to draw her bath half an hour ago," Mrs. Strode said.

Liza stood rooted to the floor.

"What is it, Miss Hastings?"

"Am I still employed?" asked Liza in a rush.

"Consider yourself on probation. Another lapse like this one and you will be dismissed. Without a reference."

Liza hurried out before Mrs. Strode could change her mind.

———

Liza put her ear to the door of the Duchess's sitting room. Her mother would be horrified, but Liza refused to walk in unprepared.

"The King thinks you look pale?" The Duchess's strident German voice sounded loudly and Liza jumped back from the doorjamb. "How dare he criticize me?"

Princess Victoria's gentler tones replied, "Mama, Uncle King only suggested I take some exercise. He is sending me a mare so I can ride." She sounded pleased. "I'll name her Rosa."

"He insults me by implying I can't give you a decent mount," said the Duchess. "Of course, if he gave us a proper allowance, I could afford a horse. We'll send it back."

Liza shook her head and sighed at the Duchess's foolishness.

"The mare is a gift for me!" Liza could hear the tears in the Princess's voice.

"Will the King's gift come with oats? I don't think so." The Duchess added, "I wish I had thought to say so to his face."

"Don't worry, Mama—you said more than enough."

On the other side of the door, Liza winced.

"Cruel, ungrateful child!" The Duchess sounded wounded. "Victoria, you have never appreciated the difficulties of my position." As if the Duchess sensed Liza's arrival, she said peevishly, "Where is that girl? You should be in your bath, not arguing with me."

Liza slipped into the room. "Your Grace." She glanced at Victoria who was staring out the window, still wearing her day dress. Even the line of her back looked sullen.

"Where have you been, Miss . . . Miss?" the Duchess asked in German.

"Excuse me, Ma'am?" Liza remembered to pretend not to understand.

In English, the Duchess said, "The Princess required you quite some time ago. Mrs. Strode is too lax. Where were you?"

Liza waited, but the Princess did not turn around.

"Ma'am, I'm sorry, but I . . . I . . . ." Liza stammered.

The Duchess said, "Answer me. Where have you been?"

Liza steeled herself to lie, but Victoria turned away from the window and spoke for her. "Oh, Mama, stop interrogating Liza, I sent her to town." Her eyes were swollen and her face blotchy.

"To town? Why?" The Duchess's eyes narrowed.

"Mama, I'd rather not say."

Liza's heart sank. The Duchess would never accept such an evasion.

"Victoria, a mother and daughter must have no secrets."

The Princess managed a coy expression. "But Mama, your birthday is coming—"

"My birthday isn't until August."

"Mama, please don't ask—you'll spoil the surprise."

Her pique forgotten, the Duchess smiled. "How nice." She click-clacked out of the room, saying as she went, "Take your bath, Victoria."

The Princess made a face at her mother's back.

"Thank you, Your Highness," said Liza, feeling like a soldier who had miraculously survived a battle.

"Did you think I wouldn't save you?" Victoria asked listlessly. "I promised."

"It's not that I didn't trust you to keep your word, but the stakes for me are very high."

The Princess sighed. Liza followed her down the hallway to the bathroom.

"Where is the Baroness?" Liza asked.

"Lehzen went to bed. She suffers from headaches, particularly after we visit the King." In the dim light of the hallway, Liza could still see the tearstains on Victoria's cheeks. "Today was especially awful."

Two scullery maids were just pouring the last of the large cans of steaming water into the porcelain claw-foot tub as the Princess and Liza entered the bathroom. They bobbed and skittered out, empty cans banging. Liza began laying out the towels and soaps.

"What happened?" Liza asked.

"First, the ride to Windsor was awful. People booed the King! Mama and Sir John loved it, of course." The Princess turned her back so Liza could unbutton her gown. Victoria gingerly stepped into the hot water in her linen chemise. "And when we arrived, Mama insulted Uncle King. Again."

"What did she say?" Liza asked, keen for more. This was the kind of detail Will Fulton's readers would crave.

"She suggested, very loudly, that my title be changed." Victoria shrank from the memory, sinking lower in the water.

"Princess?"

"Not that one." The Princess smiled wanly. "No one can take that away. I am the Heiress Presumptive. Mama, in her infinite wisdom, wants me to be the Heiress Apparent." She sat up and held out her plump white hand for a washcloth. Dipping it into the water, the Princess washed her neck and arms.

Liza unfolded a linen bath sheet as Victoria finished her bath. "Is there a difference?"

The Princess's face became somber. "All the difference to poor Aunt Queen." She stood up and Liza helped her out of the tub and wrapped her body in the sheet. "'Presumptive' means the Queen may still bear an heir. 'Apparent' means there's no hope at all," the Princess explained.

"How sad." Liza had read Queen Adelaide's babies died young.

"And tactless. Aunt Adelaide is so kind." The Princess perched on the edge of the tub and sighed. "Sometimes I wish she would have a child."

"Don't you want to be Queen?" Liza asked, astonished.

"If I weren't the heir, then Sir John would leave me alone. I could travel—see Vienna or Paris, even India." She twisted the water out of her long fair hair. "I could meet young men. Perhaps a man who might be suitable for a simple Princess, who is not destined to be Queen."

"Can't you marry whomever you wish?" Liza asked without thinking.

"Of course I can't." The Princess's laugh was bitter. "Can you marry a gentleman?" In just five words, the Princess put Liza firmly back in her place.

Eyes downcast, Liza began rubbing cream on the Princess's elbows and knees. "What is this?" she asked, noticing a puckered mark on the Princess's arm for the first time.

"It's a vaccination." The Princess pronounced the word carefully. "Against the smallpox. Mama is very progressive when it comes to matters of my health. Not many people have it yet."

Liza remembered the woman at Annie's house. The pocks on her face meant she had contracted the pox and survived. It was a risk every city dweller feared. But the Princess apparently was immune. Not for the first time, Liza thought it terribly unfair the Princess enjoyed so many privileges while her people suffered.

"Liza, are you listening to me?" The Princess sounded querulous.

"I beg your pardon, Your Highness, I was woolgathering."

"Try to pay attention, Liza." The Princess resumed her explanation. "I must marry someone of rank. But it is considered unwise to marry a British nobleman because the others would be jealous. He can't have a kingdom of his own. And he must be Protestant. And, this is the most difficult one, he must be acceptable to Mama and the King."

"That is a difficult combination," Liza admitted.

The Princess sighed as Liza towel dried her hair. "I want to marry someone strong, but would a strong man be willing to be my Consort? Without any power of his own, save what I give him?" Her voice was matter of fact; she had carefully considered the difficulties.

"Who does the King favor for you?" Liza asked.

"He liked Prince George, one of my British cousins. But then he went blind when he was only fourteen."

Liza was taken aback. "Oh my, how sad."

"I know. It was the most tragic thing. So now he can't marry anyone important, least of all me."

The girls were silent while Liza combed the knots out of the Princess's wet hair.

"Yesterday," Liza said, "I overheard your Mother and Sir John discussing the Saxe-Coburg brothers who are coming for your birthday ball. Are they suitable?"

"Mama's nephews?" The Princess's laugh was more like Dash's bark. "Ernst will inherit a dukedom in Germany, so he won't do. Albert, who is Mama's favorite, is supposed to be handsome."

"That's good, isn't it?" Liza said.

"But he's nine months younger than I am."

"Maybe you'll fall in love and it won't matter." Liza's parents' marriage had been a love match.

"Only commoners marry for love," the Princess said. "My father only married Mama to get a suitable heir." She stared at herself in the mirror. "I was destined to be myself from before I was born."

There was a long pause. Liza held out another cream for the Princess to smear on her face.

"You'll be Queen of England," Liza said finally.

"Oh Liza, you must never say that. I'll be Queen of Great Britain! Ireland and Scotland and Wales are very put out if you say only England."

Liza smiled. "The Queen of Great Britain will be the most important woman in the world."

"That's true." Princess Victoria looked happier. She dropped her towel and stepped into the luxury of the wool-lined dressing gown. "Perhaps it won't be so terrible."

A tap sounded at the door. Liza started, crushing the pen nib into a blob of ink on the page of her journal. Her caller tried to push open the door. But now that she knew the fate of the room's previous occupant, Liza was careful to shoot the bolt.

"Liza, it's Victoria."

Liza glanced longingly at her bed and sighed. She blotted the page, pulled the silk ribbon down the page to mark her place, and closed the journal. She opened the door just wide enough for the Princess to slip in. Victoria wore a turquoise dressing gown Liza had not seen before. "You shouldn't lock the door, Liza," she said. "What if I want to come in?"

"It wasn't to keep *you* out," Liza said. But if the Princess wondered what she meant, she didn't ask.

"What a tiresome day!" The Princess shivered. "It's always so cold in here. Where is your lovely shawl?"

"I don't know, Your Highness," Liza lied. She had retrieved it from Victoria's room at the first opportunity and hidden it away in her trunk.

The Princess wrapped Liza's blanket around her body. "We were having such an interesting conversation earlier I forgot to ask you about your mission. By the time I remembered, Mama was keeping me prisoner in our bedroom. What did you learn today?"

With the sensation of stepping off a precipice, Liza relayed Will's business proposition.

The Princess clapped her hands with delight. "I could finally speak directly to my subjects!"

"I told Will I wouldn't do it unless you agreed," Liza said.

"Of course you must promise not to write anything without my permission." A doubt crossed the Princess's face. "You can write, can't you?"

Liza nodded. "Of course. I keep a journal." She glanced over at the leather book on her table.

The Princess jumped up and took the two small steps to the table. "You have a journal too? I daresay yours is more interesting than mine." Paralyzed, Liza watched as the Princess opened the leather-bound book to the first page.

Her most private thoughts and dreams were in that book. But how do you tell a Princess she has gone too far?

How do you not?

"Heavens, your handwriting is hard to read." Victoria brought the journal over to the candle to read the first page of Liza's secrets. "'Today, I buried my parents.'"

Liza couldn't help herself; she snatched the journal from Victoria's hands. She clasped the book to her chest. Trembling, she sought for words to defend her private self from Victoria. But when she dared glance at the Princess, Victoria looked as shaken as she.

"Liza, dear Liza, I do beg your pardon," the Princess whispered, kneeling at Liza's feet and placing her hand over Liza's. "I should not have read that."

Liza's lungs contracted, as though there wasn't enough air to breathe. "No," she said flatly. "It was very wrong."

Victoria took her hand away. "You are my subject; you shouldn't speak to me like that."

Liza was too angry to back down. "My heart and mind are my own." She slid the book under her mattress. "You must promise never to read my journal again."

There was silence. Finally, her blue eyes dark with distress, Victoria murmured, "I forget other people are permitted the privacy of their thoughts. I shan't pry again."

"Thank you." Liza tucked her hair behind her ears and clasped her hands together.

With an air of making amends, Victoria said, "Read my journal anytime you like."

Liza stared at her. "I couldn't do that."

"Everyone else does," the Princess said simply. "I can't even use ink in my journal until my dear Mama approves what I've written."

The crisis had passed, the girls were quiet for a time. Liza wondered whether perhaps she and the Princess had moved a little closer to becoming friends.

Shaking off all that had happened, Victoria said, "What should we write about first?"

"Let me think on it."

"Tomorrow then." As the Princess put her hand on the doorknob, she glanced back. "Did you see Annie?"

Liza had dreaded the question. "I did. I gave her your money."

"My good deed for the week." Victoria's pleasure lit up her face. "I hope she looked well?"

In her mind's eye, Liza saw Annie's thick red hair covering her bruised face and the immodest way she had hiked up her skirt to hide the coins. She couldn't tell the Princess the truth. "You forget, Your Highness, I've never met her before."

"True. Goodnight, Liza." And the Princess was gone.

Liza lay down on the bed and stared at the wood rot in the ceiling. The Princess hadn't even asked how or where Annie lived. Absence did not make the Princess's heart grow fonder.

I'd do well to remember that.

Several days passed before Princess Victoria could escape her mother's watchful eye again. She was eager to begin using the press for her own advantage.

Victoria lay on her stomach on Liza's hard bed. "What should we say?"

"Don't you have any ideas?" Liza fought to hide her exasperation.

"Young royal ladies are not encouraged to have ideas." Victoria tilted her chin up doing an excellent imitation of her mother. Both girls giggled.

"I thought you wanted to speak to your subjects," Liza said. "You could discuss issues important to the common people."

"Bother the common people. I don't know any." The Princess rolled over on her back. "Liza, I'd prefer to tweak Sir John's nose."

"That doesn't seem . . . noble." Liza couldn't keep the disappointment from her voice.

"I'm not the Queen yet," the Princess said. "Liza, I'm sixteen and just want to have some fun." She smiled winningly at Liza, her head tilted to one side.

Liza crinkled her forehead. "But next time we should write about something worthwhile."

"You're in no position to dictate terms to me," the Princess said haughtily.

"Then forget about using the press, Your Highness. You can't do it without me!" Liza said, setting her jaw.

Victoria pursed her lips, but the possibility of harassing Sir John was too tempting. "Agreed. Now what can we write?"

Liza put her head to one side and brushed her pen's quill across her cheek. "Do you know anything to his discredit?"

"He's cruel and keeps me from my amusements," answered the Princess, tossing her hair back.

"The nation will hardly mind he makes you study too much," Liza said.

"He's very devoted to Mama and me," the Princess admitted reluctantly. "He's beggared himself to keep us."

Liza knew there was never enough money to support even the Duchess's small household. But Sir John always looked prosperous and fashionable. "I wonder where he gets his money?"

"Money is boring," The Princess snorted. "Everyone knows Sir John has waited all these years to get rich when I take the throne."

"What if the throne were snatched away from him?" mused Liza. "After all these years, what if Queen Adelaide—"

"Has an heir!"

Both girls smiled to think of Sir John's chagrin. "But she's not expecting a child," said Liza, dismissing the idea.

"How do we know she isn't? She did look awfully peaked when I saw her last."

"Do you think so?" Liza asked doubtfully.

"Say she was, then we'll laugh to see Sir John's face. 'Sources at court have noticed signs the King is expecting good news.'" The Princess glanced over to the writing table. "Liza, *écrivez!*"

Liza caught her bottom lip between her teeth. "Princess, I'm not certain this is a good idea."

"What harm can it do? Sir John will never suspect me! And even if he did, what can he do?"

Liza closed her eyes and sought for the right words. "He could destroy *me* with a word."

"Liza, stop worrying."

"But—"

"You're being difficult, when your job is to help me." The unspoken threat hung in the room like a London fog.

Her hand shaking, Liza dipped the quill in ink. "Should I mention the Queen's physical symptoms?" asked Liza.

"Heavens, no! How disrespectful—no one should refer to the Queen's body. It's far too personal."

———

They toiled over their article during stolen hours for the next week. One night as Liza was putting the finishing touches to their piece, Victoria asked about Will Fulton.

"How did you meet him?"

"Who?" asked Liza, distracted by a knotty spelling question: Victoria liked to sprinkle French words wherever she could and Liza couldn't remember if pregnant was *enciente* or *enceinte*.

"Your newspaper friend."

"Oh!" Aside from her brief questions about Annie, Victoria had never asked about Liza's day out. "A mutual acquaintance led me to Mr. Fulton on Fleet Street."

"Mr. Fulton, is it? You called him Will before," said Victoria shrewdly.

"Really? I hadn't noticed." Liza stared down at her quill, feeling the heat creep up her neck and face.

"Liza, you're blushing! Is he handsome?"

"Handsome is as handsome does," Liza said in a nonchalant tone. "Besides, he has no position. He works for his living."

"At the moment," the Princess pointed out, "so do you. For now, pretend he's not so unsuitable. How good-looking is he?"

"Oh, very well." Liza put down her pen and flounced onto the bed with Victoria. "He's rather attractive. Tall, but not too tall."

Both girls detested being towered over, even by handsome young men.

"Is he dark or light in complexion?" asked Victoria, clutching Liza's pillow to her chest.

"His hair is the color of sand and his eyes are beautiful. They are like the green sea."

"Green eyes would match yours." Victoria leaned back against the wall and sighed. "What about his hands?"

"They are covered with ink, but they are well shaped, with elegant fingers. In a different life, he might play the piano."

"I hate it when a boy has beefy hands," Victoria said. "Last month I had to dance with the Princes of Orange, and both of them have thick fingers and they bite their nails down to the nubs." She shuddered.

"Will you marry one of them?" Liza asked.

"Not if I have anything to say about it—they were terrible bores. Uncle King favors one of them because he doesn't want me to marry a German."

"But he married a German princess himself," Liza exclaimed.

"I know." Victoria grimaced. "But Adelaide was his last choice. Everyone else turned him down. He is a little difficult, and he always makes such scenes at parties. Poor Adelaide never knows what he'll do!"

"You have so much more to offer!" Liza said. "You will have your pick of suitors."

The Princess's eyes sparkled. "I am a Princess, so why shouldn't I dream of finding my own Prince Charming?"

"From Saxe-Coburg perhaps?" Liza was thinking of the Duchess's nephews who were arriving soon, in time for the Princess's seventeenth birthday at the end of the month.

"That would be nice," said Victoria, smiling. "And perhaps Will Fulton is the man for you!"

Liza imagined herself as the Queen's lady in waiting, dressed in a fine silk dress. She would lead Will into the royal presence. Maybe Victoria would reward him for his services to the Crown.

"You're not writing!" Victoria interrupted.

Liza shook her head to sweep away the remnants of her impossible daydream.

5 May 1836 Excerpt from the Journal
of Miss Elizabeth Hastings

Signor Lablache finally arrived. He seemed so much larger on stage. In person, he is a fussy, little man. But Victoria was enchanted and draws his likeness again and again in her sketchbook. She talks of nothing but the maestro.

The Princes from Saxe-Coburg are coming in two weeks. If anything can tear Victoria away from the opera singer—it's a potential suitor!

Unfortunately, she has lost interest in our scheme to use the press. She was so eager before; sweeping aside any doubts I had. But she is so easily distracted. Should I see this as a warning?

Will Fulton is waiting to hear from me, but until the Princess finishes the article, I have no excuse to meet him. Not that I want to see him again, but I did promise him an answer.

6 May 1836 Excerpt from the Journal
of Her Royal Highness Victoria

I like Lablache very much, he is such a nice, good-natured, good humored man and a very patient and excellent master; he is so merry too. En profile he has a very fine countenance I think, an aquiline nose, dark arched eye-brows and fine long eyelashes and a very clever expression. He has a profusion of hair, which is very gray, and strangely mixed with some few black locks here and there. I liked my lesson extremely; I only wish I had one every day instead of one every week.

10 May 1856 Excerpt from the Journal of Miss Elizabeth Hastings

The Princess has been in bed for three days. Nell tells me Victoria is always unbearable during her monthly courses. The only thing that cheers her up is the fashion papers. Today, I showed her my favorite clippings from the *Les Modes Parisiennes*. Mama and I collected sketches of dozens of dresses—none of which I'll ever wear now. The Duchess does not permit the paper at Kensington Palace, which makes sharing them with the Princess even more enjoyable. The Princess loves that she has a secret from her mother.

JB continues my linguistic lessons in flash patter. I wish I had someone to practice with. I've taken to murmuring to the walls, hoping he will answer. He still has not told me how he overhears conversations in both the Duchess's sitting room and the Princess's schoolroom. It seems impossible.

12

In Which Liza Is Fitted for a Suitable Ball Gown

VICTORIA SIGHED IN CONTENTMENT. "This is my favorite part of the week."

Dash barked happily. The spaniel was in a wash tub filled with soapy water.

Liza cupped a handful of water and dribbled it on the dog's head. "Dash likes it too. I don't blame him, I miss my baths."

"The baths at the Palace don't compare to those at Claridge's?" the Princess teased as she wrung out a cloth.

"Yours do, Your Highness," Liza said, staring down at Dash. "But the servants don't even get a bathtub."

"Heavens. Is that really true?" The Princess asked, sniffing delicately at Liza's shoulder, as though she were a scientist examining a specimen. "But you must wash sometime—you smell better than most of the lords I've met."

Liza smothered a giggle. "Mrs. Strode has a wooden wash tub filled every Friday and she uses it first. Then Mademoiselle and I take our bath. Mademoiselle thinks she should go before me, but I prefer to bathe before she gets in with all that black dye in her hair. Then the housemaids, then the scullery girls."

A grimace crossed Victoria's face. "Liza, that's not amusing at all. It's positively unwholesome."

"It's practical, Your Highness. All the water must be pumped in the kitchen and heated on the stove. It takes hours to prepare. We can't waste it on just one person."

"What about my bath?"

"Yours is fresh, of course."

"That's not what I meant, silly goose." Victoria giggled. "Use my water after I go to bed—it should still be warm."

Liza considered the idea hopefully. Even a lukewarm, once-used bath would be preferable to undressing in the dank kitchen and stepping into the tub in front of all those hostile women. "Perhaps I shall, Your Highness. Thank you."

"We should start with your bath immediately. Don't you agree, Dashy?" The Princess reached into the tub and scooped a handful of water and showered it over Liza, who froze, wanting to splash her back. But the Princess's rank, as always, stood between them.

Victoria put her damp hands on her hips. "Liza—just this once, can't you just let me be a person instead of a Princess?"

Only if I want to lose my job.

"Heavens, it's impossible to find anyone amusing in this house. I order you to splash me back!"

Liza tilted her head to listen; it wouldn't do to have Mrs. Strode walk in on this. All was quiet. "In that case, Your Highness, prepare to wage a naval war!" She slammed her flat hand on the surface of the bathwater, drenching the Princess. Dash barked wildly.

"The British navy never loses!" The Princess cried, doubled over with laughter. She put Dash's towel into the wash tub and pulled it out and snapped it hard in Liza's direction. The wall behind her was splattered with water. Liza giggled as she wiped water from her eyes.

A slow clapping silenced both girls. "How charming to see such youthful spirits in this old Palace."

Sir John stood behind them. He leaned against the doorjamb, a half smile playing across his mouth.

Liza glanced down at her damp bodice; anyone could see the outline of her chemise through it.

Victoria struggled to regain her dignity. "Sir John," she said, nodding her head almost regally.

"Princess," he said equally formally. But his eyes were not on the Princess; they were fixed on Liza's revealing blouse.

The white doors on the far side of the room banged open, revealing the tall figure of the Duchess. She stared, aghast, at her daughter, arms up to her elbows in soapy water.

"There is too much noise!" exclaimed the Duchess in German. "I could hear you all the way from my sitting room!" She noticed Sir John. "Sir John, what are you doing here?"

With all the grace of a courtier, Sir John turned his attention to her. "Madam, like yourself, I just arrived. I too, am horrified to see the Princess's undignified behavior."

Ignoring Sir John as best she could, Victoria said in English, "I'm washing Dash, Mama." Victoria held out her hand. "Liza, hand me the brush. Not that one, the one with the boar's hair bristles."

"Yes, Your Highness," Liza murmured.

"Victoria, what are you thinking? What if the nation saw you like this? This is a job for your servant." She turned an accusing glare to Liza.

"Mama, stop fussing," Victoria said wearily. "Dash is my responsibility. You always tell me I shouldn't shirk my duty."

As though she hadn't heard a word, the Duchess muttered, "It is absurd for the Princess to be washing the dog. You, girl." The Duchess looked at Liza, who kept her face blank. In her badly accented English, the Duchess said, "Why do you let the Princess dirty her hands?"

Liza clenched her teeth, just managing to hold back a sharp retort.

"Mama," Victoria interjected, "I do this every week. It is a special time for Dash and me. And I do love it so."

"Victoria, the way you spoil that dog! Sometimes I think you care more for him than your own flesh and blood."

Victoria's back snapped straight as a rod as she continued to lather Dash's silky fur. Liza understood only too well that a lonely girl, even a Princess, would take companionship wherever she could find it. Liza touched her shoulder.

"Take your wet doggy hands off the Princess!" ordered the Duchess.

Liza snatched her hand away, but not before she saw Victoria's grateful look.

"We'll discuss this later," the Duchess said. "Victoria come at once, the modiste is here to design your birthday gown."

The Princess immediately brightened. She handed the brush to Liza. "In that case Mama, Dash will have to let Liza finish his bath." Victoria stood up, stripped off her wet apron, and let it fall to the floor. She was wearing one of her oldest blue day dresses, with the simplest of silhouettes and easy sleeves which she had pushed back to her elbows. The light pouring in from the window behind her revealed she wasn't wearing a corset. "I know exactly what I want," Victoria said.

"Victoria, the modiste will make what I tell her to make."

"Mama, you don't even know what I want yet. Here, look." Dabbing her damp hands on Liza's towel, the Princess reached into the pocket of her dress. She pulled out a folded page from *Les Modes Parisiennes*, the illustrated magazine from Paris. The Princess offered it to her mother, like a cat might offer a dead mouse to her mistress. "See how pretty it is. The lace bodice, the full sleeves—and ribbons everywhere! We could design the trim together."

Holding the dripping spaniel at arm's length, Liza couldn't stifle an irritated exclamation. Victoria had taken the drawing from Liza's wall without so much as a by your leave!

That's my dress! Mama cut that page out for me!

"Girl, do you have something to say?" Sir John asked, examining Liza intently.

"No sir," Liza said, swallowing hard.

The Duchess snatched the page from the Princess's hand. "Where did you get this? I don't have such magazines in the Palace." She eyed the drawing carefully. "The gown is totally unsuitable."

"But Mama!"

"Victoria, not in front of the servants. We'll discuss it later."

A pout contorting her pretty face, the Princess followed her mother out of the room.

With a playful bark, Dash tried to twist out of Liza's grasp to follow his mistress. She dropped him in the tub and soapy water splashed all over Liza's dress and face. She groped for the towel to mop up the soap in her eyes.

"Miss Hastings, perhaps I may be of service?" Sir John's charming brogue startled her. She had assumed he would follow the Duchess. His cologne overwhelmed her nose.

"Thank you, Sir John, but I can manage," she said, dashing the suds away.

He knelt beside her. "No, let me." He dabbed the towel against her lace bodice.

Liza didn't have to look down to know her wet blouse clung to her body in a most immodest fashion. "Thank you, sir," she said. "But I wouldn't want you to spoil your fine clothes."

Fine clothes indeed. Sir John had dressed like a young dandy ready for a stroll down Rotten Row: he wore skintight trousers, a jacket tailor-made to emphasize his wide shoulders, and an impeccably knotted turquoise cravat about his throat that set off his bright lemon vest. Not for the first time, Liza thought he and the Duchess had much in common: both wore the current fashions despite their advanced age.

He must be at least forty-five!

"Your concern for my wardrobe is admirable, but let my valet worry about that. After all, what are a few drops of water between friends?" His eyes were locked on the vein she could feel throbbing at the base of her throat. His hands dabbed away at her bodice. Liza leaned away, hardly daring to breath, searching her mind for a way to get out of this predicament without alienating Sir John. She had met Annie; she knew where his "attentions" could lead.

"I have fond memories of muslin dresses at the French court. The more daring ladies imitated Empress Josephine by sponging their gowns so they clung to their bodies. It was most attractive."

"It sounds very chilly, Sir John," Liza said, edging away.

"But you have achieved a similar effect, my dear." He fingered the damp fabric of her collar between his thumb and forefinger.

"Miss Hastings," a voice lisped from the doorway. "You are required—Oh Milord, I did not see you there."

Liza exhaled in relief.

A bitter pill to swallow; to be grateful to Mademoiselle!

Swearing under his breath, Sir John got to his feet quickly. Mademoiselle leaned against the doorjamb watching them suspiciously. Her black curls stood out in sharp relief against her pale powdered face.

"What do you want, Mademoiselle?" Sir John asked.

"Miss Hastings is required in my lady's dressing room."

"I'll go at once." Liza scooped up Dash and hurried out of the room.

———

Liza paused at the doorway and peeked into the Duchess's dressing room. The Princess stood on a stool with a length of fine mauve silk draped around her neck.

"Lower, Mrs. Cavendish!" the Princess entreated, as she tugged the material off the shoulder.

The Duchess tweaked the fabric higher. "Absolutely not. It is too mature. The neckline must be higher."

Mrs. Cavendish, a tiny lady in black, retreated to the far side of the Princess. "For Her Highness's seventeenth birthday, surely a little décolletage is permissible," murmured the long-suffering dressmaker. Under her clever fingers, the skirt of the dress had already taken shape about Victoria's waist.

Baroness Lehzen sat in the corner, sneaking caraway seeds into her mouth. "Victoria, your mother is right. I don't care what the fashion says; to my mind a gown that is off the shoulder is encouraging boys to think about your breasts." She blushed as she said the word "breasts" and belched to cover her embarrassment.

"Oh, Lehzen! Not you too!" Victoria groaned. "Mama, look at the picture again." The Princess clasped her hands together. "The silhouette would be completely ruined by bringing the neckline up."

"Then ruined it must be," declared the Duchess. "This dress is for a much older girl."

"Mama, it's for debutantes!" the Princess wailed. "Most girls have already had their first season at sixteen. I'm a year older."

"I know precisely how old you are, Victoria."

"I would look foolish wearing a child's dress. You don't want me to be humiliated, do you, Mama?" Victoria asked. "It would reflect so poorly on you."

Liza hid a smile. The Princess was learning to manipulate her domineering mother.

The Duchess stopped fingering the fine fabric and stepped back. Even though the Princess stood on a stool, the Duchess had enough height to look her daughter in the eye. "Victoria, you are not like other girls. What is appropriate for them is unthinkable for you. You must always be a symbol of purity and innocence." She turned to the dressmaker and pointed toward the ceiling, "The bodice goes up, up, up."

The Princess suddenly pulled off the skirt. Pins showered down to the floor. Dressed only in a chemise, she unwound the length of silk from around her neck. She spoke slowly, emphasizing every word. "Since my wishes are of no account, then perhaps Your Grace would prefer to arrange my dress without my presence."

With a violent gesture, she threw the fabric at her mother's feet. Liza rushed forward to help the Princess down from the stool. The Princess, her chin high, and blinking back tears, held out her hand in the Baroness's direction. Startled, the Baroness Lehzen pushed herself out of her chair and rushed to help the Princess into a dressing gown. The Princess, still ignoring her mother, stomped out of the room, Baroness Lehzen following, clucking like a mother hen.

The Duchess, her face frozen, stared at the mound of fabric.

What can she say to that?

"Make the dress as I directed," the Duchess ordered and click-clacked out of the room without another word.

Liza gathered up the fabric and handed it to the dressmaker.

Mrs. Cavendish made a rude sound. "It's all fine and well for Their Royal High and Mightinesses to leave, but how am I to fit the dress without the Princess?"

"I'm nearly the same size as the Princess," Liza offered.

Running her eyes up and down Liza's body, Mrs. Cavendish murmured, "Same height, same shoulders. But I'll have to leave several more inches in the waist if the Princess is going to fit. Thank ye dearie, I'd be grateful for the help."

Liza took the Princess's place on the stool.

This should have been my fitting. Victoria has everything. Why does she have to take my dress too?

"It's a lovely dress, even with the Duchess's alterations. And this fabric is fit for a Princess!" Mrs. Cavendish chuckled at her own joke as the shape of a ball gown magically materialized from her quick hands.

"What kind of sleeve does she want?" Liza asked.

"Oh, what do all the girls want?" She looked up at Liza, and sketched the shape in the air. "Leg of mutton sleeves. I'll do them in white. They'll be tight around the upper arm, full at the elbow and then gathered at the wrist."

"May I suggest you make a separate set of sleeves with the fullness at the upper arm?" Liza said. "The Princess does not have the figure to be flattered by the sleeve you describe."

Mrs. Cavendish nodded.

"And," added Liza, feeling very daring, "do the Princess this favor, cut the armhole a trifle wider than usual. She's going to be dancing the whole night through, I'll wager. She'll appreciate being able to move her arms. And I'll be grateful if she's not sore and chafed the next morning."

The dressmaker smiled as she pushed in the pin about the waist. "Not many of my ladies think to ask for that. You know something about fashion, I daresay."

"My mama always said fashion doesn't have to be uncomfortable," Liza confided. "But still she insisted I wear a corset, that wretched torture device."

"One's about moving easy, the other's about decency." Mrs. Cavendish stepped back. "What do you think?"

"You're a marvel, Mrs. Cavendish. It is a beautiful dress," Liza said, with a sigh for the ensemble she would never wear.

The dressmaker circled around Liza, adjusting here and pulling there. "Most of my other young ladies and mamas are excited to plan a gown together," she said thoughtfully. "Not those two. Always quarreling."

Liza and her mother had enjoyed every step of designing a new dress. Her papa had teased that they had no use for him, so long as they had a dressmaker, milliner, and cobbler, but Liza would have gladly have given away all the beautiful clothes in the world if she could only have her father—her family—back.

13

In Which Liza Attracts the Notice of a Prince

"LIZA, THE PRINCES will be here any moment. Hurry up!"

Victoria's long hair slipped through Liza's fingers. She wished the Princess would sit still.

"I'm going as quickly as I can," she said.

"I must be in the hall when they arrive."

"There!" Liza pushed in the final hairpin.

"Ouch!" Victoria glared at Liza.

"You told me to hurry, Princess."

Victoria forgot all recriminations when she saw her reflection in the looking glass. She pirouetted around the bedroom. Her dress was a delightful white-and-rose satin with pale pink bows across the width of the skirt. She looked like a summer day next to Liza's plain white blouse and gray worsted skirt.

"How do I look?" Victoria asked.

"Lovely," said Liza.

"Really lovely? Or just a little lovely?"

"Princess, you look wonderful," Liza said. "These colors flatter your complexion."

The Princess looked again in the mirror. "Do you think the dress makes me look too young?"

Liza tilted her head and considered. "Well, the bodice could be adjusted a bit." She tugged at the fabric and pinned it back so that more of the Princess's bosom lay exposed.

"Liza, perfect!" the Princess cried. "Do you think he will like me?"

"Which one? Ernst or Albert?"

"Haven't you been paying attention? Albert, of course. He's the eligible one." She smoothed the ribbon around her waist. "Mama has her heart set on him."

Tears sprang to Liza's eyes.

Who will pick a husband for me?

She gave herself a bracing shake.

I'll have to arrange my own marriage.

The Duchess, followed by the Baroness Lehzen, bustled into the bedroom, her face beaming.

"Victoria, they are finally here!"

Victoria jumped up and down with delight. "We should be at the porte cochere to meet them."

"Victoria, don't be so eager. It's not dignified," scolded the Duchess, but she couldn't hide her pleasure at Victoria's enthusiasm. If she could marry Victoria to her choice, the Duchess could control her well into adulthood.

The Duchess inspected Victoria's ensemble. "I don't recall the neckline being so low," she frowned. "But there's no time now to fix it; they are arriving. I will greet them outside. You wait on the stairs."

Moments later, the Princess fidgeted at the top of the double marble staircase. Liza moved forward to take her arm.

Victoria couldn't contain her nerves. "How do I look?" she asked again.

"Charming." Liza smiled. The sparkle in the Princess's eyes made her all the more attractive.

"I think I should stand here," Victoria said. "Then he won't know how short I am until he's already admired me." She crinkled her nose at Liza's close presence. "Step back, Liza. I don't want Albert to think of me as a child who needs help going down the stairs!"

The Duchess made her entrance on the arm of a handsome man who resembled her. Behind him were two adolescent boys, clearly brothers. The eldest looked about him with an open and sunny countenance. The younger, the famous Albert, hung back. His cheeks were round and he was starting a mustache. He was grimacing and his hand rested on his abdomen as though he had a bilious stomach.

Victoria called out to them, "Cousins, welcome, welcome!"

If there were any flaws in her Prince, Victoria didn't see them.

18 May 1836 Excerpt from the Journal of Her Royal Highness Victoria

At a ¼ to 2 we went down into the Hall to receive my uncle Ernst, Duke of Saxe-Coburg-Gotha and my Cousins, Ernst and Albert, his sons. Albert, who is just as tall as Ernst but stouter, is extremely handsome; his hair is about the same color as mine; his eyes are large and blue, and he has a beautiful nose and a very sweet mouth with fine teeth; but the charm of his countenance is his expression, which is most delightful; c'est a la fois, full of goodness and sweetness and very clever and intelligent.

Tucked away in the chaperone's corner of the Duchess's sitting room, Liza decided Albert was anything but charming. After a week, even Victoria was finding conversation difficult.

The Princess asked the Prince, "Are you excited about my birthday ball?"

Without taking his eyes from his book, Albert said, "Of course."

"I love balls! I don't know which pleases me more, the music or the dancing. Which do you prefer?"

"I prefer reading," he said. "Quietly."

Victoria went perfectly still for a moment. "Hmm," she said at last. "But since the ball is in my honor, I have to dance. At least a bit, to set the tone. Imagine a birthday ball where no one danced!"

"I could only hope," answered Albert.

Victoria looked over at Liza; her eyes pleading for help. Liza made drawing motions in the air. Victoria's face brightened.

"Would you like to see my drawings?" Victoria asked. She picked up her sketchbook from the side table and thrust it in Albert's face. Albert sighed, but he put down his book and leafed through Victoria's drawings.

"I'm told I am quite accomplished," said Victoria, casually sharpening her pencil with a knife.

"Very nice," murmured Albert. "I recognize everyone. Your mother. The Baroness. Your little dog."

"Dash," Victoria supplied.

"Yes, Dash. A cunning likeness. But who is this?" Liza craned her neck to see. To while away the time one day, Victoria had sketched Liza's portrait. Her heart beat faster.

"Surely you know, Albert," Victoria said, sneaking a smile toward Liza.

"I cannot hazard a guess," he said.

"Albert, you are so unobservant." She slapped the flat side of the knife against his arm.

He drew back. "Victoria, you could have cut me."

The Princess's face assumed that stubborn look Liza knew so well. "Guess," she insisted.

Please don't, Princess.

"I don't like playing games, Victoria. We're not children."

There was a pause.

"It's not childish," Victoria said. "Look around you."

Annoyance flitted across Albert's round face. "I give up. Who is it?"

"It's Liza!" Victoria cried.

"Who?" Albert said blankly.

Victoria swung her arm wide in Liza's direction and Albert ducked away from the knife.

"Silly Albert. Liza is my maid." She gestured for Liza to step forward. Seething, Liza bobbed a curtsy.

"Your maid?" Albert raised his eyebrows as though caterpillars were crawling up his pasty forehead. "Why on earth would I know that?"

"She's with me all the time," Victoria stressed every syllable.

"You have so much to learn: in our position, we don't pay attention to servants."

Liza shifted from one foot to another. She wished Victoria would talk about something else; it made her nervous when the royals noticed her.

Albert had opened his book again, but Victoria had the bit between her teeth. "Liza is invaluable to me. *Sie spricht Deutsch.*" She speaks German.

Without looking up, he murmured, "Useful."

"She is my eyes and ears in the household."

Liza gasped for air, as though someone had punched her in the windpipe.

Victoria had finally captured Albert's attention. "A spy?"

"Not 'spy.' Such a horrid word." She shot a glance at Liza.

"That's despicable, Victoria," Albert said severely.

Victoria's mouth fell open and her eyes bulged. Liza hoped Victoria would never realize how Albert saw her at that moment.

"Does your mother know?" For the first time, Albert really looked at Liza. His face softened a bit in appreciation. Liza forced her features into a blank expression, trying to look modest and harmless. She knew Albert would betray a maid without hesitating.

Please, Victoria, tell him anything but the truth.

"Of course not. My mother is the one upon whom I am eavesdropping."

Albert began pacing around the room. "Victoria, I don't want to lecture you—"

"Then don't," Victoria said, in what Liza thought of as her Queenly voice.

But Albert didn't heed the warning. "For God's sake, Victoria, you are going to be the Queen," he scolded. "It's up to you to set an example to the nation."

"I don't need your advice," Victoria said. "After all, it is my nation."

A shutter crashed down over Albert's face. "Rather than presume again, I shall take my leave."

"Albert!" Victoria cried out in dismay, but he was gone. She turned to Liza in tears. "Look what you did, Liza. You drove him away."

"Me! Why did you tell him I speak German?" Liza shot back.

Victoria glared at her.

"Princess," Liza said in a more measured tone, "I can't help you if everyone knows our secret."

"I wanted him to recognize your likeness," Victoria said doggedly. Then her tone changed and became more guarded. "When he did finally look, he admired you."

Danger comes from unexpected quarters.

"I'm sure he did not. He had eyes only for you."

"Albert thinks pretty girls are frivolous," said Victoria spitefully.

Liza said nothing. After a few moments, Victoria asked, "Do you think he is right? Am I lessening myself by having you eavesdrop on private conversations?" She paused to consider. "My goodness, it does sound awful." Her forehead crinkled as she thought.

Liza waited on tenterhooks, while the Princess resolved her moral quandary. Under the influence of the prudish Albert, fickle Victoria might do anything.

"Do you want me to stop?" Liza asked, barely keeping desperation from her voice. "I can just be your maid."

"No!" Victoria cried. "I need your help to keep Sir John from ruining my life."

Relieved, Liza sank into a velvet armchair. She was still useful to Victoria. But if Albert said a word, Liza was as good as fired.

"Perhaps if I explain how Mama and Sir John treat me, Albert will understand."

"It might do more harm than good." Liza's fingers twisted tightly around each other.

"Albert may be my future husband, you know. I should take his advice," said Victoria. "On the other hand, we're not married yet." She tapped her fingers against her sketchbook. "What might he think about our newspaper article?"

Before Liza could answer, Baroness Lehzen appeared in the doorway to collect the Princess for tea. Without a backward glance, Victoria left Liza alone, suspended between security and disaster.

A voice from inside the wood box said, "So much for your friend, the Princess."

"That's enough from you, Inside Boy," said Liza gloomily.

21 May 1836 Excerpt from the Journal of Her Royal Highness Victoria

I sat with my dear Cousin on the sofa and we looked at drawings. Albert draws particularly well and is exceedingly fond of music. The more I see him, the more I am delighted with him and the more I love him. He is so natural, so kind, so very good and so well instructed and informed; he is so well bred, so truly merry and quite like a child and yet very grown up in his manners and conversation. It is delightful to be with him . . . he is quite an example for any young person.

21 May 1836 Excerpt from the Journal of Miss Elizabeth Hastings

There have been excursions with the Princes most every day. Queen Adelaide invited them to Windsor, but the Princess's mother (with Sir John's connivance, no doubt) refused quite rudely. And then, to cap injury with insult, the Duchess took her guests to the zoo instead! When the Duchess finally brought her nephews to see the King, he retaliated by falling asleep at dinner! (I'm sure the meal didn't agree with Albert's digestion.)

I've stayed away from Albert as much as I can. How dare he threaten my livelihood? He's here to marry into Victoria's rank and fortune, and he can't even pretend to enjoy her company. At least with me, Victoria gets what she pays for.

Yesterday, I followed the Princes during their promenade in the garden. I admit my intent was to eavesdrop; my strongest currency with Victoria is information.

Ernst, the elder (and a bit of a rogue), had little patience with the unending list of Albert's priggish complaints. His room was too small. Dinner was too rich. The evenings are too late.

Ernst said, "Brother, you must admit we've been warmly welcomed by our aunt and Cousin Victoria."

Albert grumbled he supposed so.

Then Ernst, with an intensity I particularly noted, asked, "What do you think of Victoria?"

I strained to hear the answer.

Albert said, "She is amiable enough."

Amiable! What a stuffed shirt! Victoria's journal is full of praise for him. And the best he can do is "amiable"!

Ernst warned him against offending Victoria. "The family fortunes rest on you, little brother."

I was trailing behind, ducking behind the shrubbery—very spylike!

Albert sulked in silence, then he burst out, "Ernst, she always expects me to compliment her. And she never stops talking."

"I find her prattle charming," his brother answered.

"It's all very well for you. You aren't expected to . . . to . . . you know."

"I know my duty very well. It's time you do yours."

"What kind of life will I have with her?" Albert asked. "She'll be suspicious all the time—do you know she uses her maid to spy on her good mother? I think I should tell our aunt."

I stopped dead in my tracks. Every nerve on edge, I waited for his brother's response.

"Absolutely not!" Ernst said. "Nothing could offend Victoria more."

"But—"

"You would risk an alliance with the throne of England to gossip about an insignificant maid?"

"The ethics—"

"Enough!" Ernst commanded. "Albert, I forbid it. Father will second me in this. This match is too important for you to botch with your infernal rectitude."

"Very well," said Albert, like a churlish schoolboy.

I breathed again, relieved beyond measure. But has my safety been purchased at the expense of Victoria's future happiness? Ah well, there are greater forces at work here than I can tackle. First, look after myself, then I can afford to think about Victoria.

24 May 1836 Excerpt from the Journal of Her Royal Highness Victoria

No one could be more enchanted than I was. I shall never forget it. It was Mama's birthday present for me.

24 May 1856 Excerpt from the Private Journal
of Miss Elizabeth Hastings

Today is Victoria's seventeenth birthday. The Duchess arranged for an entire opera company to come to Kensington Palace. Giulia Grisi, the finest soprano in London, sang the Princess's favorite arias. It was ostentatious, but Victoria loved every minute of it. She has been pleased with her mother all day. They are happily preparing for Victoria's ball this evening. She's so excited that she will get a chance to dance the waltz. Her mother has an old-fashioned idea that a Princess can only waltz with a member of the family. Albert had better be prepared to dance all night! The Duchess can't stop beaming. It's a nice change from their usual arguments.

I've been here almost two months now, but I am still not reconciled to my change in circumstances. I cannot help but think if Mama had lived, we would be planning my coming out ball. But instead I will dress Victoria (in the dress that should have been mine!) and wait on her convenience. The difference between what is and what might have been . . .

14

In Which Liza and Victoria Wish for the Same Thing

It was already midnight, but the party looked to go on for hours. Liza had watched the notables arrive since ten o'clock. The ball was held in the rarely used state apartments on the first floor. Laughter and music wafted up to Liza waiting in the Princess's bedroom.

Liza paced the room, her patience frayed. She fingered the Duchess's tortoiseshell combs. She tweaked the corner of Victoria's blanket. She studied the portrait of the Duchess holding the infant Victoria.

Why can't I go to a ball?

Then the orchestra below struck up a waltz, and Liza's heart constricted. She closed her eyes to listen. How often had her mother played this tune while Papa had taught Liza the dance?

One, two, three. One, two, three.

Twirling her around in his strong arms, he warned Liza she wouldn't be permitted to perform it in public until she married. They had had to stop dancing, she was laughing so hard. Then he had turned to Mama, his voice full of love, "Mathilde, may I have the honor of this dance?" Mama, not taking her eyes from his, rose from the piano and moved into his embrace. Liza had taken her place at the piano and begun to play. They swirled about the room, exquisitely matched. Perfect partners.

That was only six months ago.

Tears streaked her cheeks, but Liza didn't open her eyes until the orchestra played the last note. Dabbing her face with a handkerchief, she saw her mother's eyes reflected in the mirror and all her good sense flew out the window.

"Mama," she whispered to her reflection. "We came to England so I could go to balls. So I will." Without pausing to consider her folly, she went to Victoria's closet. The Princess had stolen Liza's gown; Liza would not hesitate to borrow one of the Princess's.

———

A bust of Victoria's long dead father presided over the ball. Slipping past his marble gaze, Liza kept a watchful eye all around her, nervous of meeting the Baroness—or anyone who knew her. She felt certain she had chosen her dress wisely. It was elegant but not distinctive. The Princess had worn the mauve dress gathered just below the bodice with silk flowers trimming the skirt when she met the Queen of Portugal a few months earlier. The dress had also had a belt of gold brocade, which marked it as a Princess's gown, so Liza had simply torn the belt off and replaced it with a length of twisted silk. A few pins at the waist tightened the dress sufficiently. She would have preferred to avoid notice, but already, several gentlemen in the crowd cast admiring glances in her direction.

The Duchess had ordered the dark-paneled rooms decorated with elaborate arrangements of pineapples and orchids. Liza glided through the cupola room with its clever ceiling that made the room seem impossibly tall. A clock standing on a pedestal in the center of the room chimed the hour: it was one o'clock. Liza arrived in the drawing room overlooking Round Pond, where the most important guests danced. She darted behind a pillar near an open window to watch.

Victoria sparkled as she danced the quadrille. Even with the Duchess's fussy alterations, the dress looked well on her. Liza had helped Victoria adjust the bodice to show her bosom to best advantage, despite the higher neckline. Victoria had also preferred Liza's choice of more flattering sleeves. Liza smiled now, watching Victoria's arms move freely as she danced. The Princess's partners were mostly old men, indistinguishable from one another. They spoke too loudly and wiped their red, perspiring foreheads as they stepped on Victoria's beleaguered toes. Fortunately for her, the quadrille demanded a frequent change of partners, so she escaped the worst bores for part of the dance at least.

For the next dance, the orchestra struck up another waltz. The Duchess had been very particular: Victoria could not dance the intimate dance with anyone of lesser rank, unless the boy was family. Victoria scanned the crowd, but Albert was nowhere to be seen. A pout crinkled her face, until Prince Ernst swept her onto the dance floor. He must have paid her very pretty compliments, because Victoria blushed a most becoming shade of pink that matched the border on her gown. But still the Princess's eyes fluttered about the room, searching for Albert.

Liza caught a glimpse of the Baroness Lehzen, her back ramrod straight, with eyes for no one but Victoria. Then Liza spied Albert studying a painting on the opposite side of the room, as far from the musicians as possible. Not once, that Liza noticed, did his eyes go to Victoria. A serving man, hired for the evening, offered him a glass of champagne from a silver tray. Scowling, Albert refused. The server turned away, bumping into a portly general. Several glasses crashed to the floor, and Albert laughed. Liza sighed for Victoria's hopes.

As the waltz ended, the Duchess, resplendent in feathers and satin, signaled the musicians. They played a flourish of notes, spreading silence among the guests. She introduced her brother, Ernst, Duke of Saxe-Coburg, Albert's father. He raised his glass and saluted the Princess's health. Outside, Liza heard cheers from Victoria's future subjects as the fireworks began. Liza remained inside while the guests began to move to the terrace to watch. From the window, Liza marveled at the beauty of the colorful explosions reflected in the water of Round Pond.

Large hands suddenly encircled Liza's tiny waist. The pins pricked her skin. Liza opened her mouth to protest, when Simon, in full formal livery, spun her around to face him.

"You look lovely tonight, Liza," he said. "Isn't that one of the Princess's gowns?"

"Take your hands off me," Liza said, but she half-smiled. "I'm not supposed to be here." Simon's easy confidence unnerved her, but it was a night for acting out of character.

"I won't tell." Grinning, he snagged two flutes of champagne from a server who was gaping at the fireworks. He handed her one.

"I shouldn't." But Liza's fingers gripped the stem of the tall glass.

"The Princess's maid should drink to her mistress's health."

Quelling her guilty conscience, she sipped. Her father had taught her to appreciate a good vintage. The Duchess had not stinted this evening. She turned back to watch the fireworks.

Simon stepped in close behind her, his breath warm on her bare shoulder. "The Princess won't leave until the musicians' fingers fall off and her last partner passes out from exhaustion. Why don't we go for a walk in the garden?"

The hairs on the back of her neck stood up. "I have to go. Mrs. Strode will have a fit if she sees me here."

"She's blind as a bat. Annie Mason and I walked out once or twice and Mrs. Strode never cottoned to it," Simon said.

"Annie Mason lost her position!" Liza snapped. "I'll not make the same mistakes."

"So, you're better than Annie, are you?" Simon's whispers turned sharp. "Are you too good for me then?"

"Of course not," Liza lied.

"Not all of us lived at Claridge's, your ladyship," he sneered.

Liza felt heat flare up her face. "That's not fair. I had to leave the hotel because I lost everything."

Simon looked down on her, the muscles in his face tight across his cheekbones. "You had more than any of us—but you don't need to rub our faces in it."

"I've never done that!"

"You're just a maid when all's said and done. Don't you forget it." Simon drained his glass in one gulp, turned on his heel and left the room.

Liza lifted her glass and saw that her hand shook. The truth was Elizabeth Hastings was impossibly above a footman, even if Liza, the maid, was not. She finished her champagne and left the glass on a table, staring at the last remnants of the fireworks. Thick smoke from the explosions billowed in the wind, streaking soot across the full moon.

The band started to play a waltz. A hand touched her elbow, she whirled around.

"Simon, I said no!" Her eyes widened. It was the prince from Saxe-Coburg—not Albert, but his handsome brother.

"I don't know who Simon is, but perhaps his loss is my gain?" he asked with a roguish wink.

Liza sank into a curtsy, her face burning with embarrassment. "Excuse me, Your Highness."

"You have me at a disadvantage, you know who I am, but I don't know your name."

"Elizabeth Hasti . . . Hastinger, Your Highness."

How could I be so stupid as to think of telling him my real name?

"Miss Hastinger, may I have this dance?"

Liza glanced around the room. All the guests were tipsy from champagne and fireworks. There was no one to notice her.

Who could resist a dance with a charming prince?

Not trusting her voice, she nodded. He swept her onto the floor. One, two, three. One, two, three. Prince Ernst's arms were strong about her waist; he was a superb dancer. For a few fleeting moments, Liza forgot who she was. Just for this little while, she was a girl dancing her very first dance at a ball, with a prince at that.

The music rose to a graceful crescendo and reluctantly, the dancers stopped. The Prince bowed.

"Thank you, Miss Hastinger, that was delightful."

Liza curtsied, not daring to look the prince in the eye.

What on earth do I say to him?

"Ernst, Ernst—there you are!" The Duchess's shrill voice broke the spell. "Where is Albert? Victoria wants to dance."

The Prince turned toward his aunt. Liza took advantage of his distraction to slip behind a pillar.

"I haven't seen him," Ernst said. He chuckled, "Am I my brother's keeper?"

The Duchess didn't smile. "Who were you dancing with? I don't know her."

Ernst turned to where Liza had been. "Where did she go?" he asked, puzzled. "Her name was Elizabeth Hastinger. A charming partner."

"Hastinger? The name is familiar, but not from my guest list."

Liza shook her head. She was the constant companion to the Duchess's daughter, and the Duchess hadn't recognized her.

Liza spied Victoria and Albert on the other side of the pillar.

"Albert, you can't leave now!" beseeched the Princess.

"It's late, Victoria."

"It's only two o'clock. The ball has just started. We only danced the cotillion. I was hoping we could waltz!"

Liza circled the column and peeked round to see Victoria clutching Albert's sleeve. He looked flushed.

"I've been here for two hours," he complained.

"You aren't supposed to leave until I do," pouted Victoria. "I'm the guest of honor."

"It's hot. I want to go to bed."

Victoria scrunched up her face. "You're being tiresome. And dull too. You have no appreciation for sophisticated society."

"And you," he retorted, "are a frivolous child."

"I'm older than you!" Stamping her pretty satin-slippered foot, Victoria said, "You should return to the provincial backwater you came from!"

"Very well." Albert drew himself up. "Good evening, Your Highness." He made a short, crisp bow and stalked away.

Victoria stared at his retreating back. She clenched her fists and blinked her eyes to keep from crying.

Liza lifted a glass of champagne from a passing tray and approached the Princess. She murmured, "Your Highness, is there anything I can do?"

"I'll have some champagne, thank you very much." Victoria took the glass from Liza's hand. Her eyes narrowed. "Isn't that my dress?"

"Yes," Liza answered. "I'm sorry that I borrowed it without your permission, but I wanted to see your ball."

"It's very naughty of you, Liza." A look of alarm clouded her flushed face. "Have Mama or Lehzen seen you?"

"Not to know me," Liza said wryly. She eyed the Princess carefully, relaxing when Victoria's face cleared—she was going to be generous. More likely, she wanted someone to commiserate with her about Prince Albert.

Gulping the champagne, the Princess said, "Prince Albert is a disappointment. He complained all night. Too warm, too crowded." She scowled. "He doesn't even like champagne."

Liza hesitated—she knew Victoria well enough not to criticize Albert. Tonight's pique would disappear if tomorrow Albert so much as smiled at her. "Perhaps he's not feeling well," she offered.

"He's been bilious since he set foot in England. What a boor!" Victoria shook her head in irritation. "I wouldn't marry Albert if he were the last prince on earth."

31 May 1836 Excerpt from the Journal
of Her Royal Highness Victoria

Poor dear Albert, who had not been well the day before, looked very pale and felt very poorly. After being but a short while in the ballroom and having only danced twice, he turned pale as ashes; and we all feared he might faint; he therefore went to bed. The rest of us kept it up for some time . . . we all stayed up until ½ past 3 and it was broad daylight when we left the room. All this dissipation does me a great deal of good.

10 June 1836 Excerpt from the Journal
of Her Royal Highness Victoria

At 9 we all breakfasted for the last time together! It was our last happy happy breakfast with these dearest cousins, whom I do love so very, very dearly. Dearest Albert is so grown up in his manners . . . and is very clever, naturally clever. Albert is the more reflecting of the two, and he likes very much talking about serious and instructive things and yet is so very very merry and gay and happy, like young people ought to be; Albert used always to have some fun and clever witty answer at breakfast. I feel this separation deeply.

12 June 1836 Excerpt from the Private Journal of Miss Elizabeth Hastings

The Princes have finally left. I was right not to criticize Albert. He paid Victoria a compliment (no doubt at his brother's urging) and she was enamored all over again. She is disconsolate now they are gone. But I have hopes her interest in our newspaper project will be restored. Mr. Fulton has waited too long for my answer.

From Miss Elizabeth Hastings
to Mr. I. B. Jones

(Left inside the wood box in the Duchess's private drawing room)

20 June 1836

IB,

*Please inform your publishing friend that I need to speak with him.
My next day out is two Sundays from today.*

L.

From Mr. William Fulton
to Miss Elizabeth Hasting

(Slipped under Miss Hasting's door after midnight)

27 June 1836

Dear Miss Hastings,

I was delighted to make your acquaintance last month when we were introduced by our mutual friend, Mr. Jones. I hope you will permit me the honor of escorting you on a promenade in Kensington Gardens Sunday next. If I do not hear from you, I will call at the servants' entrance to Kensington Palace at two o'clock.

Sincerely,
William Fulton

15

In Which Liza Puts Away Her Blacks

"You can't wear that drab old thing!"

Liza jumped. Deep in contemplation of her dreary ensemble, she hadn't heard Victoria's arrival.

"Your Highness, I don't have any other clothes," Liza said. "I'm still in mourning."

"Yet you came to my ball," Victoria said shrewdly.

Liza bit her tongue; after all what could she say?

"I've brought you one of my old gowns." The Princess held up a concoction of pale yellows and pinks, reminding Liza of a field of silken wildflowers. "It should fit you perfectly."

Liza couldn't take her eyes off the dress. "I couldn't possibly—"

"Don't you want to wear something pretty for Mr. Fulton?" Victoria asked.

Liza's back stiffened. "I'm only meeting him on your behalf."

"Of course." Victoria's blue eyes sparkled. "And since you are on a mission for me and it's summer, I command you to be lovely and gay." She thrust the dress into Liza's hands. "I must fly. Lehzen thinks I am with Mama and Mama thinks I'm with Lehzen." She flitted out, her lavender eau de cologne lingering behind her.

Liza held the gown to her shoulders and twisted to see herself in the tiny mirror. Her fingers caressed the soft silk. If she removed the childish bow at the back and pinned back the shoulders, it would suit her perfectly.

Mama would approve, I think.

"It's a royal command. What can I do?" whispered Liza. She eagerly undid the buttons of her dark gown, ignoring the pricks of guilt.

She was finishing her toilette when Nell knocked at the door.

"Miss Hastings, you've a gentleman caller." Nell sniggered. "Mrs. Strode is fit to be tied!"

"He's early!" Checking her curls were in place, she grabbed her mother's rose Kashmiri shawl. Liza took the back stairs at a run. Even before she arrived at the servants' entrance, she could hear Mrs. Strode scolding Will Fulton.

"Young man, maids at Kensington Palace are not permitted suitors."

Liza winced.

"I have official business with Miss Hastings." It was meaningless, but Will made it sound respectable.

Mrs. Strode hesitated, and Liza silently prayed that was the end of it. "Very well, she can meet you in one of the drawing rooms."

Liza made a face. She had had enough of those drawing rooms, filled with the same conversations every day.

Will unleashed more of his charm. "On a lovely summer's day, business can be transacted out of doors. We shall stay within eye-shot of the Palace. On my word of honor."

Liza fought back a giggle. Will Fulton, quarrelsome newspaper-man, was swearing an oath on his gentleman's honor.

Out of the corner of her eye, Mrs. Strode spied Liza. The house-keeper's eyes narrowed as she recognized the Princess's cast-off dress. "Miss Hastings, I see you have put aside your mourning."

"Yes, Mrs. Strode."

"You may have one hour. No more."

"Thank you, Mrs. Strode." Smoothing her skirt and adjusting the shawl around her shoulders, Liza walked through the door. Will's eyes widened at the sight of her.

"Mr. Fulton." She blinked in the bright light. Will's chin shone from a recent close shave and he had dressed in a well-cut dark blue velvet coat and vest, topped by a white cravat. His boots were polished to a high shine. A gold watch chain dangled at just the right length from his vest pocket. In his old-fashioned style, he was dressed like a solicitor or a junior banker.

He offered her his arm. "Miss Hastings." Liza let him lead her away, grateful to escape from the housekeeper's prying eyes. They walked through the gate to the public gardens.

"What a Tartar!" he said, wiping his brow.

"Mrs. Strode rules below stairs with an iron fist," Liza confided, stopping to examine an iris just past full bloom. "She terrifies me most of the time."

"She didn't half hate your gown. Jealous cat," he said. "What did she mean, you've put aside your mourning? Who are you mourning for?"

Staring at the wilted flower, Liza said, "My parents were killed in a carriage accident a few months ago."

Will whistled sympathetically. "My parents died when I was very young. I'm so sorry for your loss."

Liza looked up and offered him a small smile.

"If you abandoned your blacks to wear that dress, I must say, it was a wise choice."

Liza murmured her thanks and confided, "It was the Princess's."

He chuckled. "So I'm one step removed from royalty?"

Liza began to relax and her step grew lighter. "You look very handsome yourself," she said.

He grinned. "My uncle who raised me always said to get respect, wear the proper clothing." He looked at her more closely. "Are you surprised?"

"Ink stains are hard to scrub off," Liza said shyly.

"Miss Hastings, I'd never have embarrassed you."

"I see that now. Thank you, Mr. Fulton."

"Please, two orphans making our own way in the world needn't stand on ceremony. I've asked you to call me Will."

Liza bit her lip. What would Mama say? Would her father approve? She glanced over at Will's genial face. With a pang, she realized it didn't matter. She made her own decisions now.

"Will, call me Elizabeth," she said.

"That still seems too formal. Didn't Inside Boy call you Miss Liza?"

"My friends call me Liza."

"Then I shall certainly do so."

Forward he might be, but she could not deny he was charming too. Liza decided to give as good as she was getting and ask the question plaguing her. "Will," she asked. "How can you afford such clothes?"

"They were my father's. He worked for a bank." He fingered the watch hanging from his vest. "Is that shawl the Princess's too? The pink complements your eyes to perfection."

Blushing in earnest now, Liza said, "This one is mine. It's from India. My father had it sent to him as a sample. He asked Mama to wear it in town. He said if the Munich ladies were jealous of her, he would buy more."

"And were they?"

"Green with envy." Tears stung Liza's eyes.

"I didn't mean to upset you." Will put his callused hand over hers, where it rested on his forearm. His touch was warm. "Now I understand why you are a maid. I couldn't make it out before."

"It was either this or starve."

"Or worse," he said shortly. Without saying her name, Liza knew they were both thinking of Annie Mason. She shook her curls; today she wouldn't worry about Annie.

As they walked in companionable silence, passing gentlemen tipped their hats to Liza. For the first time in weeks, she wasn't a maid or an orphan. She was a well-dressed young lady promenading with a presentable young man.

They chatted about the news and the weather. Liza told him how her work bored her. Will offered to lend her *The Pickwick Papers,* a new serial by the writer Boz that was wildly popular. Will told her he knew the writer, a court reporter whose real name was Charles Dickens. He mentioned a new play at the Adelphi and asked if she would like to go. She said her duties at the Palace made it difficult to schedule a social engagement.

Finally, they turned to professional matters with reluctance. "Inside Boy said you wanted to see me," Will said.

"So I did." Liza sighed and came to business. "I've discussed your proposition with Princess Victoria."

"I hoped you would," said Will.

"She has given me permission—"

"Capital!"

Liza gave Will a reproving look. "But she must approve the final article."

Will's sandy eyebrows went up into his hairline. "She must be of more an independent mind than my sources suggest."

"Perhaps your informants don't know the Princess as well as they claim. Who exactly are they?" Liza asked slyly.

"Now, Liza, I can't betray a confidence."

Will looked in her eyes in a way that challenged her to outwit him. Taking on more authority than Victoria had granted her, she said, "The Princess insists you identify those who have lied about her, else she'll withdraw her patronage for your little scandal sheet."

He burst out laughing. "First, I don't need the Princess's patronage. I've built up my own business and have a circulation of over twenty-five hundred for my 'little sheets,' as you call them. Second, any newspaperman worth his salt will tell any royal to go to hell rather than do their bidding."

Good for you, Will.

"We can discuss it further after we have published our first piece together," she said tartly.

"What do you have for me?" Will asked.

Liza opened her reticule and pulled out a paper folded over three times to fit in the tiny purse. "I've written it out."

"That makes it easy for Her Highness to approve, doesn't it?" His eyes glinting with mischief, Will said, "First maid, then messenger, now secretary. How many roles do you play at the Palace?"

Liza looked toward heaven. "More than you could imagine."

He unfolded the paper and began reading. Halfway through, he looked sharply at her, opened his mouth, then changed his mind and read to the end. Liza waited anxiously.

"The Princess knows the Queen is pregnant?" he asked finally.

"Isn't that what it says?" Liza hedged.

"If it's true, it's the story of the year."

Liza's tongue darted over her dry lips. Will was taking their story too seriously. "Why?"

"If the Queen delivers an heir," he said, "then everyone's expectations change. The King is very ill and can't last much longer. A new regent for the baby would not be as popular as Victoria would be. The country has barely recovered from last year when the King tried to defeat the Reform Bill."

Before Liza could ask, Will explained, "The Reform Bill gave more rights to the people. The people didn't half like the King's opposition to the bill. Victoria's become a symbol to the people for change. We're due. We've had drunken reprobates for the past fifty years! George III was mad as a hatter. His son, the Regent, was a spendthrift and a womanizer. And now we've got Silly Billy."

"Don't call the King that," Liza said. "It's disrespectful."

He smiled at her. "Anyway, if Victoria is pushed aside, the people might take to the streets."

"I saw riots in Munich," Liza said, wincing at the memory.

"And in the Netherlands, Italy, and Spain. The entire continent is a hotbed of unrest. England has been spared so far, but it wouldn't take much to light a spark."

Surely he was exaggerating. England was the most civilized place on earth. A harmless prank played by two seventeen-year-olds couldn't possibly cause a revolution!

Will glanced down at her worried face. "So, is it true?"

"The Princess dictated the article," she said at last.

Will said wryly, "If Her Highness vouches for it, I'll consider her a reliable source." He reached into his pocket and brought out some coins. "For you."

Liza stared at his hand. "I can't take it, Will."

"Why not? I promised to pay you. If you write other articles, I'll pay you even more."

"I thought we were friends," she said uncertainly.

"I'm Inside Boy's friend too." Will smiled winningly. "Can you afford to turn down hard cash?"

She shook her head. "I can't accept it."

"Suit yourself," he said, replacing the coins in his pocket.

Liza glanced toward the brick Palace. The Princess's fair head pressed against a third-floor window, watching Liza's promenade. She's a prisoner, Liza thought. This prank was her only way of striking back. But Liza had so few friends. Could any good come from lying to one of them?

16

In Which Liza Meets a Royal Personage

LIZA WAS DUE TO ESCORT the Princess to her piano lesson. As she peered into her tiny mirror to pin up her hair, she heard a scratching at her door. The hall was empty, but a broadsheet, rolled up tight, lay on the floor.

Thank you, Inside Boy.

She secreted the paper in the top of her stocking, then ran to fetch the Princess. On their way to the music room, Liza and Victoria were startled by a screech, followed by a crash of breaking glass. Sir John threw open the door to the Duchess's sitting room, throwing angry remarks inside.

"You're right, Madam. We have wasted the past sixteen years. But you would've had to raise the brat anyway!"

He stopped short when he saw Victoria. Swearing roundly, he shouldered past Liza. Before Sir John's angry steps had faded away, Victoria's voice was inside the room complaining to her mother.

"He called me a brat! Mama, he has gone too far."

The Duchess was pacing by the windows looking out at the gardens. She twisted a handkerchief in her hands.

Liza wrinkled her nose; the smell of liquor was thick in the air. Rivulets of fine brandy, kept for the exclusive use of Sir John, still ran down the wall and shards of glass littered the floor.

"Victoria, we've heard terrible news," the Duchess said peevishly.

"Enlighten me, Mother. After all, I am seventeen now, practically old enough to rule the country." Victoria welcomed every opportunity to emphasize her age.

"Sir John and I have done everything to safeguard your throne, but now all our work is for naught."

"What's happened, Mama?" Victoria could not conceal her anticipation as she settled herself primly on the couch.

"Queen Adelaide is . . . expecting a child." The Duchess could barely form the words.

Shooting Liza a triumphant glance, Victoria said, "But Mama, how lovely! Queen Adelaide's been so sad to disappoint Uncle King." Liza wondered the Duchess didn't hear the malice in Victoria's voice.

The Duchess whirled around and stared at her daughter. "You stupid girl! Our plans are in ruins. You won't be Queen of anything. I won't be regent. Sir John won't get the peerage he deserves. After all this time!"

The Princess could hardly contain her delight. "Oh Mama, don't take on so. Perhaps it is not true?"

Liza's stomach was roiling.

The Duchess ran her hands through her elaborate hairdressing. "It's in the newspaper."

"Mama, sometimes the papers print lies. You know that."

You minx!

The Duchess opened her mouth to protest, but then snapped her lips together. "Victoria, you are right. Something might be done. I must talk to Sir John." The Duchess rushed out of the room, calling his name.

The Princess glanced at Liza and smiled in triumph. "It worked! Did you see Sir John's face?"

"I did." Liza hesitated, then pulled out the broadsheet. "Do you want to see your handiwork?"

"You have it?" The Princess ran her eyes down the text. "Oh excellent, Liza! Your friend printed every word."

"He's not my friend. He's just a business acquaintance," Liza protested.

"He's been a friend to me!"

"What did your mother mean when she left? Could she really undo what's been done?" Liza said. "Thousands of people will read this article."

"Thousands?" the Princess asked. "Truly?"

Liza closed her eyes for a moment. "It's a newspaper. He'll sell two thousand copies and those papers will be passed on and read by others who can't afford to buy their own."

"I'd almost forgotten real people read the newspaper." The Princess giggled.

Liza pressed her fingernails into the palms of her hands. This was all a game to the Princess, but the stakes were life and livelihood for Liza. Somehow Queen and country paled in comparison.

———

Ten days later, Liza ran her hands behind the cushions in the Duchess's sitting room. The Princess had lost her embroidery again. Her finger encountered the Princess's needle.

"Ouch!" She sucked on her fingertip. A muffled chuckle could be heard from the wood box.

"Boy, is that you?" she whispered.

"Who else?" came a disembodied voice. She heard his latch being drawn back. The lid lifted. "Any body snatchers about?"

"That's one I don't know," Liza giggled.

"Anyone about to blow the gab?" he said.

Liza tiptoed to the door and peered up and down the hall. "There's no one."

Inside Boy emerged and stretched, as if he had just awoken from a nap.

"Miss Liza," he said, "I've got somethin' for you."

"From Will?" The pain in her finger was forgotten.

"Yeah, it's a sheet 'bout the Queen."

Liza put her hands on her hips. "You already gave it to me."

"Not both sides, I didn't."

"Sides?" Liza wasn't sure she had heard correctly.

"Sides of the story. There's usually two."

"Not this story," Liza said with decision.

"Will found 'imself a new source and put out a second edition with two pages. The first page is about the Queen increasin'."

"That's ours," said Liza without thinking.

Inside Boy nodded as if a suspicion had been confirmed.

"But what's this about a second story?" Liza asked.

"Read for yerself." He handed her a rolled broadsheet, grimy with his fingerprints. "All 'ell's goin' to break loose." He heard a noise. "Someone's coming. Hop the twig!" With a thump, he pulled the door closed.

Boy's panic was contagious. Liza hid the pages in her stocking. *Two stories?*

She had no time to worry about it now. She started for the far door. Despite her sensible shoes, she tripped over a buckled square of parquet and lost her head start.

"Miss!" Nell's voice brought Liza to a halt.

"Nell, you frightened me," said Liza, her heart beating frantically. Her constitution wasn't strong enough for all this sneaking around. "What is it?"

"It's Miss Frenchy's day out, so Mrs. Strode says you're to fetch the Duchess to the visitor's parlor," Nell said, breathing quickly. "Queen Adelaide is here."

"The Queen!" Liza gathered her skirts together, checking the newspaper was secure. The Queen hadn't visited in all the time Liza had been at the Palace. It couldn't be a coincidence. "I'll go at once."

Her stomach sinking, Liza climbed the narrow flight of stairs to the Duchess's bedroom. She opened the bedroom door without knocking. The Duchess was reclining on her large mahogany bed, shoving toffees in her mouth. Victoria lay on her smaller bed, staring rebelliously at the ceiling.

"Yes?" The Duchess sounded bored.

"What's happened, Liza?" said Victoria.

"The Queen's here," Liza blurted out, not daring to look at Victoria. "She's waiting for you, Your Grace."

A sharp rat-a-tat came at the door, and without waiting for an invitation, Sir John came in. Liza stepped back into the shadow of the wardrobe. The Duchess sat up quickly, tugging the front of her lacy peignoir over her ample bosom.

"Sir John, I'm *déshabillée*," she said, with a quick look at Victoria.

"The Queen is here," he said.

"I know. I'll go to her as soon as I dress."

"Are you sure that's wise?"

"Wise?" The Duchess, Victoria, and Liza stared at him.

"The Queen wants to curry favor. With you. After the latest news reports, she needs all the friends she can get." He glanced over at Victoria, who was hanging on every word.

"I've heard the rumors about the Queen's baby," Victoria said pointedly.

"You know what we permit you to know," Sir John said. "The latest scandal is not suitable for your ears."

"What scandal?" Victoria was dying to know. So was Liza. Inside Boy had tried to tell her, but the warning had come too late.

"It's not for your ears, Little Woman," said Sir John.

"I insist you tell me." Victoria's voice pitched high, a sure sign she was losing her temper.

"Not now, Victoria," said her mother. Remembering Liza, the Duchess switched to German. "Sir John, what must I do?"

"Refuse to see her," he said with decision. "It's presumptuous for her to come without an invitation." The Duchess began to nod, like a puppet responding to Sir John's masterful pulling of strings.

"The Queen requires no invitation to our home." Victoria glared at Sir John.

"Don't contradict Sir John," said her mother.

"But, Mama," said Victoria, "Auntie Adelaide used to be your friend."

"Envy has ruined her," said Sir John with a pious air.

The Duchess nodded vigorously. "Because I have a daughter and she does not. No doubt, that led to her . . . indiscretion."

What on earth are they talking about?

"You must not see her," Sir John said. "Send the girl to say you are indisposed."

"But Mama, Aunt Adelaide isn't some social climber who hasn't been introduced—she's the Queen!" Neither Sir John nor the Duchess paid Victoria any attention.

"Miss Hastings," said the Duchess in English. "Tell the Queen I am indisposed."

Liza nodded. Closing the door behind her, she pressed against the wall. Her thoughts were racing.

The door opened and Sir John appeared. He stopped short when he saw her.

"What are you still doing here? Her Grace gave you an order!"

Liza pushed her palms away from the security of the plaster wall. "Yes, sir," she muttered and turned to go.

He grabbed her arm as she tried to pass him in the narrow hall. His blue eyes narrowed when he saw her face. "Why do you look so flushed, girl?"

"I think I have a touch of the influenza," Liza said, dragging her gaze away from his.

"Hmmm, perhaps you should get some rest. I can arrange for you to stay in bed." He ran his fingertip from under her chin to the hollow at the base of her neck. His meaning was unmistakable.

Liza jerked away from his touch.

"I'm fine, sir. I must deliver the Duchess's message." She ran down the stairs as quickly as she could; the danger behind her was greater than her fear of the Queen.

She stopped only to smooth her hair before entering the parlor. A woman, standing alone by the mantle, was looking at a portrait of the Duchess and Victoria as a toddler. Dressed in fine gray silk, she wore an unflattering bonnet shading both sides of her face. Impossibly dowdy, nevertheless she was Queen Adelaide.

"Your Majesty." Liza dropped into a deep curtsy.

The Queen's blotchy face looked out at her from under a mass of untidy hair. "Yes?"

Liza opened her mouth, but no words emerged.

"Girl, speak up. Are you the Duchess's maid?"

"No, Ma'am. I serve the Princess, but I have a message from the Duchess."

"Well?"

"The Duchess . . . is . . ." Liza spoke past the embarrassment in her throat. "Indisposed."

The Queen turned away, but not before Liza caught a glimpse of the flush sweeping up from her neck to her hairline. Her back to Liza, she asked, "How indisposed is she?"

"I beg your pardon, Your Majesty?"

"What lengths will she go to insult me? Will she be riding in the park when I leave or will she have the decency to keep to her room?"

The Queen's fingers were twisting a handkerchief around her bony knuckles. Liza noticed she wore no jewelry.

"Ma'am, I only know what I was told to say."

The Queen turned and smiled wanly at Liza. "My dear, I know you're only following orders." She peered at Liza's face. "You're very pretty—it must be pleasant for Victoria to have you about her."

"I hope so, Your Majesty."

"I came to see the Princess, but as His Majesty and I have discovered, you can't see the daughter without the mother." The Queen sank down on a settee and slouched against the velvet cushion. Her protruding teeth gave her the look of a melancholy rabbit. "How is the Princess? Is she in good health?"

"She is well, Ma'am."

"Good. I was afraid she might have been upset by the rumors."

Liza wished the floor would open and swallow her up. Will had warned her about revolts—but she had never thought about the Queen's feelings.

A racking cough shuddered across Her Majesty's body. In German, she muttered, "What I wouldn't give for a glass of sherry."

"I'll get it for you, Your Majesty." Liza went to the buffet in the corner and poured a glass.

The Queen took a cautious sip. "You speak German?" she asked.

"Yes, Ma'am." Liza cursed under her breath. Five months and she hadn't tripped up once, but this mousy woman had slipped under her guard.

The Queen began coughing again, and Liza poured her another glass.

"Perhaps just one more, thank you, my dear," said Queen Adelaide. She finished the glass of sherry in one gulp. She held out the glass for Liza to fill again.

"In my position, there are always stories, you know," Queen Adelaide hiccoughed. "But this one was particularly hurtful."

"I'm sorry!" Liza clapped her hands over her mouth as soon as she said it.

"It's not your fault. A foreign queen is an easy target. At first the paper said I was *enceinte*." The Queen looked over at Liza. "That means pregnant."

Liza nodded.

"As if the King and I need to be reminded of our tragedy—my tragedy—since the King has so many children already."

Liza nodded again. The Duchess always referred to the King's ten illegitimate children as "the bastardy," and worried that their lack of morals could contaminate the innocent Princess. Tears rolled down the Queen's cheeks. She dabbed them with a damp handkerchief. Liza handed her a newly laundered piece of linen from her own pocket.

"Thank you, I'm sure you are a comfort to the Princess," she sniffed. "Will you take a message to her? Away from the Duchess's ears, if you don't mind."

"I would do anything for you."

Anything, but confess what the Princess and I did.

"Tell Victoria *all* the stories are false." The Queen brushed a strand of hair back into her simple bun. "Her position as the heir is safe."

The Queen blew her nose in Liza's handkerchief and stood up. She staggered a little and put her hand on Liza's shoulder. "My goodness, the Duchess's sherry is very potent."

"Go slowly, Your Majesty," Liza said, ashamed of her lies about this harmless old woman.

"Call my carriage."

Liza rang the bell. Nell's arrival was suspiciously quick, her curious eyes darting to the Queen's face and back to Liza's.

"Her Majesty's carriage, Nell."

Bobbing, Nell scurried out. The Queen's eyes were closed and she was deep in thought; Liza waited patiently.

Finally, Queen Adelaide said, "I have to send some message to the Duchess." Her eyes began watering again.

Liza's words spilled out before she could stop them. "Your Majesty, the Duchess meant to hurt your feelings. Why give the satisfaction of leaving a message?"

"A girl with a mind of her own." The Queen raised her eyebrows and peered more closely at Liza.

"I'm sorry, Your Majesty."

"Nonsense, very few people stand on ceremony with me." The Queen pressed her fingers to her eyelids. "What's your name, dear?"

"Elizabeth Hastings."

"Miss Hastings, take good care of my niece."

"I will, Your Majesty."

Liza lay the Queen's cloak on her shoulders. As Adelaide left, she glanced back at the Duchess's portrait above the mantle. "We were such friends once," she sighed.

Liza watched the Queen walk down the stairs. The rolled up newspaper in her stocking pressed against her thigh, accusing her of plotting against the Queen. Liza knew she was guilty as charged.

———

Liza had to wait until after dinner to reach the safety of her room. Bolting the door behind her, Liza pulled out the broadsheet. There was her story. She turned it over. The moment she saw the title, she groaned. "A Cuckold in the Palace?" Will had accused the Queen of having another man's baby.

"But there never was a baby," Liza whispered. She read on, sick at heart. The father was supposed to be Lord Howe, who ran the Queen's household, and, according to the broadsheet, took a great many other liberties besides. Relations were strained, the paper went on to report, between the Queen and Lord Howe's wife.

Shaken, Liza lay the paper down.

How could Will do this?

Just when she was beginning to like him, he ruined it by writing a vicious lie. Of course, the Princess had started it, with Liza's help. Tonight, when Victoria came for her midnight visit, Liza was determined they would both shoulder the blame for hurting the kind Queen Adelaide.

———

"Finally, we are *tête-à-tête*," said Victoria later that night in the security of Liza's room. "Tell me—what did the Queen say?"

"First you must read this." Liza handed her Will's broadsheet. She waited as Victoria, making tiny distressed cries at each accusation, read it through.

The Princess's mouth gaped open in dismay. "For heaven's sake, what has he done?" she cried. "This wasn't what I wanted!" Tears welled up in her eyes.

Liza handed the Princess a clean handkerchief. "The Queen is unpopular. She can't give her husband the only thing he married her for—an heir. We used her tragedy against her."

"I only wanted to tease Sir John. I never thought about Auntie Adelaide."

"Neither of us did," Liza said. "But we should have."

"Liza, you shouldn't speak to me that way," Victoria said uncertainly.

"We only thought of hurting Sir John, but other people suffered for our thoughtlessness."

"I won't stand to be scolded by my maid." Victoria's cheeks were bright pink and her nostrils flared. "Take it back, or you are finished working for me."

Without pausing, Liza shot back, "I'd rather be on the street like Annie Mason, than lie for you again."

"What does Annie have to do with this?" Victoria demanded crossly. "You are the one being impertinent and rude. Take it back."

"You never thought what might happen to Annie after she left. You didn't consider the Queen's feelings. You put *me* at risk all the time."

"Remember who you are speaking to, Liza." Victoria's voice was sharp as a shard of crystal.

"You are impossibly above me, but that's all the more reason you should do the right thing and admit you were wrong." All her prospects rested on Victoria's good will, but Liza was tired of mincing her words. "We behaved badly, Your Highness."

The Princess's perfect posture seemed to slump a little. She rubbed at her cheek with the back of her plump hand. "Perhaps you are right," she said in a low voice.

Liza wasn't sure she had heard correctly. "What did you say?"

"I shouldn't have done it," the Princess said. "I'm going to be the Queen, and I should take responsibility for my actions." She nodded as though something momentous had been decided. "But you were very rude, Liza."

"Forgive me, Princess." An apology was a small price to pay for the Princess's admission.

"And I'm sorry I threatened to fire you. It was unworthy of me." The Princess threw herself on Liza's bed and pounded the thin pillow with her small fists. "Our article was such a lovely idea, but somehow, Sir John wins again!" she cried. "I hate him. If I didn't know better, I would suspect him of fabricating that second rumor himself."

Both girls turned toward each other.

"Could he?" asked the Princess.

"It's part of his plan to use the press," Liza exclaimed. "Why not write the story he wants himself?"

"But Liza, how? Isn't it too remarkable a coincidence your friend would publish both stories?"

Liza remembered Will's thoughtful look after he had asked her if the article were true. "Not if Sir John is Will's other source. He must have commissioned the second article to counter ours."

"Sir John took our little musket shot and turned it into a cannon ball." The Princess's father had been a soldier and she liked military metaphors. "But that means he must have written the one saying I was feeble-minded!"

Liza bit her lip to keep from smiling at the Princess's outrage.

"I don't think much of your Mr. Fulton for printing all these falsehoods," the Princess said.

Liza's first instinct was to agree, but she had to be fair. "Perhaps Mr. Fulton doesn't think much of us for telling all these lies. He prints what will sell. We ought to know better."

"What do we do now?" the Princess asked.

"We must be sure Sir John is behind this," Liza said. "There have been enough unsupported accusations."

"When will you see Mr. Fulton again?"

"He invited me for tea on Sunday, but the Baroness said I can't have the day out."

"I wish I could go." The Princess sounded wistful. Of all the things she could ever do, meeting a young man at a teahouse was among the least likely. "I'll take care of Lehzen. You go to town and get the truth out of him."

17

In Which Liza and Will Have a Private Quarrel in a Public House

STORM CLOUDS THREATENED, casting an ominous gloom over Fleet Street.

"Where are we going?" Liza asked again. Will's grip on her arm was fierce and his face was forbidding. "I won't take another step unless you tell me."

"Somewhere we can talk," he said gruffly. He dragged her along even faster, turning down a tiny alley she had never noticed before. She glimpsed a metal sign creaking in the wind. Fat raindrops began to splash the pavement as they arrived at Ye Olde Cheshire Cheese, a public house. Will pulled open the oak door, but Liza held back.

Will muttered, "It's respectable enough."

Taking a deep breath, Liza followed him into a gloomy passage strewn with sawdust. To her right was a bar with a sign proclaiming No Females Allowed. On her left, a chop room was filled with patrons, including, she was relieved to see, some ladies. She sniffed the air, surprised at the rich smells of meat and puddings.

The hostess led them to a table near the unused fireplace in the chop room. Liza sat down, adjusted her shawl, and placed her reticule on the table. Will sat with his back to the wall, his forefingers pressed together in a steeple.

Liza pulled off her gloves, finger by finger. Will watched her, his face impassive. Finally, she could bear the silence no more.

"You should be ashamed of publishing that awful story!" she exclaimed.

"Which awful story are you referring to?" he asked, his tone dangerously quiet.

"Those lies about the Queen! She's no more an adulteress than I'm the Empress of Persia." Liza was trembling, but she met his gaze squarely.

Will's green eyes saw right through her. "How was my story any less true than your little concoction?"

Liza's eyes dropped to her own hands. "I don't know what you mean," she said.

Will brought his fists down hard on the well-worn table. Liza was glad they hadn't been served. "Lies don't become you, Liza Hastings." The cutting edge in his voice made Liza jerk as though Will had slapped her. "You knew the Queen wasn't pregnant. You lied to my face."

"I didn't tell you she was an adulteress," she said, tilting her chin up defiantly. "That was despicable."

"You're a hypocrite," he shot back. "I had sources, of dubious reliability grant you, for both stories. I did my job and printed them. It was a popular edition; I sold twenty-five hundred copies."

"You don't care what you publish so long as you turn a profit."

"Oh, I made a tidy sum off both." Will reached into his pocket and counted out five sovereigns into his hand. "Here's your share." He tossed them in front of Liza.

Liza stared at the coins. One heavy gold coin spun on its edge a few times then toppled over. The coins were what she'd earn in two months at the Palace. She would have given everything she owned to take the money honestly.

"I didn't do it for the money." Her shoulders slumped.

"Didn't you?" asked Will. "Or are you claiming it was your duty to Victoria?"

"It was the Princess's idea," Liza found herself stammering, "but I knew it was wrong." To her dismay, one tear, and then another, and then another rolled down her cheeks.

Faced with tears in a public house, Will's face lost some of its grimness. "Don't cry, Liza." He pulled out a handkerchief and handed it to her. "Please, don't cry."

His kindness cut Liza worse than his anger had. Liza sobbed as though a sluice had been opened; all the fear and tension of the past few months poured out. Will waited her out patiently, then waved the server over.

"Tea for two," said Will. The server hurried away.

With a final sniff, Liza noticed the ink stains on the handkerchief, "Heavens! Will, do I have ink on my face?"

He shook his head, trying unsuccessfully not to smile. Liza marveled that harmony could be restored so quickly between them. The server set two china cups in front of them. Staring down at the willow pattern painted on the saucer, Liza sipped the steaming pale brown liquid. The tightness in her chest eased.

"Will, I apologize for such a display."

"Accepted." Will began spooning sugar into his cup. "I'm sorry I threw money at you. That was cruelly done. You didn't deserve that."

"No, I did. Will, I hated lying to you, but Victoria wanted to make mischief."

"At the Queen's expense?"

"She didn't think about Adelaide, I'm afraid," said Liza. "She just wanted a little revenge against her mother and Sir John Conroy." At Will's skeptical look, she rushed on. "Everything depends on Victoria, but they treat her like she's an idiot child. They plot against her to steal the throne. She wanted to punish them." Liza sighed. "But *I* knew better."

Will settled back in his chair and stretched his arms above his head, frowning a little as his coat tightened across his shoulders. "You can't blame yourself entirely: I knew it wasn't true."

Liza's jaw dropped. "Then why did you print it?" she asked.

"It was a legitimate rumor." Will shrugged. "The people may not like Adelaide, but they want to read about her. I sold out of three print runs. The second sheet sold twice as many as the first."

"We're back where we started. That awful story about the Queen and her Lord Chamberlain." She watched him closely over her teacup. "Will, who gave you that story?"

"Liza, I've sworn not to reveal my source."

"It's Sir John Conroy, isn't it?"

"I cannot say."

"Will, it must be!" Liza insisted. "Who has more to lose if the Queen bears a child? And accusing the Queen of adultery is the quickest way to discredit a new heir."

"What about Victoria?" said Will with a mischievous smile. "She would lose everything."

"She knew none of it was true."

"What about her mother?"

Liza's eyes grew wide. "The Duchess gave you the story?"

"I didn't say so."

"Will!"

He relented. "Liza, I've never met Sir John." Liza started to protest, but Will held up his hand. "I receive the information under my print shop door in the night." He saw her face and chuckled ruefully. "It sounds ridiculous, but until now the stories have been accurate enough."

"The Princess can't trust anyone in that house."

"Liza, nor can you." He put his hand over Liza's. "And you should not trust the Princess either. You are dependent on the royals for your living. It's different for me. If Sir John, or someone else close to the Princess, wants to tell tales out of school, then I'll publish them and make my fortune."

"That story about the Princess throwing her books could only come from Sir John."

"Then, it's Sir John. It matters not a whit to me."

"But he's using you!"

Will lifted his eyebrows. Liza had the grace to look embarrassed.

"Liza, we all use each other. Sir John sends me a story for his own reasons, and I sell broadsheets. Many, many broadsheets."

"You print his lies for money. You work for him." Liza's distress wiped the smile from his face.

"Victoria pays you," he said reasonably. "What's the difference?"

"She's my future Queen for one thing," Liza pointed out. "And I won't let her use me to do something despicable again. But you spread Sir John's lies to hundreds of people through your paper!"

"Thousands," he corrected her with pride.

"Thousands then. He's evil. I couldn't bear to be your friend if you work for him."

Will was staring at her, his brow furrowed, as though he didn't believe what he had heard. "You'd end our . . . association because I print Conroy's stories?"

Liza nodded. Will picked up one of the coins and rubbed his fingers across the engraving. Liza forced herself to keep still, while Will made his decision. Would he choose Liza or profit? She blinked against more tears. Until she had risked losing his friendship, Liza hadn't admitted to herself how much she valued it. Will was decent and kind, and her only friend outside the Palace. Oh, why had she issued that ultimatum?

Will drained his tea cup. "Liza, give me some time to think on it. I've my livelihood to consider. And my employees. Sir John's stories sell a lot of papers. I told you before; I'm not rich enough to be high-minded."

Liza considered how to reconcile her needs with Will's. A scrap of a conversation and a fragment of a letter came to her mind. She weighed the sovereigns in her hand and thought about Annie Mason. "What if we could sell just as many papers and hurt Sir John at the same time?" she asked slowly.

Warily, Will asked, "How?"

———

Liza didn't know how Will kept his bearings in the maze of filthy streets. "Thank you for taking me to Annie's house," she said.

"First, you don't know how to get there on your own," he said.

"And second?"

"A pretty girl like you wouldn't last five minutes out here alone."

Liza might have protested, if she could have caught her breath. Will thought she was pretty.

She looked around, her eyes widening at the number of dirty children swarming the streets. "Don't they go to school?" she asked.

"Education costs," Will said over his shoulder. "Who would pay?"

"You managed."

"I was lucky. My uncle thought it worthwhile to invest in me. He was right, I've paid him back every penny." Will drew his back straight and his chest puffed out.

"Will, you've been successful. Tell me how can I earn a lot of money?" Liza asked.

Will stopped short. Ignoring the passersby trying to maneuver past them, he asked, "Are you in trouble, because I—"

"My father left me nothing but debts." She tugged on his arm, and they began to walk again.

"A daughter isn't responsible for her father's obligations," he said.

"Daughter or not, I'll pay what's owed," Liza said with determination, but then the grim reality returned. "Unfortunately, I don't know how to do it. I've nothing but my clothes and some jewelry. And Claridge's is holding them until I pay forty-three pounds and two pence."

Will whistled. "Your parents' things must be worth more than that. Why don't you sell them and pay Claridge's with the proceeds?"

"It's all I have of my family."

"You really have nothing else?" asked Will.

"Papa's solicitors told me there was nothing."

"Did your father have a man of business?" He lifted her by the elbows over a noxious puddle, and steered her down a narrow street. "Maybe he embezzled your money."

"Mr. Ripley was practically a member of the family. But he's in India and I've no way to reach him."

He tried another tack. "What about back home, in Munich?"

"The lawyer told me there was nothing," Liza said. "I'm resigned to making my own way."

"Liza, that's all fine and well, but how? What does a maid earn?"

Staring at the cobblestones, Liza said, "Thirty pounds a year, but I owe almost four hundred and fifty."

Will whistled again. "You might want to start by keeping those sovereigns I gave you."

"Not if I earned them with a lie." Liza was certain. "I'd rather spend it to buy the truth about Sir John Conroy. Annie wouldn't tell me what she knew, but perhaps she'll sell it to me." They had arrived at Annie's building.

"What if she doesn't know anything?"

"She must," Liza said. "In any case, she needs the money more than I do."

Will lifted one foot and examined something slick and yellow on the sole. He scraped it off on the doorstep. "What's Annie to you?"

"I have her position. I sleep in her room."

"You're nothing like Annie," Will said with warmth in his voice. "You're a lady."

"I *was* a lady," Liza corrected him. "Now I'm a maid like she was. She belonged to no one; I have no family. Am I so different? What wouldn't I do to survive?"

Will took her hands in his and said fiercely, "Liza, you have friends. I'd never let anything happen to you."

Marveling that Will didn't hear her heart beating so loudly, Liza said, "Thank you, Will."

She knocked on the door to the ramshackle house.

The same pock-faced woman opened the door. When she recognized them, she scowled. "Annie Mason don't live 'ere no more." She smelled of cheap gin. "Good riddance to bad rubbish." She began to slam the door, but Will pushed it back open with the heel of his hand.

"We'll make it worth your while." He jingled some coins in his pocket and brought out ten shillings. "Just tell us how to find her."

Staring at the coin, the landlady said, "I don't rightly know. 'er fancy man, Barnabas, 'e threw 'er out."

Liza asked, "Did they quarrel?"

"Never did anything but. She kept shouting she wouldn't do it, whatever it was. 'e roughed 'er about some, then told 'er to get out. Gave me 'er clothes in exchange for rent."

"That's despicable!" Liza exclaimed.

"'e paid for 'em, didn't he?"

Will flipped the coin in the air with his thumb. "Surely you have some idea where she is?"

Her eyes fixed on the glint of metal, the old woman said, "You might try the Mary Magdalene 'ouse."

Will handed the woman the coin. She snatched it away and shut the door. Without a word, Will led Liza back through the warren of streets. Waste floated in the grooves of the street that served for sewers. Liza began to cough and gag from the vile smells. She pulled out Will's handkerchief to cover her mouth.

They were jostled by filthy children, but larger, more adult menaces stood in doorways. Mindful of Inside Boy's warnings about pickpockets, Liza held her reticule in front her, clasping it tightly with both hands. Will stayed comfortingly close.

A group of large boys chased an undersized boy in front of them. He tried to escape by darting around Liza and running off in the other direction. He slipped on the uneven cobblestones, slicing his knee open. The boy howled when he saw his blood dripping onto the street.

"Oh, poor boy!" Liza exclaimed, leaning down to place Will's handkerchief over the wound. The boy was struck dumb and his eyes widened as he took in Liza's dress. The other children backed away, just as silently.

"Liza, that's my handkerchief," Will protested, glancing around warily. There were eyes everywhere.

"Will, if the wound isn't bandaged, it will fester." She tied the cloth round the child's knee, then stood up and examined her handiwork.

Will shook his head. "He'll sell it as soon as we're gone."

"Covered in blood?"

"In this neighborhood, it wouldn't matter."

She opened her reticule and handed a coin to the boy. "Buy a sweet."

"Ta, Miss." Her patient ran off without even a limp, Liza watched dismayed. The other children stared and then began to clamor for a coin for themselves.

"Liza, put your money away!" Will whispered fiercely. He stepped closer and took her arm. "Let's go. It's not safe."

He piloted her deftly down a twisting street ending in a small cul-de-sac. Liza shivered as she looked up at the brick house with black wooden trim. A plain bronze plaque next to the door read Mary Magdalene House for the Reformation of Prostitutes. Liza tightened her grip on Will's arm.

"We don't have to go in." His tone did not sound hopeful.

Liza shook her head. She lifted the huge knocker. A panel of wood on the door, just above eye level, slid back to reveal a small peephole.

"Who is it?" A voice filled with suspicion asked.

"My name is Elizabeth Hastings. I am here to visit Annie Mason, one of your . . ." She glanced at Will. "What do I call them?"

"The penitents are not allowed visitors," the voice answered.

"But I must see her," said Liza.

The panel began to close.

"Wait!" Liza cried. "Her Royal Highness Princess Victoria sent me!" Will inhaled sharply. The door swung open. The doorkeeper was a shrunken old man, whose few wisps of black hair lay pasted across his otherwise bald head. He looked them up and down and grudgingly let them into a dark hallway, bare of any decoration except an oil painting of Mary Magdalene receiving blessings from Jesus Christ.

"This way." He showed them to a parlor with two lumpy armchairs, which sat side by side, and no other furniture. "Someone will come."

Liza sat at the edge of her chair, reluctant to let her dress encounter the moth-eaten upholstery. "Why would Annie come here?" she whispered.

Will's face was severe. "The poorhouse is worse."

A tall, gaunt woman dressed in black appeared in the doorway. Her voice was unexpectedly deep. "I'm Mrs. Russell. You're here from the Princess?"

Liza hesitated, knowing she mustn't implicate Victoria further. "I've come from Kensington Palace," she said. "I have a message for Annie Mason."

"So, Annie was telling the truth about her friends in high places." Mrs. Russell's face twitched. "Give me your message."

"I must deliver it personally," said Liza firmly.

For a moment, she thought Mrs. Russell was going to deny her, but then with a little sigh, the woman said, "I'll take you to her. Sir, you have to wait here."

Will got out of his chair and stood behind Liza. "No, I'll go with Miss Hastings."

"It's not allowed." Mrs. Russell's tone allowed no argument. "We offer the penitents refuge from men here."

Liza murmured, "I'll be fine, Will."

Mrs. Russell led Liza into the hall and up a flight of steep stairs. At the landing, she paused and pointed to a door. "Annie Mason is working in there. Don't take up too much of her time."

Liza thanked her. Smoothing her hair back, she opened the door.

Annie was seated at a table alone next to a window, a length of pink silk cloth draped in front of her, across a table. She glanced up at Liza's entrance, but then bent her head to her sewing. Her magnificent hair was bound up in a bleached handkerchief.

Steeling herself, Liza stepped closer.

"Hello, Annie," she said softly. "Do you remember me?" Annie was sewing a seam for a wide skirt.

"I remember you, Liza Hastings," Annie replied sourly.

Liza licked her lips, wondering what to say. She fingered the fabric Annie was working on. "This is good quality."

Annie looked up. "There's not many here with enough skill to work on cloth this fine." She added with a quick, lopsided grin, "And I miss the first two hours of Bible reading."

"If you can sew, why didn't you get work doing that?" Liza asked.

"After I left the Palace, I got plenty of sewing for hire. But it nearly killed me. I'd work from dawn 'til dark sewing a pair of pants to sell for a pound and I'd get tuppence."

"It's honest work, though," said Liza uncertainly.

"Honest?" Annie finally looked up. The words tumbled out of her mouth as though they had been trapped for months. "When you are starving, honest don't matter much." Annie carefully slid the needle into the finished seam and rubbed her nose with the back of her hand. "I was desperate. I met Barnabas, and he offered me a room, for a percentage of the takings. I hated what Barnabas wanted me to do, but I did it."

And I whine I might lose my fancy dresses and baubles.

"What happened then?"

Indignation had raised Annie's color. Her skin was still beautiful, despite the yellow bruises across her cheek and half-healed cut over her eye. "He wanted me to do something I wouldn't do."

"After all you'd done, what could be so awful?"

Annie shot her a hostile glance. "Something against God."

"And prostitution isn't?"

"Mary Magdalene was redeemed in the end—but God wouldn't have forgiven me what Barnabas wanted." She shoved back the wooden chair and stood up. Liza gasped when she saw the unmistakable bulge. Annie placed her hand on the top of the swelling in her abdomen. "'e wanted me to abort my babe. I couldn't do it."

"Why would he want you to—" Liza broke off as the answer came to her. "Oh."

Annie rubbed her back with one hand. "Yes, Miss High and Mighty—I cannot be takin' clients in my condition. Barnabas gave me a choice. Get rid of the baby or get out. I couldn't do it, so I left."

"Who is the father?" Liza didn't know how to ask the question with any delicacy.

"What's it to you?" Annie snapped.

"I live in your old room."

Annie's eyes grew bleak. "Stay away from Conroy."

Liza felt her stomach sink. "He's the father?" she asked faintly.

Bitterness twisted Annie's face. "I asked Mrs. Strode for a lock, but she said servants weren't permitted privacy."

A picture of the shiny, new bolt on her bedroom door came into Liza's mind. Mrs. Strode had learned her lesson.

Liza glanced around the bare room. The walls were solid and the house was quiet. "What's it like here?"

"They read the scripture too much and keep poor fires—but I've got a bed, food, and they'll help me when the baby is born."

"I'm glad."

As though she had just remembered she didn't like Liza, Annie burst out, "Why did you come? You didn't get enough of my shame before? Victoria didn't send you, I'm sure of that."

"The first time we met," Liza said. "You hinted you knew something about Sir John. Something that could hurt him. I have a way to use such a weapon. Will you tell me what it is?"

Glancing down at her stomach, Annie shook her head. "No. Before, I thought he might punish me. And now, I've got something even more precious to lose."

"I have money."

She pulled out the five sovereigns and held them in her hand where Annie could see, much as Will had tried to convince Annie's former landlady.

This time Annie did not grab the coins. She stared. "So much?" she asked.

"It's yours," said Liza.

"No. 'e'd come after us for sure."

Annie's jaw was set and Liza saw there was no budging her. Nor could Liza blame her. She handed Annie the money. "Take it anyway," she said. "For the baby."

"For the baby." Annie tucked the coins in a pocket at her skirt.

"When will the baby arrive?" Liza asked.

"In the autumn. You'll be away; the Princess always goes to Ramsgate." Annie looked out the narrow window.

"Will you stay here afterwards?" Liza asked.

"I've got kin in Wales. They don't look down on a bastard child as they do in London. It'll be a better life for my baby."

Mrs. Russell appeared at the door and tapped her foot with impatience.

"Miss, I don't think we should meet again," Annie said. She sat back down and picked up the needle. "Goodbye."

As Will and Liza left the house, Liza glanced into another room. Inside sat eight dejected women around a long table, listening to another penitent read to them in a monotone. It sounded like The Book of Job. Liza understood why Annie preferred to sew.

Will took her arm. "Are you all right?"

Placing her hand on top of his, Liza told him what had happened upstairs.

"It's a common enough story," he said.

"Will, she asked for help, and no one would protect her. But there's a lock on the door now. I'm safer because of Annie."

He interrupted her. "If that bastard Conroy ever tries to interfere with you, I'll kill him."

She gripped his hand tightly. "Will, you mustn't. I'm perfectly safe."

But as they walked away from the Mary Magdalene House, Liza wondered how strong her lock really was.

2 August 1836 Excerpt from the Journal of Her Royal Highness Victoria

At a ¼ to 4 we went with Lehzen to Chiswick to the Children's Friend Society. It was a most interesting and delightful establishment founded entirely by Miss Murray. It is for poor vagrant girls, who are received under the age of 15; and Miss Murray says they have never had a girl 6 months who did not become a perfectly good child. Miss Murray told us many curious stories of the depraved and wretched state in which many arrive and how soon they become reformed and good.

From Miss Elizabeth Hastings
to Mr. Richard Arbuthnot

7 August 1836
Kensington Palace

Dear Mr. Arbuthnot,

I am grateful for your forbearance regarding my outstanding obligation to Claridge's Hotel. Your offer to hold my belongings for six months before selling them to satisfy my debt was extraordinarily generous.

However, Her Royal Highness Victoria of Kent is of a different mind. She is certain only a heartless management would sell an orphan's only mementos of her parents for the repayment of a minor debt. Her Royal Highness insists I have misunderstood your terms.

The Princess and I would be beholden to you if you could clarify Claridge's proposal. A letter addressed to me at Kensington Palace will reach me.

Sincerely,
Elizabeth Hastings

From Mr. Richard Arbuthnot
to Miss Elizabeth Hastings

12 August 1836
Claridge's Hotel

Dear Miss Hastings,

Claridge's is pleased to extend you every accommodation. We shall hold your belongings indefinitely.

Please convey our best wishes to Her Royal Highness. Should the Princess ever require lodging for her distinguished visitors, Claridge's Hotel is happy to oblige.

Sincerely,

Richard Arbuthnot
Manager

From Miss Elizabeth Hastings
to Mr. William Fulton

22 August 1837
Kensington Palace

Dear Will,

Unfortunately, I will not be able to accompany you to the theater next month. The Duchess has decided Victoria must tour the country. And where Her Highness goes, I go.

If this were the time of Queen Elizabeth, it would be a royal progress. The Duchess is planning cannon salutes and the use of the King's barge. No doubt she'll raise the royal standard at every house they visit! The King is reportedly apoplectic. Victoria feels the slight to him very much, but the Duchess has turned a deaf ear to her daughter's protests.

The house has been so tense the Duchess cannot bring herself to speak civilly to her daughter. Although they share a room, she wrote the Princess a letter explaining the necessity for the trip. I thought you might be interested, so I've copied it and included it with this letter. Naturally, this is not for publication!

The Princess gave in, as she always does, but not graciously. We will be going to Oxford first. You can write to me at Chatsworth House.

Sincerely,
Liza

From the Duchess of Kent to
Her Royal Highness Victoria

Undated

. . . I am disappointed and grieved that you feel so averse to traveling, but nevertheless, you must try to recognize that it is of the greatest consequence that you should be seen, that you should know your country, and be acquainted with, and be known, by all classes. If the King was another man, and if he really loved you, he would welcome the tour.

Can you be dead to the calls your position demands? Impossible! Reflect—before it is too late. . . . Turn your thoughts and views to your future station, its duties, and the claims that exist on you.

Mama

From Mr. William Fulton to
Miss Elizabeth Hastings

1 September 1836
London

Dear Liza,

The news at home is all about your so-called royal progress. Your Princess stays only with the richest and most powerful families. She would do better to spend some time with the common people who will also be her subjects.

Reports from Court say His Majesty is indecent in his wrath about the liberties the Duchess takes. Is it true the Princess was served her breakfast in a jeweled crown at Eaton Hall? Perhaps the Duchess hopes to make the King expire from outrage and ensure her regency that way?

All the royal gossip in the world cannot reconcile me to the loss of our day together. Please write, as it is a great consolation.

Fondly,
Will

6 September 1856 Excerpt from the Journal of Her Royal Highness Victoria

Oh! What a business was there, there!! The people, of whom there was a dense mass, insisted upon dragging us through the town & in spite of every effort which was tried to prevent them from so doing, they obstinately persisted. . . . Not only through it, did they drag us, but round it, so, that we were detained exactly 1 hour & a ¼ in Lynn! I could see nothing of the town; I only saw one living, dense mass of human beings! We unfortunately drove over a poor man just as we stopped but he is not materially hurt, I hear.

From Miss Elizabeth Hastings
to Mr. William Fulton

6 September 1836
Norfolk

Dear Will,

I have little time to write. We've just arrived in Norfolk and I am required to help the Princess change her clothes for the 5th time today. But during our travels, in a town called Lynn, a man was run over by the Princess's carriage. I haven't been able to hear how he fares. Can you look into the matter for me?

Fondly,
Liza

From Mr. William Fulton to
Miss Elizabeth Hastings

18 September 1836
London

Dear Liza,

I regret to inform you Mr. Josiah Smith, in his eagerness to view the elusive Princess, ventured too near her carriage's wheels. He was killed instantly. The common man should be wary of interrupting the royal progress!

I hear the King was furious the Duchess demanded royal salutes from the men-of-war and the forts along the Solent. He has ordered all the popping must cease. Finally, in a state of great excitement, he prohibited the firing of royal salutes to any ships except those that carried the reigning sovereign or his consort. Somehow, I think the Duchess will find another way to harass the King.

Please write again soon. Your letters are a poor substitute for your presence, but I will be grateful for any word from you.

Fondly,
Will

From Miss Elizabeth Hastings to
Mr. William Fulton

28 September 1836
Oxford

Dear Will,

We are leaving Oxford today. The crowd waited for hours to hear Victoria speak, but her mother insisted on speaking in Victoria's place in her dreadful English. The day was not a loss for all: Sir John Conroy was presented with an honorary doctorate in civil law. No doubt this was done at the Duchess's prompting, since I cannot imagine in what way Sir John has earned such a prize. The Duchess is keeping him sweet since their hopes for a regency grow dimmer every day.

The Baroness Lehzen tells me Sir John has set his sights on becoming Victoria's private secretary. As I understand it, this is a role that demands the sovereign have the utmost trust and confidence in the bearer of the title. I do not think much of his chances.

Today I accompanied Victoria to the Bodleian Library. She was shown the notebook in which Queen Elizabeth did her Latin exercises. Victoria has been inspired and vows to study harder. I wish we were going home soon as the Princess does not look well. She has lost her appetite (no small thing for a Princess who loves her food) and is so fatigued she nearly fell asleep over dinner at Holkham. This travel is too much for her.

Will, since we've left Kensington, I've seen so many different kinds of British people. In the Midlands, the coal miners were actually black with soot and the children were dressed in filthy rags. But the Oxford streets are filled with black robed undergraduates filled with high spirits and academic excess. Perhaps there is an opportunity for your printing press in the diversity of the British people? Each one of these groups needs a newspaper for their special needs. I could write the articles for distressed gentlewomen!

I look forward to seeing you when we return. Next we go to Ramsgate for the autumn but I will return to Kensington by Christmas.

Fondly,

Liza

25 September 1836 Excerpt from the Journal of Her Royal Highness Victoria

I am much tired by the long journeys and the great crowds we have to encounter. We cannot travel like other people, quietly and pleasantly, but we go through towns and crowds and when one arrives at any nobleman's seat, one must instantly dress for dinner and consequently I never rest properly.

From Miss Elizabeth Hastings
to Mr. William Fulton

30 September 1836
Ramsgate

Will,

A brief note is all I have time for. We arrived in Ramsgate this morning. The town was all assembled for a triumphant arrival, but the Duchess disappointed them by entering town through a little used entrance and going directly to the house.

I am troubled by the Princess's fatigue. The Baroness Lehzen is worried too. I will write when I can.

Liza

From Mr. William Fulton
to Miss Elizabeth Hastings

18 October 1836
London

Dear Liza,

It has been two weeks since I had a letter from you. There is a rumor the Princess is seriously ill. Please write and let me know you are well.

Will

From Mr. William Fulton
to Miss Elizabeth Hastings

26 October 1836
London

Liza,

It has been three weeks. I pray you, write to me. My sources hint the Princess is on her deathbed with typhoid fever. I have seen what the fever can do to those who care for its sufferers. Your duty to the Princess is not worth your life.

In your absence, I have discovered how very much your welfare touches my heart. Please take care of yourself until you come back to me.

Very fondly,
Will

**From Miss Elizabeth Hastings
to Mr. William Fulton**

5 November 1836
Ramsgate

Will,

This has been my first opportunity to write. Your sources were unexpectedly accurate. The Princess nearly succumbed to typhoid. The Baroness and I nursed her night and day these last three weeks. The Duchess, like an ostrich, preferred to believe Victoria was malingering and refused to call in a doctor until it was almost too late. We all knew the diagnosis—after all there are only so many causes of high fever and that scarlet rash—but the Duchess refused to acknowledge the danger. She never even visited her daughter once. The Princess told me once the Duchess had her inoculated against the pox. At one time, her daughter's welfare meant everything to her. Alas, the Duchess has lost her way. If she's not careful, she'll lose Victoria for good.

Sir John, his prospects declining along with Victoria's health, visited every few hours. Last week I returned from the kitchen in the middle of the night to find him in the Princess's chamber. He was twisting her arm to make her sign a letter appointing him her private secretary. His nerve knows no boundaries. I tore the letter from his hands while the Baroness called for help. He knows now I am his enemy. But the King's health is so poor and Victoria is so near to her majority—only six more months—I do not think he can harm me.

Mademoiselle Blanche, the Duchess's lady's maid, a sly boots if ever I met one, has condescended to inform me all the servants have a holiday the day after Christmas. Will you meet me at Kensington Palace at noon?

Do not think I am insensible to the concern you showed in your letters. I was very touched.

Until Christmas,
Liza

5 November 1836 Excerpt from the Journal of Her Royal Highness Victoria

Dear good Lehzen takes such care of me and is so unceasing in her attentions to me after my illness that I shall never be able to repay her sufficiently for it but by my love and gratitude. I never can sufficiently repay her for all she has borne and done for me. She is the most affectionate, devoted, attached and disinterested friend I have and I love her most dearly. I feel that I gain strength every day.

18

In Which Liza Receives an Intriguing Offer

THE DAY AFTER CHRISTMAS was a perfect English winter day. Icicles glistened from the evergreens in Kensington Gardens. The Round Pond sparkled with icy splendor. Gentleman in elegant long coats skated gracefully while ladies, cocooned in ermine, admired from sleds on the ice. Several ladies who were not afraid of exercise skated with the men.

Liza wore a winter coat of dark maroon wool, a cast off from Victoria. The crisp air was intoxicating, especially after the stuffiness of the Christmas celebrations at Kensington Palace.

"Will, why is today called Boxing Day?" Liza asked.

"In some houses, employers put Christmas money in a box for the servants." Will, dressed in his handsome green velvet coat, looked prosperous and confident.

"Not the Duchess of Kent." Liza wrinkled her nose. "She's too stingy."

Will smiled and placed her gloved hand firmly on his arm. "I'm just glad you're back from Ramsgate. When I heard there was typhoid, I was frightened for you."

Pulling up her collar to hide the blush warming her face, Liza reassured him. "I was fine. It was the Princess who was so ill."

"Is she fully recovered?"

Liza laughed. "Are you asking me as a reporter or my friend?"

"Does your answer change?" he countered.

"She's much better, but she nearly died. And Sir John's treatment of her made it worse."

"Forget the scoundrel. She didn't sign his letter. Once she's Queen, she'll be done with him."

Liza couldn't forget those long weeks in the Princess's sickroom or the night Sir John tried to force Victoria to put herself in his power. "But Victoria—"

"Liza, stop talking about them. This is our day." Will turned to look at her and shaded his eyes from the dazzling sun. "Your red coat makes your hair look like spun gold."

"Victoria's lost her beautiful hair—we had to cut it all off." Liza twirled one of her own curls around her gloved finger.

"Vanity, thy name is woman!" said Will.

"For her whole life, she's been told her hair is her best feature—and now it's gone!"

"It'll grow back," Will said. "There are worse problems."

"Her fairness is gone though," Liza said. "She'll be a brunette from now on."

"Alert the royal portraitist!" cried Will in mock alarm.

"Stop!" Liza slapped his arm. "It's a tragedy for any girl."

"Liza, if you mention the Princess again, I'll throttle you. I've been waiting for months to see *you.*"

"Oh, I'm sorry, Will." Liza brushed a lock of hair away from her forehead. "Kensington Palace is like an ornate birdcage. We flit from one perch to another, chattering about the same things over and over again. I forget what freedom is."

Will led her to a small stand where a man was renting ice skates. "Shall we?"

Liza nodded eagerly; she knew she was a pretty skater. Will helped her strap the metal blades onto her shoes and led her on to the ice. To her great pleasure, Will skated as well as she did. They glided across the pond, attracting appreciative looks from the other skaters.

"Did you enjoy Christmas?" Will asked.

"We ate well, but it was a lot of work. Victoria's mother received guests all day; Victoria received carriages full of gifts. We needed three tables to display it all. And every table had an evergreen tree." Liza sighed. "It reminded me of home."

"I heard the royal family decorates dead fir trees."

"Don't the English have Christmas trees?" Liza asked. "In Germany we always did."

"A waste of a good tree, if you ask me. A better use would be to make paper. They're trying to see if wood pulp can be used instead of rag." He neatly dodged a slower skater.

"No one could ever accuse you of being sentimental." Liza pulled away from Will and spun, her full skirt flaring out around her. He caught her up and they circled the pond several times. Breathless, but happy, they sat down on a small bench. Will pulled a small package out of his pocket.

"Maybe you'll think I'm sentimental now," he said, almost shy. "I brought you a Christmas present."

"You shouldn't have!" Liza was relieved beyond measure she had not been the only one to bring a gift. "I've something for you too. Open mine first." She reached inside her coat and handed him the flat package wrapped in soft fabric.

"I didn't expect . . ." He pulled the package open and stared at the set of linen handkerchiefs, each painstakingly embroidered with his initials in dark thread.

"To replace the one I gave to the boy that day—do you remember?"

"How could I forget?" Will lifted his head and looked her straight in the eyes. "They're very handsome, Liza; I'll treasure them."

"Then you shouldn't ever lend them to me!" Liza laughed.

"Now open mine," he said.

Liza opened the package and exclaimed with delight at the gift: a small, glass snow globe on a wooden base. The silver snowflakes floated inside the globe over a scene of a frozen lake, much like the one in front of them.

"Will—it's exquisite," Liza gasped.

"I asked a German glassmaker what to give a girl from Munich."

She shook it gently and watched the snowflakes jumble and settle inside the globe. "Last Christmas, my mother and I shopped in town and all the nicest stores had snow globes." A familiar bubble of grief welled up in her throat, and the watering in her eyes was not from the cold. "Will, it's wonderful."

Will brushed away a tear from her cheek. "Don't cry, Liza." He leaned in to kiss her on the lips. Without an instant's hesitation, Liza kissed him back.

"I knew you would taste like honey," he said softly.

Liza trembled and shifted slightly away.

Will fixed his eyes on a gentleman putting a fine gelding through his paces in the distance. "It's a shame your father was a knight," he said with the air of someone saying something aloud that had long been in his thoughts.

Liza tilted her head to one side in surprise. "Why would you say such a thing?"

"Daughters of gentry don't mix with tradesmen."

"No, he was in trade himself," Liza hurried to correct him. "King George knighted him because his sauerkraut was far superior to any in England. And it was a very minor knighthood. We weren't true gentry at all."

"Why was his sauerkraut the best?"

Liza loved how Will's curiosity always got the better of him, no matter what the circumstances.

"It's a secret ingredient," she said, narrowing her eyes.

"It shall remain confidential, I swear."

"You didn't hear it from me," she whispered.

"Of course not!" A wide grin spread across his face.

Hiding her mouth with her hand, and glancing about for eavesdroppers, Liza revealed her father's secret, "It might be cardamom, from India."

"Cardamom." He nodded as though he was filing the information away. But then his eyes came back to her. "I would have liked to have met your father."

"He would have liked you. He appreciated self-made men."

"And your mother?"

That one is harder.

"Mama hoped I might get to court one day," she answered with an evasion.

"And so you did."

Liza laughed ruefully. "Not precisely as she planned."

Will brushed a lock of her hair off her forehead. "She wouldn't have approved of me."

"Mama approved of me being happy," Liza said. But her voice betrayed her uncertainty. Mama had been ambitious for her only daughter.

"So there is no family at all? No uncles or aunts? A distant cousin?"

"No, I'm quite alone in the world." Somehow, when she was with Will, it didn't seem true.

"Liza, love, I'm at a loss," Will said with a slow smile. "Whose permission should I ask to court you?"

Liza trembled from the inside out. She managed to say, "You could ask me."

Will suddenly grew serious. "Miss Elizabeth Hastings, you know I am smitten with you." His large hands took hers. "I've worked hard my entire life, but until I met you, I never knew why. You're intelligent, beautiful, loyal, and brave. Everything I admire. Liza, will you have me?"

Caution returned in a rush. She could almost hear her mother's voice warning her against inappropriate alliances. She frowned. "Will, you could do much better than a maid."

Will shook his head and a lock of sandy hair fell over his eye. "You could do better than a newspaperman."

"I'm worse than penniless. I owe money all over London."

Will swept away that consideration with a quick gesture. "I've plenty saved. I can pay your debts."

"No!" Liza pulled her hand back. "They're my obligations, not yours. I won't cost you a penny."

Will stood up and took a step back, looking down at her. "That's not why you won't marry me. You think I'm beneath you." He stated it as though it was a fact.

"No, no," Liza stammered. "I think you're wonderful. And after all, I'm only a servant."

"Not for long, Liza my dear. I know why you serve Victoria so loyally. You want her to restore your fortunes."

Were my motives so transparent? Are they still my motives?

"Then you could marry whomsoever you wish," Will continued.

"But I don't want to marry anyone else," Liza protested.

"Liza, you don't know what you want," he said.

Liza opened her mouth to protest, but the raw vulnerability on his face warned her to be honest.

"Maybe I don't," she confessed.

Will's face was stern, although there was a hint of a smile on his lips. "I can wait for you to figure it out, so long as you promise not to marry anyone else."

"You're too patient," Liza said, feeling guilty.

"I'm not a saint," Will warned. "I'll wait until your precious Victoria is Queen. Time enough then for you to make your choice."

With a flash of her old self, Liza said tartly, "On the one hand, Will Fulton, publisher of scandal sheets, or on the other, confidant to the Queen of the British Isles?"

He grinned and reached out to take her hand. "For such a clever girl as you, the choice should be easy."

31 March 1837 Excerpt from the Journal of Miss Elizabeth Hastings

Spring is here—finally an end to the long, frozen winter. The anniversary of my parents' death passed with no ceremony except from me. The Duchess's greenhouse has roses, Mama's favorite. I slipped out and dropped rose petals into the Serpentine River for her and Papa. The river is beautiful, but I can never forget it claimed their lives.

Since the household returned from Ramsgate, the inhabitants of Kensington Palace are like angry ghosts of themselves. Six months after her bout with typhoid, Victoria has lost too much weight. She still has no appetite. Her limbs are always cold. Each morning and night the Baroness and I rub her icy feet. Until Victoria recovers, there are not even lessons to enliven her days, much less balls or the opera. She relies only on the Baroness and myself for companionship and entertainment.

I've accomplished my goal to be indispensable to Victoria; never did I think I could be so necessary to her. However, I much preferred her when she was insouciant and imperious. Sir John and the Duchess should pay for how they have diminished her spirit.

I would be quite bored myself, but Will comes to see me on my afternoons out. And IB is teaching me his flash patter. I would teach Victoria (I think she would find it amusing), but it would lead to too many questions.

19

In Which Liza Witnesses a Fall from Grace

APRIL BREEZES freshened the room, and the sunny morning promised a perfect spring day. Victoria and her mother ate their breakfast in silence. Since the Princess's brush with typhoid, she clearly preferred the Baroness Lehzen's company, so the Duchess excluded Lehzen whenever possible. Victoria, her face pinched and her once beautiful hair a wispy dark shadow of its former self, stared out the open windows. Dash pressed his head against his mistress's leg.

The Duchess said, "Victoria, you should eat more."

"I still find my appetite is lacking. It's very good for my waistline." The Princess sliced off the top of a soft-boiled egg and fed Dash a bit of egg white.

"Victoria!" the Duchess exclaimed.

"Dash still has *his* appetite," Victoria said. She pushed her food about on her plate. "I think I shall go riding today on Rosa."

The mare, Rosa, the King's gift to the Princess, was still a sore subject between mother and daughter.

"No, Victoria, you're still too weak," said the Duchess.

Victoria spooned out the soft yolk and smeared it on her toast in one economical motion. "It's kind of you, Mama, to be concerned about my convalescence, when you were so nonchalant during my actual illness." She never missed a chance to remind her mother of the events at Ramsgate.

The Duchess tut-tutted. "You shouldn't ride. Take the carriage."

Liza could hear the effort it took for the Duchess to keep her tone even. These days Liza liked to pass the time wagering with herself on when the Duchess's control would snap.

"Mama, I shall ride if I want to." Victoria too, was a model of restraint. Gone were the tantrums; an icy politeness now defined relations between mother and daughter.

"Victoria, I forbid it," the Duchess said.

"I heard you the first time, Mama. But I'm old enough to make my own decisions." Mother and daughter stared defiantly at each other; the Duchess's eyes dropped first.

"Liza, tell the stables to be ready," Victoria said. "You shall accompany me."

"Yes, Your Highness," said Liza from her corner, startled at being spoken to. She hurried out, smiling. She had feared she would be trapped in the Palace on this fine day. But first she detoured to the Baroness's room. Like the Princess, Liza had grown closer to the Baroness during those long nights of illness and fear at Ramsgate.

"Good for Victoria. She should stand up to her mother," Lehzen said after Liza had reported the conversation at breakfast. "But Rosa is a spirited mare. Perhaps Victoria isn't strong enough yet."

Liza shrugged. "She's determined."

"Watch over her, Liza." The Baroness waved Liza off, her right hand already fishing in her pocket for caraway seeds.

Liza hesitated in the doorway.

"Well?" the Baroness asked.

"I don't have any riding clothes, Baroness."

"The Princess's chaperone must be properly dressed." Lehzen thought for a moment. "Victoria has outgrown a blue velvet riding habit. Take that one."

Liza bobbed a curtsy and ran to the Princess's room, a lightness in her step.

———

"Faster, Liza!" Victoria leaned forward in the saddle, pressed her heels into Rosa's sides, and sped off. "I want to gallop!" she called gaily. Escaping the Palace gave Victoria no less pleasure than Liza.

"Your Highness, slow down, please," Liza called. Her mount, a staid gelding named Rex, reluctantly obeyed Liza's command to canter.

The riding habit, secondhand though it was, suited Liza as though tailored just for her. The velvet jacket had dark blue piping and fit to perfection. The skirt must have been made with three yards of fine wool; it was longer on the right side to drape gracefully over the pommel of her saddle. Liza's mother had a similar ensemble in the same dark blue. Mama would revel in this moment: her daughter riding with royalty in a beautiful park on a crisp spring morning.

And the color favors my complexion.

At the sound of hoof beats behind her, Liza glanced back through the veil attached to her elegant hat. Two sober-faced grooms in the Duchess's green livery followed on a pair of matched gray horses. The Duchess's open landau carriage, complete with a driver and footman, followed the grooms. Perhaps the Duchess thought Victoria might succumb to exhaustion and would have to be driven home. The Princess's liberty was an illusion.

Victoria reined in, her soft face hardening as she noticed the grooms. She trotted past Liza and spoke to them directly. "I don't require you. Go home."

"Sir John gave orders—"

"Is Sir John your future monarch, or am I?" Victoria asked icily.

The grooms stirred uneasily.

"Princess," Liza said. "They could lose their jobs if they let you ride alone." Liza, also charged with Victoria's protection, was rather glad they were there.

"Oh, bother," Victoria said impatiently. "Be sure to keep out of my sight." She pulled Rosa's reins hard to the right and spun off down the bridle path. The groomsmen and carriage followed at a slower pace, trying to keep trees between themselves and the Princess.

Liza trailed behind Victoria across the bridge over the Serpentine River. Suddenly a small figure leapt out of the shrubs near Victoria.

"Liza!" Inside Boy cried.

Rosa reared up, her hooves pawing the air, but Victoria was an expert horsewoman and quickly brought her under control.

"Are you mad?" cried Victoria. "You don't startle a horse that way. We could have been killed."

Liza was too overcome by memories to speak. Her parents' carriage had been dragged, helter-skelter, by a frightened horse plummeting into this very river. She ducked her head down and patted Rex's withers.

Inside Boy ignored the Princess. "Liza, please."

"Don't you know who I am?" Victoria asked, her mood hovering between irritation and curiosity.

"'ullo, Your 'ighness," said Inside Boy, doffing an imaginary cap. "Can I borrow your lady's maid?"

"Liza, do you know this, um, gentleman?"

Liza found herself making the most improbable of introductions. "Your Highness, may I present . . . ," For the first time Liza realized she didn't know Inside Boy's first name. "Inside Boy Jones."

"Inside Boy? What an interesting name." Victoria's curiosity was sharper than one of her embroidery needles. She leaned forward in her saddle. "How do you know Liza?"

"We've met around the Palace," he said.

A gulp started deep in Liza's throat and threatened to become a giggle.

The grooms cantered up and flanked Liza and the Princess. "You, boy! You're not to bother the Princess."

"Nonsense. He's not bothering me at all." She fixed her protectors with a glare. "And I can see you! Off with you!" The grooms backed their mounts out of earshot and the Princess turned to Liza expectantly.

Cursing Inside Boy's foolhardiness, Liza asked, "What's happened, Boy?" Liza asked. "Has something happened to Will?"

Oh please, not Will.

"It's Annie."

Liza had often thought of Annie increasing in the Mary Magdalene House for Penitent Prostitutes. She must have had the baby in November.

"What's wrong?"

"Dunno. Maybe it's the baby. She got a message to me, don't ask 'ow, and she wants you to come to 'er."

"Why me?"

"Annie? Annie Mason?" Victoria interrupted. "She's having a child? Liza, you didn't tell me she had married. I would have sent a card."

"Princess, a moment, please," begged Liza. "Boy, she doesn't even like me."

"Annie said she was ready to tell you what you wanted to know. But it 'as to be this morning. She said she won't be there past noon." He paused and Liza saw the anxiety in his eyes. "Liza, she sounds right desperate."

If Annie was ready to give up her secrets, Liza couldn't pass on this opportunity to discover evidence against Sir John. "Princess, I apologize, I've no time to explain," she said. "But it's important I go." She lowered her voice. "Annie could have the kind of ammunition we've been looking for against You Know Who." To Inside Boy she said, "How can we get there?"

"Let's take my carriage. I'd love to see Annie again," the Princess said eagerly.

"No!" Liza and Boy exclaimed in unison.

The Princess's posture stiffened. "I shall go, if I want to." She dismounted and beckoned to one of the guards to take her reins.

Liza slipped down from Rex's back and threw the reins to the puzzled groom. Tripping over her long skirt, Liza cried, "Your Highness, it is not possible."

244 PRISONERS IN THE PALACE

"Why not?" called Victoria over her shoulder. Simon, a bewildered expression on his face, held the carriage door open.

"It's a dangerous neighborhood," said Liza. "You cannot go there."

"Nonsense," Victoria said. "I'll be Queen of all Britain soon; there's no place I cannot go." At the mention of danger, groom, driver, and footman exchanged uneasy looks. Simon, the highest ranked, spoke for the group. "Begging your pardon, Your Highness, we cannot permit you to leave the park."

"Of course you can."

"We have our orders," Simon said doggedly.

Victoria glared at them.

Liza knew bone-deep that what Victoria proposed was unthinkable. "Princess, you mustn't try to come."

"I never get to have adventures," the Princess complained.

Simon and the others looked miserable.

"And I would lose my job for certain," said Liza.

I'll lose it anyway.

The grooms took their orders from Sir John; he would learn how Victoria tried to leave. Fault would be laid squarely on Liza's shoulders.

Damn Annie for starting this.

Victoria's lips pulled together in a pout. "But—"

"Princess, be reasonable." Liza echoed the Baroness: "Remember who you are."

The Princess's shoulders slumped. "Duty can be very vexing," she sighed. "Very well. I'll stay. You take the carriage. Liza, do you promise to tell me everything when you return?"

"I will, but you must go back to the Palace." She glanced at Inside Boy, who was watching the negotiations with growing impatience.

Victoria turned to Simon. "Take Miss Hastings wherever she wants to go. Accompany her at all times."

With a marked lack of enthusiasm, Simon said, "As you wish, Your Highness."

As Liza and Inside Boy climbed in the carriage, she noticed the Duchess's prominent crest on the door. "Should we cover your mother's crest?" said Liza.

"Don't be foolish, it's my crest too," said Victoria. "You are on an errand for me."

May as well be hanged for stealing a sheep as stealing a lamb.

Everyone in the Palace, from the Duchess to the least scullery maid, would know about this escapade, why not the people of London too? She pressed her gloved fingers to her eyes and carefully removed her hat and veil.

"Annie's information had better be worth it," she muttered to Boy.

———

As they approached town, the driver asked, "Where to now, Miss?" Before Liza could answer, Inside Boy clambered over to the driver's seat and began to direct him.

Despite her worries about what lay ahead, Liza enjoyed seeing the city from an open carriage instead of the stuffy omnibus. The streets seemed cleaner and London's air fresher from the velvet carriage seat. They turned down Haymarket to Fleet Street. Shoppers rushed up and down the streets, but either their driver possessed exceptional maneuvering skills, or as Liza suspected, respect for their royal carriage cleared a path. Suddenly they stopped and Inside Boy hopped down.

"Are we there?" she asked. She recognized nothing.

"The house is down that street, but it's too tight for the carriage. We'll hoof it." He started to open the carriage door, but Simon got there first.

As Liza adjusted her too-long riding skirt, Simon murmured in her ear. "Liza, I don't like the looks of this. I won't leave your side." Though Simon and Liza had been very formal ever since the Princess's birthday ball, she was glad to have him with her.

"What about the driver?" she asked.

"He can wait here," Simon said.

"As long as we go now," said Inside Boy. "C'mon, Liza." He ran off.

The driver looked resigned; as she ran after Inside Boy, Liza hoped they would be able to find the driver for a ride home. Outpacing Simon, who was built to be more imposing than quick, Liza hurried to catch up to Inside Boy. She spotted him weaving around pedestrians as though they stood still. In a few minutes, they arrived at the Mary Magdalene House. This time, Liza didn't hesitate to knock loudly.

"You've come back, have you?" Mrs. Russell opened the door herself this time. She peered down at them. "And with another young man this time." She recognized Boy. "I thought you looked familiar. Mr. Jones, if that is your real name, the girls are not permitted gentleman visitors. You're too late anyway. She's gone."

Not daring to look at Boy, Liza asked, "Do you mean she's dead?"

"Lord have mercy, I'd have said so. Although if she's gone back to her old ways, she might as well be dead." She shook her head piously. "The Lord will forgive a penitent once, but not twice."

"Where is she?" Inside Boy nearly shouted.

Mrs. Russell drew back and pulled the door halfway closed. "I don't like your tone, young man. Why are you asking all these questions about a whore?"

Wishing she were taller, Liza pointed to Simon, in his green livery, who had just lumbered up the narrow street. "He is the Duchess of Kent's footman. Not an hour ago, Princess Victoria sent me to inquire about Miss Mason."

Mrs. Russell was quick to become respectful. "I beg your pardon, Miss. We never know whom we are dealing with. Sometimes a girl's procurer comes, wanting her back. I remember once—"

"The Princess is concerned only with Annie Mason," Liza interrupted, imitating Victoria's haughtiest vowels. Inside Boy flashed Liza an admiring look.

"I don't know where she is."

"What about her baby?" asked Liza.

"Dead."

Liza had to wait a moment before she could trust her voice. "When?"

"It sickened a few days ago and died yesterday." Mrs. Russell crossed herself. "Annie was quite hysterical, refusing to let us take the body. As if she could bury it decently."

Liza wished she would stop calling the baby an 'it.'

As if he could read Liza's thoughts, Inside Boy said bleakly, "Her name was Prudence."

"She was better off dead," Mrs. Russell said in her queer deep voice. "What could a bastard child have to look forward to? She would end up no better than her mother."

"Is that what you told her?" Liza asked shaking her head and glaring at Mrs. Russell. She remembered Annie's hand resting on her stomach as she planned a better life for her baby. But her mind's eye drew back from imagining a pale and frantic Annie grabbing at the little girl's corpse.

"Her sort never listens. She cried for a bit, and when I came back in with her supper, half an hour ago it was, she was gone. I don't expect we'll see her again."

"Did she leave anything behind? A letter or a package?" asked Liza.

"No," Mrs. Russell said.

"There must be something," Liza insisted.

"Nothing. But you might look for her by the Fire Monument. It was her favorite place."

Inside Boy turned to Liza. "The old biddy's useless to us."

"I don't care if you are from the Princess, I'll not stand to be insulted." The heavy door slammed in their faces.

"Where's the Fire Monument?" Liza asked.

"It's not far." He tugged her sleeve.

Liza glanced over at Simon who was waiting respectfully out of earshot.

"Should we take the carriage?"

Boy ran down the alley, calling over his shoulder, "Quicker on foot."

He plunged into the crowd at the busy cross street. Liza and Simon followed. A few hundred yards later, Boy turned onto Cannon Street, and there, the Monument loomed over them. Liza couldn't believe the height of the white stone column; she'd wager you could see Kensington Palace from the top. A man collected money at the bottom to climb to the viewing platform.

"Wait here," said Inside Boy and he disappeared into the crowds of people surging around the base.

Liza and Simon stood on the edge of the square, panting from the pace Inside Boy had set. Liza searched the crowd carefully, but saw no sign of Annie.

Simon said, "Liza, I could help if I knew who you were looking for."

Now Liza regretted herself for bringing Simon along; he knew Annie from her days at the Palace.

He saw her dismay and reassured her. "A footman is trained to be discreet about his employer's business."

With a little nod, Liza bowed to the inevitable. "We're looking for Annie Mason."

The muscles in Simon's face tightened. "How do you even know her?" he asked.

"It's a long story." Liza remembered he once had told her he and Annie had courted. "But I need to find her, urgently."

Simon towered above the crowd by a good head. He had sharp eyes too.

"Liza, look there." Simon pointed up to the copper urn on top of the Monument. "There's a woman there. On the edge of the platform. She's got red hair."

Liza heard the anxiety in his voice and she was grateful to him for it.

"I'll get her," Simon said. And without a word, he pushed through the crowd, and past the line of people waiting to climb the Monument. A gatekeeper tried to stop him, but Simon pushed him aside with one hand and lumbered up the spiral staircase, three steps at a time.

"Look!" shouted a fruit seller, jabbing an apple toward the tower. "She's going to jump!"

A ripple of morbid anticipation washed over the crowd. Liza's heart sank; if anything would drive Annie to the worst, it would be these ghouls. Liza prayed Simon would reach Annie in time. Where was Inside Boy?

Not daring to tear her eyes away, Liza clasped her hands together.

Please Lord, you tried her too hard; it's not her fault she broke. This sin is too much. Save her.

Far above her head, the redheaded figure turned to say something to someone inside.

Without any warning, Annie hurled herself, backward, away from the safety of the platform. Her white gown billowed out as she plummeted silently down. Liza stared. Not breathing, not feeling, she was suspended in that instant, eyes fixed on the falling angel. The crowd scattered, voiding a spot of pavement to receive her body.

Annie hit the ground with a sickening thud. A stout woman swooned and had to be carried away. A mother pulled her young son to her skirts and covered his face. A rush of people swarmed into the empty space around Annie's body, like water filling a bowl. Liza hadn't believed it could happen. Not to anyone she knew.

A ragged old woman at the edge of the square began to shriek, "She was pushed!" She said it again and again.

A man shouted at her, "Shut up, you old hag, you're too blind to see that far."

Liza's hands went cold as ice and her heart beat so loud it drowned out the crowd. She staggered toward Annie's body, pushing at the crowd. "Let me through, I know her." She began to sob, pounding at the tall backs with her fists. "Please move!"

"Liza, we have to go." Simon spoke at her back, panting and perspiring. "You can't be here."

"No! Help me get to her!" she begged.

Something in her face weakened his resolve. He nodded. "Let her through!" His stentorian voice, combined with his hefty forearm, cleared her a path. She knelt down and took Annie's warm hand. Her eyes were open, fixed on nothing at all and her face was peaceful, save for the trickle of blood at the corner of her mouth. Her red hair had been cut short. Liza dared not lift Annie's head; the blood's widening pool told its own story. With the tips of her fingers, Liza gently closed Annie's eyes.

Two men pushed forward and examined the body.

"Usually they scream," said one, with a bushy beard.

"There have been too many suicides at the monument," said his companion, a thin man with a narrow, pointed chin. "These girls get into trouble and can't face the consequences."

Liza turned to stare at them, tears running down her face. With their morality and fine waistcoats, they had no idea of Annie's tragic circumstances.

What did she have to live for?

"We should raise a question in Parliament," said the bearded man. "It's disrespectful to the monument."

"It's the local council's responsibility. Perhaps they should install a gate over the viewing area."

"It's a shame to ruin everyone's view for the weakness of a few girls."

Liza couldn't bear it anymore. "You hypocrites!" she screamed. "Instead of a gate, perhaps you could make it illegal for a gentleman to ruin a decent maid."

"You're blaming us? The girl was unbalanced, and she fell." The bearded man nudged the thin man in the ribs.

"Not a bad jest, that. Unbalanced."

"You could have saved her, if you wanted to." Liza didn't recognize her own voice.

The two men stared at her as though she was an escapee from an asylum.

Simon stepped forward. "That's enough gawking. Move along. Gentlemen like yourselves have better things to do with your time."

The thin man began to take offense, but stopped short when he noticed Simon's royal livery. He grabbed his friend by the sleeve and moved on. Liza closed her eyes in relief.

The blood seeped into Liza's riding skirt and the small stones embedded in the pavement dug into her knees. She reached out to brush a lock of Annie's short red hair from her cheek.

"They even took away your lovely hair," whispered Liza. No doubt the Mary Magdalene House had considered it sinful. "It was your best feature." As if it mattered to Annie now.

Annie's left hand gripped a cheap woolen scrap of cloth. Liza pried it out of her hand. It was a baby blanket, embroidered with pretty blue flowers. Blinking against the sunlight, she looked up to the top of the monument.

Such a long way to fall.

20

In Which Liza Disrespects Her Betters

"LIZA." Will's comforting voice finally roused her. His familiar figure was kneeling at her side.

"You shouldn't be here," he said somberly.

"Will, it's Annie. She's dead," Liza cried.

"I know," he said. "Let me take you away." He tried to pull her up, but she knelt rooted to the ground.

"The baby died." Her voice sounded thin, as though coming from far away. "Annie couldn't bear it. She threw herself off the monument."

Will's hand tightened around hers.

"What did she have to lose?" Liza's voice had grown louder and more strident.

"Liza, stop, people are staring."

"What do I care?" She spoke over Will's attempts to hush her. "What happens to Annie now? She can't even be buried properly— not a suicide!" Liza began to cry, great sobs racking her body. "They bury suicides at crossroads."

"Liza, forgive me, but . . ." Will slapped her face hard.

The world came sharply, unhappily back into focus. "You didn't have to do that," Liza said dully.

Will's eyes darted around the curious crowd staring at them. "Yes, I did. Let's get you cleaned up."

"I can't leave her alone."

Will cast about for a solution. His eyes lit upon Simon who stood on the other side of Annie's body, keeping the crowd back.

"You, in the Duchess's livery!"

Simon looked over and then behind him, as if he couldn't believe Will was talking to him.

"His name is Simon," said Liza.

"Simon, come here."

Simon stalked over. "Who are you to be ordering the Duchess's man about?" He towered over Will by at least half a foot.

"I'm a friend of Miss Hastings. Find a constable and tell him this . . ." He looked down at Annie's peaceful face, shorn of her magnificent hair, "this woman should be decently buried."

Simon's eyes hardened and he crossed his arms over his chest.

Will added, "Tell him the royal family is concerned and it must be done quietly."

Simon hesitated a moment longer. "Very well," he said, relenting. "Where will you take the young lady? The Princess has charged me with her safe return."

"We'll be at the coffee house on the corner."

Simon nodded. "I'll return with the carriage."

Will lifted Liza to her feet by her elbows. Her knees buckled when she stood up and Will tightened his hold on her, supporting more of her weight.

"My skirt," she said faintly. The long riding skirt was soaked in Annie's blood.

"Can you lift it, fold it over or something?"

The practicalities of walking preoccupied Liza until they reached the coffee shop. The expression on Will's face and the obvious quality of Liza's dress convinced the restaurant owner to seat them, despite the blood on Liza's hands and clothes.

"Black coffee," Will ordered when the server approached. "And a measure of brandy in it."

"Two?" the server asked, giving Liza a worried look.

"Two. And bring some cloths and warm water. The young lady witnessed an accident. She's had a bad shock."

Liza slumped against the high-backed chair. The rags came and Will gently wiped the worst of the blood and grime from her palms. When the coffee came, he placed a cup of steaming liquid in her hands.

"Drink."

She took a sip and coughed at the bite of the brandy. "Will," she began.

"Keep drinking."

Liza obeyed, taking several more sips with Will watching. Finally the tightness in her chest began to ease. "How did you know to come for me?" she asked.

"I heard there was a suicide. I came—" he faltered.

"To see if there was a story," Liza finished.

He took a sip of his own coffee and grimaced at the bitter taste. He added three heaping spoonfuls of sugar and stirred. "You've a knack for finding yourself in difficult situations, Liza. Why were you there? And dressed like you were riding with the Princess herself." "I was." Her morning ride seemed an eternity ago. "Then Inside Boy came."

Will shoved the table away from him, sending coffee sloshing out of his cup into the saucer. He glowered at the scandalized couple sitting next to them, who suddenly became very interested in the bottoms of their tea cups. "Liza, have you no thought for yourself? You're risking everything. And for who? Annie Mason? Inside Boy?"

"He said," Liza touched Will's hand to claim his attention, "he said Annie was ready to talk to me about Sir John. She wouldn't before, because she was afraid he might hurt her or the baby. But what did she have to lose now?"

"You should have stayed home."

Liza raised her eyebrows. "You know me better."

Will gave her a sour look. "And the Princess? Don't tell me she consented?"

"Yes." Thank goodness Victoria had not come with them.

"Where is Mr. Inside Boy Jones now? Don't tell me he just left you there?" The look on Will's face augured ill for Boy.

"Will, calm down. Boy must have seen her fall. He'd be terribly upset. You know he really cared about Annie. And I wasn't alone. Simon was with me."

"So now you've dragged the Duchess's footman in it too." Will tapped his spoon against his cup. "Liza Hastings, you're in deep waters."

"Stop scolding me," she begged. "I have to decide what to do."

"You'll go home with that oversized fellow, and hope you still have a job. But I doubt it."

"I'm not thinking about myself." Liza put her coffee down, surprised at how sincerely she meant it. "We have to punish the people responsible for what happened to Annie."

"That would be half the men in London."

"I'll start with the first one," said Liza. "Sir John has to suffer for what he did to her."

"The Conroys of the world don't suffer for the likes of Annie." Will shook his head. "Liza, love, he's out of reach."

Liza was thinking furiously. "Except for the press. He can't stop your broadsheets. You came to the monument for a story, Will. Let me write it for you."

"There's no profit in it," he said. "A gentleman taking advantage of a maid is too common a tale." Will took another sip of syrupy coffee.

"This ending isn't. Nor are the players. A powerful man, close to the Princess, abusing his power over a poor maid until she destroys herself? Your readers would pay for that."

He shrugged.

"Please? It's the right thing to do, regardless of how many sheets you sell."

Exasperated, he said, "We're back to this. You want me to choose a side: Sir John's profits or your justice."

"Will," Liza said simply, "you've already chosen."

———

Liza slumped against the side of the carriage. She didn't look up as the gravel of the Palace drive crunched under the horses' hooves. Kensington Palace looked eerie and quiet. Could it only have been a few hours ago she had left Victoria in the park?

Simon jumped down and opened the door.

"Thank you for your help," Liza said in a low voice.

He shook his head sadly. "What happened ought not to have. But there's nothing more to be done for Annie now."

"You might be surprised." As Liza turned toward the servants' entrance, she said, "Sir John may discover it's a mistake to ruin a maid."

Simon looked about and leaned down to whisper in her ear. "Liza, watch yourself. Sir John is not a man to cross. The lass, God rest her soul, will still be dead."

Liza raised the knocker on the servant's door, but before she let it fall, the door swung open and a hand reached out and pulled her inside the Palace. Nell's eyes glowed like a cat's in the dim hallway. "They want to see you the moment you return."

"Who?"

"Sir John, the Duchess, Mrs. Strode, and the Baroness," Nell answered.

"Of course. And I want to see them."

Looking sidelong at Liza, Nell noticed her skirt. "What happened to the Princess's riding habit? Is that blood?"

Liza looked down at the soiled fabric. "There was . . . an accident."

"Oh, Miss Liza," Nell moaned, shaking her head.

On the family's side of the green baize door, the rooms were blazing with light. Liza's shadow preceded her in sharp relief, as though eager for the coming scene. Angry voices could be heard in the Duchess' drawing room. Nell squeezed her hand and scurried away. Liza took a deep breath and opened the door.

The Duchess was pacing. Her face was flushed, and coils of hair were tumbling out of her elaborate coiffure. Mademoiselle Blanche stood in the corner, her lips curved in a sly smile, holding smelling salts at the ready. Mrs. Strode's formidable head was cast down and her hands clasped together at her waist. The Baroness sat in the corner methodically chewing on caraway seeds. The Princess was nowhere to be seen.

Sir John, the one Liza most dreaded seeing, stood at the fireplace as though he owned the Palace. When she saw him, her stomach began churning and bile rose in her throat.

"You! You wicked girl," The Duchess shrieked at Liza. For once, she remembered to speak English. "You let the Princess consort with a commoner!"

Before Liza could answer, the Duchess went on, "And if that wasn't enough, the Princess wanted to go off on some adventure in the slums." She jabbed a finger at Liza. "And you, Miss . . . Miss . . . would have let her go!"

"No, I didn't—" Liza began.

"And you stole my carriage! I'll have you jailed!"

Liza tried again. "The Princess lent it—"

"As if the Princess has any authority in this house!" The Duchess turned her ire on the Baroness. "Lehzen, you assured me the girl was of good moral fiber, but she's a liar and a thief."

"Your Grace, once again the Baroness has placed someone unsuitable around the Princess," drawled Sir John. "Remember the previous maid? Lewd, she was. The Baroness lacks the necessary judgment to be Victoria's governess."

The Baroness said nothing, but her broad shoulders tensed from fear. Liza's heart sank. She had expected to be blamed, and rightly so. Her friendship with Inside Boy and her curiosity about Annie had led her to this moment. But now her rashness had put Baroness Lehzen at risk, too. Sir John might find a way to get rid of the Baroness once and for all. Victoria would be left friendless and alone.

With Annie's lifeblood on her skirt, Liza could not bear to let Sir John win again. She cleared her throat and said as firmly as she could, "It's not the Baroness's fault Sir John seduced Annie Mason."

The room was silent.

Liza spoke quickly before Sir John could deny it. "Annie Mason was dismissed because she was carrying Sir John's child."

The Duchess's mouth dropped open, and slowly her eyes turned from Liza to Sir John. The Baroness stared ahead fixedly. Mrs. Strode's mouth moved as though she were praying.

"It's a lie!" exploded Sir John. "The slut was thrown out; she'll say anything to discredit the family."

"It's not a lie. She delivered the baby in November!"

Sir John stepped closer to Liza. "Lying piece of baggage!" He raised his hand as if to hit her in the face. Liza stood her ground. For the first time, her eyes were not afraid to meet his.

"Sir John!" The Duchess's face paled. "There will be no violence in my drawing room!"

"I beg your pardon, Duchess, but these accusations are absurd." With obvious effort, he brought his hand to his side and composed himself. "That baby could be anyone's."

"You deny you ruined her?" Liza asked. Her stomach ached with all of her anger.

"Of course I do." He fidgeted under Liza's stare. "And even if I did—what does it matter?"

Unexpectedly, the Duchess contradicted him. "It would matter to me," she said. "Lehzen, what do you know of this?"

"Nothing, Your Grace. Mrs. Strode told me Annie was dismissed only after she was gone," said the Baroness grimly. "I was not consulted."

The Duchess's face puckered in confusion. "Mrs. Strode—why did you dismiss her?"

"Sir John said it was necessary," Mrs. Strode said in the intonation of the perfect servant. No one looked at Sir John.

The door opened and Nell came in. Everyone's eyes followed her as she handed a folded note to Sir John. He slowly read it through. A smile crossed his lips before he controlled his face again. He shoved the note in his vest pocket.

"Let this Annie accuse me to my face," he said smoothly.

The Duchess looked doubtful. "If she's just had a baby, can she travel? When I had Victoria, I was laid up for months. The Duke made me come from Germany during the final month of my confinement so Victoria would be born in Britain. Sir John, do you remember?"

"Your Grace, I do recall." Sir John closed his eyes for a moment. "But to the matter at hand, bring the girl here so everyone can see how ridiculous these charges are."

Liza stared at him in dismay.

How does he know Annie can't bear witness against him?

"She's dead," Liza muttered. Her hand touched the still moist blood on her skirt.

"What? What did you say?" asked the Duchess.

"Annie Mason killed herself today."

"If she would do such a wicked thing, then she would not hesitate to lie about Sir John." The Duchess glanced over at Sir John, looking for his agreement. His expression was so smug, Liza wanted to slap his face.

The Baroness spoke in her gravelly voice, "What about the child?"

Sir John glared at her, but sounded unconcerned as he said, "I don't believe there ever was a baby."

"Well girl? What about this mythical baby?" asked the Duchess.

"Dead," muttered Liza.

"No girl. No baby. Sir John is completely cleared." The Duchess beamed. "The only thing left is to punish you for your wicked tale telling."

"Your Grace, she cannot remain here," said Sir John.

"I agree, Sir John. She's a liar and a bad influence on the Princess. Mrs. Strode, send her packing."

Liza had expected it, even thought she deserved it, but now it had happened. She was on the street. Like Annie.

Why don't I care?

"Yes, Your Grace," Mrs. Strode said.

"Very well." The Duchess had lost interest. "Come, Sir John." He placed her hand on his forearm and escorted her out. Mademoiselle Blanche followed her dutifully, but she could not resist giving Liza a triumphant smile on the way out.

Liza remained standing alone. The little security she had found after her parents' death was gone. She barely heard Mrs. Strode conferring in whispers with the Baroness. Mrs. Strode left without a word, leaving the Baroness alone with Liza.

"Liza," the Baroness said.

"Yes, Ma'am?" said Liza, her voice as tired as she felt.

"Are you certain it was Sir John who did this to Annie?"

"Yes. She told me so."

Heaving herself out of her chair, the Baroness sighed. "Victoria told me you prevented her from accompanying you today. It cannot have been easy; she's headstrong. I've prevailed upon Mrs. Strode to let you stay the night. And I'll write you a good character."

That was more than Annie had. Bitter and exhausted, Liza knew she needed to express some sort of gratitude. "Thank you, Baroness."

"Get some sleep, child. Do you know where you will go?"

"No." But she did know who would help her. Will would be relieved if she left the Palace. If only she didn't feel as though she had failed everyone: Annie, Inside Boy, Victoria, and even Baroness Lehzen. "May I say goodbye to the Princess?"

"That would not be wise," said the Baroness.

So Victoria was to lose another friend without a word of explanation.

"Goodbye, Liza."

"Goodbye, Baroness."

Liza forced herself to walk to her room. She removed the blood-stained riding jacket as quickly as she could undo the buttons. She couldn't quite reach the hooks in the back of the skirt. A moan burst from her throat; the dress had become intolerable to her. Another angry tug and the fabric tore away from the hooks. She balled it up and threw it the corner where the slope of the gable met the floor.

Liza pulled out her trunk but couldn't face packing. She threw herself on her narrow bed, pulled her blanket over her head and cried until she slept.

———

"Liza, wake up!" The Princess's high-pitched voice pierced Liza's sleep.

Liza tried burrowing deeper under the blanket, but the Princess wouldn't give up. She knocked again. Liza stumbled to the door and slid back the bolt.

"Princess, leave me alone!" Liza's aching body made her tactless.

Princess Victoria stood in the doorway, her eyes closed, counting silently.

"What are you doing?" asked Liza.

"Lehzen tells me to count to ten if I'm going to lose my temper. I'm up to twenty-five, Liza."

Hearing the unmistakable royal warning, Liza asked wearily, "What do you want?"

"You've no idea of the trouble you caused," the Princess said coming in and closing the door carefully behind her. "Mama and I have been fighting all day. I don't know why I should suffer Mama's temper while you have all the fun."

Fun.

Liza sank back to her bed and began to cry silently. The Princess sat next to her and awkwardly placed her arm around Liza's shoulder.

"Tell me what happened, Liza," she insisted.

Liza shook her head. "You don't want to know."

"But I do. Tell me." Even when the Princess was kind, she couldn't help issuing orders. So Liza laid out the sordid tale for the Princess. Annie's seduction by Sir John was no surprise. But when Liza began to talk of Annie's life of prostitution, Victoria moved her arm away from Liza's shoulder. Liza didn't care. The more Liza spoke, the more outraged she became. She described in detail how Annie was beaten because she refused to abort the baby. Sir John's baby.

"Liza, stop," the Princess cried. "I've changed my mind, I don't want to hear anymore."

"Princess, you told me you liked Annie. You need to hear the end." Liza described the Mary Magdalene house, and Annie's dead child. The Princess clasped her hands over her ears and squeezed her eyes tightly together. Past caution, Liza pulled the Princess's hands away from her ears and recounted every awful moment until Annie's body plummeted to the ground.

At the end, the Princess's face was pale. She stood up and smoothed her nightdress. "Is there anything I can do for Annie now?"

"You're too late," Liza answered brutally.

"Why are you angry with me? I had nothing to do with Annie's death."

"She was your friend, but you never cared what happened to her. The day she asked you for money, you lost interest in her."

"Everyone wants something from me!" the Princess cried. "Even you are working only for what I might do for you someday."

Liza stared at her—wondering why she ever thought Princess Victoria was her friend. "Your Highness, rest easy. I'll never ask you for anything again."

The Princess noticed Liza's trunk. "Where are you going?" she asked in a small voice.

"Sir John has sent me packing."

"He can't dismiss you!" The Princess's whisper became a wail. "You work for me."

"I leave at first light. And if you don't mind, I still have a lot to do."

"Liza, I need you."

"You found a new Annie. You'll find a new Liza."

The Princess stomped her foot. "I don't want a new Liza, I want you. Sir John had no right to fire you. You weren't foolish enough to let Sir John seduce you."

"He forced her!" Liza cried.

"How do you know? I saw how she smiled at him. He's very attractive in his sinister way—my mother thinks so. So do you."

Liza didn't deny it. But it didn't change anything. She placed her few books and journal at the bottom of the trunk.

"Once Annie gave in to him, her days were numbered," said the Princess. "I couldn't help her. But I can help you. I told Sir John you were under my protection."

Liza slowly straightened up and stared at the Princess. "You said that, Princess?"

"I did!" Victoria said drawing herself up to her full height. "When I was sick, you stayed by me and protected me from Sir John. Even today, you only went to see Annie for my sake. We both know what you have risked for me." She paused, then said, "In private, you may call me Victoria. Friends should not stand on ceremony."

Liza sank down on her bed, touched. Victoria didn't have many ways to reward loyalty.

"Thank you, but in the morning I'll be gone."

Victoria placed her small hands on the bed, and pushed herself upright—only her lack of inches saved her head from brushing against the sloped ceiling. "I won't permit it."

"Victoria," Liza relished saying the Princess's name out loud. "You saw what happened this morning: the guards followed his orders, not yours."

"Leave it to me, Liza." Victoria held out her arms. After a moment, Liza realized the Princess wanted to embrace her. She stepped forward and Victoria hugged her clumsily.

"Don't worry." As the Princess turned to leave, she saw the crumpled riding habit in the corner. "I hope you don't treat all my old clothes so shabbily." She walked out.

Liza shook her head, full of exasperation and affection. Victoria was deluding herself; she was as powerless as Liza. There would be no reprieve. But before she packed her bags, she would show Sir John he couldn't throw people away like so much rubbish.

Liza pulled out a piece of foolscap paper and dipped her pen in the inkwell. Her father's watch said it was two o'clock. She had plenty of time to write before getting thrown out of Kensington Palace in the morning.

21

In Which Liza Taunts a Tyrant

"**YOUR BREAKFAST, MISS,**" said Nell.

Liza's body ached from fatigue. She had written a draft of her article while her anger was fresh. Then she had forced herself to finish packing. Only when the trunk was tied with twine had she slept. She sat up and sniffed. "Is that hot chocolate?"

"Yes, Miss." Nell handed Liza a cup of the coveted beverage. "None of us dare say so, but we all feel so terrible for what happened." Her face was troubled.

Liza accepted the offering from below stairs and took a sip. "Thank you."

"Miss, where will you go?"

"I'll be fine," she said, with more confidence than she felt.

First things, first. Get out of Kensington Palace with my dignity.

"The Princess's riding dress is in the corner; I don't know if it can be salvaged," Liza said.

"I'll do what I can," Nell said miserably.

"That's all we can hope for," said Liza. "Nell, thank you for everything."

"Here's your wages and a character from the Baroness." Nell handed over an envelope.

Liza tucked it away in her reticule. "It's more than Annie got."

Nell wouldn't meet her eyes. "Take care, Miss."

Half an hour later, Simon knocked on her door, his wig freshly powdered and his green livery immaculate. "Miss, your hansom cab is waiting."

Liza pulled her cloak around her shoulders against the chill of the April morning. She followed Simon downstairs as he carried her trunk on his back, awkwardly maneuvering the narrow stairs.

"Where is everyone?" Liza asked, her voice sounding loud in the empty hallway. She couldn't admit to herself she was looking for Victoria.

"The staff has been instructed to wait in their dining room until—"

"I vacate the premises? I had no idea I was so dangerous. Tell me, did Sir John take the same precautions when he dismissed Annie?" A muscle in Simon's face twitched. Liza stopped harassing him: it wasn't his fault Sir John was a tyrant. And it was an ill omen to remember Annie's departure from Kensington Palace.

They reached the servant's door. Still no Princess. Ah well, for all Victoria's promises, Liza hadn't truly expected to see her. Victoria didn't know how to risk herself for someone else. Liza lifted her chin high, as she had seen Victoria do, and walked out into the courtyard. An ordinary hansom cab was waiting for her. Simon handed her trunk up to the driver. Shivering, Liza took a last look at Kensington Palace. The shadowy figure of Sir John watched from the window.

Liza climbed into the carriage and settled herself. Suddenly she heard Victoria's high, laughing voice. Liza poked her head out of the carriage and looked toward the Palace. The voice came not from inside, but from the gardens. Victoria rode into the courtyard on her mare, Rosa. Trailing behind her was a group of fine gentlemen, all riding even finer animals. The Baroness Lehzen, looking sleepy, followed in the Duchess's landau carriage.

"Liza!" Victoria called gaily. "Where are you going?"

Had Victoria forgotten what happened the night before? Had Liza dreamed their conversation? "Your Highness, I'm leaving."

"I forbid it." And still Victoria's voice was light and filled with mischief. She turned to the best-dressed gentleman in the group. Liza recognized him as one of the partygoers at the Princess's ball.

"Lord Liverpool," said Victoria. "My maid has been dismissed because she spoke the truth to my mother's comptroller. Doesn't that seem unfair?" Victoria's face was shining and she looked handsome in her green velvet riding habit. Her dark hair, still short, peeked out from under a charming hat.

Liza leaned farther out of the carriage to hear better. The Princess's confidence gave Liza hope for the first time that morning.

"Devilishly unfair, Your Highness, if you'll forgive my language. Our future Queen should be surrounded by honesty at all times!" Lord Liverpool inclined his head to the Princess.

The door slammed open. Sir John, as well-groomed as ever, burst into the courtyard. "What is all this?"

His gaze moved from Liza to Victoria. He took a step back when he recognized Lord Liverpool. "Liverpool, Princess," he said more civilly. "Perhaps someone would tell me what is happening?"

"By chance, I met Lord Liverpool while I was out riding this morning," said Victoria. "I invited his party home for breakfast."

"If the weather is fine, I ride every morning in this park," said Liverpool. "But this is the first time I've had the honor of meeting the Princess."

"Perhaps because Her Highness never rides this early." Sir John spat out the words.

"That must be it," laughed Victoria. "But isn't it a happy happenstance that this morning I should decide to go out before breakfast?"

Victoria dismounted from her horse and handed the reins to a groom. She beckoned to Sir John to join her, just within Lord Liverpool's earshot if she spoke loudly. "Sir John, before we go in, there seems to be a horrible mistake," she said in a strong clear voice. "My maid, Liza, has been unfairly dismissed. See to it she is reinstated."

Liza caught her breath; could Victoria's boldness save her?

Sir John's eyes went from the Princess to Lord Liverpool. In a low voice, he asked, "And if I refuse?"

Just as quietly, Victoria said, "Lord Liverpool's morality is legendary. He might wish to know why you dismissed not one, but two of my maids."

"I don't know what you think you know—"

"I know everything," Victoria interrupted, still whispering. "Including the ending. Lord Liverpool will find it terribly sordid, I'm afraid. Not at all the proper atmosphere for the heiress to the throne." Victoria was smiling as though she was discussing the breakfast menu. Every so often she would lift her riding crop and wave at Liverpool, who smiled back indulgently.

"So?"

"My Lord Liverpool has the King's ear, and he's very vocal in Parliament. If he chose, he could wreck what is left of your prospects."

Sir John glanced sideways at Lord Liverpool. "And if I let the wench stay?"

"That's the end of the matter."

Liza clasped her hands together tightly, waiting for his answer.

Finally, through teeth so tightly clenched Liza thought they might break, Sir John said, "Agreed."

"Liza, bring your things inside," ordered the Princess for the benefit of everyone listening.

Simon looked at Sir John, who hesitated, then gave a curt nod. Once his back was to Sir John, Simon grinned broadly at Liza. He hoisted the trunk onto his shoulders as though filled with feathers.

"After you, Miss," he said. Liza climbed down from the carriage, dizzy, as though someone had twirled her round and round the cobblestone courtyard.

Sir John returned to Lord Liverpool and said, "Shall we take this delightfully impetuous Princess into breakfast?"

His voice had an edge that worried Liza. For Liza's sake, Victoria had bested him. What would it cost them both?

8 April 1837 Excerpt from the Journal
of Miss Elizabeth Hastings

Victoria has paid a high price for her impudence. Her mother barely speaks to her. The Duchess and Sir John scheme in corners, springing apart when I enter the room. I fear we have showed our hand too plainly. Although they do not know I understand their words, they know I am Victoria's ally.

Sir John's plot to become private secretary, like the one to extend the regency, has melted away like the snow in Hyde Park. So far, I haven't any idea of what he plans next. The newspapers report that the King's health declines every day. We are all waiting.

JB has returned to the Palace. He is very melancholy but angry too. He's more than willing to play courier between Will and me. Will has promised to print my article by Monday next. I cannot wait to see Sir John's mortification.

The following Monday, Liza laid out Victoria's evening clothes as quickly as possible, then stole down to Sir John's office. She wanted to be there when Sir John read Will's broadsheet. She heard Sir John in his office, speaking to someone whose voice Liza couldn't distinguish. She crept closer to the door to overhear. The first scrap of conversation prickled the hairs on Liza's skin.

"I'm running out of time," Sir John said. "In a few days, she turns eighteen. My leverage is almost gone."

His voice grew louder then faded a bit, then grew again. He must be pacing back and forth, Liza thought. He went on, "She cannot leave the Palace or correspond with anyone without my permission."

Liza heard the jangle of keys coming toward her from down the corridor. Mrs. Strode! She ducked behind a floor-length curtain and closed her eyes. The heavy steps passed without stopping. With a sigh of relief, Liza moved back to her listening post.

Sir John was still speaking. "If I have to, I can bring more pressure to bear." Liza shivered at the menace in his voice. Sir John's voice stopped. Liza pictured him staring out the window.

A muffled voice asked a question. Sir John answered, "I have to convince the Duchess anew every morning. But it will end soon. The Princess is weak. She'll give in."

So he's not speaking with the Duchess.

She edged closer to the open door—a little nearer and she would see Sir John's fellow conspirator. Too late. The other door to the room was closing. Disappointed, she turned to go and stepped on a square of warped parquet that creaked. Though she tried to hurry away, Sir John appeared in the doorway at once. He dragged Liza into the room.

"If it isn't the Princess's little spy," he said as he released her arm. He twisted a lock of Liza's golden hair around his finger.

"I must admit, you've shown more stamina than I expected. I hope you don't expect Victoria to reward you for your service—she's as stingy as the rest of her family."

Click-clack, click-clack. Liza backed away from Sir John and smoothed out her skirt. "Her Grace seems to be in quite a hurry," Liza said with a slow smile. "Perhaps she has been reading the papers?"

"What do you mean?" Sir John asked, his eye narrowed and menacing.

The Duchess's heels grew louder. She burst into Sir John's office, so agitated her hair came down out of its pins in bunches. She clutched a broadsheet in her hand. She spoke in German.

"Sir John! That horrible story has appeared in the newspaper!"

Sir John shot a venomous look at Liza; she met his eyes and smiled even more broadly.

The Duchess went on, "You assured me it was a lie!"

"Let me see." Sir John grabbed the paper out of the Duchess's grasp. He smoothed it out, his eyes moving back and forth rapidly over the page. His nostrils flared.

Liza recognized Will's distinctive printing style. He had devoted half the page to a dramatic sketch of Annie plunging to her death from the top of the Fire Monument. Wonderfully, tragically eye-catching.

When Will chooses a side, he does so with a vengeance.

Sir John's hands shook as he scanned the article.

The Duchess saw Liza in the corner. "We dismissed her, but she is still here. Why is that?" she asked Sir John peevishly.

"Shut up," Sir John's color was rising with each paragraph.

Liza's hand flew to her mouth.

"Sir John!" the Duchess cried. "How dare you speak to me like that!"

Sir John blinked, as though the Duchess had slapped him. "My dear Duchess, I beg your pardon. I was distracted."

The Duchess was not so easily placated. "That's no excuse for incivility."

He pulled her hand to his lips and covered it with quick sensual kisses. Liza's stomach soured at the sight.

"Where did you get this tissue of falsehoods?" Sir John asked, his voice muffled against the Duchess's hand.

"On the desk in my sitting room," said the Duchess, reluctantly forgiving him.

Only one person could put a newspaper on the Duchess's desk. Nothing could bring Inside Boy solace from the pain of Annie's death, but humiliating Sir John was bound to help.

"Sir John, I'll ask you only once. Is this story true?" Through half closed eyes, the Duchess watched Sir John shrewdly.

Without hesitation, Sir John said, "It's a vicious lie."

The Duchess pointed at Liza and spoke in English. "The newspaper printed the same accusation you made against Sir John. What do you know about this?"

"Me, Ma'am?" Liza tossed her head. "How could I tell a newspaper what to print?"

"Impudent girl!" But the Duchess accepted Liza's powerlessness without a second thought. "Get out; I have private things to discuss with Sir John."

"Of course, Ma'am. Sir John." Liza sank low in a curtsy, looking up at Sir John from under her eyelashes. With satisfaction, she saw he could hardly contain his rage. She left the room.

That was for you, Annie.

22

In Which Liza Learns to Not Underestimate Sir John

THE DREARINESS of April gave way to sunny May. Victoria's eighteenth birthday drew near. The King's health worsened, but not quickly enough for the Duchess and Sir John. Now they were plotting to have Victoria name Sir John the keeper of the privy purse.

"As if Victoria would have that man in her household once she's Queen," said the Baroness while Liza brushed her hair. The phrase "Once She Is Queen" was repeated several times a day.

"Why does he want to keep the privy purse?" Liza asked. "It doesn't sound very important."

The Baroness snorted, a small shower of caraway seeds spraying Liza's image in the mirror. "The Queen's privy purse is four hundred thousand pounds."

"Per annum?" Liza had never imagined so much money in her life.

"She will have to run her palaces, pay her servants, take care of all the hangers-on—she'll spend it, don't worry."

Liza pulled the steel comb through the Baroness's long gray hair. "And if Sir John gets the privy purse?"

"He'll loot the treasury and rob Victoria blind."

"Where is everyone?" Liza asked Nell. It was late on a Thursday afternoon, but Nell was in her second best dress and tying on a bonnet.

"Sir John gave everyone a 'oliday," Nell said.

Liza was immediately wary. "Everyone?"

"Almost. A few scullery maids 'ave to stay, but even Mrs. Strode is visiting 'er sister in town. Simon is still 'ere." Nell sighed. "I'd fancy 'im, but footmen are too grand for parlor maids."

"Has Sir John ever given everyone a day off before?"

"No—and I'm 'urrying out in case 'e changes 'is mind." Nell took a second look at Liza in her working dress. "Don't you 'ave the day off too?"

"No one has told me so."

"Perhaps the Princess needs you in Northumberland?" Nell asked.

"Northumberland?"

Nell looked puzzled. "Isn't she going with 'er mother?"

"When?" Liza hadn't heard about any excursions.

"Today."

"Enjoy your day out, Nell," Liza said as she hurried away to the Princess's schoolroom. Events were coming to a head; she must warn Victoria.

The Baroness hovered outside the closed door. At Liza's approach, she put her finger to her lips. Liza whispered her intelligence into Lehzen's ear.

"The servants dismissed and the Duchess going too? I don't like it," said Lehzen. "It's his doing, have no doubt."

"I know, but why?" Liza asked.

"Hush."

The Baroness pressed her ear to the door. Without hesitation, Liza did the same. Victoria and the Duchess were arguing loudly.

"Mama!" Victoria cried. "Why isn't Signore Lablache coming?"

"We have decided—" It was impossible to mistake the Duchess's strident tone.

"You mean Sir John has decreed!"

"You're so emotional lately. Some discipline will be good for you, especially now the King is so ill."

"Any more discipline and I might as well be in jail!"

Liza and the Baroness exchanged knowing glances.

"Jail, indeed. Victoria, don't be so melodramatic."

The strain of keeping her temper made Victoria's voice quaver. "I'm not permitted to leave the Palace. We have no visitors, not even family. I have no friends. My 'amusements' are the only thing that make life worth living. And you have stripped them from me one by one."

"Nonsense, Victoria," said the Duchess. "We're protecting you. Of course, if you listened to reason, you could have your amusements back again."

"You mean, if I do what Sir John demands, I'll get my music lessons back?"

"Is it so much to ask? After all, you wouldn't extend the regency, despite the obvious advantages to you. And you ungratefully refused to appoint Sir John as your private secretary—something he had counted on particularly. The least you can do is name him keeper of the privy purse."

"The keeper of the privy purse spends the Queen's money. And it is so much money! I can't give the office to someone I don't trust." Victoria's voice changed, became softer, but bitter too. "He's just an employee, Mama. I'm your daughter. Why won't you take my side?"

"Sir John has been my dearest friend for the past eighteen years. Ever since your father died, he is the only man I can depend on. You're a selfish child not to reward him."

"He's horrid to me! And my own mother does nothing to stop it!"

Liza had heard a dozen versions of this argument in the past week alone. So far, Victoria had refused to give Sir John what he wanted, but it was taking a toll on her health. She wasn't sleeping and she ate too many sweets. Her normally clear skin was spotted with blemishes.

Liza sighed. If only the Duchess would listen to her daughter, truly listen. Victoria only wanted to be loved. If the Duchess became her champion, Victoria would be generosity itself. Liza indulged in a memory of her own mother, perched in her favorite armchair, her blue eyes fixed on Liza's face, concentrating on what mattered to her daughter.

The Duchess said, "I'll be staying with the Duchess of Northumberland in town for a few days."

"Why can't I come too?"

"You shall stay here and think about your lack of gratitude." Her loud footsteps approached the door. Liza backed away, dragging the Baroness with her. The Duchess stopped in the open doorway and said meaningfully, "I'll come home when you have seen reason."

The Duchess started when she saw Liza and the Baroness.

"Lehzen," the Duchess said, peering at the Baroness. "Pack your things. You will accompany me to town." Without waiting for a reply, her heels click-clacked down the hallway. The long feathers on her hat bobbed as she walked away.

The Baroness clasped her hands and pressed them against her mouth. *"Mein Gott.* She won't let us return until the Princess agrees."

"What can we do?" Liza asked.

"I have no choice but to go with Her Grace," Lehzen whispered fiercely. "Sir John is growing desperate—it is up to you to protect Victoria. Don't leave her side!"

"What if he . . . threatens me?" asked Liza.

"Better you should suffer than Victoria," the Baroness said, deadly earnest. She squeezed Liza's hands tight, then followed the Duchess.

Liza slipped into the room. The afternoon sun shone through the windows, but Victoria had sunk into a chair in the darkest corner of the room. With her pale complexion and the dark smudges of fatigue around her eyes, she looked like a wraith.

Without looking at Liza, Victoria said, "She boasts of sacrificing everything for me. But she won't protect me against him."

"Sir John is a subtle enemy," Liza answered. "He has poisoned the Duchess's mind for so long, she doesn't see what he's doing. Just hold on a little bit longer."

"It can't be long, I know. If only Uncle King would finish dying!" Victoria inhaled sharply. "Listen to me! They've turned me into a monster."

"Not at all, Victoria. You can't help the circumstances. The moment King William dies, their power over you is gone forever."

"But what if the King doesn't die for months? I'm so tired!" Victoria's eyes welled up with tears. "Perhaps I should just give in.

Appoint him and be done with it." She slumped even lower in her chair.

Liza knelt at the Princess's feet. "Victoria, don't let them beat you." She held the Princess's hands tightly between her own.

"There is so much money—what does it matter if he takes some?"

Liza considered her words carefully. She had her own score to settle with Sir John, but she also knew how important this moment would be to Victoria in the future. "If you give in now, when you are so close to winning, that failure will be with you all your life."

"Now who is being melodramatic?" Victoria emphasized the syllables of the last word just as her mother did. "Why should I give up Signore Lablache?"

"Will you trade your honor for a singing lesson?"

Victoria pulled her hands away and gave Liza a sour look. "You make me sound so frivolous."

The sound of carriage wheels echoed up to them from the courtyard below. Both girls went to the window and watched as the Duchess was handed into the carriage. The Baroness stepped into the carriage slowly, and once settled, she twisted her body to look up at the sitting room windows.

Victoria lifted a hand in a forlorn gesture of farewell. The girls watched the carriage drive away, a small cloud of dust blowing behind the wheels. Victoria stood there long after the carriage had disappeared over the hill into the park.

"I told the Queen everything," said Victoria.

Liza glanced sharply at the Princess. "How?"

"I was very cunning. I hid the letter amongst some of my mother's." Victoria sighed. "I can't imagine why no one has come to help me."

Liza had often seen Sir John glance at each letter before handing them to Simon to post. A letter in Victoria's handwriting, addressed to a powerful relative, would have alerted a man far less calculating than Sir John. Liza would wager her precious hoard of sovereigns that the letter had been destroyed.

Why didn't Victoria ask me to post the letter for her?

"What's going to happen now?" asked Victoria in a low voice.

"Sir John will come to persuade you. That's why your mother left." For Victoria's sake, Liza wished she could think better of the Duchess. "He's dismissed the servants too. We're alone."

Just as Liza was beginning to panic at the forces aligned against them, Victoria suddenly took heart.

"I am a Hanover, descended from kings!" She began pacing, her strides growing stronger and more resolute with each step. "I won't be afraid of him any longer."

"Victoria, he's out of time and he's desperate," warned Liza.

"You are so defeatist, Liza."

"Just in case, Victoria," Liza said. "We should have a signal if you want me to get help."

"You said everyone is gone."

"The footman, Simon, is still here. And the porter is outside. I'll find someone."

"Very well, if I touch my brooch like this . . ." Victoria put her fingers to a cameo brooch of her dead father. "Then get help. But not before."

"Perhaps I should go now," Liza suggested. "Just to be safe?"

"No, Liza. And that's an order. The future Queen of Britain must prove herself."

23

In Which Liza Finds
Flash Patter a Useful
Language to Know

TWO HOURS LATER, Victoria's resolution was not so steady. She fidgeted and paced and talked to herself. "When will he come?" she cried. "I'd rather face Sir John than this interminable waiting!"

As though she had made a bargain with the devil, the door swung open and he appeared. There was a new tension about him, like a coiled spring.

This man might do anything.

"Your Highness," said Sir John. "I hope I didn't startle you?"

"Sir John," said Victoria, inclining her head.

His eyes narrowed when he saw Liza. "Leave. The Princess does not require you."

Victoria held up her hand. "Please don't give orders to my maid."

"I need to speak to you privately." There was an edge to his charming brogue. "Send her away."

"It wouldn't be seemly for me to be alone with a gentleman, even one so devoted to my mother." Victoria's voice was laden with delicate innuendo.

Liza's eyebrows rose.

"So I am," he said. The muscles in his face tightened. "I am also devoted to you."

"You've always said the heir must be above reproach," Victoria said. "My maid stays."

Liza deliberately stepped nearer to the Princess.

His lips curved in a half smile, Sir John gave in. "As you wish. We shall speak German to be private."

Victoria glanced at Liza and then gave a slight nod to Sir John. He walked to the side table and poured himself a glass of brandy.

"You see how tedious your life can be, if I choose to make it so," he said in German.

"Really?" said Victoria. "I hadn't noticed."

"I'm sure that's not true." Sir John searched her face. "The little Princess is lost without her opera and her amusements!"

"While Uncle King is so ill, it's appropriate I am in seclusion—I don't want to seem heartless."

Liza couldn't help smiling at the Princess's apt answer. Sir John scowled and Liza made her face blank.

"Soon you will be Queen," he said. "You've refused a regent, so you will be burdened by thousands of decisions. Without a private secretary, you will be overwhelmed with paper. As keeper of your privy purse, I can relieve you of some of your onerous responsibilities." The vein beside his left eye was throbbing.

"Sir John, I wouldn't think of imposing on you." Victoria's chin tilted up, but her hands clenched and unclenched, like a cat unsheathing its claws. Liza moved so Victoria could see her.

"Before his death, your father promised me I would have the post." Sir John's voice grew silkier.

Liza held her breath and waited; Victoria was foolishly sentimental about her father.

"Eighteen years ago," Victoria said thoughtfully. "I'm not certain my father would approve of your attentions to my mother since then."

Well done, Victoria!

Sir John frowned slightly.

Victoria went on, "You are a charming man and my mother is still a handsome woman. The situation was inevitable, I suppose."

Sir John looked at her with fresh eyes. He had neither credited Victoria with the will to fight him, nor that her mother's conduct would be her choice of weapon. "You're bluffing. You'd never expose your mother to scandal."

Victoria sniffed. "I've been sorely tried."

"You wouldn't do it." His voice was confident.

They stared at each other. Victoria looked away first.

"I thought not," he said with satisfaction. "Appoint me to the post, and I shall forget you said it."

Victoria considered for a moment, putting her finger alongside her nose. Then she smiled sweetly. "I'll see you in hell first, Sir John."

Liza watched Sir John's hands. She didn't think he would forget himself so far to strike Victoria.

But has Victoria ever been so brave before?

"In your situation," he said, delicately accenting the final word, "you would do better not to offend me."

"My situation?"

"I control Kensington Palace: what quarters you have, whether the cook takes a holiday, if you have any company. No one will question my orders."

"My mother . . ."

"Has given me *carte blanche.*"

Victoria's face blanched. "My uncles . . ." she said faintly.

Sir John pressed his advantage. "Your Uncle the King is practically dead—he can't protect you. And your correspondence with your other relatives has been intercepted."

Victoria sank into a chair.

"Now you see my plan." Sir John went on. "This past year, I've cut you off from your social and family connections. It will be weeks before anyone realizes you are *incommunicado.*" He refilled his glass.

Liza stared at the cameo on Victoria's dress, her anxiety growing. Why didn't Victoria signal for help? Like a bird mesmerized by a snake, Victoria sat paralyzed by Sir John's scheming.

"There is no one to care what happens here . . . or to you," continued Sir John. He downed the glass of liquor in one gulp.

"It's not true!" Liza said loudly, hoping to pierce Victoria's trance. "The Princess has powerful friends." Only after the words flew out of her mouth, did Liza realize she had spoken in German.

Dismay flooded Victoria's face. Liza inhaled sharply.

"*Sprechen Sie Deutsch?*" Sir John started toward Liza, and she could see he was remembering all his indiscretions in her presence. "You're a filthy spy!" he said. His fist swung out and smashed Liza's face; his signet ring cutting her cheek. Her body reeled with the impact, and she fell against the mantle. Blood trickled down her cheek and dripped onto the coal scuttle.

"Liza!" cried Victoria.

Sir John stared down at Liza's prone body. "I should have gotten rid of you long ago."

"Stop hurting her," ordered Victoria. She ran to the door and called, "Help! Help!"

Abandoning Liza, Sir John caught up to Victoria in a few strides. He grabbed her arm. "I've sent everyone away." He pulled her back into the room and kicked the door shut.

Victoria stood stock still, staring at Sir John's hand on her arm. Behind them, Liza staggered to her feet, her face throbbing. She didn't take her eyes off Victoria.

"Princess, do what I want and this ends," said Sir John. His fingers tightened around the flesh above Victoria's elbow.

"No, I won't do it," said Victoria. Tears streamed down her face. To Liza's relief, Victoria lifted her hand to touch her cameo. Liza edged her way along the wall, toward the door.

Sir John murmured persuasively, "Write the letter and everything returns to what it was."

Victoria spoke to keep Sir John's attention. "Once I am Queen, I'll tell everyone what you have done." She avoided looking in Liza's direction.

"It will be my word, and your mother's, against that of a hysterical young girl," he sneered. "Don't you read the newspapers? Everyone thinks you are an imbecile. If you start making wild accusations, Parliament just might insist your mother be named regent after all."

Sir John's entire attention focused on the Princess. Liza took her chance. She felt the doorknob behind her back. She turned it, and slipped out of the room. She ran downstairs to the servant's hall.

Simon sat on a bench, his shirt loosened at the collar. He was drinking a large glass of ale.

"Simon!" she called. "Come, we need you."

He sprang up, wiping the foam from his mouth with the back of his hand. "Liza, what's the matter? What happened to your face?"

Liza touched the wetness on her cheek. "Never mind. The Princess is in danger."

"Take me there," he said simply.

Taking comfort in Simon's powerful build, Liza hurried back to the schoolroom. The tableau had not changed: Sir John still gripped the Princess's arm.

Sir John glanced up. "Good work, I was afraid the maid might cause trouble."

Liza stared at Sir John, afraid to think of what his words meant. Slowly she turned and saw Simon standing in front of the closed door. Guarding it for Sir John.

"Simon?" Her voice faltered.

"Liza, I'll have to ask you not to interfere with Sir John again." Simon looked through her, as though she was a total stranger.

Everything fell into place. Now Liza understood how Sir John knew so quickly about Annie's death. She shivered realizing she and the Princess were alone except for their enemies.

Sir John's scornful voice broke the silence. "This is all very touching—but I have more important concerns. Victoria, there will be no cavalry coming to the rescue. Write the letter."

"No, Victoria—don't write anything," cried Liza. "He can't force you!"

"Can't you control the wench?" Sir John asked Simon irritably. Simon grabbed hold of Liza and placed his beefy hand over her mouth. Liza thrashed under his grip, but he was like a block of stone.

Victoria seemed to have found her courage with Liza's words. "I'll be Queen any day now. To hurt me would be high treason. You don't dare."

"You have no idea what I will dare, Princess," said Sir John. "Simon!"

Simon stirred uneasily. "I won't hurt the Princess," he said.

"We don't have to," said Sir John with a wicked smile. "The Princess is vulnerable in a way I hadn't considered." He dragged Victoria to the desk in the corner. "Oh foolish Little Woman. Always looking for someone to love. Even a maid. I never dreamed it would be so useful."

Liza saw his meaning first and her heart sank. She clawed at Simon's hand with all her might, but he was too strong.

"You don't mean . . ." Victoria said, her eyes darting toward Liza. Sir John pushed her down in the chair.

"You aren't as stupid as I told everyone you were. I can't hurt you, but who cares about your maid? Girls like her disappear every day. Look at the last one."

Liza knew Sir John meant every word. Her life was worth nothing to him. But Victoria could purchase it back, at a steep price. Liza stopped struggling—she didn't want to be the cause of Victoria's surrender.

Slowly, Victoria asked, "What do you want?"

"Six months as the keeper of the privy purse."

"Can you steal enough in half a year?" Victoria asked with bitterness in her voice.

"I'm not greedy."

"And after six months?"

"I shall leave. We need never see each other again."

Sir John began rummaging in the desk, but could find no paper. "Damnation!" he exclaimed. "What kind of schoolroom doesn't have paper?" He hauled Victoria out of her chair and headed to the Duchess's sitting room next door. Simon followed, dragging Liza along.

What can I do to help her? And myself?

Sir John pushed Victoria into the Duchess's desk chair. He dipped the quill into the inkwell and pressed it into Victoria's limp hand.

"It must be entirely in your handwriting," he said.

The Princess looked over at Liza. Under Simon's hand, Liza's eyes entreated Victoria not to do it. Victoria winked at Liza, and poised her hand over the page, ready to write.

Sir John dictated, "'I, the Royal Highness Victoria Kent, hereby appoint Sir John Conroy to be the keeper of my privy purse on the occasion of my accession to the Crown. I swear he shall occupy this post for six months. I make this oath in grateful appreciation of' "

Victoria made a gagging noise in her throat.

Sir John scowled. "Keep writing, girl."

"I can't write that."

Sir John placed his hand on Victoria's shoulder. Liza could see the marks where his fingers pressed against the bone. Victoria winced and began to write again.

"'In grateful appreciation of his years of dedicated service and selfless devotion to my person.' Now sign it."

The Princess penned her neat signature to the letter. Liza watched, puzzled. What did Victoria think she was doing?

Brushing her aside, Sir John blotted the letter and held it up to the light from the window. Like a figure from a pantomime, his satisfaction turned to rage.

"I hereby do *not* appoint Sir John—did you really think I wouldn't read it through?"

Victoria slumped in her chair, crushed at the failure of her stratagem.

Liza's mind was working frantically.

I've only got one advantage. How can I use it?

Sir John crumpled the false letter in his hand. "Take the girl away," ordered Sir John. "My business with the Princess is better done without witnesses."

"Where?" Simon asked.

"There's a box room on the far side of the cupola room. No one will hear anything there." He reached in his pocket and threw a set of keys to Simon, who caught it with his left hand.

Liza took her chance and wrenched her mouth away from Simon's other hand. "Boy!" she cried. "Simon's a Tartar. He's earwig with the bark. If you can, undub the jigger to the crib and save my bacon. But if you can't, blow the gab to Will."

"What is the wench blathering about?" Sir John said. "I must have hit her harder than I thought."

"Who are you talking to?" Simon asked, tightening his hold on Liza's arms.

"Get her out of here!" Sir John commanded.

"What are you going to do to her?" cried Victoria.

"I won't hurt her—if you do as I ask. No more tricks."

With Victoria's defeated eyes following her, Simon hauled Liza out of the room. She hoped Inside Boy had received her message.

Simon dragged her down the corridors to the cupola room. The tall windows looked out on a world of safety and normalcy as remote to her present circumstances as Kashmir. He lifted his hand from Liza's mouth; there was no one to hear her cry out.

"You're despicable, Simon," Liza said coldly.

Simon snorted. "After Conroy makes me a gentleman, no maid will ever turn her nose up at me again." A spasm twisted his face. Liza wondered she'd never seen how dangerous he was.

"He's a monster and you're no better."

"I do as I'm told, just like you," Simon said stolidly.

"So when you helped me that day, with Annie—"

"Just looking out for my employer's interests."

Liza stared at him, feeling sick as she reconsidered that awful day. The figure of Annie backing away on the platform—backing away from what? Perhaps that old woman had seen more clearly than Liza had: was Annie pushed?

"You killed her! She was a threat to Sir John. And not just about the baby. She knew something damaging about him, perhaps even had proof. He faced ruin if she talked to me." If her suspicions were correct, then Liza had contributed to Annie's death, as surely as Sir John and Simon had.

"Perhaps she fell." Simon's grin dared her to prove his guilt.

"What did she know?"

"Let's just say that Sir John hasn't been as scrupulous with the Duchess's accounts as he might have been," Simon said. "You'd think Conroy would be grateful. But no, he was furious you found out about the baby. Any scandal does Sir John no good. Especially when you managed to get it in the newspaper!"

Oh Will! I promise I'll listen to you next time.

They reached the box room. Simon unlocked the door and opened it into darkness.

"It's your last chance," he said. "If you cared to be more obliging, I might leave you with a candle."

Liza spat at him. He looked down at the spittle dripping down his livery.

"You shouldn't have done that," he said in a calm voice but his eyes burned with fury. Liza backed away from him, into the darkness of the box room.

"Nobody to hear you, Miss High and Mighty. You think you're so much better than the rest of us. Where are all your airs now?"

He shoved her against the wall and grabbed the back of her head. In a shower of pins, her hair came down from its bun. He bent his head to kiss her, his thick lips pressed against hers.

"Help!" Liza cried, pushing him away with all her strength. She scratched his face, drawing blood. "Help me!"

She drew breath to scream again—afraid it was hopeless. Then at the door, she saw a shadow. Simon began to turn. A heavy iron poker came crashing down on his head. Simon fell to the floor.

Liza looked into the light. Inside Boy stood there with a wide smile plastered over his grimy face.

24

In Which Liza Dons a Peculiar Outfit to Rescue the Princess

LIZA STEADIED HERSELF against the wall. "Thank you, Boy."

"I got your message," Inside Boy said. "You're a quick study, Miss. You patter flash like you was born to it. Lucky for us, Simon came from the country. 'e don't know the first thing about flash."

She nudged Simon's unconscious body with the toe of her boot.

"Where is the Princess?"

"Crying in her room. I thought you needed my 'elp more."

Recalling the pressure of Simon's lips, Liza nodded. "We have to help Victoria now." She started to leave, but Inside Boy's hand on her sleeve stopped her.

"What about 'im?" He delivered a sharp kick to Simon's posterior. "Can't we lock the door?"

Inside Boy shook his head. "This room would've 'eld you—but 'e's a mite stronger. Let's tie 'im up."

Liza rummaged around the box room shelves filled with old livery and moth-eaten curtains. A shiver ran across her body thinking of being imprisoned in this tiny space. "This will do," she said, holding up the scarlet velvet ties from the curtains.

"Too fine for the likes of 'im," said Inside Boy, taking the makeshift rope to wind around Simon's unconscious frame. "I know a back way to the Princess. But Miss Liza, maybe you should change your dress first," Inside Boy said.

Liza looked down at her dusty skirt. "What does it matter?" she said.

"I was thinking about the livery," he said, pointing at a pile of page's uniforms. "No one 'ill be looking for a couple of boys."

"I couldn't!"

"Desperate times call for desperate measures."

Liza stared at the boy's breeches and dark green tailored coat. Holding it up to her shoulders, she thought it might fit perfectly.

———

Inside Boy's "back way" was a maze of tunnels inside the walls of the Palace, which he navigated like an experienced rodent. The passage was scarcely wide enough for Liza to crawl through on her knees. Thank goodness for the Duchess's livery; Liza couldn't imagine making this journey in her skirts.

Grates let in air and light every fifteen feet or so. Liza recognized some of the rooms. Now she understood how Inside Boy could overhear so much. But then they made a few turns and she was hopelessly lost.

Trust Inside Boy.

He had rescued her; now they would rescue Victoria.

If only I could see!

"Can't we have a light?" she whispered.

"The grates open into the public rooms—a candle is just begging to be caught."

"The Palace is empty," Liza pointed out.

"Better safe than sorry," came Inside Boy's voice.

Just when she thought her knees might give out, Inside Boy stopped. "We're 'ere."

"Here" was a metal grate. Liza looked through into the pitch-black room. Victoria's sobs filled the dark space.

Liza shoved at the grate, but it was screwed to the wall.

"Who's there?"

"Victoria, it's Liza."

"Are you dead? Liza, are you a ghost?" Victoria's voice rose in hysterics. "I tried to save you!"

Liza clenched her fists.

Sir John has much to answer for.

"Calm yourself, Victoria," she said. "I'm alive and I'm here to save you."

"Where are you?" Some of the terror left Victoria's voice. "I've never been alone in the dark before."

"Victoria, I'll be right there." Liza whispered to Inside Boy, "I can't open the grate."

"'old on, let me help." She heard him grunting and muttering as he turned himself around like a contortionist. Liza pushed with both hands while he shoved hard with his feet against the metal grate. One of the fasteners popped off.

"Boy, it's working!" whispered Liza.

Another kick and the grate fell to the floor. Victoria cried out at the noise. Liza fell a few inches into the room.

"Ouch," she said, rubbing her elbow where she had landed. "Victoria?"

"Here," came a muffled voice. "Sir John locked the shutters. And he took the candles away."

"Did he take the lantern too?" Liza asked.

"I don't know how to light it."

Inside Boy made a rude noise.

"What was that sound?" Victoria called out.

"Shhh," hissed Liza in Inside Boy's direction. Of course Victoria couldn't light a lantern; Princesses were not encouraged to do anything practical. She felt her way to the shelves.

"Liza, don't leave me!" Victoria cried.

"I'm lighting the lantern." Liza felt along the shelf for the box of lucifers.

"Mother doesn't like to use it; she says the oily smoke leaves marks on the ceiling."

"With all due respect, Your Highness," said Liza. "Your mother can—"

"Stick it up her arse!" chimed in Inside Boy.

"Who's that?"

"You've met Mr. Jones," Liza said soothingly. "That day in the park."

A lifetime ago.

Liza struck the bulb of phosphorus at the end of the lucifer against the rough edge of the box. The first one didn't light. The second one flamed quickly, throwing out sparks and Liza almost dropped it. Holding it high, she lit the paraffin lantern. The wick flared and bathed the room with ghostly luminescence. The Princess was huddled against her headboard, the coverlet around her shoulders. Her pale face was the only visible part of her body.

Liza gestured to Inside Boy to wait. She put her arm around Victoria and rubbed her back until the Princess stopped shaking.

"I signed his letter. I imagined terrible things were happening to you," sobbed Victoria. But then her back straightened and she peered at Liza. "But you aren't hurt at all. Did I give away the treasury for nothing?"

Smiling at the return of the old Victoria, Liza said, "I got away, with Inside Boy's help."

"What on earth are you wearing, Liza? It looks like my mother's livery."

Inside Boy pantomimed looking at a watch.

"Why is he in such a hurry?" asked Victoria with her usual imperiousness. "Does he have somewhere to go?"

Inside Boy stepped forward. "I'm sorry for your troubles, Your 'ighness," he said, with a deep bow. "I'm 'ere to give you an escape route, a road we must take right soon."

Victoria got up and extended her hand. "Mr. Jones, thank you for your efforts. But I won't run away."

"Are you a bloomin' idiot?" he asked, then he caught himself. "Sorry, Princess."

"Victoria, we must get you to safety," said Liza.

"No," Victoria said loudly. "The future Queen of Britain is not going to flee her own home."

Boy and Liza looked at each other helplessly.

"Victoria," began Liza. "Sir John is a desperate man. He can't turn back now."

"He has what he wants." Victoria sat at her dressing table and began to brush her hair with carefully controlled strokes. "But Liza, you are in danger. You must leave. You can fetch help for me."

"I won't go without you," Liza replied, determined to protect the Princess.

"You have to. Go to the King at Windsor or better yet, to the Queen, she knows you."

"I can't just walk into Windsor Castle and demand to see the Queen," Liza said.

"I'll give you a token." Victoria went to her jewelry box and pulled out a dark blue velvet garter, with gold lettering across it. "Only the royal family and trusted advisers have the Order of the Garter. Trust me, you'll be admitted."

Liza took the garter and held it up to the light. Her fingers traced the lettering: *Honi soit qui mal y pense*. Shame upon him who thinks evil of it.

"Take it, Liza," said Victoria. "The Queen will make sure we're safe."

Inside Boy's patience was running out. "Can we go now?" he asked. "Or do you two want to chatter some more?"

Liza said, "Victoria, you must hide until I can bring help."

"But where?" Victoria asked.

"I know just the place," Liza said with a mischievous twinkle in her eyes.

Inside Boy needed only a scant second to appreciate the joke. "Sir John will never look for her there," he agreed.

"Where? Liza, what are you two talking about?" asked Victoria.

"You'll have to come with us, Victoria," Liza said.

"Through the walls? Are you mad?" said the Princess. She peered into the opening in the wall. "Where does it lead?"

"There are passages all through the Palace," Inside Boy explained. "Don't know why. Maybe to catch rats. Or maybe servants used to be smaller."

"Just how are you so familiar with the inside of my house?" asked Victoria peering closer at Boy.

Liza smothered a giggle. For once, Boy had no words. "Liza, douse the glimm and let's go." He ducked into the narrow opening and disappeared into the wall. Liza extinguished the lamp, and she and Victoria followed.

Later, Liza would make light of the journey through the walls with the Princess, but in reality, it was nightmarish. Sandwiched between Inside Boy and Liza and crawling on her hands and knees in the dark tried every nerve the Princess had left. Liza bit her lip and counted to ten more than once, trying to keep her temper, and gently encouraged Victoria whenever she lost her courage.

Finally they arrived in the Duchess's sitting room. The three sat on the floor, stretching their cramped muscles.

"Your 'idey 'ole, Your 'ighness," said Inside Boy, opening his box for Victoria. "You'll 'ave all the comforts of 'ome."

"Home indeed." Victoria was stunned. "How long have you lived here? The things you must have heard!" She examined the contents of the box. "This is my blanket. I wondered where it went to. And are these my mother's caramels?"

Liza giggled at the blush blooming across Inside Boy's face. "Princess," she said. "Sir John will be looking for us. You have to get out of sight."

"Can you get me something to drink?" Victoria asked. "I'm parched after that awful tunnel."

Boy gave her a crooked look. "Princess, take it from me, my nest lacks certain . . . amenities."

Victoria's eyes widened as she took his meaning.

"I'll bring help as soon as I can," Liza promised Victoria.

"Oh, Liza, please hurry!" Victoria hesitated, then embraced Liza with both arms. She nodded to Inside Boy and climbed into the box.

"Don't forget to lock it," Inside Boy said.

She nodded and pulled the door down over her head. Inside Boy and Liza listened carefully for the sound of the bolt being shot into place. They both felt an enormous burden lift with the Princess safely hidden.

"How shall we go to Windsor?" he asked.

Liza shook her head. "You would never be allowed to see the Queen. You have to stay here, Boy, and look after Victoria."

He grimaced. What could Inside Boy do against Simon and Sir John? "I'll try." He paused. "After what you did for Annie—I owe you." His voice had became rougher.

"I couldn't save her," said Liza.

"Once she had made up her mind, no one could save her." Tears welled up in his eyes, to be struck away by the back of his dirty hand.

Liza hesitated, but Boy had the right to know. "She might not have jumped. I think Annie was running away from Simon. He may even have pushed her—"

Boy's face reddened and he formed a fist with one hand and hit the wall. "I should have hit him harder."

Inside the wood box, Victoria yelped at the pounding.

"Princess, you mustn't make a sound," Liza warned.

"Are you sure I won't run out of air?" asked the Princess's muffled voice.

"Stow it, your 'ighness," Boy ordered.

"Very well," Victoria said meekly.

"When I bring help," Liza said, "Simon will get his comeuppance. You can be sure of that." Liza grabbed Boy's arm. "Now, promise you'll keep the Princess safe."

Boy's face had hardened with hatred, but he relented when he saw Liza's distraught expression. "I promise."

Liza twisted her long hair up in a knot and tucked it under the page's cap. Her black shoes could pass for a boy's. Victoria's garter was tucked inside her coat. "How do I get out?" she asked.

"Crikey, Miss, it ain't 'ard. Come with me." He led the way through the Palace's empty hallways to the Duchess's morning room. He pointed to the window. "See, it's got a broke latch, and it opens next to a strong tree. Shin down the tree and bob's yer uncle."

Liza looked down. She was fifteen feet off the ground but the tree was within reach. "Really, Miss. It's easy," Inside Boy said.

"I'll manage."

Inside Boy gave her a short mock bow and opened the window. He helped her step out onto the ledge. She held out her hand to the nearest bough, said a prayer, and pulled herself into the air. Her feet found purchase and with no long skirt to hamper her, she climbed down the tree as easily as she might a ladder. Once she reached the safety of the ground, she wanted to leap in the air. Not only her person had been liberated, but her body too.

Boys' clothes are so comfortable.

The sound of men talking brought her back to her mission. It was two grooms from the stable. She pressed her body against the tree, grateful the Duchess's livery was a dark color.

"'tis a bother to be searchin' the garden for a lady's maid instead of muckin' out the stables as we ought," one said.

"I don't believe Miss 'astings stole from the Duchess. She's a lady, she is," the other said. "And I don't 'alf like taking orders from Simon Gooding."

"Did you see the bandage on his 'ead?"

"Aye, and the scratches on 'is face. If the maid did that, I'm not surprised 'e's looking so murderous," his companion replied. "God 'elp 'er if 'e gets his 'ands on 'er."

So, Simon was free and Sir John had recruited the stable lads to search for her. Since there were no guards at Kensington Palace, Sir John's resources were limited. A phrase of her father's came to mind: "Penny wise and pound foolish." Sir John and the Duchess might regret their cheeseparing on the Princess's security.

Easily avoiding the grooms, Liza made her way to the stable. As she had hoped, it was almost empty. Only an ancient groom, who had served the royal family for decades, was on duty.

Carefully lowering her voice, and adding a bit of gravel to it for good measure, Liza said, "The Duchess has sent me for her daughter's mare, Rosa."

"At this hour?" The old man peered at her through his rheumy eyes. "You must be new," he said.

"I just entered Her Grace's service," Liza said, smiling to herself.

Minutes later, the groom had saddled Rosa and handed the reins to Liza. She led the horse to the mounting block. Just as she was about to get onto Rosa sidesaddle, Liza remembered her disguise; she had to ride astride, not sidesaddle. Before the clock struck six o'clock, she was galloping into the setting sun toward Windsor. She had an urgent message for the Queen of England.

25

In Which Liza Negotiates with Sir John

THE TOWN CLOCK RANG OUT the nine o'clock hour as Liza finally rode up the spiral road leading to Windsor Castle. The temperature had dropped since she had left Kensington and her ice-cold hands made unclenching her fingers from the reins painful. She had never ridden so long or so hard and knew her body would be sore tomorrow.

When she made the final turn to enter the tower gates of the castle, Liza's jaw dropped. She had become used to the scale of poor, dilapidated Kensington Palace, so the King's glorious stone castle dazzled her. A round tower dominated the sky, rising above the medieval ramparts. The royal standard flew to tell the world the King was home.

"Halt." A sentry stepped in front of Rosa and held up his hand. "What is your business?"

Dressed in the Duchess's livery, it would be simpler if the guard assumed she was a boy. Liza kept her voice low and rough. "I've a message for the Queen from Kensington Palace."

"She's praying for the King. You'll have to wait until morning," said the guard. "Move on, boy."

Liza pulled out the garter from inside her coat and held it out to the guard. "I've a token from the Princess Victoria," she announced. "It is vital I see Her Majesty."

His eyes widened and he stood at attention. "You can go into the chapel."

That's some token.

Outside, the courtyard glowed with the light of gas lanterns. But when she entered the church, Liza's eyes needed a moment to adjust to the dimness. The only light came from iron candelabrum illuminating the nave at intervals. Liza made her way into the center of the nave and despite her worries for the Princess, she couldn't help but stare upward into the space above her. There were no pillars to support the wide roof—just an intricate system of stone vaulting, as if only God's grace held it up. There was no sign of Queen Adelaide.

Suddenly, by a trick of sound or architecture, she could hear a murmuring. Then it was gone. She moved past the huge organ in the center of the nave and found herself in a doorway between two great, throne-like chairs. Along the walls were rows of wooden seats. A crest and a pole hung above each seat, and armored helmets perched on each pole. Liza read the motto, *Honi soit qui mal y pense,* on the chapel's walls, chairs, tapestries—no one could mistake this room for anything but the chapel of the Knights of Garter.

Tonight I'm a Knight too.

The Queen knelt on a wooden prie-dieu in front of the altar. Her silhouette against the colored stained glass was a portrait of quiet tragedy. Statues of angels peered down from the upper windows, chiding Liza for disturbing the Queen's prayers.

Poor Queen hausfrau. *Away from her homeland, no children, and now her husband lay dying. She was alone.*

Not even for Victoria would Liza interrupt Queen Adelaide at such a moment.

While she waited, Liza let the serenity of the chapel wash over her. She wished her mother could see this place. When they visited a new city, the first two places they went were the cathedral and the opera. Mama had said one could worship God in both places. Liza closed her eyes and sent a prayer heavenward to her parents.

"Young man, why are you intruding on my prayers?" A forbidding voice at her elbow said.

Liza's eyes flew open. "Your Majesty." She quickly curtsied. Then realizing her mistake, she bowed like the page she was dressed to be. She was lucky not to trip over her feet.

The Queen, dressed in a blue silk dress, a dark shawl wrapped around her shoulders, was scowling. But then she looked a little closer at Liza's face under her page's cap and smiled.

"Aren't you Victoria's girl?" The Queen stressed the word 'girl.'

Liza nodded.

"You look adorable, my dear." Her rabbit eyes, soft and brown, blinked at Liza's ensemble. "Are you helping the Princess with a theatrical?"

"The Princess is in trouble. She needs your help."

Queen Adelaide seemed to shrink. "Come into the Palace." She led Liza through a private door, into a passageway that led into a long paneled hallway within the castle. Waiting at the door were two ladies. Their eyes were full of curiosity about Liza, but they fell in behind the Queen without saying a word. The procession wound up an imposing staircase which led to a long gallery hung with large portraits of Napoleonic War heroes. Except for their own muffled footsteps, Liza did not hear another sound in the castle. After many more twists and turns, through doors opened and closed behind them by royal guards, Liza, the Queen, and the ladies in waiting came to a sumptuous sitting room. Liza glanced around curiously. The carpet was a rich silk oriental in muted shades of green and blue. There were overstuffed velvet chairs scattered about the room. The turquoise curtains at the windows completed the color scheme.

So this is what a royal palace should look like.

Although Liza was fidgeting with impatience, the Queen insisted on ordering tea.

"Now, tell me all about it," the Queen spoke in German, reminding Liza of their first meeting.

In a cocoon of soft green velvet, sipping fine China tea, Liza told the Queen everything. "Oh my goodness," said the Queen when Liza was finished. "This is appalling. I never thought Sir John would dare lay hands on the Princess, nor that her mother would permit it."

"He's not lost to all reason," Liza admitted. "Even when Sir John was most angry, he hurt me instead." The cut on her cheek still throbbed.

"You are not there to be her whipping boy, I mean girl, now," the Queen pointed out.

"No, I'm not," Liza said ruefully.

"Are you sure she is safe?"

Thinking of Victoria tucked away in a wood box, Liza half-smiled, "She's well hidden."

Queen Adelaide spoke. "This will put the King in such a temper, and he's not at all well tonight." She lifted herself out of her comfortable chair. Liza leapt to her feet. The Queen paused at the door. "Liza, I know you have had a long and frightening day. I'll order your horse fed and I'll send my ladies to attend you."

Liza curtsied gratefully until the Queen's steps faded. As she rose, the weight of her fear and fatigue pressed heavy on her body. One of the Queen's ladies bustled in, flanked by two maids. Liza happily let them lead her to a bathroom. She wriggled in delight when she saw the deep tub filled with steaming water, destined only for her. Liza lingered in the lavender-scented hot water as long as she dared, surrendering herself to the expert hands of the Queen's attendants as they washed her dusty hair. Clad in a fur-lined dressing gown, the maids combed and set her hair in a simple chignon. Then they helped her into a dark red silk gown with pale yellow trim. Looking in the mirror, Liza barely recognized herself. This was Miss Elizabeth Hastings, daughter of a knight, however minor.

What would Will think? Might he miss Liza the maid?

One of the Queen's ladies led her back to Her Majesty's boudoir to wait. After her exertions, the quiet and warmth proved irresistible. She was awakened by the Queen's hand at her shoulder.

Rubbing her eyes, Liza said, "Your Majesty. I do beg your pardon. What time is it?"

"It's almost three in the morning. I've spoken with the King. He and the Lord Chamberlain are drafting a letter for you to deliver to the Princess."

"You want me to go back there?" Liza swallowed hard. "Alone?"

"Lord Conyngham and a full complement of guards will accompany you. We've been sorely tried by that man." The Queen clucked in disapproval. "It ends today."

"But why me?"

"The King does not want the Princess's situation to be a subject of gossip. He wants to involve as few people as possible. Lord Conyngham will explain the details to you."

The Queen pulled a silky rope attached to the wall. Liza heard chimes ringing faintly elsewhere in the Castle. "The King's business will take some time. While we wait, tell me about yourself."

No matter how Liza wanted to rush back to Victoria, there was no hurrying the King. So she sat back and told Queen Adelaide the story of her life. About her parents' death. How she had to leave Claridge's and find a job. Even about spying for Victoria.

"I'm glad Victoria has a friend in her time of need." The Queen sighed. "She is like the child we never had."

With a thump in her chest, Liza remembered all the pain she and Victoria had caused. Queen Adelaide's kindness was too much for Liza's conscience. "Your Highness, I must confess something." Smoothing her new silk skirt, she told her story. "We tried to use the press against Sir John. My friend, Mr. Fulton, publishes broadsheets. We wrote a story Victoria might not inherit the crown."

The Queen became very still. "Because I might have a child?"

"Yes." Liza rushed on, "We're so sorry. We didn't think how it might hurt you. And we never expected Sir John to spread that awful story about your Lord Chamberlain." Feeling as though a heavy load had been lifted off her chest, Liza covered her face with her hands, afraid to look at the good Queen.

To her great surprise, she heard a gurgle. Peeping through her fingers, she saw the Queen was laughing, her mouth open and her head thrown back.

"To think, all this fuss was a prank of Victoria's!"

"Your Majesty?"

"Of course it was very naughty," the Queen said, wagging a finger at Liza. "But it's good to know Victoria is not all milquetoast and spun sugar."

"We never intended to cause you pain."

Adelaide patted her knee again. "I know. In the long run, there was no harm done." The Queen looked closer at Liza. "Don't look so stricken. You've confessed, which is good for your soul. I've forgiven you, which is good for mine. Victoria has learnt a lesson, which is good for the nation." A thought struck her. "Was Victoria also responsible for the tragic story about Sir John and the maid?"

"That was mine." Liza looked at the fine portrait above the fireplace, at the chandelier, at anything but the Queen. "And every word was true."

"I can't tell you how the King relished that one." The Queen's hand flew to her mouth. "Not the fate of the poor girl, of course, but Sir John's humiliation."

The maid arrived with a large tray and began to arrange the food on a small table.

"Now, eat something."

"Thank you, Ma'am." Liza's wits were befuddled. A few hours ago, she had feared for her life and virtue. Now, she was dining with the Queen!

Just as they finished their meal, Lord Conyngham, the King's Lord Chamberlain, appeared in the doorway. "Your Majesty, we are ready to go."

"Thank you, Lord Conyngham." The Queen rose. She held out her hand to Liza, a mark of favor. "The Princess is very dear to me. Take care of her."

Liza sank down in a curtsy and kissed the Queen's fingers. "Good luck, Miss Hastings."

———————

Lord Conyngham explained the King's instructions to Liza, then promptly fell asleep in the stifling carriage. Liza looked through the velvet curtains, wondering if she was brave enough to play the part the King had assigned to her.

The clock tower chimed six o'clock when the carriage wheels crunched the gravel in front of Kensington Palace. The sun's first rays were beginning to chase away the darkness. It was going to be a beautiful morning. Liza took note of the candles burning in every window of the Duchess's apartments. She imagined Sir John's frantic searching for Victoria and smiled.

Flanked by Lord Conyngham, Liza lifted the knocker. The door was opened by Simon, looking bedraggled with a bandage on his head. He glared at Liza, then silently led them to the vestibule, where Sir John awaited them. The Duchess of Kent, wearing the same dress from the day before, stood behind him, wringing her hands.

Lord Conyngham didn't waste time on civilities. "Conroy, I've heard about unpleasant goings-on here."

"Conyngham, I've no idea what you mean. We have been searching for this girl." With a dismissive gesture he indicated Liza. "She's been upsetting the Princess with her hysterics."

"Is that so?" Lord Conyngham drawled. "Where is Her Royal Highness?" He was enjoying Sir John's predicament.

"She's asleep, of course." Sir John gestured behind him. "Ask her mother."

"I wasn't aware you had returned home, Your Grace."

Liza watched the Duchess closely. She was Sir John's last line of defense.

"I don't know what you mean, Lord Conyngham," the Duchess said, "I'd never leave Victoria alone."

"Who's with her now?" Lord Conyngham asked pointedly.

"Baroness Lehzen, of course. What is this about?"

"I'd like to see Her Royal Highness. At once."

"She can't be disturbed," said the Duchess, a tremor in her voice. Seeing her distress, Liza felt a twinge of pity. It must be terrible for a mother to lose her child. But then she remembered the Duchess had willingly placed Victoria in danger.

"His Majesty has given me a letter for her." Lord Conyngham pulled a long envelope out of his coat pocket. The King's wax seal lay crimson like a drop of blood on the white paper.

The Duchess, looked over to Sir John in a panic, then held out her hand. "I'll take it to her."

Lord Conyngham shook his head slightly. "My instructions are to deliver it to her in person."

"That's absurd. I'm her mother," declared the Duchess. "All her correspondence is read by me."

"The King has given a direct order," said Lord Conyngham implacably. "Duchess, while you wake the Princess, I have private business to discuss with Sir John."

Sir John gave the Duchess a curt nod, "Fetch the Princess while I talk with our visitors," he ordered. The Duchess's eyes widened as she tried to decipher his meaning.

"You may wait in the red drawing room," she said before hurrying off. Liza wondered what she planned to do. If they hadn't already found Victoria, the Duchess was not going to be able to produce the Princess now.

Sir John gestured to Lord Conyngham to precede him. The Lord held out his arm to Liza. Sir John's face reddened, but he held his tongue. Nell met them in the red drawing room with a hastily assembled tray of tea. She caught Liza's eye and winked.

The rarely used room's uncomfortable chairs and Grecian sofas smelled of damp. Lord Conyngham's guards stood with their backs to the doorway. Simon took up a post just inside the room, his face impassive. Sir John settled himself on a gold brocade settee.

"Miss Hastings, will you pour?" Lord Conyngham said, deferring to Liza as if she were the young lady of the house. Glancing over at Sir John, he said, "Conroy, let's not mince words. The King is unhappy with your mistreatment of his niece."

"Has this lying maid been telling wild tales?" Sir John stretched out his legs, admiring the reflective polish on his boots.

Lord Conyngham sipped his tea. "We found her tales very credible," he said. "It's over, Conroy. His Majesty will not leave Victoria defenseless again."

"The Princess has named me the keeper of the privy purse. I have it in writing." Sir John patted his jacket pocket. "You can't do anything about it."

With a twinkle in his eye, Lord Conyngham said, "On that subject, this young lady has business with you, Conroy."

Sir John's face twisted. "I won't deal with a servant."

"Don't think of her as a servant," said Lord Conyngham. "Rather, think of her as the King's envoy." He couldn't contain his glee. Part of the King's plan to humiliate Sir John was to force him to negotiate with Victoria's maid.

Liza wasted no time. She reached into her reticule and pulled out a stiff piece of paper. "I have a warrant for your arrest, signed by the King."

Sir John said, "Silly Billy roused himself from the death bed?" Lord Conyngham stiffened, but Sir John paid no attention to him. "A warrant? Why? I've done nothing wrong."

"You assaulted the Princess, for a start," Liza said. "And you committed bodily injury upon my person. I'm a witness."

"It's my word against yours."

"Victoria was a witness too." Liza reminded him.

"Not one, but two, hysterical girls," he sneered. "No one will credit your story."

Liza made a tut-tutting sound. "Sir John, the King already does. And I am sure there are others in this household who would be more than happy to tell their story to the courts."

Sir John tapped his fingers against his impeccably tailored trousers; the only sign he was not sure of the outcome of this conversation. "How unseemly to drag the Princess into the courts . . . just as she is poised to start her reign."

"As it happens, the King agrees with you," Liza said.

Sir John raised his eyebrows and glanced over at Lord Conyngham, who studiously stared at the dregs in his teacup.

"I'll tear up the warrant, if you give me the letter you forced Victoria to sign." Liza's voice was firm, even though the hand holding the warrant trembled.

Sir John's eyebrows lifted. "That's not much of a bargain. My letter is exceedingly valuable."

"It would be difficult for you to claim your appointment from Newgate Prison." Liza made a show of thinking hard. "I don't think you rate the Tower of London. That's only for noble criminals." She was beginning to enjoy herself.

Sir John's eyes rested on the warrant in Liza's hand. His tongue darted out and he licked his lips. Whether or not he was prosecuted, a stint in prison would finish his ambitions forever.

"I need more," he said finally.

This was Lord Conyngham's cue. "Miss Hastings, the negotiations have reached a point where I may be of service."

Liza nodded. She gratefully leaned back in her hard chair.

Lord Conyngham faced Sir John, not hiding his disdain, "How much, Conroy?"

Sir John said, "Ten thousand a year."

Liza gasped.

Lord Conyngham didn't turn a hair. "Absolutely not. One thousand. It's a handsome income—it more than compensates you for your years of service."

"I have expenses. Seven thousand."

"Two thousand. You can supplement that with what you have stolen from the Duchess over the years." Sir John started. Lord Conyngham chuckled. "You thought the King didn't know? His accountants surmise you have robbed her of at least forty, perhaps fifty thousand pounds."

Liza's jaw dropped.

Annie must have discovered proof of his embezzling.

Poor Annie.

Lord Conyngham continued, "Since His Majesty cannot abide the Duchess, he did not interfere."

"Five thousand," said Sir John.

"Three. My final offer."

Sir John calculated. Three thousand was an enormous amount, but he wanted more. "I want a peerage."

"Perhaps an Irish one," Lord Conyngham countered. "There are none available, at the moment. But if one becomes vacant—"

"Agreed."

Lord Conyngham extended his palm, and Sir John reluctantly handed over his letter appointing him as keeper of the privy purse. Lord Conyngham checked it through, scowling, then gave it to Liza. She ceremoniously tore it into two pieces, relishing the wince on Sir John's face.

"The warrant," Sir John said.

Without a word, Liza gave it to him.

"Just a moment," she said. She pulled out another official piece of paper. "Lord Conyngham, perhaps you could call the guards to make an arrest."

"We had an agreement!" said Sir John coldly.

"So we did," said Liza. She handed the warrant to the guard. "This is for the arrest of Simon Gooding, Footman, for the unlawful restraint of Elizabeth Hastings, and on suspicion of the murder of Miss Annie Mason."

Simon began to back out of the room.

"He's right there!" Liza cried, pointing.

The guards seized him.

———

The mood in the drawing room varied among the inhabitants. Lord Conyngham dozed on the least uncomfortable sofa. Sir John sulked in the corner. Liza hugged herself with the knowledge she had done what she had set out to do: Sir John wasn't a threat to Victoria any longer, Annie was avenged, and best of all, the Duchess and Sir John still didn't know where Victoria was.

Half an hour later, a miserable Duchess click-clacked in. An exhausted and anxious Baroness Lehzen followed. A wave of guilt washed over Liza; how could she have forgotten Lehzen? She must be sick with worry. Liza smiled at Lehzen hoping to reassure her, but Lehzen looked too frantic to understand the message.

"The Princess is ill," the Duchess said flatly. "She cannot see anyone."

"Are you sure?" asked Lord Conyngham.

"Of course. I'm her mother."

"Madam, that is odd indeed," he said, with a wink at Liza. "Because my sources tell me the Princess has been missing since yesterday afternoon."

The Duchess's face went pale and a snarl came from Sir John's direction.

Lord Conyngham continued scolding Victoria's mother. "You have one job, madam, for which you receive an allowance and a home. How difficult is it to keep track of one seventeen-year-old girl?"

The Duchess began to weep, while the distraught Baroness sank down into an armless chair.

Lord Conyngham turned to Liza. "Miss Hastings, if you would be so kind . . ."

A broad smile on her face, Liza jumped up and ran out of the room. She flew to the Duchess's sitting room and knocked on the lid of the wood box.

"Victoria, wake up," Liza said.

There was silence, then a sleepy voice, "Liza, just a minute more."

"Now, Victoria!"

"Very well." The bolt was slid back and the Princess unfolded herself from the box. "This hidey-hole is very snug but rather confining." She stretched and yawned. "Liza! Look at you! What a lovely dress."

"The Queen gave it to me, Your Highness. And Sir John, none too happily, gave me this," Liza said, holding up the pieces of Sir John's letter.

Victoria was very still, then she reached out and hugged Liza. "Thank you, Liza. I owe you an enormous debt. And Inside Boy too. You know his lair is quite comfortable. I don't blame him for living there."

"You can thank us later. Right now you have guests." Liza quickly explained Lord Conyngham's mission and her negotiations on behalf of the King. She ended with the King's letter.

"I'm tempted to make Mama wait even longer; it would serve her right for leaving me in Sir John's clutches," Victoria said spitefully. "But I can't wait to read Uncle King's letter. It's high time I opened my own mail."

Stopping only to make a much needed visit to the water closet and to wash her face, Victoria led the way back to the drawing room. When she swept in, the Duchess's face was filled with relief, which was quickly chased away by anger. Baroness Lehzen began to fuss over Victoria's dusty dress. Sir John's face hardened like granite and the glare he threw at Liza was murderous.

"What a naughty girl you are to hide from us," the Duchess said. "You have kept all of us waiting with your childish game." Her voice trailed off as she realized no one in the room was fooled. "Victoria, my brother-in-law, the King, has written you a letter."

Victoria broke the seal, dropping bits of red wax to the carpet. She read the letter quickly, her lips parted and her breathing grew rapid. She read it again more slowly. "Uncle King proposes to give me an income of ten thousand pounds! And my own household!"

The Duchess flinched. "She is too young," she said to Lord Conyngham. "She refuses."

"Mama, I think I should consider his kind offer."

"It is for Her Highness to decide," Conyngham said. "Without coercion."

The Duchess put her hand to her ample chest. "Lord Conyngham, what are you accusing us of?"

"Your Grace, I think you know."

Victoria spoke up, startling them out of their battle. "How is the King's health, Lord Conyngham?"

"Very poor, Your Highness. The end will come in days, not weeks."

Victoria shook her head sadly. "Then I think it would be more suitable to remain in my mother's house for the time being."

"You see!" said the Duchess triumphantly. "Tell the King Victoria prefers to stay with me." She looked toward Sir John for his approval, but he had lost too much this evening to cater to her feelings.

Lord Conyngham said, "I am also instructed to say the King deeply regrets the Princess has had difficulty communicating with him. To remedy the situation, Lord Liverpool will visit the Princess daily and speak with her. Privately."

"That is completely unnecessary," protested the Duchess.

"Be that as it may, Your Grace, the King has ordered it." Lord Conyngham's manner did not brook any argument.

"Lord Conyngham, let me show you to your carriage," Victoria offered prettily.

"Victoria, don't be common," the Duchess scolded. "It's not appropriate to escort a gentleman outside."

"Nevertheless," said Victoria. "I shall." Taking Lord Conyngham's arm, she beckoned to Liza and the Baroness Lehzen to attend them. Outside the sun had just risen and the park was fresh and new.

"Forgive me for saying so, but you look a trifle peaked, Your Highness," Lord Conyngham said quietly.

"I've been worrying so about Uncle King." She sighed. "Tell Uncle I meant no disrespect by refusing his kind offer. I just think it is more fitting to stay here."

"If I may be so bold, Your Highness," Lord Conyngham took Victoria's hand and bowed respectfully over it. "The King understands completely. His offer was a gesture of his affection."

Victoria squeezed his hand. "And perhaps to irk Mama and Sir John as well?"

With a twinkle in his eyes, Lord Conyngham said, "Perhaps."

"Please assure Queen Adelaide I am praying for her and Uncle King." Victoria dashed a tear from her cheek.

Lord Conyngham bowed and climbed into his carriage.

Victoria, flanked by Liza and the Baroness Lehzen, stood in the doorway until his carriage disappeared into the park.

"Go inside, Victoria," said the Baroness. "We wouldn't want you to catch cold."

Victoria smiled at Liza. "No, Lehzen, that wouldn't be amusing at all."

20 May 1837 Excerpt from the Journal
of Miss Elizabeth Hastings

Will is furious! He couldn't even get the words out, he was so angry. Finally, I think I made sense of his complaints.

Firstly, I should not put myself between the Princess and bodily harm. (Fortunately, the bruise on my cheek was cunningly hidden by powder, else he might have exploded.)

Secondly, I don't appreciate the dangers of riding alone to Windsor in the middle of the night.

Thirdly, how could I neglect to go to him for help?

And finally, how could I be so cruel as to tell him, in strictest confidence, the story of the century? Don't I understand how exasperating it is to know the intimate details of a scandal so close to the throne and not be able to print a word?

What I love about Will is that his concern for me and his regret at missing the story of the century are equivalent in his mind. He does me the inestimable honor of treating me as an equal.

From Her Majesty, Queen Adelaide, to Miss Elizabeth Hastings

2 June 1837
Windsor Castle

Dear Miss Hastings,

His Majesty and I are very grateful for your services to our niece. The Princess is very dear to us and we are not unaware of the risks you took to ensure her message reached us. The enclosure is a small token of our appreciation for your bravery and your discretion, upon which we know we can rely.

With Sincere Affection,

Her Royal Majesty
Adelaide R

Enclosure: £ 500

24 May 1837 Excerpt from the Journal
of Her Royal Highness Victoria

Today is my 18ᵗʰ birthday! How old! And yet how far am I from being what I should be. I shall from this day take the firm resolution to study with renewed assiduity, to keep my attention always well fixed on whatever I am about, and to strive to become every day less trifling and more fit for what, if Heaven wills it, I'm someday to be!

The demonstrations of loyalty and affection from all the people were highly gratifying. The parks and streets were thronged. Numbers of people put down their names and amongst others good old Lablache inscribed his. . . . The Courtyard and the streets were crammed . . . and the anxiety of the people to see poor stupid me was very great, and I must say I am quite touched by it.

From the Duchess of Kent
to Her Royal Highness Victoria

24 May 1837
Kensington Palace

. . . But as there is no joy without pain in this world, so even between us, for moments only, have these feelings been blended, I advert to the grief I experienced from some little misunderstandings which clouded our happy intercourses and which never should occur between a beloved child and Her only parent.

Enclosed is a keepsake for your birthday, a lock of my hair, the last perhaps of its natural color.

Mama

From the Firm of Ratisbon and Ratisbon, Esq.
to Miss Elizabeth Hastings

9 June 1837
Temple Inn

Dear Miss Hastings,

We trust this letter finds you well.

We are delighted to report the clipper ship Fortuity has docked at Portsmouth. The manifest indicates a container of shawls from Kashmir. Your father's man of business, Mr. Ripley, has been in Kashmir for two years, supervising the native production of the clothing. Mr. Ripley was grieved to learn of the death of your parents. He hopes you will meet him at our offices so he can make suitable arrangements to handle the sale of the apparel on your behalf. According to Mr. Ripley, the sale should realize several thousand pounds. His Royal Majesty's Custom Board agrees with this generous appraisal.

Mr. Ripley is prepared to make arrangements to retrieve your family's belongings from storage in Munich once you decide where you wish to live.

Ratisbon and Ratisbon will be happy to act for you in this matter. We look forward to seeing you at your convenience.

Sincerely,
Gerald Ratisbon, Esq.

15 June 1837 Excerpt from the Journal of Her Royal Highness Victoria Kent

The news of the King is so very bad that all my lessons are put off, including Lablache's . . . and we see nobody. I regret rather my singing lesson, though it is only for a short period, but duty and proper feeling go before all pleasures. 10 minutes to 1, I just heard the doctors think my poor Uncle the King cannot last more than 48 hours! Poor man! He was always kind to me, and he meant it well, I know; I am grateful for it, and shall ever remember his kindness with gratitude.

At about ½ past 2 came Lord Liverpool, and I had a highly important conversation with him—alone.

26

In Which Liza Curtsies to the New Queen of England

THE ORMOLU clock on the Duchess's mantle chimed five o'clock in the morning. The sitting room had a view of the main gate and Liza had been keeping watch with Inside Boy. He had grown bolder since Victoria had agreed to let him stay in his hidey hole. She relished having a secret friend in the walls.

"When will we hear?" Liza asked him. "The messenger from Windsor came at seven o'clock last night to say it would happen at any moment."

Boy shrugged. He poured her a glass of the Duchess's sherry from the side table. "'e'll kick off when 'e's ready."

Liza yawned. "Victoria is worn out with the waiting. First the King was alarmingly ill. The next morning he

was at death's door. And that was a week ago!" Liza sipped gratefully. "I don't think she has slept in days."

By the pearly predawn light, Liza saw dozens of people on the
great lawn in Kensington Gardens. They had been there for the past
week. "What are they waiting for?"

Inside Boy lay down on the Duchess's settee and rubbed his
eyes with the back of his grimy fist. "Dunno. It's not often the King
pegs out and we get a new Queen. Some people likes to say they
was there."

"Boy, something's happening!"

Four gray horses drew a large carriage lit by two hanging lanterns. The crowd of commoners moved to the road like a swarm of
bees. The carriage didn't slow until it drew up to the iron gates of
Kensington Palace. The gatepost lamps flickered in the early morning light. A footman dismounted and rang for the porter.

"For once in your lazy life, be awake, you old git," muttered Boy.

"That porter is practically a myth," said Liza. "But today of
all days!"

The footman knocked again. He returned to the carriage and
delivered a message to the passengers. The carriage door slammed
open and an imposing figure stumbled out. Swearing loudly, he
stomped over to the pedestrian gate and rang the bell. "Open up,
we're on state business!"

"This is absurd," said Liza. Wrapping her shawl around her dressing gown, she hurried down the stairs and opened the front door.
The man spied the pool of light from the house and Liza in the
doorway.

"Girl, where is the bloody porter? Is everyone asleep?"

Liza recognized the voice. "Lord Conyngham?"

"Miss Hastings! Thank goodness someone sensible is awake."

"I'll find the keys."

"The porter's sleeping, is he?"

"More likely drunk, sir." She opened the door to the porter's little box. He was slumped in his chair, snoring and reeking of gin. Liza held her nose and plucked the keys off his belt. She opened the gate and the carriage rolled in.

"A thousand thanks, my dear." Lord Conyngham gave her an approving nod.

"Is the King—" Liza started to ask.

He held up his hand. "I cannot say, Miss Hastings." But his face was solemn and his voice heavy.

Another man climbed down from the carriage. He was short and stout, wearing a greatcoat of even finer quality than Lord Conyngham's. "Miss Hastings, the Archbishop of Canterbury."

Liza curtsied to the highest priest in the land.

"Let us in, young lady," he said in low voice. "We have urgent news for Her Royal Highness."

"Yes, sir." Liza led them into the house to the red drawing room. Sir John waited there, immaculately attired despite the hour. Liza wouldn't have been surprised if he had never gone to bed.

Lord Conyngham made a strangled noise in his throat. "Conroy. You're still here."

"Conyngham." Sir John nodded. "I shall remain until the Duchess no longer requires my services." Then he caught sight of the other man. "Your Excellency."

"We need to see the Princess," said Lord Conyngham.

"She's asleep."

"I hope for your sake she's truly in her bed this time. Wake her."

The Duchess's arrival in soft, silent slippers surprised them all. She wore a shimmering turquoise dressing gown Liza had never seen before. Liza wondered if the Duchess had purchased it specifically for this occasion.

"Lord Conyngham, Archbishop," she said in a high voice, as though she were surprised.

The visitors stifled their impatience and formally greeted the Duchess. Lord Conyngham repeated his demand to see Victoria.

"It's too early. You'll have to wait," said the Duchess, after a quick glance at Conroy.

"You refuse to wake her?" asked the Archbishop, his bushy eyebrows lifting high above his tired eyes.

"If the Duchess says you have to wait, then you wait," said Sir John.

"For God's sake, Conroy," snapped the Archbishop. "We have news for the Queen!"

The Duchess gasped and Sir John's face grew sterner. The King's death, long anticipated, had finally happened.

Lord Conyngham continued. "Take your losses like a man, Conroy. Send the girl down."

Liza had heard enough. She backed out of the drawing room and ran up the narrow back stairs to the Princess's chamber. She burst in. Victoria was sitting on her bed, whispering with the Baroness.

"Has it happened?" asked the Baroness.

"Is Uncle King gone?" asked Victoria at the same moment.

One word answered them both. "Yes."

The Baroness Lehzen jumped up and clapped her hand over her mouth to keep from exclaiming. Victoria sat perfectly still, her eyes brimming with tears.

"What's wrong?" Liza asked.

"Why are you crying, *Liebling*?" The Baroness hurried over. "You're finally the Queen. It's the beginning of everything."

Tears rolling freely down her cheeks, Victoria said, "He's dead, Lehzen. He was kind to me. And poor Aunt Adelaide, she must be so sad."

"The King is dead. Long live the Queen," Liza said quietly.

"Remember who you are," said the Baroness to Victoria. "Let me be the first to say it . . . Your Majesty." The Baroness burst into tears, but Victoria, dabbing at her eyes with a handkerchief, began to smile.

"Liza, my white dressing gown," she said.

Baroness Lehzen agreed. "It's very flattering."

"And Lehzen, my hair needs doing."

"Your Majesty, perhaps you should leave it down?" Liza said. "You can't help your youth; use it to charm and disarm their lordships."

"Down," Victoria agreed.

The Baroness brushed the Princess's dark hair. It was still thin from her illness, but Lehzen arranged it flatteringly over her shoulders.

"Who is downstairs, Liza?" asked Baroness Lehzen, as Liza tweaked the bows on Victoria's dressing gown.

"Lord Conyngham and the Archbishop of Canterbury."

"My mother knows?" Victoria asked.

"She's trying to make them wait." Liza allowed herself a giggle. "They are very vexed by the delay."

Lehzen snorted, but Victoria lifted her chin, her eyes gleaming. "Let her, darling Lehzen. It is the last time she shall infringe upon my prerogatives."

An iciness in her voice made Liza realize the Princess was gone forever.

Queen Victoria indeed.

———————

Voices in the hall made all three look sharply to the door. Then Victoria gave herself a little shake and smiled at herself in the mirror. "I have no reason to fear Sir John or my mother ever again."

The Duchess let herself in. She held a silver candlestick. The solemnity of her expression gave way to irritation when she saw Liza and Lehzen dressing Victoria.

"I suppose the maid has already told you?" she asked.

"Yes, Mama. Aren't you very sad about Uncle King?" Victoria asked. She swiveled round from her dressing table to look at her mother.

"Of course." The Duchess straightened Victoria's collar and smoothed her hair. "You should put your hair up," she said. "It will make you seem more mature."

"The difference one poor old man's death makes! You never wanted me to look mature before." Victoria's tone was deceptively light. Liza saw the Duchess's back stiffen and the hand stroking her daughter's hair froze.

"I admit I made some mistakes, Victoria," the Duchess said finally. "But can't we put that aside? I've sacrificed my whole life for yours."

"And I'm grateful, of course." Liza didn't think Victoria sounded grateful. "However, from this point forward, I'll make my own decisions, Mama. I shall wear my hair down because I choose to. I shall meet my ministers privately. When I address the council, I will do so alone. You will never have any influence over affairs of state."

The Duchess burst into tears. "You are so cruel. What have I done to make you be so hateful?"

Victoria's face might have been sculpted from alabaster, she showed so little emotion. "Mama, it is what you didn't do. You never protected me from Sir John. You never, ever, placed my happiness above your own, as a mother ought."

The Duchess stared speechless at her daughter, who returned her gaze steadfastly. This new Victoria was impressive, though Liza wished she could warn Victoria not to say anything unforgivable. Liza had lost her parents to a tragic accident. Did Victoria want to lose her mother to her anger and bitterness?

As if she knew of Liza's concern, Victoria relented a little. "Of course, you shall always make your home with me. As my mother, you'll never want for anything."

The Duchess blew her nose loudly.

The tableau was broken by a loud thumping. Victoria gestured to Liza, who opened the door. Sir John loomed in the doorway. He brushed past Liza as though she didn't exist.

"How long are you going to keep us waiting?" he asked.

The four women in the room gaped at his astonishing rudeness.

The new Queen looked at him with nothing short of hatred. "In a few moments, Sir John, the Archbishop of Canterbury is going to inform me that I am the Queen." She drew herself up to her full height. "And once I am, you are never to enter my royal presence again."

"Victoria!" The Duchess cried.

"Mama, stay out of this."

Sir John sneered down at his former charge. "You aren't even crowned yet and already you are abusing your power."

"I had an excellent teacher."

Liza wanted to applaud and the Baroness Lehzen's plain face was split by a wide smile.

"History will attribute any success of yours to my Kensington System," said Sir John. "You'll never escape my upbringing."

"You forget once I am Queen, mine is the only story people will care about. Everyone will know the truth about your wretched System." Victoria smiled triumphantly. "Pack your bags today and go."

"I work for your mother. You've no authority to remove me."

Victoria tossed her head. "Lord Liverpool assures me the exorbitant pension you extorted will only be paid when you quit my mother's service and I am rid of you forever. You are dismissed."

"It's not so easy to get rid of me," Sir John warned.

"Liza," Victoria said, without taking her eyes from Sir John. "I'm sure Lord Conyngham has come with a retinue of guards. Please fetch one."

"Gladly, Your Majesty." Liza stressed Victoria's new title.

His face flushed with humiliation, Sir John turned on his heel and stalked out. The door banged behind him.

Victoria watched his back with satisfaction. "And that is the end of Sir John."

"Victoria," her mother began weakly. "How can you be—"

Victoria silenced her mother by holding up her hand. "Mama, if you want to be part of my life, don't ever take his side again."

The imposing Duchess seemed to shrink while tiny Victoria grew taller.

"You look bedraggled, Mama," Victoria said. "You should repair your face before we go down."

The Duchess, as if in a trance, moved to her own dressing table and began to powder her tear-streaked face.

Victoria turned to Baroness Lehzen. "While I am meeting my ministers, darling Lehzen, please arrange a new bedroom for me. And one for you nearby. Tonight, I will sleep alone."

"Victoria!" The Duchess's protest was half-hearted.

"Mama, you may stay in our former rooms." Victoria paused before the mirror. "Lehzen, Liza, how do I look?"

The Baroness had been silent since the Duchess's arrival, but now she burst into excited speech. "Lovely." Her voice faltered. "To everyone else you will be the Queen, but you'll always be the daughter of my heart."

"Oh, Lehzen! We shall never be parted." Victoria embraced her. The Duchess averted her eyes as her daughter embraced her governess.

Victoria said to her mother, "Shall we go, Mama?" Then she picked up the silver candlestick and walked out the door, her mother trailing behind. Liza thought the Duchess did it rather well, considering how unaccustomed she was to being in her daughter's shadow.

———

While Victoria spoke with her guests privately the staff prepared the house to mourn King William's passing. The clocks were stopped in honor of the dead King and Mrs. Strode ordered black crepe be draped over all the mirrors.

To show their respect for their new monarch, the servants lined up on the landing outside the red drawing room. As always, Mademoiselle Blanche tried to bully her way to her accustomed spot at the head of the line. But Mrs. Strode shook her head firmly. With a gracious gesture, she invited Liza to take the first place.

Although Liza knew it was unworthy of her, as she moved to the front of the line, she could not resist saying, "Mademoiselle, I think there is no question about precedence now?"

Nell was listening at the door. "She's coming!"

Victoria appeared in her youthful dressing gown, her hair loose over her shoulders. The servants sank into their deepest curtsies or bowed until their foreheads scraped the floor. It was the first curtsy Liza had done with her whole heart since she arrived at Kensington Palace.

20 June 1837 Excerpt from the Journal of Her Majesty, Queen Victoria

I went into my sitting room (only in my dressing gown) alone and saw them. Lord Conyngham then acquainted me that my poor Uncle, the King, was no more, and had expired at 12 minutes past two this morning and consequently that I am Queen.

27

In Which Liza Gives Up Her Heart's Desire for Her Heart's Desire

LIZA WAS MORE EXHILARATED than tired as she slipped out of the Palace into the crowds thronging the gardens. She looked back at Kensington Palace; the staid, old house seemed to quiver with new energy. The windows to the state apartments flung open and the tiny figure of Victoria appeared in the opening. Cheers erupted from the crowd; Liza thought her ears might explode.

One moment she was fighting the sea of people, the next she was alone. She saw Will's tall, but not too tall, figure leaning against the chestnut tree. He bowed and she curtsied.

"You look lovely in your dark dress. Is this another of Victoria's castoffs?"

"No, this one is mine." Liza stroked her taffeta skirt. "Victoria has barely enough mourning for herself. The dressmakers are queuing. The Queen insists the court mourn for twelve weeks." She made a face. "Ten more than I was allowed to wear my own blacks."

"The royals have different rules," he said. "You of all people should know that." His eyes went to the hollows of her neck. "I like that locket. I don't think I've seen you wear jewelry before."

"I wasn't permitted to as a maid. But that's all changed now."

She admired the cut of his dark coat. "You. In mourning, for King William?"

"I harried the man enough when he was alive, a show of respect is the least I could do." He smiled ruefully. "Besides, my best girl works at the Palace."

"Your best girl?" asked Liza archly. "There are others?"

"Well, my first choice has kept me waiting. Now we have a new Queen, I hope she'll marry me."

Liza looked off in the distance at Kensington Palace.

His smile faded. "That was our agreement, wasn't it?"

There was a long silence.

"I just never thought past this morning," Liza admitted, matching Will's gaze.

"The day's arrived. Will you marry me now?"

She took a deep breath. "Will, when my parents died, I was left alone to fend for myself."

"And you did."

"I know! I found a job, good friends, and a new life."

"And me." Will thumped his chest.

"And you." She smiled. "But I wanted my old life back. I couldn't see past everything I had lost."

"And now?"

"I don't want the life I led before. I want the life I'm going to build with you."

"Ah, finally!" He tilted her chin and kissed her gently. "And you'll let me help with your debts?"

"That won't be necessary," Liza assured him. "I've heard from Papa's solicitor. You are looking at the sole owner of a large boatful of very expensive and fashionable scarves from Kashmir."

"Ship," he corrected.

"Boat, ship." Liza shrugged. "What matters is I possess a moderate fortune. Not to mention a reward from a grateful Queen."

"Victoria?"

"No, Adelaide!" She laughed at his surprise. "A thank-you for helping Victoria."

"She wants you to keep quiet?" Will guessed.

Liza nodded.

"She's a clever and generous woman. I'm sorry I wrote all those stories about her. Well, she's out of it now. No scandal sheets will bother with her now that she's the Dowager Queen." He grabbed Liza's hand and brought it to his lips. "Are you sure you aren't too rich for me now?" He never took his eyes from hers.

"Just rich enough, Mr. Fulton. Now I can come to you without liabilities." She sighed. "I feel terrible. I blamed my parents for leaving me destitute, but all the while, my inheritance floated to me on the Indian Ocean. I should have trusted them better."

But without this year, I wouldn't have met Will. And I wouldn't have learned what I am capable of.

With the intuition she loved about him, Will let her thoughts take their course. After several moments, he handed her one of the handkerchiefs she had embroidered for him. Dabbing her eyes, she said, "Thank you."

"It was my honor."

She smacked her forehead with a gloved hand. "How could I forget? Speaking of honors—Victoria has offered me one."

Will looked wary.

"She wants to make me her gentlewoman of the bedchamber."

"I've never heard of such a position."

"Victoria made it up," Liza laughed. "I don't have birth enough to be a true lady in waiting, but this way I can be a lady and still be close to her."

"Liza," Will said slowly. "A lady can't marry a newspaper man."

Watching him closely, Liza said, "She could marry a minor knight. How would you like to be William Fulton, Esquire?"

He rocked back on his heels. "A knighthood? For what?"

"You took her side when she had no one."

"But I also took the other side!" he exclaimed.

"Victoria doesn't see it like that," Liza assured him. "I've told her all about you. Perhaps she just wants to make it easier for us to marry. All the Queens in England are paving the way for us."

He shook his head. "I can't take it."

"Will—it's rank! You won't get another chance like this."

"Liza, the kind of honor I want, no one can give." His face set in a stubborn look Liza knew well.

"Not even me?" Liza asked, watching him closely.

"Not even you."

Liza kissed him lightly. She had chaffed him long enough. "I knew you would refuse."

He looked at her sharply.

"Your pride is one of the things I love about you," Liza said. "I already told Victoria thank you, but no."

"For both of us? You refused being lady of the chamber pot?"

"Gentlewoman of the bedchamber!"

"And my knighthood?" He growled, but his eyes were smiling. "You gave that up without even talking to me?"

"Will, you can't be proud in both directions at once!" Liza laughed. "She offered Inside Boy a garnet brooch. I couldn't bring myself to tell her he's probably stolen much more valuable items from her mother's jewelry box. He should just be grateful she didn't shop him to the peelers."

Will burst out laughing. "Living at Kensington Palace has had a terrible effect on you—you're pattering flash, stealing horses, playing bailiff." He stopped laughing. "You've come so far this year. Are you sure you still want to marry me? You are giving up so much."

"Will, I want to marry you more than anything," Liza said firmly. "If I've learned anything this past year, it's riches and rank don't make you happy."

"What about Victoria?" he asked. "Will she be happy now she has everything?"

Liza shrugged. "She's never had a chance to make her own choices before. It may go to her head."

"But you're well out of it?"

Liza nodded. "She doesn't need me anymore."

"Are you certain?"

"Will, if you keep asking me that, I may have to reconsider! You are my choice." She brushed a lock of sandy hair off his forehead. "I haven't said that for the longest time. My choice."

Will held out his hand. Liza could see a faint imprint of ink stains. Without hesitation, she took his hand in her own.

"What do we do now, dear Liza?" he asked.

"I've the rest of the day to myself. Will you take me to Claridge's Hotel? I've an account to settle."

She glanced back at Kensington Palace. The setting sun bathed the red brick house in golden light.

"Don't look back," said Will.

"Why not? Mama was right; it was a year like no other."

The End

Author's Note

At the end of *Prisoners in the Palace*, in 1837, the eighteen-year-old Victoria ascended the throne. She reigned for sixty-three years, longer than any other British monarch. While she was Queen, England became an empire of over four million square miles and one hundred twenty-four million people. She was dearly loved by the public and is credited with restoring the faith of the British people in the monarchy itself.

You may be dismayed to learn Victoria married Prince Albert, although by all reports his disposition and looks had improved by the time they met again (three years after their first encounter). It was a successful marriage and they had nine children. Albert became her closest adviser. Through his efforts, Victoria and her mother were eventually reconciled. When Albert died of overwork at the age of forty-two, Victoria was inconsolable. She built an enormous (some people think it's quite tacky) memorial to his memory not far from Kensington Palace. She retreated from public life as much as possible and wore mourning until her death in 1901. The image of the tiny dark Victoria, dressed in mourning, is the way most of us know her. I wanted to write about the girl with fair hair (before she contracted typhoid) who loved to dance and reveled in staying up late.

Although Victoria died over a century ago, I hear her voice quite clearly in my head because I've read her diaries. It is great fun trying to find the teenager hiding in the words "Mama would find proper." She made her entries in pencil, which were only to be inked over when her mother approved them. The Baroness Lehzen looms large in the diaries as "dear, dear Lehzen," but the Duchess is just "Mama." Victoria never lost the habit of journaling, and by the time she died she had written over one hundred volumes. The excerpts of Victoria's journal entries and the Duchess's letters to her daughter in the novel are authentic, although I've taken the liberty of rearranging some dates.

Victoria's childhood was incredibly restrictive. She was permitted few friends, had a limited allowance, and knew very little about the outside world. Her sketches of the most important people in her life, including Lehzen, her mother, and Signor Lablache, still exist. Her spaniel Dash was one of her few friends. She washed him weekly, doing the dirty work herself. In fact, the day she was crowned Queen, she returned from the coronation and started to wash her dog.

The Duchess had a terrible relationship with the King, although Victoria was very fond of him. To understand their animosity, you must look at the history of the family.

The Duke of Kent, Victoria's father, was one of fifteen children of King George III (who lost the American Colonies and was widely considered insane). The royal children were despised by the public as expensive drains on the treasury. George IV, the oldest son, became Prince Regent for his father in 1810 and succeeded him in 1820. This period is called the Regency. His only child, the young, healthy Princess Charlotte, was confidently expected to inherit. However, when she died in childbirth in 1817, the succession was opened to the King's numerous siblings. The next three brothers immediately rushed out to get married and have a legitimate heir. Because of the Royal Marriages Act of 1772, any descendent of the King could not marry without the monarch's consent.

The Duke of Kent, Victoria's father, was especially profligate and spent most of his life in debt. In fact, he had so many debts, he fled to France to live in Paris. After Charlotte's death, he abandoned his French mistress of twenty-five years to marry Victoria's mother in 1818. (His mistress learned he had left her through the newspapers.) When the Duchess became pregnant, he insisted they travel to Britain, despite terrible traveling conditions, so his child could be born on British soil. When they arrived, King George IV refused to pay his brother's debts, so the family moved into shabby quarters at Kensington Palace. The Duke racked up more debts to renovate his rooms, including designing the famous double staircase where Victoria first sees Albert. Victoria was born on May 24, 1819.

There is a story the Duke consulted a psychic who told him he would never become King, but his daughter would be the greatest Queen England had ever known. The psychic knew what she was talking about, because the Duke died when Victoria was eight months old. She idealized her father's memory and one of her first acts as Queen was to pay all his debts. He is buried in St. George's Cathedral, in the same chapel of the Knights of the Garter, where Liza finds the Queen to tell her of Victoria's plight.

William IV succeeded his brother George IV in 1830. He was a sailor and a buffoon. No one took him very seriously. He proposed to three women before poor Adelaide accepted him. His wife was never appreciated by the British people, who saw her as a dowdy German housewife. Although he had ten illegitimate children with his mistress, a notorious actress, William and Adelaide never had children. He often complained bitterly the Duchess was keeping Victoria from his court.

Sir John Conroy worked for the Duke of Kent. After the Duke's death, Sir John appointed himself the Duchess's comptroller. Speculation at court and in the press claimed Sir John was the Duchess's lover, but people close to the household felt their relationship was more complicated. The Duchess was a handsome woman who was left very lonely by her husband's death. She was alone and afraid in a strange land. She spoke English very poorly. Sir John exploited her vulnerability until she was totally under his thumb.

Sir John is a great character because he really was a villain. After she became Queen, Victoria called him a demon and noted his cruel and abusive treatment of her in her diaries, especially during her illness at Ramsgate and in the months just before she became Queen. But he was clever enough to fool the outside world; his Kensington System was considered a great success by everyone except Victoria. She thought of her childhood as the worst time of her life.

Unfortunately, because Sir John was her mother's employee, Victoria couldn't just wave her royal scepter and get rid of Sir John when she became Queen. He delayed his departure, holding out for his Irish peerage (a higher rank which would entitle him to be called Lord Conroy). He never got it, although he did enjoy spending his enormous pension. He was never called to account for his embezzlement of the Duchess's funds.

Liza Hastings lived only in my imagination, but a maid named Annie Mason was dismissed from Kensington Palace for lewdness and immorality. What happened to maids like Annie, without a character reference, was almost inevitable. Annie's death was inspired by accounts of young maids throwing themselves off the London Monument. A broadsheet, much like the one Will prints for Liza, showed a drawing of a young girl diving off the top. In 1842, a cage was built at the top to prevent any more suicides. You can climb to the summit today, but I recommend it only for the stout of heart: there are 311 steps!

The duties I assigned to Liza were typical of the time. A lady's maid was required for status, not for hard work. She was supposed to be young and pretty, preferably French or Swiss. She would wear her mistress's discarded clothing and her rank was just below a housekeeper or butler. There wasn't much of a career path; a successful lady's maid was one who married before she lost her looks. Often, she married a footman. These male servants were chosen for their handsome looks and how well their thighs looked in tight breeches. They often behaved arrogantly, so Simon, although a fictional character, runs true to type.

Only a lady of fine birth could be expected to be a lady in waiting to the Princess or the Queen. However, there is precedent for Victoria's extraordinary offer to Liza of the post of gentlewoman of the bedchamber. Victoria created this job to reward the daughter of her tutor, the Reverend Davys. I took the liberty of offering Liza the same.

Will Fulton is a fictional character but very representative of the new class of entrepreneurial publishers emerging in Britain at this time. Broadsheets were very profitable and used to publicize everything from the latest scandal to a political point of view. I invented the broadsheets about Victoria and Queen Adelaide, but they were typical of the time, as were wickedly funny political cartoons. Liza envisions an enormous Victoria chasing a tiny Sir John out of the room with her royal scepter. I took this image from a political cartoon of the time.

Newspapers in 1837 were heavily taxed, making them too expensive for the working class. In the next few years, the newspaper tax would be eliminated, paper made from inexpensive wood pulp would become available, and public education would be made compulsory, dramatically increasing the literacy rate. The resulting explosion in publishing would produce tens of thousands of specialized periodicals by the 1860s. So Will's prospects are rosy.

The real Inside Boy Jones was discovered lurking in the royal nursery at Buckingham Palace, after Victoria came to the throne and had her first child. He was imprisoned but soon after his release he returned and broke into the Palace again. This time he was shipped off to sea. The last history hears of him, Inside Boy was jumping ship off the coast of Algiers for reasons unknown. I took the liberty of starting his career as a royal housebreaker when Victoria was still at Kensington Palace.

Flash patter is a documented language (search for "flash dictionary" at www.victorianlondon.org), which is closely allied to cockney rhyming slang in London's East End. In case you are interested, Liza's message to Inside Boy can translate as "Simon is a villain. He's conspiring with the Irishman (Sir John). If you can, save me and unlock the door to the storage room. But if you can't, tell the whole story to Will."

Many of the events described in the book took place over a

three-year period before Victoria became Queen. I condensed these events to fit into a single year. The public events, such as Albert's visit, Victoria's birthday ball, and Victoria's brush with typhoid, are all documented. It is also true that the King received secret messages shortly before his death about Sir John's treatment of Victoria. From his sickbed the King wrote to his niece offering her an independent income and her own house. Victoria refused the King's offer, probably because she knew it was only a matter of weeks before she inherited the throne and an enormous fortune.

The morning Victoria was informed of the King's death happened much as I described it. Lord Conygham and the Archbishop had a difficult time gaining entry to the Palace and the Duchess, in a last desperate bid to keep her self-importance, tried to make them wait. Victoria finally came to meet them, dressed simply, with her hair down. She carried a silver candlestick. Many years later, this same candlestick was sold by Sir John's son, suggesting that Conroy was up to his thieving tricks even on that momentous night.

True to her word, Victoria always met her ministers alone and her mother was never permitted a voice in affairs of state. Queen Victoria's first official piece of correspondence was a letter of condolence to her aunt, which she signed as Victoria, omitting Regina, or "Queen," as a gesture of respect to the former Queen. The mourning dress she wore that day was very shabbily made and is preserved with all its fraying seams in the Royal Costume Archives.

One last note about Kensington Palace: within a month of becoming Queen, Victoria left Kensington, vowing never to return. Refusing to go to Windsor Castle because she didn't want to intrude on her Aunt Adelaide's grief, Victoria insisted Buckingham Palace be completed a year ahead of schedule so she could live there. Her ministers demanded she live under the same roof as her mother until Victoria married. She acquiesced, but placed her mother's room on the opposite side of the Palace from her own. The Baroness Lehzen was allotted the room next to the Queen. The Baroness would stay with Victoria until forced out of the household by Albert after the birth of Victoria's second child.

Victoria was persuaded to come back to Kensington on her eightieth birthday when the state apartments, the site of her seventeenth birthday ball, were restored. They are open to the public. The rest of the Palace has been used to this day as living quarters for members of the royal family, most notably Diana, the Princess of Wales, and her two sons, Prince William and Prince Henry.

For Further Reading

I consulted many sources to write *Prisoners in the Palace*, including biographies, novels by Dickens, books about publishing and histories of Kensington Palace and London. If you are interested in learning more, I suggest you start with the following books:

Queen Victoria: A Personal History by Christopher Hibbert. Basic Books, New York (2000).
Hibbert writes obsessively readable history, and this is no exception. He also draws heavily on Victoria's diaries and letters.

Queen Victoria: An Illustrated Biography by Lytton Strachey. Harcourt Brace Jovanovich, New York (1978).
This was originally published in 1921, but I recommend the illustrated edition because it has wonderful pictures of Victoria and her intimate circle. You can find the text online by searching for "Strachey and Victoria."

Queen Victoria: Born to Succeed by Elizabeth Longford. Harper and Row, London (1964).
Perhaps the most popular and enduring of Queen Victoria's biographies.

Victoria and Albert by David Duff. Taplinger Publishing Company, New York (1973).
A fascinating discussion of Victoria's love affair with Albert. Duff is very opinionated and paints a convincing portrait of the two young people who are destined to be together.

Her Little Majesty: The Life of Queen Victoria by Carolly Erickson. Simon and Schuster, New York (1997).
Erickson writes fun biographies and tries to capture the heart of a teenager being groomed to be Queen.

Life Below Stairs: Domestic Servants in England in Victorian Times by Frank Huggett. Book Club Associates, London (1977).
A useful reference for the duties and responsibilities of a servant.

For primary sources about Victorian London, I cannot recommend a Web site more highly than www.victorianlondon. org. Whenever I needed a flash patter dictionary, a restaurant recommendation, or pictures of young maids throwing themselves off the Monument, I started here.

Acknowledgments

Thank goodness I don't write in a vacuum! I must thank . . .

My writing group: Sari Bodi for always finding romantic comedy in a scene, Christine Pakkala for making me figure out what my main character has lost, and Karen Swanson for forcing me to get rid of all that history and focus on the story.

Krista Richards Mann who helped me to fully develop Liza's character, strengthening the book immeasurably. Elizabeth George who flew with me all the way to Kensington Palace and waited patiently through a ridiculous number of tours. Patricia Reilly Giff, a patient teacher and mentor—I've learned more than I can say from her.

My fabulous agent, George Nicholson, and the incomparable Erica Silverman, who held my hand every step of the way.

Victoria Rock, my editor, for understanding right away what I wanted to achieve and helping me get there, and Sara Gillingham and Amelia Mack for their lovely designs.

My mom, Barbara Burns, who has always shown by example that it's never too late to follow a dream; my dad, Robert Wieboldt, whose love of history and politics were constant companions in my childhood; and my aunt, Susan Richardson, for inspiring me to travel.

Rosemary Nichols who read and reread the manuscript and was an invaluable resource for all things Victorian.

My husband, Rob, whose insistence that I was a professional writer finally convinced me.

And most of all, my two beautiful daughters, Rowan and Margaux—they inspire me every day and I hope that maybe, just a little, I inspire them.

Our faithful tomcat, Simba, who passed away as I was finishing this book. He was a noble cat and a constant writing companion.

Prisoners in the Palace
Discussion Guide

1. In the Victorian era, clothes could tell you a lot about a person's social status. During the course of *Prisoners in the Palace*, Liza's clothes tell us not only about her changing social status, but also her state of mind. What does it mean when Liza borrows the Princess's ball gown? Or when Liza puts on her mourning dress in the final scene? How do we judge people by their clothes in modern times?

2. When Liza first sees Kensington Palace, she is dismayed. How did Kensington Palace, and Victoria's life, differ from what you expected? What do you think will change when Victoria becomes Queen?

3. "Don't be familiar with the servants," the Baroness Lehzen warns Victoria. Why doesn't the Baroness want the Princess to make friends with servants?

4. Liza feels connected to disgraced maid Annie Mason. What does Liza do to put herself on a different path than Annie's?

5. Will Fulton, newspaper man, is quickly attracted to Liza. She likes him from the beginning, too. Why does Liza resist his charms for so long? How did Liza and Will's relationship differ from typical romantic relationships in the Victorian era? How does it show the ways in which society was changing? How is their relationship different than those in modern times?

6. Annie Mason, Princess Victoria, and Queen Adelaide have well-defined roles in society that determine how they behave. Discuss ways they broke free of these roles and followed their own minds.

7. Inside Boy lives between the walls of Kensington Palace and has no established place in society. Liza envies him his freedom, but he tells her not to romanticize his life. Which character in *Prisoners in the Palace* has the most freedom to determine his or her own destiny?

8. In real life, soon after Victoria became queen, she married Prince Albert. Their match was considered one of the great romances of the nineteenth century. What qualities did the prince have that you think captured the heart of the future queen?

9. Victoria's relationship with her mother is complicated. How was the Duchess's treatment of Victoria self-serving, and how was it well-meaning? Put yourself in the Duchess's shoes: How would you justify her actions and behavior? What are the consequences of how Victoria treats the Duchess at the end of the novel?

10. At the start of the story, Liza is looking for someone to save her. How does she change over the course of the story?

11. At the end of the novel, Liza has made some important decisions, but we don't know exactly what she is going to do next. What do you think she does when she walks away from Kensington Palace?

For more discussion guides and book club guides, visit chroniclebooks/educators.

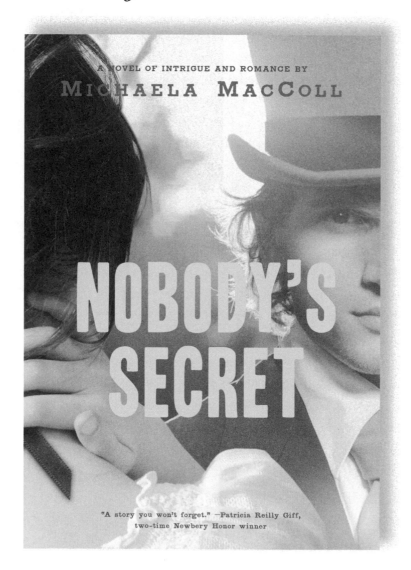

NOBODY'S SECRET

BY MICHAELA MACCOLL

Emily lay perfectly still, hidden in the tall grass, her eyes closed tight. A chain of wildflowers lay wilted around her neck. But no matter how quiet she was, the bee would not land on her nose. Emily, she told herself sternly, bees are special. You can't expect the first one to accept your invitation.

The bee thrummed. A delicate brush of wings tickled her cheek. Pollen drifted into Emily's nose. She sneezed. She didn't need to open her eyes to know that her quarry had flitted away.

The crunch of nearby footsteps made her sigh. Had her mother sent Vinnie to fetch her already? In Mother's view, to play truant from housekeeping was a terrible crime. Especially on laundry day. But this was the first day Emily had felt well enough to wander; she wasn't going home yet. She willed herself to become as invisible as the blur of hummingbirds' wings.

The footsteps came closer. A shadow came between her and the sun. Someone was standing over her. She squeezed her eyes closed even tighter and thought only of the bees.

"A young lady lying hidden among the wildflowers. . . . How unexpected."

Emily's eyes flew open. A young man towered over her. Hastily, she sat up, craning her neck to see him. His silhouette was rimmed with sunlight and his fair hair glistened like strands of fine silk. Her sun-warmed skin suddenly felt chill.

"Hello," she answered warily, glancing toward the stand of white pines that stood between her and home. Then she took a closer look at his fine clothing and her confidence returned. From the high polish on his black shoes and the gold watch peeking from the left pocket of his vest, she could tell he was from a city, perhaps Boston or even New York. He couldn't be more than twenty—twenty-two at the oldest. Harmless, she thought. "Are you a student at the college?"

The college on the hill dominated Amherst's landscape as well as the rhythms of the Dickinson family. Emily's grandfather was one of the founders of Amherst College, and her father was its treasurer.

"I'm no scholar," he said, grimacing. "I've never had any interest in a formal education."

"I'm eager to go to Mount Holyoke Seminary next year." She looked at him curiously, unable to fathom not wanting to learn everything about everything. "I've never met anyone who didn't want to go to school."

"I've been too busy living." He shrugged. "What could I learn in college that I couldn't learn traveling the world?"

The world! Rather than let her envy show on her face, Emily's glance traveled from his well-trimmed hair to his shined shoes. "The civilized parts, I presume."

"I'm off to California as soon as I've finished my business here," he said.

Emily couldn't imagine the courage it would take to go to the wilds of California. "You'll need more rugged clothes if you are going West," she pointed out, gesturing to his tailored coat.

He burst out laughing, but it was a good laugh, not high-pitched and not too hearty.

"May I assist you?" He offered his hand. After a brief hesitation, she put her hand in his. He easily pulled her off the ground. She was small and he was very tall. Her hand lingered on his and for just a moment she could feel the roughness of his skin.

"Your hands prove you aren't a student," she said. "Amherst students rarely work hard enough to callus their hands."

"You're the local expert on college students?" he teased.

"I know all of them," she sighed. "My father is . . . connected with the College."

To her pleasure, the stranger didn't seem interested in her father. As if it were of no importance, he asked, "What were you doing down there, anyway?"

She paused, considering his intelligent eyes. Finally, she told the bald truth without explanation: "Hoping a bee would land on my nose."

He nodded, as though that made all the sense in the world. The silence lengthened while Emily waited for the inevitable question. Finally she said, "You aren't going to ask me why?"

He pursed his lips. "I suspect you want to know what it feels like."

His easy understanding was like a blow to the body. She nodded, speechless.

"But aren't you afraid of being stung?" he asked.

"I don't know. It hasn't happened yet." She paused. "But I'm sure it will be excruciating."

His forehead crinkled and his mouth twisted to stop a smile. "And that's a good thing?"

"It's a new experience. If you are sequestered at home, as I am, new experiences are to be savored."

"Perhaps you'll be lucky," he said. "I have a relation who keeps bees. He doesn't even notice the beestings."

"I'm very sensitive to natural poisons," Emily assured him. "Of all the girls in my botany class, I reacted most to poison oak. So if I'm stung, it's bound to be painful. But I still hope a bee will visit."

"You've picked a good spot," he said, "with all these wildflowers about."

"So far the bees have decided my nose is not the place for them." She picked a long blade of grass from her braid of red hair and smoothed   ches above he   ger dresses tl   ally chose th   day she wisl

"Lav   ied a purple   Try this."

She   ave the plea:

He s   tter of it. "T   of straight

Emily   wn fathers a

How   ling very mis